CW00739184

Robert Barr (16 September 1849 – 21 October 1912) was a Scottish-Canadian short story writer and novelist. Robert Barr was born in Barony, Lanark, Scotland to Robert Barr and Jane Watson. In 1854, he emigrated with his parents to Upper Canada at the age of four years old. His family settled on a farm near the village of Muirkirk. Barr assisted his father with his job as a carpenter, and developed a sound work ethic. Robert Barr then worked as a steel smelter for a number of years before he was educated at Toronto Normal School in 1873 to train as a teacher. After graduating Toronto Normal School, Barr became a teacher, and eventually headmaster/principal of the Central School of Windsor, Ontario in 1874. While Barr worked as head master of the Central School of Windsor, Ontario, he began to contribute short stories—often based on personal experiences, and recorded his work. On August 1876, when he was 27, Robert Barr married Ontario-born Eva Bennett, who was 21. (Source: Wikipedia)

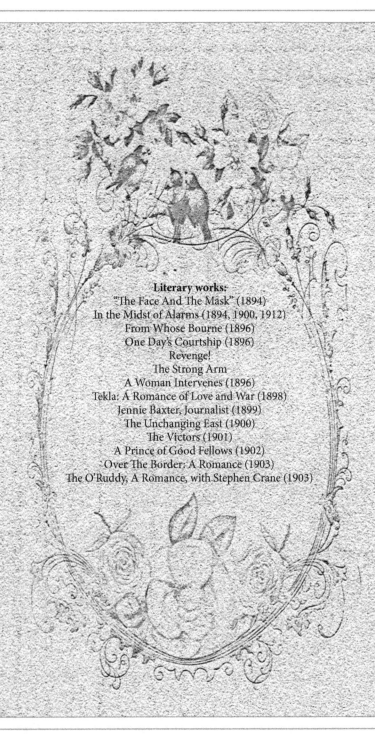

Literary works:
"The Face And The Mask" (1894)
In the Midst of Alarms (1894, 1900, 1912)
From Whose Bourne (1896)
One Day's Courtship (1896)
Revenge!
The Strong Arm
A Woman Intervenes (1896)
Tekla: A Romance of Love and War (1898)
Jennie Baxter, Journalist (1899)
The Unchanging East (1900)
The Victors (1901)
A Prince of Good Fellows (1902)
Over The Border: A Romance (1903)
The O'Ruddy, A Romance, with Stephen Crane (1903)

OVER THE BORDER
&
YOUNG LORD STRANLEIGH

ROBERT BARR

PRINCE CLASSICS

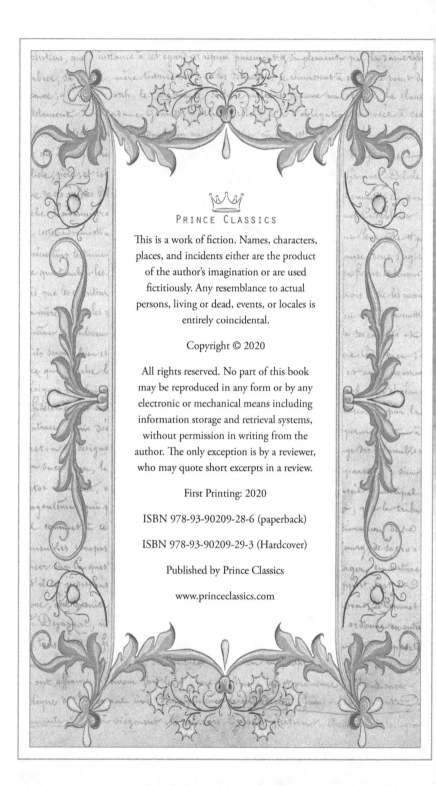

PRINCE CLASSICS

First Printing: 2020

ISBN 978-93-90209-28-6 (paperback)

ISBN 978-93-90209-29-3 (Hardcover)

Published by Prince Classics

www.princeclassics.com

Contents

OVER THE BORDER
&
YOUNG LORD STRANLEIGH

OVER THE BORDER

TO

FREDERICK A. STOKES

WITH WHOM MY LITERARY LIFE HAS BEEN PLEASANTLY ASSOCIATED

SINCE I BEGAN TO WRITE BOOKS.

BOOK I.—THE GIRL.

CHAPTER I.—ASSERTION.

The end of October had been more than usually fine, and now the beginning of November was following the good example set by its predecessor. In the Home Park, the only part of the extensive grounds surrounding Hampton Court Palace that was well wooded, the leaves had not entirely left the branches, and the turf beneath was green and firm, as yet unsodden by autumnal rain.

Along one of the forest aisles there walked a distinguished party, proceeding slowly, for the pace was set by a disease-stricken man whose progress was of painful deliberation. He was tall and thin; his body was prematurely bent, though accustomed to be straight enough, if one might judge by the masterful brow, now pallid with illness, or by the glance of the piercing eye untamed even by deadly malady. That he was not long for this earth, if Nature had her way, a scrutinizer of that handsome, powerful face might have guessed; yet he was singled out for destruction even before his short allotted time, for at that moment his enemies, hedged in secrecy behind locked doors, were anxiously planning his ruin. They were wise in their privacy, for, had a whisper of their intentions gone abroad, the Earl of Strafford would have struck first and struck hard, as, indeed, he intended to do in any case.

Thomas Wentworth, Earl of Strafford, was accompanied by an imposing train. On either side of him, accommodating their slow steps to his, were some of the highest in the land, who waited on his words and accorded him a deference more obsequious than that with which they might have distinguished the King himself; for all knew that this shattered frame was more to be dreaded than the most stalwart personage who that day trod English soil.

Behind this noble circle followed a numerous band of attendants, alert for beck or call, each having place according to his degree. A huntsman was surrounded by dogs kept in thrall by fear of the whip. Falconers with hooded hawks attested a favorite sport of the Earl, who loved to have the birds near him even though he made no trial of their flight. And here he walked the grounds of the King as if he owned them; as though he were permanent master instead of transient guest. Here he rested for the moment, hoping to recover some remnant of health by the placid Thames, after his troublous journey from Ireland, which turbulent country lay numb under his strong hand, soon to be vocal enough when the hounds were upon him. No echo of London's clamour came to this green paradise. He knew the mob was crying out against him, as in truth the whole country cried; but he heeded not the howl, despising his opponents. Better for him had he been more wary or more conciliatory.

Among those now in his company was young De Courcy, one of the numerous band of Frenchmen smilingly received at Court because the consort of Charles had a predilection for her countrymen,—a preference unshared by any save her husband. The French contingent thought little of the scowls of the English so long as those in authority smiled on them and the smile brought profit. They were regarded as titled mercenaries; spies probably, anxious to feather their own nests at the expense of the Treasury; possibly the propagating agents of a Church of which England had a deep distrust; certainly possessing an overweening influence at Court, dividing still further the unfortunate King from his suspicious people. It might have been imagined that so thoroughly English, so strenuous a man as Strafford, the last to be deluded by suave manners or flattery, although he had an insatiable appetite for cringing deference, yet uninfluenced by it (as witness his crushing of Lord Montmorris in Ireland), would have shown scant friendship for frivolous French nobles; but it was a fact that he bore from young De Courcy a familiarity of address that he would have suffered from none other in the kingdom. Courtiers find a ready reason for every action, and they attributed Strafford's forbearance to the influence De Courcy possessed with the Queen, for his lordship was well aware that his sovereign lady showed small liking for the King's most powerful minister. Strafford was too keen a politician not to make every endeavour to placate an enemy who at all hours had access to the private ear of his master, on whose breath depended his own elevation. Therefore it may well be that he thought it worth while to conciliate one of the haughty lady's favourites.

The conversation under the trees was lightly frivolous, despite the seriousness of the time. Strafford was not one to wear his heart on his sleeve, and if he was troubled that the King insisted on his presence in London, refusing to him permission to return to Ireland, where he was safe,—the wielder of the upper hand,—his manner or expression gave no hint of his anxiety. A cynical smile curved his bloodless lips as he listened to the chatter of De Courcy, not noticing the silence of the others, who disdained a conversational contest with the voluble Frenchman.

"I give your lordship my assurance," insisted the young man, "that his Majesty was much perturbed by the incident. All Scots are superstitious, and the King has Scottish blood in his veins."

"As to superstition, I have never learned," said Strafford, speaking slowly, "that the French are entirely free from some touch of it."

"That's as may be," continued De Courcy airily, "but her Majesty, who is French, advised the King to think nothing more of the encounter, so she regards but lightly any predictions of doom from an old gipsy hag."

"There were no predictions of doom, and no gipsy hag. The case was of the simplest, now exaggerated by Court gossip," amended the Earl.

"My lord, I have it almost direct from the King himself."

"Your 'almost' will account for anything. It was merely a piece of youthful impertinence which should have been punished by one of the park rangers, had any been present. The King had honoured me with his company in the park. We were alone together, discussing problems of State, when there suddenly sprang out before us a smiling, froward girl, who cried, 'Merry gentlemen, I will predict your fortunes if in return you tell me where I may find the Earl of Strafford.' His Majesty looked at me, and the hussy, quick to take a hint, evidently saw that I was the person sought. In any case the King's remark must have confirmed her suspicion. 'Your predictions are like to prove of small value,' said his Majesty, 'if you ask such a question. Here you have two men before you. Choose the greater.' Whereupon the wench seized my hand before I was aware, and the King laughed."

"It was an uncourtierlike proceeding," said De Courcy. "That young woman will not advance in a world which depends on the smile of the mighty for promotion."

"The choice shows her a true prophet," muttered one of the nobles; but Strafford, paying no heed, went on with his account.

"The words which followed were more diplomatic than the action. 'You are the King's best friend,' she said, examining the palm she had taken. Then his Majesty cried, 'What do you read in my hand?' 'You are the King's worst enemy,' said the pert hussy. This nonplussed Charles for the moment, who replied at last, 'I think you are more successful with my comrade. Read all you find in his palm, I beg of you.' Then the gipsy, if such she was, went glibly on. 'Your fate and that of the King are interwoven. If you overcome your enemies, the King will overcome his. If you fall, the King falls. Your doom will be the King's doom; your safety the King's safety. At the age you shall die, at that age will the King die, and from the same cause.' His Majesty laughed, somewhat uneasily I thought, but said jauntily, 'I have the advantage of you, Strafford, for you may die at any moment, but I am given seven years to live, being that space younger than you.' I was annoyed at the familiarity of the creature, and bade her take herself off, which she did after making vain appeal for some private conversation with me."

"Was she fair to look upon? In that case I do not wonder at your indignation. To learn that a handsome and young woman was searching for you in the lonely forest, to meet her at last, but in company of a King so rigid in his morals as Charles, was indeed a disappointment. You had been more favoured with any other monarch of Europe beside you. Had you no chance of getting one private word with her; of setting time and place for a more secluded conference?"

A slight frown ruffled the broad, smooth brow of the statesman, but it vanished on the instant, and he shrugged his shoulders nonchalantly.

"I but gave you a brief account of a very simple incident that you were inclined to make much of. You have now the truth, and so may dress the retailing of it in the guise that best pleases you. I make no doubt 'twill be fanciful enough when next I hear it."

"Were it any other monarch than Charles, I should say he was annoyed to find his minister so favoured; but in his mind the prediction will take more space than thought of the prophet, be she never so young or so fair. But all good wishes go toward you, my lord. It is my prayer that when next you meet the woodland sylph you are alone in the forest."

As if to show how little profit follows the prayer of a French exquisite, there stepped out from behind a thick tree in front of them the person of whom they spoke. She was tall and slender, with dancing eyes of midnight blackness, which well matched the dark, glossy ringlets flowing in profusion over her shapely shoulders. Her costume betokened the country rather than the Court, yet its lack of fashionable cut or texture was not noticed in a company of men, and the almost universal gaze of admiration that rested on her showed that in the eyes of the majority she was well and tastefully garbed.

"My lord of Strafford," she said in a sweet clear voice, "I crave a word with you in private."

De Courcy laughed provokingly; the others remained silent, but turned their regard from the interloper to the Earl, whose frown of annoyance did not disappear as it had done before. Strafford spoke no word, but his underlings were quick to interpret and act upon his black look. Two attendants silently took places beside the girl, ready to seize her did his lordship give a sign. The huntsmen let loose the dogs that had been snarling at the newcomer. They made a dash at her, while she sprang nimbly to the tree that had concealed her, having first whisked from the scabbard of an astonished attendant the light sword with which he was supposed to guard himself or his master.

"Call off your hounds, you villain!" she cried in a voice that had the true ring of command in it; indeed, to many there the order had a touch of the

Earl's own tones in anger. "I ask not for my own escape from scath, but for theirs. I'd rather transfix a man than hurt a dog. You scoundrel, you shall feel the sting of this point if you do not instantly obey."

The thin shining blade darted here and there like an adder's tongue, and as painfully. Yelp after yelp showed its potency, and the dogs, quick to learn that they were overmatched, abated their fury and contented themselves with noisy outcry at a safe distance from the semicircle of danger, jumping sideways and backward, barking valorously, but keeping well clear of the rapier. At a glance from the Earl the huntsman whipped them back into their former places.

"Yes, lash them, you whelp, but it's over your own shoulders the cord should go, had I the ordering, thou meanest of the pack."

"Madam," said the Earl of Strafford sternly, "I would have you know that none give orders here but me."

"In that you are mistaken, my lord. You have just heard me give them, and furthermore have seen them obeyed. But aside from the ordering of either you or me, I understand this to be the King's park." Again De Courcy laughed.

"She hit you there, my lord," he had the temerity to say.

Strafford paid no attention to his gibe, but gazed darkly at the fearless intruder.

"What do you want?" he asked.

"I have told you, my lord. I wish a word in your private ear."

"Speak out what you have to say."

"'T is to be heard by none but the Earl of Strafford; no, not even by the King himself; for, you should know, were it other fashion, I would have spoken when last I encountered you."

"I have no secrets from the King."

"Nor need this be one. 'T is yours to proclaim to the world at your pleasure. But first it is for your ear alone. Send that painted popinjay to the rear with the dogs. The others are gentlemen and will retire of their own accord when they learn a lady wishes to speak privily with you."

It was now the turn of the English nobles to laugh, which they did merrily enough, but De Courcy seemed less pleased with the rude suggestion. He fumbled at his sword-hilt, and muttered angrily that if any present wished to make the girl's reference his own, a meeting could be speedily arranged to discuss the question. Strafford, however, had no mind for any by-play. His glance quelled the rising difference; then he said harshly to the young woman,—"What do you here in the King's park, lacking permission, as I suspect?"

"Indeed," cried the girl with a toss of the head, "they say, where I come from, that everything seemingly possessed by the King belongs actually to the people, and being one of the people I come to my own domain asking permission of none."

"You are young to speak treason."

"'T is no treason of mine. I but repeat what others say."

"Still, how came you here?"

"Easily. Over the wall. I was refused access to you by any other means, so I took the method that suggested itself."

"You were feigning yesterday to be a gipsy. Who are you?"

"That is what I wish to tell your lordship when I get the opportunity. As for yesterday, I feigned nothing. I but retold what an old gipsy once said to me regarding the King and Lord Strafford. I wished to engage your attention, but, like the underlings of this palace, you turned me away."

"Your persistence shall be rewarded, but with this proviso. If the news you make so much of is not worth the telling, then shall you expiate your impudence in prison. If you fear to accept the risk, you had better begone while there is yet time, and let us see no more of you."

"I accept the hazard freely, my lord."

The Earl of Strafford said no more, but turned to his followers, who at once withdrew to the background, except De Courcy, who, not having forgiven the insult placed upon him, and unconscious that his reluctance to quit the spot was giving point to the girl's invective, cried angrily,—"Beware, Lord Strafford. There may be more in this than appears on the surface. She has shown herself expert with a stolen blade. That blade is still in her hand."

The Earl smiled coldly; he was unused to disobedience even where it concerned his own safety.

"'Tis but fair," he said, "that I should take some risk to equal hers. I'll chance the stroke. Your prayer was that I should meet this damsel alone in the forest. Do not, I beg of you, prevent fulfilment of your devout petition by further tarrying."

But before this was spoken the girl had flung the borrowed rapier far into the forest glade, then waved her disencumbered hand to the departing Frenchman, saying mockingly,—"Farewell, popinjay. The treacherous ever make suggestion of treachery." To the Earl she added, "My lord, I am entirely unarmed."

"What have you to say to me?" replied Strafford severely, bending his dark gaze upon her.

"Sir,"—her voice lowered so that none might by any chance overhear,— "Sir, I am Frances Wentworth, your lordship's eldest daughter."

CHAPTER II.—RECOGNITION.

The Earl lowered upon the girl, and the black anger upon his brow might have warned a more intrepid person than even she appeared to be that there was peril in trifling. When at last he spoke, his voice was harsh and menacing.

"What do you expect to gain by a statement so preposterous?"

"I expect to gain a father."

The girl's answer trod quick upon the heels of the question, but her colour changed from red to pale, and from pale to red again, and her hurried breathing hinted of some knowledge of her hazard, which nevertheless she faced without flinching.

"My eldest daughter, say you? My eldest daughter is Ann, aged thirteen, a modest little maid. I take you to be older, and I should hesitate to apply to you the qualification I have just coupled with her name."

"I am sixteen, therefore her senior. Thus one part of my contention is admitted. If she is modest, it doth become a maid, and is reasonably to be expected, for she hath a mother's care. I have had none. If you detect a boldness in my manner, 't is but another proof I am my father's daughter."

Something resembling a grimace rather than a smile disturbed the white lips of Strafford at this retort. He bent his eyes on the ground, and his mind seemed to wander through the past. They stood thus in silence opposite each other, the girl watching him intently, and when she saw his mouth twitch with a spasm of pain, a great wave of pity overspread her face and brought the moisture to her eyes; but she made no motion toward him, held in increasing awe of him.

"Boldness is not a virtue," he muttered, more to himself than to her. "There's many a jade in England who can claim no relationship with me."

This remark, calling for no response, received none.

"Sixteen years of age! Then that was in——"

The Earl paused in his ruminations as if the simple mathematical problem baffled him, the old look of weariness and pain clouding his downturned face.

"The year 1624," said the girl promptly.

"Doubtless, doubtless. 1624. It is long since; longer than the days that have passed seem to indicate. I was a young man then, now——now——I am an aged wreck, and all in sixteen years. And so in you, the spirit of youth, the unknown past confronts me, demanding——demanding what?"

"Demanding nothing, my lord."

"Humph. You are the first then. They all want something. You think I am an old dotard who is ready, because you say you want nothing, to accept your absurd proposal. But I am not yet fifty, nor as near it as these fell maladies would have me appear; and a man should be in his prime at fifty. Madam, it will require more convincing testimony to make me listen to you further."

"The testimony, irrefutable, stands here before you. Raise your eyes from the ground, my lord, and behold it. If, scrutinizing me, you deny that I am your daughter, I shall forthwith turn from you and trouble you no more."

Strafford slowly lifted his gloomy face, prematurely seamed with care, and his heavy eyes scanned closely the living statue that confronted him. The sternness of his features gradually relaxed, and an expression near akin to tenderness overspread his face.

"Any man might be proud to claim you, my girl, no matter how many other reasons for pride he possessed. But you have not come here merely because someone flattered the Earl of Strafford by saying you resembled him."

"No, my lord. I am come to return to you this document which once you presented to my mother."

She handed him a paper, which he read with intent care. It ran thus:

"I have, in little, much to say to you, or else one of us must be much to blame. But in truth I have that confidence in you, and that assurance in myself, as to rest secure the fault will never be made on either side. Well, then; this short and this long which I aim at is no more than to give you this first written testimony that I am your husband; and that husband of yours that will ever discharge these duties of love and respect toward you which good women may expect, and are justly due from good men to discharge them; and this is not only much, but all which belongs to me; and wherein I shall tread out the remainder of life which is left to me——"

Strafford looked up from his perusal, blank amazement upon his countenance.

"How came you by this paper?"

"I found it among the documents left by my grandfather, who died a year ago. It was sent by you to my mother."

24

"Impossible."

"Do you deny the script?"

"I do not deny it, but 't was written by me eight years since, and presented to my third wife, whom I married privately."

"Your third wife? Who was she?"

"She was Mistress Elizabeth Rhodes, and is now Lady Strafford."

"Then she is your fourth wife. You will see by your own inditing that this letter was written in March, 1624."

The date was unmistakably set down by the same hand that had penned the bold signature, "Thomas Wentworth," and the bewilderment of the Earl increased as he recognized that here was no forgery, but a genuine letter antedating its duplicate.

"Is it possible," he murmured to himself, "that a man has so little originality as to do practically the same thing twice?" Then aloud to the girl he said:

"Who was your mother?"

"I had hoped the reading of this document would have rendered your question unnecessary. Has a man such gift of forgetting, that the very name of the woman he solemnly married has slipped his memory as easily as the writing of the letter she cherished?"

"She was Frances, daughter of Sir John Warburton," murmured the Earl.

"His only daughter, as I am hers, my lord."

"But when Sir John wrote me coldly of her death, he made no mention of any issue."

"My grandfather always hated you, my lord. It is very like that he told you not the cause of my mother's death was her children's birth."

"Children?"

"Yes, my lord. My twin brother and myself."

An ashen hue overspread the Earl's face, and the hand that held the letter trembled until the fateful missive shook like one of the autumn leaves on the tree above it. Again his mind wandered through the past and conjured up before him the laughing face of his supposedly only son, whose position was thus unexpectedly challenged by a stranger, unknown and unloved. A daughter more or less was of small account, but an elder son promised unsuspected complications. The ill favour with which he had at first regarded the girl returned to his troubled countenance, and she saw with quick intuition that she had suddenly lost all the ground so gradually gained. Cold dislike tinctured the tone in which the next question was asked.

"If, as you say, you have a brother, why is he not here in your place; you in the background, where you properly belong?"

"Sir, I suppose that her good name is thought more of by a woman than by a man. She wishes to be assured that she came properly authenticated into this world, whereas a man troubles little of his origin, so be it he is here with some one to fight or to love. Or perhaps it is that the man is the deeper, and refuses to condone where a woman yearns to forgive. My brother shares our grandfather's dislike of you. He thinks you cared little for our mother, or you would not have been absent during her last days when——"

"I knew nothing of it. The times then, as now, were uncertain, requiring absorbed attention from those thrown willingly or unwillingly into public affairs. What can a boy of sixteen know of the duties thrust upon a man in my situation?"

"Sixteen or not, he considers himself even now a man of position, and he holds your course wrong. He says he has taken up the opinions you formerly held, and will do his best to carry them to success. He is for the Parliament and against the King. As for me, I know little of the questions that disturb the State. My only knowledge is that you are my father, and were you the wickedest person in the world I would come to you. A man may have many daughters, but a daughter can have but one father; therefore am I here, my lord."

26

Like the quick succession of shade and sunshine over the sensitive surface of a lovely lake, the play of varying emotions added an ever-changing beauty to the girl's expressive face; now a pitiful yearning toward her father when she saw he suffered; then a coaxing attitude, as if she would win him whether he would or no; again a bearing of pride when it seemed she would be denied; and throughout all a rigid suppression of herself, a standing of her ground, a determination not to give way to any rising sentiment which might make the after repulse a humiliation; if a retreat must come it should be carried out with dignity.

The Earl of Strafford saw nothing of this, for his eyes were mostly on the ground at his feet. That his mind was perturbed by the new situation so unexpectedly presented to him was evident; that he was deeply suspicious of a trap was no less clear. When he looked up at her he found his iron resolution melting in spite of himself, and, as he wished to bring an unclouded judgment to bear upon the problem, he scrutinized the brown sward at his feet. Nevertheless he was quick to respond to any show of sympathy with himself, even though he was unlikely to exhibit appreciation, and he was equally quick to resent the slightest lack of deference on the part of those who addressed him. If the girl had made a thorough study of his character she could not have better attuned her manner to his prejudices. Her attitude throughout was imbued with the deepest respect, and if the eye refused to be advocate for her, the ear could not close itself to the little thrill of affection that softened her tone as she spoke to him. He raised his head abruptly as one who has come to a decision.

"November is the stepmother of the months, and the air grows cold. Come with me to the palace. In a world of lies I find myself believing you; thus I am not grown so old as I had feared. Come."

The girl tripped lightly over the rustling leaves and was at his side in an instant, then slowed her pace in unison with his laboured mode of progression.

"Sir, will you lean upon my shoulder?"

"No. I am ailing, but not decrepit."

They walked together in silence, and if any viewed them the onlookers were well concealed, for the park seemed deserted. Entering the palace and arriving at the foot of a stairway, solicitous menials proffered assistance, but Strafford waved them peremptorily aside, and, accepting now the support he had shortly before declined, leaned on his daughter's shoulder and wearily mounted the stair.

The room on the first floor into which he led her overlooked a court. A cheerful fire burned on the hearth and cast a radiance upon the sombre wainscoting of the walls. A heavy oaken table was covered with a litter of papers, and some books lay about. Into a deep arm-chair beside the fire Strafford sank with a sigh of fatigue, motioning his daughter to seat herself opposite him, which she did. He regarded her for some moments with no pleased expression on his face, then said with a trace of petulancy in the question:

"Did your grandfather bring you up a lady, or are you an ignorant country wench?"

She drew in quickly the small feet out-thrust to take advantage of the comforting fire, and the blaze showed her cheek a ruddier hue than heretofore.

"Sir," she said, "the children of the great, neglected by the great, must perforce look to themselves. I was brought up, as you know, without a mother's care, in the ancient hall of a crusty grandfather, a brother my only companion. We played together and fought together, as temper willed, and he was not always the victor, although he is the stronger. I can sometimes out-fence him, and, failing that, can always outrun him. Any horse he can ride, I can ride, and we two have before now put to flight three times our number among the yokels of the neighborhood. As to education, I have a smattering, and can read and write. I have studied music to some advantage, and foreign tongues with very little. I daresay there are many things known to your London ladies that I am ignorant of."

"We may thank God for that," muttered her father.

"If there are those in London, saving your lordship, who say I am not a lady, I will box their ears for them an they make slighting remarks in my presence."

"A most unladylike argument! The tongue and not the hand is the Court lady's defence."

"I can use my tongue too, if need be, my lord."

"Indeed I have had evidence of it, my girl."

"Queen Elizabeth used her fists, and surely she was a lady."

"I have often had my doubts of it. However, hereafter you must be educated as doth become a daughter of mine."

"I shall be pleased to obey any commands my father places on me."

The conversation was interrupted by a servant throwing open the door, crying:

"His Majesty the King!"

The girl sprang instantly to her feet, while her father rose more slowly, assisting himself with his hands on the arms of the chair.

CHAPTER III.—MAJESTY.

There was more of hurry than of kingly dignity in the entrance of Charles. The handsome face was marred by an imperious querulousness that for the moment detracted from its acknowledged nobility.

"Strafford," he cried impatiently, "I have been kept waiting. Servants are at this moment searching palace and park for you. Where have you been?"

"I was in the forest, your Majesty. I am deeply grieved to learn that you needed me."

"I never needed you more than now. Are you ready to travel?"

Strafford's gloomy face almost lighted up.

"On the instant, your Majesty," he replied with a sigh of relief.

"That is well. I trust your malady is alleviated, in some measure at least;

still I know that sickness has never been a bar to duty with you. Yet I ask no man to do what I am not willing to do myself for the good of the State, and I shall be shortly on the road at your heels."

"Whither, your Majesty?" asked the Earl with falling countenance, for it was to Ireland he desired to journey, and he knew the King had no intention of moving toward the west.

"To London, of course; a short stent over bad roads. But if you are ailing and fear the highway, a barge on the river is at your disposal."

"To London!" echoed the Earl, something almost akin to dismay in his tone. "I had hoped your Majesty would order me to Ireland, which I assure your Majesty has been somewhat neglected of late."

"Yes, yes," exclaimed the King brusquely, "I know your anxiety in that quarter. A man ever thinks that task the most important with which he intimately deals, but my position gives me a view over the whole realm, and the various matters of State assume their just proportions in my eyes; their due relations to each other. Ireland is well enough, but it is the heart and not the limbs of the empire that requires the physicians' care. Parliament has opened badly, and is like to give trouble unless treated with a firm hand."

The hand of the Earl appeared anything but firm. It wavered as it sought the support of the chair's arm.

"Have I your Majesty's permission to be seated? I am not well," Strafford said faintly.

"Surely, surely," cried the King, himself taking a chair. "I am deeply grieved to see you so unwell; but a journey to London is a small matter compared with a march upon Dublin, which is like to have killed you in your present condition."

"Indeed, your Majesty, the smaller journey may well have the more fatal termination," murmured the Earl; but the King paid no attention to the remark, for his wandering eye now caught sight of a third in the conference, which brought surprised displeasure to his brow. The girl was standing behind the high back of the chair in which she had been seated, in a gloomy angle where the firelight which played so plainly on the King and Strafford did not touch her.

"In God's name, whom have we here? The flippant prophet of the forest, or my eyes deceive me! How comes this girl in my palace, so intimate with my Lord Strafford, who seemed to meet her as a stranger but yesterday?"

The slumbering suspicion of Charles was aroused, and he glanced from one to the other in haughty questioning.

"I never met her until I encountered her in the forest when I had the honour to accompany your Majesty. To-day, as I walked with De Courcy and others, there came a second accosting from her, as unexpected as the first. The girl craved private speech with me, which I somewhat reluctantly granted. The upshot is, she brings me proof, which I cannot deny, that she is my eldest daughter."

"Your eldest daughter!" cried the King, amazed. "Is your family then so widely scattered, and so far unknown to you, that such a claimant may spring up at any moment?"

"I was married privately to the daughter of Sir John Warburton. Circumstances separated me from my wife, and although her father curtly informed me of her death he said nothing of issue. There was a feud between us,—entirely on his part,—I had naught against him. It seems he has been dead this year past, and my daughter, getting news of her father among Sir John's papers, comes thus southward to make inquiry."

"You fall into good fortune, my girl. Your extraordinary claim is most readily allowed."

Frances, finding nothing to say, kept silence and bowed her head to the King, whom she had regarded throughout with rapt attention.

"Where got you your gift of prophecy? Is prescience hereditary, and has your father's mantle already fallen on your shoulders? He is my best friend, you said, and I my worst enemy. God's truth, Madam, you did not lack for boldness, but the force of the flattery of your father is lessened by my knowledge of your relationship, hitherto concealed from me."

"Your Majesty, it has hitherto been concealed from myself," said the Earl wearily.

"Has the girl no tongue? It wagged freely enough in the forest. Come, masquerader, what have you to say for yourself?"

"Your Majesty, I humbly crave your pardon. The words I used yesterday were not mine, but those of a gipsy in the north, who told me I was the daughter of the Earl of Strafford at a time when such a tale seemed so absurd that I laughed at her for connecting my name of Wentworth with one so exalted as the Earl of Strafford. Later, when I received proof that such indeed was the case, her words returned to me. I had no right to use them in your august presence, but the entourage of the Lord Strafford prevented my meeting him; thus, baffled, I sought to intercept him in the forest, and was willing to use any strategy that might turn his attention toward me, in the hope of getting a private word with him."

"I knew you had a tongue. Well, it matters little what you said; your mission seems to have been successful. Do not think I placed any weight upon your words, be they gipsy-spoken or the outcome of a spirit of mischief. My Lord Strafford, you will to London then?"

"Instantly, your Majesty."

"I will consult with you there to-morrow. And have no fear; for on my oath as a man, on my honour as a king, I will protect you."

The King rose and left the room as abruptly as he had entered it.

For some moments Strafford lay back in his chair, seemingly in a state of collapse. The girl looked on him in alarm.

"Sir, is there anything I can do for you?" she asked at length.

"Call a servant. Tell him to order a coach prepared at once, and see that it is well horsed, for I would have the journey as short as possible."

"My lord, you are in no condition of health to travel to London. I will go to the King and tell him so."

"Do that I requested you, and trouble me not with counsel. There is enough of woman's meddling in this business already."

Frances obeyed her father's instructions without further comment, then came and sat in her place again. The Earl roused himself, endeavouring to shake off his languor.

"What think you of the King?" he asked.

"He is a man corroded with selfishness."

"Tut, tut! Such things are not to be spoken in the precincts of a Court. No, nor thought. He is not a selfish monarch, other than all monarchs are selfish, but——discussion on such a theme is fruitless, and I must be nearing my dotage to begin it. I am far from well, Frances, and so, like the infirm, must take to babbling."

"Do you fear Parliament, my lord? How can it harm you when you have the favour of the King?"

"I fear nothing, my girl, except foolish unseen interference; interference that may not be struck at or even hinted against. Did they teach you the history of France in your school?"

"No, my lord."

"Then study it as you grow older; I'll warrant you'll find it interesting enough. Ruined by women. Ruined by women. Seven civil wars in seventeen years, and all because of viperish, brainless women. Well, we have one of the breed here in England, and God help us!"

"You mean the Queen, my lord?"

"Hush! Curses on it, will you be as outspoken as another of your sex is spiteful and subtle? Mend your manners, hussy, and guard your tongue. Could you not see you spoke too freely to the King a moment since?"

"Sir, I am sorry."

"Be not sorry, but cautious."

Strafford fell into a reverie, and there was silence in the room until the servant entered and announced that the coach was ready, whereupon his master rose unsteadily.

"Sir," said the girl, "will you not eat or drink before you depart?"

"No." Then, looking sharply at his daughter, he inquired, "Are you hungry?"

"Yes, my lord."

"Bring hither some refreshments, whatever is most ready to hand, and a measure of hot spiced wine. I had forgotten your youth, Frances, thinking all the world was old with me."

When the refection came, she ate but sparingly, despite her proclamation, but coaxed him to partake and to drink a cup of wine. He ordered a woman's cloak brought for her, which, when she had thrown it over her shoulders, he himself fastened at her throat.

"There," he said, when the cloak enveloped her, "that will protect you somewhat, for the night grows cold."

Strafford himself was wrapped in warm furs, and thus together they went down the stairs to the court, now dimly lighted. A cavalier, who seemed to have been standing in wait for them, stepped out from the shadow of the arches, and Frances recognized the French spark whom she had so frankly characterized earlier in the day.

"My lord," protested De Courcy jauntily, "you have your comrades at a disadvantage. You have captured the woodland nymph, and, I hear, propose spiriting her away to London. I do protest 't is most unfair to those who are thus left behind."

"Sir," said Strafford, with severity, pausing in his walk, "I would have you know that the lady to whom you refer is the Lady Frances Wentworth, my eldest daughter, ever to be spoken of with respect by high and low. Native and foreign shall speak otherwise at their distinct peril."

The Frenchman pulled off his bonnet with an impressive sweep that brushed its ample feather lightly on the stones. He bent his body in a low obeisance that threatened, were it not so acrobatically accomplished, to pitch him forward on his nose.

"If I congratulate your lordship on finding so rare a daughter, rather than offer my felicitations to the lady in the attainment of so distinguished a father, it is because I am filled with envy of any man who acquires a companionship so charming. My lady, may I have the honour of escorting you to the carriage?"

The girl shrank closer to her father and made no reply. On the other hand the father offered no objection, but returned—rather stiffly, it is true— the bow of the foreigner, and De Courcy, taking this as an acceptance, tripped daintily by the girl's side, chattering most amiably.

"I hear on the highest authority that our sovereign lady is tired of Hampton, and that we are all to be on the march for London again; to-morrow, they tell me. London delights me not. 'T is a grimy city, but if, as I suspect, a new star of beauty is to arise there, then 't will be indeed the centre of refulgence, to which worshippers of loveliness will hasten as pilgrims to a shrine. I take it, my lord, that you will introduce your daughter to the Court, and hide her no longer in the cold and envious northland?"

"My daughter has already been presented to his Majesty, and doubtless will take the place at Court to which her birth entitles her."

"And to which her grace and charm no less lay claim. I hope to be present when the lady is greeted by the Queen we both adore. The meeting of the Lily of France with the Rose of England will be an occasion to be sung by poets; would that I were a minstrel to do justice to the theme."

Their arrival at the carriage, with its four impatient horses, postillion-ridden, saved Strafford the effort of reply had he intended such. He seated himself in the closed vehicle, and his daughter sprang nimbly in beside him, ignoring the proffered aid of De Courcy, who stood bowing and bending with much courtesy, and did not resume his bonnet until the coach lurched on its lumbering way, preceded and followed by a guard of horsemen, for the Earl of Strafford always travelled in state.

Nothing was said by either until the jingling procession was well clear of the park, when the girl, with a shudder, exclaimed:

"I loathe that scented fop!"—then, seeming to fear a reproof for her outspoken remark, added, "I know I should not say that, but I cannot see what you have in common with such a creature that you are civil to him."

To her amazement her father laughed slightly, the first time she had heard him do so.

"When we travel, Frances, safe out of earshot, you may loathe whom you please, but, as I have warned you, 't is sometimes unsafe to give expression to your feelings within four walls. I may find little in common with any man, least of all with such as De Courcy, whom I take to be as false as he is fair; but there is slight use in irritating a wasp whom you cannot crush. Wait till he is under my hand, then I shall crush ruthlessly; but the time is not yet. He has the ear of the Queen, and she has the ear of her husband."

"Sir, what reason have you to suspect that the Queen moves against you?"

"One reason is that I am this moment journeying east when I would be travelling west. In truth, my girl, you seem resolved unconsciously to show you are your father's daughter with that uncurbed tongue of yours, for a lack of lying is like to be my undoing. If I had told the King I must to London, 't is most like we were now on our way to Dublin."

"But it may be the King himself who thus orders you contrarywise."

"I know the King. He is not, as you think, selfish, but ever gives ear to the latest counsellor. He is weak and thinks himself strong; a most dangerous combination. With trembling hand he speaks of its firmness. Now, a weak monarch or a strong monarch matters little; England has been blessed with both and has survived the blessing; but a monarch who is. weak and strong by turns courts disaster. 'War with the Scots,' says the King. He will smite them with a firm hand. Very good; a most desirable outcome. But our captains, promoted by a woman's whisper and not by their own merit, trust to the speed of their horses rather than the ingenuity of military skill, and so escape the Scots. Our army is scattered, and there is panic in Whitehall. I am called, for God's sake, from Ireland, and I come scarce able, through illness, to sit my horse. I gather round me men of action and brain, and send Madam's favourites to the rear, where they will gallop in any case as soon as the enemy shows front. What is the result? A portion of our Scottish friends are cut up, and those whose legs are untouched are on the run. Very good again. The dogs are rushing for their kennels. What happens? An added title for me, you might suppose. Not so. A censure comes post haste from London. 'Leave the Scots alone, the King is negotiating with them.' In the face of victory he embraces defeat. A peace is made that I know nothing of; all their demands are granted, as if they had environed London! I am left like a fool, with a newly inspired army and no enemy. They termed it 'negotiating' in London, but I call it 'surrender.' If you intend to submit, keep the sword in its sheath and submit. If you draw the sword, fight till you are beaten, then submit when there is nothing else to do. God's name! they did not need to hale me from Ireland, where I had wrenched peace from chaos, to encompass a disgraceful retreat! Even De Courcy could have managed that with much greater urbanity than I."

"And you think the Queen is responsible?"

"Who else? Her generals were disgraced and whipped like dogs. Unvaliant in the battle-field, they are powerful in the ante-chamber, and their whines arise in the ears of the Lily of France, who would rather see her husband wrecked than saved by me. But I was never one to hark back on things that are past. My duty was to save the King from future errors. One more grave mistake lay open to him, and that was the summoning of Parliament at such a moment. It was a time for action, not for words. 'If you meant to concede, why did you not concede without bloodshed?' was a question sure to be asked; a question to which there could be no answer. Very well. I accepted in humbleness the censure that should have been placed on other shoulders, and sent back by the courier who brought it a message imploring the King to call no Parliament until we had time to set our house in order and face Lords and Commons with good grace. I then arranged my command so that if the Scots broke forth again they would meet some examples of military science, and not view only the coat-tails of the Queen's favourite generals. No reply coming from the King, I mounted my horse, and, with only one follower, set forth for London. Pushing on through darkness on the second night of my journey, I heard the galloping of a horse behind me, and drew rein, fully expecting that the greedy Scots, asking more than could be allowed, had taken to the field again. 'Good friend,' I cried, 'what news, that you ride so fast?' 'Great news,' he answered, breathless. 'A Parliament is summoned, and as I am an elected member I ride in haste. Please God, before the month is done we have Strafford's head in our hands and off his treacherous shoulders.'"

The girl gave utterance to a little cry of terror.

"Oh, 't was nothing but some braggart countryman, knowing not to whom he spoke so freely, and big in the importance of his membership, dashing on to London, thinking the world rested on his speed; and thus I learned how my advice had been scorned. When I met the King he was all panic and regret. He had conjured up the Devil easily enough, but knew not how to allay him. He bewailed his mistakes and called himself the most unfortunate of monarchs, eager to please, yet constantly offending. He was in a contrite mood, but that soon changed. 'T is my head they want,' I said. 'Do with it as you please. If it is useless to you, toss it to them; if useful, then send me to Ireland, where I shall be out of the way, yet ready to afford you what service lies in my power.' He swore he would concede them nothing. He was done with unappreciated complaisance, and now it was to be the firm hand. They should learn who was ruler of the realm. He gave me permission to return to my post. I was his only friend; his truest counsellor. That was yesterday. You heard him speak to-day. It is still the firm hand, but I must to London. There indeed exists a firm hand, but it is concealed, and so directed by hatred of me that it may project the avalanche that will overwhelm us all."

"And what will you do in London?" asked his daughter in an awed whisper.

"God knows! Had I the untrammelled ordering of events, I would strike terror into Parliament, as I struck terror into the Scots or the Irish, but——but if, after that, there was a similar sneaking underhand surrender, why then the countryman would have my head, as he hoped. I fear there are troublous times before us. This alternate grip of the firm hand, and offering of open-palmed surrender, each at the wrong time, is like the succeeding hot and cold fits of an ague; 'T will rend the patient asunder if long continued. Frances, be ever a womanly woman. Never meddle with politics. Leave sword and State to men."

Tired with long converse and the jolting of the vehicle, Strafford sank into a troubled sleep, from which he was at last awakened by the stopping of the carriage in front of his town house.

CHAPTER IV.—PROPOSAL.

Frances Wentworth crossed the threshold of her father's house with more trepidation than she had experienced on entering the palace of the King at Hampton Court. Here probably awaited a stepmother with her children, and Frances doubted the cordiality of the approaching reception. The ever-increasing fear of her father, a sentiment felt by nearly all those who encountered him, mingled with hatred, usually, on their part, but with growing affection on hers, prevented the putting of the question whether or no Lady Strafford was now in London. Their journey together had been silent since he ceased the exposition of the difficulties which surrounded him,—a man whom all England regarded as being paramount in the kingdom, yet in reality baffled and almost at bay. Looking back over the day now drawn to its close, she marvelled at her own courage in approaching him as she had done, light-heartedly and confident. Were her task to be re-enacted her mind misgave her that she would not possess the temerity to carry it through, with her new knowledge of the man. Yet if Strafford were hated in the three kingdoms, he seemed to be well liked in that little despotism, his home, where servants clustered round, for each of whom he had a kind word. Whether they knew of his coming or not, the house was prepared for his reception, fires blazing, and a table spread in the room to which he conducted his daughter. Outside, the night was cold and damp, and the inward warmth struck gratefully upon the senses of the travellers.

"Mrs. Jarrett," said the Earl to his housekeeper, who looked with wonder at the new-comer he had brought, "have you aught of woman's trappings that will fit my daughter here?"

"Your daughter, my lord?"

"Yes, and as you will be consumed by curiosity until you know how it comes so, I will add that she is newly found, having lived till now with her grandfather in the North, and is the child of my second wife, Frances Warburton, married by me some seventeen years since. Any further particulars my daughter herself will supply, if you question shrewdly, as I doubt not you will; but postpone inquiry, I beg of you, until to-morrow. Meanwhile robe her as best you may with the materials at hand, and that quickly, for I wish her company at supper."

Frances was then spirited away to the apartment assigned to her, and when presently she reappeared she was costumed more to her father's liking than had hitherto been the case. They sat down together to the meal that had hastily been prepared for them.

"To-morrow, if I remember aright what you said, is your birthday."

"Yes, my lord."

"Is it difficult for you to say 'Father'? My other children pronounce the word glibly enough. When you and I first met, and even since then, you seemed not backward in speech."

"Sir, I find myself more afraid of you than I was at the beginning."

Strafford smiled, but answered: "I assure you there is no need. I may be an implacable enemy, but I have the reputation of being as staunch a friend. So to-morrow is your birthday, saddened by the fact that it is also the date of your mother's death. That is a loss for which a man in my onerous position cannot even partially atone, but it is a loss which you perhaps have not keenly felt. It seems heartless to speak thus, but the fact remains that we cannot deeply deplore the departure of what we have never enjoyed. One thing I can covenant; that you shall not hereafter know the lack of money, which is something to promise in a city of shops."

"I have never known the lack of it, my lord."

"Have you indeed been so fortunate? Well, there again you bear a resemblance to your father. Sir John was reputed comfortably off in the old days, and I infer he harboured his wealth, a somewhat difficult task in times gone by. Are you then his heir?"

"One of two, my lord."

"Ah, yes! I had momentarily forgotten the brother who favours his grandfather rather than his sire. I am like to be over-busy to-morrow to attend the mart of either mercer or goldsmith, and if I did, I should not know what to purchase that would please you. But here are all the birthday presents of London in embryo, needing but your own touch to bring forth the full blossom of perfect satisfaction. Midas, they say, transmuted everything he fingered into gold, and it is the province of your sex to reverse the process. Buy what catches your fancy, and flatter your father by naming it his gift."

He held forward a very well filled purse, through whose meshes the bright gold glittered.

"Sir, I do not need it, and you have been very kind to me as it is."

"Nonsense! We all desire more than we can obtain. It is my wish that you take it; in any case it is but part payment of a debt long running and much overdue."

Fearing again to refuse, she accepted the proffered purse with evident reluctance, now standing opposite her father, who said:

"I am very tired and shall not rise early to-morrow. Do not wait breakfast for me. Good-night, daughter."

"Good-night, father."

Although he had said the last conventional words of the day, he still stood there as if loath to retire, then he stooped and kissed her on the lips, ruffling her black, wayward, curly hair so like his own in texture, colour, and freedom from restraint, and patting her affectionately on the shoulder.

"You will not be afraid of me from this time forward, child?" he asked. "Indeed, Frances, I grow superstitious as I become older, and I look on your strange arrival as in some measure providential. There is none of my own kind to whom I can speak freely, as I did to you in the carriage; my daughters—my other daughters—are too young. My Lady Strafford takes much interest in her garden, and dislikes this London house and this London town, for which small blame is to be imputed to her. In you, a man's courage is added to a woman's wit, and who knows but my daughter may prove the reinforcement I lacked in my baffling fight with the unseen. Do you speak French, my girl, or are you as ignorant of the language of that country as of its history?"

"I speak it but haltingly, sir, though I was taught its rudiments."

"We must amend that. It is to our tongue what the thin rapier is to the broadsword. Good lack! there was a time when one language served the English, yet great deeds were done and great poems written; but that time is past now. I must get you a master. I have likely used the broadsword overmuch, but who knows? You may be the rapier by my side."

"I hope I shall not disappoint you, sir, though I am but a country maid, with some distrust of this great city and its Court."

"City and Court are things we get speedily accustomed to. Well, again good-night, sweetheart, and sleep soundly. I see those fine eyes are already heavy with slumber."

But sleep came not so quickly as he surmised to the eyes he had complimented. The day had been too full of rapid change and tense excitement. The strange transformation of the present, and the dim, troubled vista of the future which opened out to her, cherished thought and discouraged slumber. Was it possible that she was thus to be transplanted, was to stand by the side of the greatest man in England, his acknowledged daughter, his welcome aid? God grant she might not fail him, if he had real need of her. And so she planned the days to come. She would be as subtle as the craftiest. She would cover all dislikes as the cloak had covered her, and her lips should smile though her heart revolted. Her tongue must measure what it said, and all rural bluntness should disappear. She slipped from these meditations into a hazy, bewildering conflict; her father, somehow, was in a danger that she could not fathom, she lacking power to get to him, restrained by invisible bonds, not knowing where he was, although he called to her. Then it seemed there was a turmoil in the street, a cry for help, a groan, and silence, and next Mrs. Jarrett was moving about the room and had drawn curtains that let in a grey, misty daylight.

"Is my father yet arisen?" she cried.

"Oh, good lack! no, your ladyship, nor will he for hours to come."

The girl's head fell back on her pillow, and she said dreamily, "I thought there had been trouble of some sort, and men fighting."

"Indeed, your ladyship, and so there was, a rioting going on all the night. I think the citizens of London are gone mad, brawling in the street at hours when decent folk should be in their beds. 'T is said that this new Parliament is the cause, but how or why I do not know."

Although the Earl of Strafford did not quit his chamber until noontide, he was undoubtedly concerned with affairs that demanded attention from the greatest minister of State. There were constant runnings to and fro, messengers despatched and envoys received, with the heavy knocker of the door constantly a-rap. It was two hours after mid-day when Strafford sent for his daughter, and she followed his messenger to the library, where she found her father in his chair beside a table, although he was equipped for going forth from the house. There had been seated before him De Courcy, but the young man rose as she entered and greeted her with one of his down-reaching bows which set her a-quake lest he should fall forward on his face.

"My child," said the Earl, "I am about to set out for Parliament, and it may be late before I return. Yet I think you shall sup with me at seven if all goes well and debate becomes not too strenuous; but do not wait in case I should be detained. I counsel you not to leave the house to-day, for there seem to be many brawlers on the streets. Any shopman will be pleased to wait upon you and bring samples of his wares, so send a servant for those you wish to consult. My friend De Courcy, here, begs the favour of some converse with you, and speaks with my approval."

Strafford looked keenly at the girl, and her heart thrilled as she read the unspoken message with quick intuition. He had some use for De Courcy, and she must be suave and diplomatic. Thus already she was her father's ally; an outpost in his vast concerns now committed to her. The young man saw nothing of this, for he had eyes only for the girl. The broad rim of his feathered hat was at his smirking lips, and his gaze of admiration was as unmistakable as it was intent.

"Sir, I shall obey you in all things, and hope to win your commendation," said Frances with inclination of the head.

"You are sure of the latter in any case, my child," replied Strafford, rising. "And now, De Courcy, I think we understand each other, and I may rely upon you."

"To the death, my lord," cried the young man, with another of his courtly genuflections.

"Oh, let us hope 't will not be necessary quite so far as that. I bid you good-day. To-morrow at this hour I shall look for a report from you. For the moment, good-bye, my daughter."

No sooner was the Earl quit of the room, and the door closed behind him, than De Courcy, with an impetuous movement that startled the girl, flung himself at her feet. Her first impulse was to step quickly back, but she checked it and stood her ground.

"Oh, divine Frances!" he cried, "how impatiently I have waited for this rapt moment, when I might declare to you——"

"Sir, I beg of you to arise. 'T is not seemly you should demean yourself thus."

"'T is seemly that the whole world should grovel at your feet, my lady of the free forest; for all who look upon you must love you, and for me, who have not the cold heart of this northern people, I adore you, and do here avow it."

"You take me at a disadvantage, sir. I have never been spoken to thus. I am but a child and unaccustomed. Only sixteen this very day. I ask you——"

"Most beauteous nymph! How many grand ladies of our Court would give all they possess to make such confession truly. Aye, the Queen herself. I do assure you, sweetest, such argument will never daunt a lover."

"I implore you, sir, to arise. My father may return."

"That he will not. And if he did, 't would pleasure him to see my suit advancing. I loved you from the first moment I beheld you; and though you used me with contumely, yet I solaced my wounded heart that 't was me you noticed, and me only, even though your glance was tinged with scorn."

Notwithstanding a situation that called for tact, she was unable to resist a touch of the linguistic rapier, and her eyes twinkled with suppressed merriment as she said, "You forget, sir, that I also distinguished the keeper of the hounds with my regard;" but, seeing he winced, she recollected her position and added, "In truth, I was most churlishly rude in the forest, and I am glad you spoke of it, that I now have opportunity to beg your pardon very humbly. I have learned since then that you stand high in my dear father's regard, and indeed he chided me for my violence, as 't was his duty to do by a wayward child." The gallant was visibly flattered by this tribute to his amour propre. He seized her hand and pressed his lips to it, the tremor which passed over her at this action being probably misinterpreted by his unquenchable vanity. The tension was relieved by a low roar from the street, a sound that had in it the menace of some wild beast roused to anger. It brought to the girl a reminiscence of her disturbed dreams.

"Good heaven! What is it?" she exclaimed, snatching away her hand and running to the window. Her suitor rose to his feet, daintily dusted the knees of his silken wear with a film of lace that did duty for a handkerchief, and followed her.

The street below was packed with people howling round a carriage that seemed blocked by the press. The stout coachman, gorgeous in splendid livery, had some ado to restrain the spirited horses, maddened and prancing with the interference and the outcry. Cudgels were shaken aloft in the air, and there were shouts of "Traitor!"

"Tyrant!" and other epithets so degrading that Frances put her hands to her ears in horrified dismay.

"Whom are they threatening so fiendishly?" she whispered.

"That is your father's carriage," answered De Courcy.

Before she could make further inquiry there came up to them the cold, dominating tones of her father's voice, clear above that tumult,—

"Strike through!"

The stout coachman laid about him with his whip, and the curses for the moment abandoned the head of Strafford to alight on that of the driver. The horses plunged fiercely into the crowd. The cruel progress changed the tenor of the cries, as if a wailing stop of a great organ had suddenly taken the place of the open diapason. The press was so great that those in front could not make for safety, and the disappearing coach was greeted with screams of terror and was followed by groans of agony. Men went down before it like ripe grain before a sickle.

"Oh! oh! oh!" moaned the girl, all color leaving her face.

"It serves the dogs right," said De Courcy. "How dare they block the way of a noble, and the chief Minister of State."

"I—I cannot look on this," lamented Frances, shrinking back to the table, and leaning against it as one about to faint, forgetting her desire to avoid further demonstration from her companion, in the trepidation which followed the scene she had witnessed.

"Indeed they were most mercifully dealt with, those scullions. The King of France would have sent a troop of horse to sabre them back into their kennels. 'Strike through!' cried his lordship, and, by God! 't is a good phrase, most suitable motto for a coat of arms, a hand grasping a dagger above it. 'Strike through!' I shall not forget it. But 't was a softer and more endearing theme I wished to——"

"Sir, I beseech your polite consideration. I am nigh distraught with what I have seen, and am filled with a fear of London. 'T is not the courtly city I expected to behold. I am not myself."

"But you will at least bid me hope?"

"Surely, surely, all of us may hope."

"Why, 't was the last and only gift left in Pandora's casket, and London were grim indeed to be more bereft than the receptacle of that deceitful woman. May I make my first draught on Madam Pandora's box by hoping that I am to see you at this hour tomorrow?"

"Yes—to-morrow—to-morrow," gasped the girl faintly.

CHAPTER V.—EXACTION.

A 'drizzling rain had set in and had driven the crowds from the streets. Frances drew a chair to the window of the library and sat there meditating on the strange events in which she was taking some small part, so different from the tranquil happenings of the district she had known all her life. She had imagined London a city of palaces facing broad streets, fanciedly, if not literally, paved with gold; a town of gaiety and laughter: and here was the reality, a cavernous, squalid, gloomy, human warren, peopled with murky demons bent on outrage of some sort, ill-natured and threatening. As the day waned, she saw that in spite of the rain the mob was collecting again, its atoms running hither and thither, calling to each other; bedraggled beings labouring under some common excitement. And now its roar came to her again, farther off than before,—a roar that chilled her while she listened, and the wave of sound this time seemed to have a fearful note of exultation in it. She wondered what had happened, and was anxious for her father if he were at the mercy of it. Mrs. Jarrett came into the room, followed by a man-servant, and also by one of her father's secretaries, as the woman whispered to the girl:

"My lady, we must close the shutters and bar them tightly, for the ruffians are threatening again, and may be here in force at any moment, to stone the windows, as they have done before."

The secretary seated himself at the table and was arranging papers. The man-servant opened the windows, from which Frances drew back, and now the cries came distinctly to her. "Death to Strafford!"

"Down with the tyrant!" "To the block with the King's Earl!" were some of the shouts she heard lustily called forth.

"Oh! I fear my father is in danger. Do you think they have him in their power, that they exult so?"

Good Mrs. Jarrett, anxiety on her own honest face, soothed her young mistress, and the secretary came forward.

"Be not troubled, Madam," he said. "While they cry 'To the block' it shows they have not possession of his lordship's person, but hope to stir up rancour to his disfavour. While they shout for process of law, his lordship is safe, for the law is in his hands and in those of the King, whose behests he carries out."

This seemed a reasonable deduction, and it calmed the inquirer, although there remained to her disquietude the accent of triumph in the voice of the mob.

"Death to Strafford!" was the burden of the acclaim; but now one shouted, "Justice on Strafford!"—though his meaning was clearly the same as the others. There was no dissenting outcry, and this unanimous hatred so vehemently expressed terrified at least one listener. Why was her father so universally detested? What had he done? Stern he was, undoubtedly; but just, as his reception of herself had shown, and courteous to all to whom she heard him speak; yet the memory of that phrase "Strike through!" uttered with such ruthless coldness, haunted her memory, and she heard again the shrieks of those trampled under foot. It was an indication that what he had to do he did with all his might, reckless of consequence. If any occupied his path, the obstructor had to stand aside or go down, and such a course does not make for popularity.

The windows being now shuttered and barred securely, and the tumult muffled into indistinct murmur, lights were brought in. Mrs. Jarrett urged the girl to partake of some refreshment, but Frances insisted on waiting for her father. The secretary, seeing her anxiety, said:

"Mr. Vollins went out some two hours ago to learn what was taking place, and I am sure if anything serious had happened he would have been here before now with tidings."

"Who is Mr. Vollins?"

"His lordship's treasurer, Madam."

As the words were uttered, the door opened, disclosing John Vollins, the expression of whose serious, clean-shaven face gave little promise of encouragement.

"What news, Mr. Vollins? The mob seems rampant again," spoke up the secretary.

"Disquieting news, or I am misled. The rumour is everywhere believed that his lordship was arrested in Parliament this afternoon, and is now in prison."

"Impossible! 'T would be a breach of privilege. In Parliament! It cannot be. Did you visit the precincts of Parliament?"

"No man can get within a mile of it, the mass of people is so great. It seems as if all London were concentrated there, and one is swept hither and thither in the crush like a straw on the billows of the sea. Progress is out of the question except in whatever direction impulse sways the mob. There are so many versions of what is supposed to have happened that none can sift the truth. It is said that Parliament, behind closed doors, impeached his lordship, and that when he demanded entrance to his place he was arrested by order of the two Houses acting conjointly."

"But even if that were true,—and it seems incredible,—the King can liberate him at a word."

"They say even the King and Court have fled, and that hereafter Parliament will be supreme; but one cannot believe a tithe of what is flying through the streets this night. The people are mad,—stark mad." Mrs. Jarrett hovered about the young lady in case an announcement so fraught with dread to all of them should prove too much for her; but Frances was the most collected of any there. "If that is all," she said calmly, "'T will be but a temporary inconvenience to my father which he will make little of. He has committed no crime, and may face with fortitude the judgment of his peers, certain of triumphant acquittal. He is in London by command of the King, his master, and his Majesty will see to it, should all else fail, that he suffers not for his obedience."

This conclusion was so reasonable that it had the effect of soothing the apprehensions of all who heard it, and, young as she was, Frances seemed to assume a place of authority in the estimation of those present, which was to stand her in good stead later in the evening.

The headless household, barricaded in, with frequent testimony of public execration in the ominous impact of missiles flung against doors and shutters outside, went about its accustomed way in an anxious, halfhearted manner, continually on the qui vive. As the girl wandered aimlessly about the large house, nothing gave her so vivid a sense of insecurity as the dim figure of the secretary seated in the ill-lighted hall, with his cheek against the front door, listening for any hint of his master's approach, ready to undo bar and bolt with all speed and admit him at the first sign of necessity; ready, also, to defend the portal should the door be broken in by the populace, a disaster which the blows rained against it sometimes seemed to predict, followed by breathless periods of nonmolestation. The secretary's sword lay across his knee, and, like a phantom army, backs against the wall, stood in silence, similarly armed, the menservants of the household. The one scant twinkling light had been placed on a table, and a man sat beside it, his pale face more strongly illumined than any other of that ghostly company, radiant against a background of darkness. He was prepared to cover the light instantly, or to blow it out, at a signal from his leader the secretary, seated in the chair by the strong oaken door.

It was after nine o'clock, during a lull in the tempest, that there was a rap at the door.

"Who is there?" asked the secretary through the grating.

"A messenger from the Court," was the reply. Frances had come up the hall on hearing the challenge.

"What name?" demanded the secretary.

"De Courcy. Open quickly, I beg of you. The mob has surged down the street, but it may return at any moment."

"Open," said Frances with decision, and the secretary obeyed.

De Courcy came in, unrecognizable at first because of the cloak that enveloped him. The door was secured behind him, and he flung his cloak to one of the men standing there. His gay plumage was somewhat ruffled, and the girl never thought she would be so heartily glad to see him.

"Is it true that my father is sent to the Tower?" were her first words.

"No, Mademoiselle; but he is in custody, arrested by order of Parliament, and at this moment detained in the house of James Maxwell, Keeper of the Black Rod, who took his sword from him and is responsible for his safety. 'T is said he will be taken to the Tower to-morrow; but they reckon not on the good will of some of us who are his friends, and they forget the power of the King. Mon Dieu! What a night, and what a people! One walks the streets at the risk of life and garments. I was never so mauled about, and despaired of reaching this door. I've been an hour outside screeching 'Death to Strafford!' with the rest of them, else I were torn limb from limb."

Frances frowned, but said:

"What were the circumstances of my father's arrest? What do they charge against him?"

"God knows what the indictment is; chiefly that he is Strafford, I think.

He entered the House of Lords this afternoon, and walked with customary dignity to his place, but was curtly ordered to withdraw until he was sent for, as the Commons were at that moment enunciating their formula against him. He withdrew in the face of this loud protest, and at last, being recalled, stood before them; was commanded to kneel, which with some hesitation he did, while the articles to his disparagement were read from the Woolsack. He was then dismissed, and, once in the outer room again, the Black Rod demanded his sword, and so conducted him, under restraint, to a carriage; no man of all then present capping to him, although they had been obsequious enough when he entered. A scurvy lot!"

"Were you among them?"

"Not I; I give you the account as 't was told to me, but had I been in that contemptible company, my hat would have gone lower than ever before."

"You have not seen my father, then; he has sent no message by you?"

"I have not seen him, but I come to crave a few words with you in private."

"Sir, you must excuse me. I am so tense with anxiety about my father, I can think of naught else."

"'T is on that subject I wish to discourse. He has set in train a series of events in which I hoped to aid him, but it is like to go awry through this most unlooked-for arrest. That is why I was here this morning, and the commission was to have been completed to-morrow. Did he say anything to you about it?"

"You heard all he said to me to-day. I saw him for but a moment, and that in your presence."

"I had hoped his lordship made a confidant of you, so my mission were the easier of accomplishment."

"If it has to do with his welfare, I am ready to confer with you. Come with me to the library." But before they could quit the hall, they were aware that another was taking advantage of the lull in the street to seek entrance to the mansion. Frances paused to learn the result. This time it was an envoy from Strafford himself, and he brought a letter addressed to "Mistress Frances Wentworth." She opened and read the note with eager anticipation, forgetting, for the moment, all who were standing there.

Sweetheart:

"You have heard before this what hath befallen me; yet trust thou in the goodness of God that my enemies shall do me no hurt. I am troubled that you should be in London at this time, where I can be of no help to you. It would please me to know that you were safe in the home where you have lived until this present time. Think not that you can assist me other than by obeying, for I trust in God and the King, and in the assurance that I am innocent of the charges malice hath brought against me. Therefore be in no way alarmed, but betake yourself straightway to the North, there to wait with your brother, as heretofore, until I send a message for you, which I hope to do right speedily. Travel in comfort and security, and take with you such of my household as will secure both.

"My treasurer, John Vollins, will give you all money you require, and this letter is his assurance to fulfil your wishes in this and every respect. Trust in God; give way to no fear; but bear yourself as my daughter.

"Your loving father,

"Strafford."

The young woman folded the letter without a word, except to the secretary, to whom she said:

"My father writes in good confidence, seeing no cause for alarm, having assurance of his innocence and faith in God and the King."

Then she led the way to the library, followed by De Courcy, hat in hand. Vollins arose and left them together, whereupon the Frenchman, with some slight hesitation, possibly remembering a different plea on that spot a few hours before, began his recital.

"This morning his lordship, your honoured father, requested my assistance in a business which he thought I was capable of bringing to a satisfactory conclusion. It concerned a highly placed personage, whom it is perhaps improper for me to name, and perhaps unnecessary for me to particularize further. His lordship's intention was to present this exalted lady with some gift which she would value for its intrinsic worth no less than its artistic quality, and, as he professed himself no judge of such, preferring to depend upon the well-known taste of my nation in delicate articles of merit, also so far complimenting me as to believe that I could, in suitable manner and phrase, present this token to the gracious accepter of it, he desired my intervention, and I promised so to pleasure him to the best of my poor abilities. On leaving you this morning I made selection of the gift, and furthermore gave hint to the recipient of its intended presentation,—a hint, I may say, which was received with palpable delight. Judge, then, my consternation when I heard of the Earl's arrest, for he had promised to pay me the money to-morrow."

The young man paused, his listener pondering with her eyes on the floor. She had such a deep distrust of him, and was so well aware of the prejudice, that she struggled against it, praying for an unbiased mind. Yet much that he had said coincided with certain things she knew,—her father's desire that the Queen should cease from meddling in affairs of State to his disadvantage and theirs; his seeming friendship for De Courcy, although he despised him; his intention that she should be civil to him; his disclaimer of all knowledge regarding what a woman valued in a gift when he presented her with a full purse the night before,—all these fitted with the Frenchman's story. The suppliant, scrutinizing her perplexed brow, seemed to fear that his chance of getting the money was vanishing, as he continued on the line most likely to incline her to favour his present demand.

"Of course, I should not have troubled you in this matter did I not think that if the arrangement your father wished to make was important this morning, it is ten times more important to-night. Indeed, his liberty may depend upon it. I am well aware that it is open to me to say to the lady, 'Lord Strafford is in prison, and is unable to carry out his generous intentions,' but I fear the deep disappointment will outweigh the force of the reasoning. Your charming sex is not always strictly logical."

"What was the sum agreed upon?" asked Frances, looking suddenly up.

"A thousand pounds in gold."

The question had been sprung upon him, and he had answered without thought, but as he watched her resolute face a shade of disappointment passed over his own, as if of inward regret that he had not made the amount larger, should her determination prove his ally.

"I shall see that you get the money, if not to-night, at the time promised."

She sent for Vollins and placed the case before him. The treasurer stood by the table, with inscrutable face and listened in silence, his somewhat furtive look bent on the Frenchman.

"Has Monsieur De Courcy some scrap of writing in which my lord signifies that so considerable a payment is to be made?"

"My dear fellow, this relates to business that is not put in writing between gentlemen," said the foreigner hastily.

"I am not a gentleman, but merely the custodian of his lordship's purse. I dare not pay out gold without his lordship's warrant over his own signature."

De Courcy shrugged his shoulders and spread out his hands, as though he had washed them of responsibility.

"Mr. Vollins," pleaded the girl eagerly, "my father's life and liberty may depend on this disbursement. I will be your warrant. I have money of my own in the North, many times the sum I request you to pay. Should my father object, I will refund to you the thousand pounds; indeed I will remit it to you in any case, and my father need know nothing of this transaction, therefore you cannot be held in scath." Vollins shook his head.

"I must not do it," he said. "His lordship is a very strict man of business and will hold me to account. He would forgive you, Madam, but would be merciless with me did I consent to so unheard of a proposal. I dare not count out a thousand pounds to the first man who steps from the street and asks for it, giving me his bare word."

"Do you dispute my word, sir?" demanded De Courcy, bristling.

"Assuredly not. I am but putting a case, as his lordship would undoubtedly put it to me were I to consent,—and what would be my answer?"

"But you have my word as well, Mr. Vollins," urged the girl.

"Madam, I beseech you to consider my position. I am but a servant. The money is not mine, or you were welcome to it. Yet why all this haste? His lordship can undoubtedly be communicated with tomorrow, and then a word or line from him is sufficient."

"You have an adage, sir, of striking while the iron is hot; the iron may be cool enough by the time your scruples of legality are satisfied," warned De Courcy.

"His lordship can be communicated with; you are quite right, Mr. Vollins," cried Frances, remembering. "He has communicated with me. I ask you to read this letter, and then to pay the thousand pounds required of you."

Vollins read the letter with exasperating slowness, and said at last:

"There is nothing here authorizing me to pay the gentleman a thousand pounds."

"True, there is not. But my father says you are to pay me what moneys I require. I require at this moment a thousand pounds in gold."

"The money is for your safe conduct to the North."

"You have read my father's letter more carelessly than I supposed, by the time you took. He says you are to fulfill my wishes in this and every respect. Do you still refuse me?"

"No, Madam. But I venture to advise you strongly against the payment."

"I thank you for your advice. I can certify that you have done your duty fully and faithfully. Will you kindly bring forth the gold?"

Vollins weighed the five bags of coin with careful exactitude and without further speech. De Courcy fastened them to his belt, then looked about him for his cloak, which he at last remembered to have left in the hall. Vollins called upon a servant to fetch it, taking it from him at the door. The Frenchman enveloped himself, and so hid his treasure. The cautious Vollins had prepared a receipt for him to sign, made out in the name of Frances Wentworth, but De Courcy demurred; it was all very well for the counting-house, he said, but not in the highest society. The Earl of Strafford would be the first to object to such a course, he insisted. Frances herself tore the paper in pieces, and said that a signature was not necessary, while Vollins made no further protest. She implored De Courcy, in a whispered adieu, to acquit faithfully the commission with which her father had entrusted him, and he assured her that he was now confident of success, thanking her effusively for the capable conduct of a difficult matter of diplomacy. Then, with a sweeping gesture of obeisance, he took his courteous departure.

Mr. Vollins deferentially asked Frances to sign a receipt which he had written, acknowledging the payment of a thousand pounds, and to this document she hurriedly attached her signature.

CHAPTER VI.—ORDEAL.

Frances made her way to the North as her father had directed, and everywhere found the news of his arrest in advance of her; the country ablaze with excitement because of it. The world would go well once Strafford was laid low. He had deluded and misled the good King, as Buckingham did before him. Buckingham had fallen by the knife; Strafford should fall by the axe. Then the untrammelled King would rule well; quietness and industry would succeed this unhealthy period of fever and unrest.

The girl was appalled to meet everywhere this intense hatred of her father, and in her own home she was surrounded by it. Even her brother could not be aroused to sympathy, for he regarded his father not only as a traitor to his country, but as a domestic delinquent also, who had neglected and deserted his young wife, leaving her to die uncomforted without even a message from the husband for whom she had almost sacrificed her good name, bearing uncomplaining his absence and her father's wrath. During the winter Frances saw little of her brother. Thomas Wentworth was here and there riding the country, imagining, with the confidence of extreme youth, that he was mixing in great affairs, as indeed he was, although he was too young to have much influence in directing them. The land was in a ferment, and the wildest rumours were afloat. Strafford had escaped from the Tower, and had taken flight abroad, like so many of his friends who had now scattered in fear to France or to Holland. Again it was said the King's soldiers had attacked the Tower, liberated Strafford, and the Black Man was at the head of the wild Irish, resolved on the subjugation of England. Next, the Queen had called on France for aid, and an invasion was imminent. So there was much secret preparation, drilling and the concealing of arms against the time they should be urgently needed, and much galloping to and fro; a stirring period for the young, an anxious winter for the old, and Herbert Wentworth was in the thick of it all, mysteriously departing, unexpectedly returning, always more foolishly important than there was any occasion for. Yet had he in him the making of a man who was shortly to be tried by fire and steel, when greater wisdom crowned him than was at present the case.

One by one the sinister rumours were contradicted by actual events; no French army crossed the Channel; the Irish did not rise; the grim Tower held Strafford secure in its iron grasp. Parliament seemed hesitating to strike, piling up accusations, collecting proof, but staying its hand. Everyone was loyal to the King, so grievously misled. The King could do no wrong, but woe to the Minister who could and did. So, this exciting winter passed and springtime came, ringing with news of Strafford's approaching trial. A stern resolve to be finally rid of him, proof or no proof, was in the air, tinctured with the fine silken hypocrisy that all should be done according to the law; that the axe should swing in rhythm with a solemn declaration of judgment legally rendered. And there was no man to say to the hesitating King, "When that head falls, the brain of your government is gone."

Since the letter she had received on the night of his arrest, the daughter heard no word from the father. Had he again forgotten, or were his messages intercepted? She did not know and was never to know. She had written to him, saying she had obeyed him, but there was no acknowledgment that her letter had reached its destination. Thus she waited and waited, gnawing impatience and dread chasing the rose from her cheeks, until she could wait no longer. Her horse and the southern road were at her disposal, with none to hinder, so she set forth for London, excusing herself for thus in spirit breaking her father's command, by the assurance that he had not forbidden her return. She avoided her father's mansion, knowing that Lady Strafford and her children were now in residence there, and went to the inn where she had formerly lodged. She soon learned that it was one thing to go to London, and quite another to obtain entrance to Westminster Hall, where the great trial, now approaching its end, was the fashionable magnet of the town. No place of amusement ever collected such audiences, and although money will overcome many difficulties, she found it could not purchase admission to the trial through any source that was available. Perhaps if she had been more conversant with the ways of the metropolis the golden key might have shot back the bolt, but with her present knowledge she was at her wit's end.

Almost in despair, a happy thought occurred to her. She wrote a note to John Vollins, her father's treasurer, and asked him to call upon her, which the good man did at the hour she set.

"Your father would be troubled to know you are in London, when he thinks you safe at home," he said.

"I could not help it, Mr. Vollins. I was in a fever of distraction and must have come even if I had walked. But my father need never know, and you remember he wrote that you were to help me.' I wish a place in Westminster Hall and cannot attain it by any other means in my power than by asking you."

"It is difficult of attainment. I advise you not to go there, for if his lordship happened to catch sight of you in that throng, who knows but at a critical moment it might unnerve him, for he is a man fighting with his back to the wall against implacable and unscrupulous enemies."

"Could you not get me some station where I might look upon my father unseen by him?"

"Seats in the Hall are not to be picked or chosen.. If a place can be come by, it will be because some person who thought to attend cannot be present."

"Do you think that where there are so many faces a chance recognition is possible? I should be but an atom in the multitude."

"Doubtless his seeing you is most unlikely. I shall do my best for you, and hope to obtain an entrance for to-morrow."

And so it came about that Frances was one of the fashionable audience next day, occupying the place of a lady who had attended the trial from the first, but was now tired of it, seeking some new excitement, thus missing the most dramatic scene of that notable tragedy. Frances found herself one of a bevy of gaily dressed ladies, all of whom were gossiping and chattering together, comparing notes they had taken of the proceedings, for many of them had dainty writing-books in which they set down the points that pleased them as the case went on. It seemed like a gala day, animated by a thrill of eager expectancy; a social function, entirely pleasurable, with no hint that a man stood in jeopardy of his life. Although the body of the hall was crowded, draped benches at the upper end were still untenanted, except that here and there sat a man, serving rather to emphasize the emptiness of the benches than give token of occupancy.

The lady placed at Frances's right, observing that the girl was a stranger and somewhat bewildered by the unaccustomed scene, kindly made explanation to her.

"On those benches will sit the Lords, who are the judges; on the others the Commons, who are the accusers. They have not yet taken their stations."

"Will the King be present?"

"Technically, no; actually, yes. The Throne, which you see there, will be vacant throughout, but the King may be behind that latticed screen above it, where he can see but cannot be seen. The King must not interfere at a State trial, but he may overset its verdict, and he will, if it should go against the Earl, which is not likely."

"I—I do not see my——I do not see the Earl of Strafford."

"He is not here yet, and will not arrive until the Houses sit."

The girl listened to the hum of conversation going on round her, and caught understandable scraps of it now and then. She was in an entirely new atmosphere, for here every one seemed in favour of Strafford, thought him badly used, and was certain he would emerge triumphant from the ordeal. Then let his enemies beware! Feminine opinion was unanimous that all those who were concerned in this trial against his lordship would bitterly regret the day they had taken such action. The spirits of Frances rose as she listened. The invariable confidence by which she was environed had its inspiring effect on her depressed mind. She no longer thought the gathering heartlessly frivolous, as at first she had resentfully estimated it. She was in the midst of enthusiastic champions of her father, and realized now, as never before, the great part he played in the world.

Suddenly there was a movement in the upper part of the Hall, and Lords and Commons filed in to their places. A silence fell on the audience, maintained also in dignified state by the judges, but to the section occupied by the Commons was transferred the rustle of talk which had previously disturbed the stillness of the auditorium. Men bustled about, whispering to this member of Parliament or that. Papers and notes were exchanged, while by contrast their Lordships seemed like inanimate statues.

Once again the centre of attention changed. The Hall resounded with the measured tramp of armed men. Two rows of soldiers took their stand opposite each other, leaving a clear passage between, and slowly up this passage, with four secretaries and some halfdozen others behind him, came a bowed and pallid figure, dressed in black, a single decoration relieving the sombreness of his costume, which hung, loosely unfitting, about a frame that had become gaunt since its wear began.

"That is the Earl of Strafford," whispered the lady on the right, but the remark fell upon unlistening ears. How changed he was! No trace now of that arrogance of which she had caught chance glimpses during her brief acquaintance with him; a broken man who had but a short time to live, whatever might be the verdict of this court. Sentence of death was already passed on him by a higher tribunal, and all this convocation might do was to forestall its execution. He stood in his place for a moment, and bowed to his judges, but gave no sign that he had knowledge of the existence of his accusers, and the girl began to doubt if the old arrogance had, after all, entirely departed from him. Then, leaning heavily on the arm of one of his secretaries, he sank into his seat and closed his eyes, as if the short walk from the barge to the hall of judgment had been too much for him. As he sat thus there stole down to him a boy leading two children. Strafford's eyes opened, and he smiled wanly upon them, put an arm around the boy's neck, and fondled the girls to his knee, both of whom were weeping quietly.

"Who—who are those?" gasped Frances, yet knowing while she asked, and feeling a pang, half jealousy, half pain, that she must hold aloof unnoticed.

"They are his son and his two daughters. The third daughter is not here."

"The third!" she' cried in surprise. "Does he then acknowledge a third?"

"The third is an infant too young to know what is going on. Hush! We must not talk."

The girl's eagerness fell away from her; she reclined back in her seat and sighed deeply. The preliminaries of the day passed her like a dream, for she knew nothing of the procedure, but at last her attention was aroused, for she saw her father on his feet, and before she was aware he began to speak, the voice at first cold and calm, penetrating the remotest corner of that vast room, in argument that even she recognized as clear, logical, and dispassioned as if he were setting forth the case of another. He was listened to with the most profound respect by enemies and friends alike. He seemed to brush away the charges against him as if they were very cobwebs of accusation. As he went on, he warmed more to his theme, and by and by the girl, leaning intently forward, drinking in every word, knew that she was listening to oratory such as had never before greeted the ears of England, and probably never would again. A breathless tension held the audience spellbound, and it seemed impossible that his direst foe could remain unmoved. The belief in his acquittal now became a certainty, and it was every moment more and more evident that this acquittal would also be a triumph. He stood, one man against three kingdoms thirsting for the blood, yet turning the crisis to the dumfounding of his enemies by the overwhelming force of eloquence. Not a chord on the harp of human sentiment and passion was left unsounded. The deft hand swept every string and fascinated his hearers. When he spoke of his children, pleading more for them than for himself, they weeping at his knee, his own voice broke into a sob more touching even than his living words. From the eyes of Frances gushed the pent-up tears. And she was not alone in her emotion, for the flutter of lace at the eyes of fair ladies broke like white blossoms everywhere. And yet——and yet she became reluctantly convinced that her father in this crisis had entirely forgotten her, and when he spoke of his children, remembered only those that had been all their lives about his knees. She was but the daughter of a day!

Recovering himself, the speaker went on to his peroration. "And now, my lords, I thank God, I have been, by His blessing, sufficiently instructed in the extreme vanity of all temporal enjoyments, compared to the importance of our eternal duration. And so, my lords, even so, with all humility and with all tranquillity of mind, I submit clearly and freely to your judgments. And whether that righteous doom shall be to life or death, I shall repose myself, full of gratitude and confidence, in the arms of the Great Author of my existence. Te Deum laudamus, te Dominum confitemur."

The Latin phrase pealed forth like the solemn tone of a chant, and the speaker subsided into his chair almost in a swoon, for physical weakness had at last overcome the indomitable spirit.

On none of the vast visible throng had the effective oration exercised greater power than upon an unseen listener. The awed stillness was suddenly broken by a splintering crash, and the startled audience, looking up, saw the frail lattice work of the alcove shattered, and the King standing there like a ghost enframed by jagged laths. Stern determination sat on that handsome countenance; a look which said as plainly as words, "This man shall not die!" His hands clutched the broken framework beneath him, and he moistened his lips as if to give utterance to the words his expression foreshadowed. But before he could speak, a tall, angular figure sprang out from among the Commons and held up a sinewy hand. His face was ablaze with anger; his stentorian voice dominated the Hall, envenomed with hatred, striking the ear with terror as does the roar of a tiger.

"The might of England, in Parliament assembled, gives judgment untrammeled and unafraid. The King is not here. The King cannot be here. The Throne is vacant, and must remain vacant until justice is done."

As the last words rang out, the long index finger, shaken menacingly, pointed at the empty chair. There was defiance of King or Minister in words, and tone and gesture; a challenge to the Throne. The pale face of the King became ghastly white, his hand trembled, and fragments of the lattice-work fell from beneath it. Irresolution took the place of former determination, and he glanced pitifully from right to left, as if seeking human support, of which, in the amazed stillness, there was no indication. Then the fine white hand of an unseen woman showed for a moment on his arm like a snow-flake, and Charles, with one look of haunting compassion on the prisoner, disappeared from sight. The phantom picture had vanished from its ragged frame without a sound, and blank darkness occupied its place. Truly the King was not present, conjured away by the strenuous hand of the fierce combatant on the stage, and the soft hand of the woman behind the scenes.

"Who is that man?" whispered Frances, gazing in frightened fascination on the rude interrupter.

"That is John Pym, the chief prosecutor and deadly personal enemy of Lord Strafford."

As the girl gazed at this dominating individuality, all the froth of confidence in her father's acquittal, whipped up by the chatter of conversation at the beginning, evaporated. There stood the personified hatred of England against the Earl of Strafford. No wavering in accent or action there, but a determined man, knowing what he wanted and bent on having it. To her excited imagination the resolute face took on the semblance of a death-mask, and the clenched hand seemed to grasp the shaft of an axe. It was as if the headsman had suddenly stood forth and claimed his own, and a chill as of the grave, swept over the audience with a shudder in its wake.

A low wailing cry went sobbing across the silence; a cry that tugged at

Strafford's heart when he heard it. What memory did it stir in his troubled mind? A reminiscence of something that had escaped him, crowded out by matters of more pressing moment.

"What is that?" he asked anxiously.

"It is nothing, my lord," answered Vollins, stepping between his master and the commotion among the women. "A lady has fainted, that is all. They are taking her out."

CHAPTER VII.—APPEAL.

Once out in the open air, Frances Wentworth came again into control of herself, ashamed that, for the moment, her emotions had overwhelmed her. She had no desire to re-enter Westminster Hall, even if the doorkeepers would have permitted her, so she wandered slowly back to the inn which was her temporary home. In the evening John Vollins came to see her, and offered money which she told him she did not need. He gave some account of Pym's speech, and said that the Commons had not asked the Lords for judgment, which was taken by Strafford and his friends as an indication that they knew the weakness of the evidence and feared the effect of his lordship's speech in his own defence. The refusal to ask for judgment was regarded as a good omen, and for some days Frances felt the revival of hope, when she could forget the grim figure of John Pym, but the Commons speedily disillusioned the Straffordian party. A bill of attainder was brought in, and they showed their determination to have the head of the unfortunate Earl by act of Parliament, if not by legal procedure. At last the bill, passing its third reading, was sent up to the House of Lords. There were many who said the Lords would never assent to it; that the Commons should have asked for judgment at the close of the trial; that if they could not hope to have the verdict as they wanted it then, it was not likely the Lords would allow themselves to be cozened by a side wind now. These predictions were quickly falsified. The Lords gave their consent to the bill of attainder, and nothing stood between Strafford and the block but a scrawl from the King's pen.

The Lords, it was said by those who defended them, had been coerced by the populace. The mob had gathered again and had clamoured around the House of Peers, crying for justice on Strafford; now they transferred their loud-throated exclamations to Whitehall, for success with the nobles foreshadowed success with the King.

It was late on Saturday night when John Vollins made his way to the inn at some jeopardy to himself, for the streets were wild with joy at the action of the Lords. He told Frances that her father's life depended solely on the firmness of the King. If Charles signed on Monday, Strafford was to be led to the block on Wednesday. Vollins was in deep gloom over the prospect. The Earl, he said, had some time previously written to the King, absolving him from all his promises, offering his life freely if the taking of it would advantage his Majesty in dealing with his obstreperous subjects.

"But the King is trebly perjured if he signs. He cannot sign," cried Frances.

Vollins shook his head.

"If all the Lords in England are held in terror by the people's clamour, and so let the greatest of their number slip through their fingers to the axe, how can one weak man be expected to withstand the concentration of the popular will brought against him? 'T is blinded folly to look for it."

"But the people dare not coerce a King."

"Dare they not? Go down to Whitehall and you will find them doing it. This very day they have all but stormed the palace."

"I will see the King, throw myself at his feet and implore him to keep his word. I was present when he bade my father take this fateful journey to London, and when he promised full protection. A King's word should stand against the world, for he is the source of truth and honour in a nation."

"You cannot get to see him. Every entrance to the palace is strongly guarded. Highly placed friends of my lord, friends when all others had fallen away from him, have sought admission to the royal presence in vain. He has refused to see the Earl of Bristol, whose son, Lord Digby, spoke out against the conclusiveness of the evidence, and his Majesty has let it be spread abroad that he gives no approval of Lord Digby's plain words, and so the people cry 'God save the King!' and revile Lord Digby."

The girl stood aghast at this intelligence, remembering the scene at the trial, when royalty in the person of Charles Stuart, and the people in the person of John Pym, opposed their wills to each other. Then royalty had faded from the sight of men, and the strong champion of the people held his ground alone and triumphant. "Trust in God and the King," wrote the prisoner. What a conjunction! Almighty power, and a bending reed! "Nevertheless, I will see the King," she said.

On Sunday the immensity of the swaying crowd, shouting and moving like a slow resistless flood through the streets, daunted her. There was no employment that day to keep any one within doors, and it seemed as if that labyrinth of human warrens called London had emptied itself into the narrow thoroughfares. She hesitated like a timid swimmer on the brink of a raging torrent, yet if she was to win access to the King she must trust herself to the current, which had this advantage, it set toward the direction in which she wished to go. If the streets could be compared to sluggish streams, the broad avenue or square of Whitehall might be likened to the lake into which they emptied. It was a packed mass of humanity, surging to and fro, as if influenced by mysterious tides, but making no progress. Way through it in any given direction might well seem an impossibility; but an alert atom, by constantly watching opportunity, could edge here and there, through chance openings, and, by a constant devotion to a given direction, ultimately attain any chosen point. Thus the girl, buffeted about, often well-nigh exhausted and breathless, came by the entrance to the palace that stood next the banqueting-house. The gates, however, were tightly closed, and guarded on the outside by a double row of soldiery, who stood the hustling of the mob with great good humour, being evidently cautioned not to exasperate the populace by any hostile act. The crowd itself seemed good-natured enough, although constant fighting took place here and there along its choking surface; but the great bulk of those present appeared to be out on a larking holiday, although they all riotously lent breath to the unceasing roar, calling for justice on Strafford. Occasionally there were shouts for the King, and demands that he should speak to them, but the windows of Whitehall Palace were blank and gave no sign of human occupancy.

Suddenly Frances found herself in new danger through one of those unexplainable heaves of the many-throated beast at whose mercy she stood.

"To the gates!" went up a shout. "We will make the King hear," and a great human wave, overwhelming the soldiers, struck against the shuddering portal. The mere pressure of the multitude was deadly and irresistible. There were shrieks and appeals for forbearance, but the unreasoning mass behind pressed on, unheeding, cheering, and shoving. A crash of rending timbers, and the gates flew inward; then the mob, as if frightened at what it had done, paused, giving the soldiers time to collect themselves and help the wounded. There was as yet no malice in the crush; it was more like a conglomeration of irresponsible children, bent on mischief of any kind, but temporarily scared at the breaking of something. This fact seemed to be recognized by a man in authority who came through the gate and with some difficulty secured a precarious footing on one of the stone pillars which stood in a row between the pathway and the road, thus giving him a position which towered over the heads of the assemblage. He held up a hand for a hearing, and the crowd cheered him, not in the least knowing who he was or why he was there. Comparative silence followed the cheer, and the nobleman spoke.

"My good people," he said, "there is little use in the breaking of gates that the King may hear you; for the King has heard, and is taking the requests of his faithful subjects into his august consideration."

"Where is the King?" demanded an auditor.

"His Majesty is in the banqueting-house, where, as you know, he is in touch with his people. 'T is a prayerful subject he has to meditate on, and I beg of you not to disturb his devotions by further——"

"Is the Queen at her devotions too? In that hall she began masked revels on a Sunday, and six good men were done to death for protesting against the desecration, each life more valuable than the wicked Earl's. Let the King say that he will sign, and we will disperse!"

These and other cries more or less to the purpose baffled the orator, and the air quivered with denunciations of Strafford. The man on the stone post had cast his eyes behind him several times, as if to see what progress was being made with the readjustment of the gate, and from this his hearers quickly divined that he was but deluding them to gain time, which was more than likely his purpose, so the shout went up to move through the breach and surround the hall. Meanwhile reinforcements had been summoned from within, and a hand-to-hand fight ensued with the encroachers. Frances, panting and nigh worn out in the struggle, nevertheless saw her opportunity. There were few women in the throng, and such as came near them the soldiers sought to protect. She attempted appeal to the officer, but that harassed dignitary could harken to none, and thrust her rudely but effectually through the opening, saying,—"You will find egress at one of the other gates. Take care of yourself. I cannot help you."

Breathing a sigh of thankfulness, she cowered and ran along the end of the banqueting-hall, turned at the corner, then down the side, entering an archway that let her into a passage. She knew that she must turn to her right, but where after that she had not the slightest notion. The tumult at the gate was so frightful that she expected every moment to hear the victorious assaulters at her heels. Her joy at finding herself thus unexpectedly within the precincts of the palace, unimpeded, caused her to overlook the fact that this was scarcely a propitious moment in which to implore the King to disregard the lusty giant rudely beating at his doors. A frightened waiting-maid came hurrying along the corridor, and to her she directed inquiry regarding the entrance to the banqueting-hall.

"Turn to the right and up the stair."

"Take me there, I beg of you."

"I cannot. I bear a message."

"But I bear a message to the King, so yours must wait."

At this the maid turned and conducted her to the door of the hall, saying to the man at arms,—"This lady has a message for his Majesty."

The first thing that struck her on entering the great painted chamber was that the nobleman on the stone outside had not spoken the truth when he said the King heard the demands of his people. A growl as of an angry lion penetrated the closed windows, but the words spoken were not to be distinguished.

The King was sitting at a massive table, his head in his hands. Behind him were grouped a number of bishops in their robes, and it certainly seemed that his Majesty was engaged in devotional exercises, as had been stated by the orator. But if this were the case they were of a strangely mixed order, for behind the lady who was talking volubly to the King, stood two Capuchin monks with folded arms. Excepting the bishops none of the English nobility were present, but several Frenchmen, among whom she recognized De Courcy, held aloof from the cluster at the table, so the girl quite correctly surmised that the lady bearing the whole burden of the conversation was no other than the Queen herself, and that these foreigners were members of her train.

Her Majesty spoke sometimes in French, sometimes in English, the latter with broken accent, and her eloquence was rather puzzling to follow, for the flow of her conversation was of extreme rapidity. Palpably she supposed herself talking in English, but whenever she came to a difficulty in the choice of a word she made no attempt to surmount it by any effort of thought, but swam swiftly round it on the easy current of her native tongue. Translated, her discourse ran thus:

"My God! These good men have made it perfectly plain; for, as they say,—and who shall question the dictum of the Church in such matters,—you have two consciences, the conscience of the Prince and the conscience' of the man; and where the consciences come into conflict that of the Prince must of necessity rule, as is the axiom in all civilized Courts. Is it right that you, a King, should jeopardize yourself in a useless effort to save one condemned by his peers, because your private conscience as a man urges you to keep a promise which he himself has relieved you from, holding you guiltless before God and the nations, and further advised by these good men, lords of their Church, that such action would not make toward peace of the realm. It is not a subject to be hesitated upon for a moment, the good of the ruler being paramount always——"

"Oh, my lord, the King, listen not to such sophistry, be it from the lips of priest or woman. The given word is the man, and he stands or falls by it. If the foresworn peasant be a cringing craven, ten thousand times worse is the perjured Prince. You pledged your faith to Lord Strafford, and now, in his just Heaven, God demands the fulfilment of your word."

The dishevelled girl had flung herself at the feet of the frightened monarch, who started back, gazing wildly about him, shaking as one struck with palsy, so startling and unexpected had been the interruption. Red anger flushed the face of the no less amazed Queen, speechless with indignation at the words and the tone of them, addressed to her exalted husband. The sage bishops were astounded at the lack of diplomacy on the part of the petitioner, who had thus rudely thrown herself counter to the expressed wishes of the highest lady in the land; but Frances, with an instant intuition more subtle than theirs, saw that the Queen was an enemy not to be cajoled by deference or flattery, so she determined that the war between them should be open and above board.

The King had reason for agitation greater than the surprise that had made breathing statues of those about him. The accents that disturbed him were the accents of Strafford himself, softened as they were by the lips that uttered them. The boldness of the address was Strafford's, and, until he saw that a woman knelt before him, it almost seemed that the dominant spirit of the prisoner had burst the bonds of the Tower and sped hither to reproach him for meditated treachery.

Frances, gathering breath, took advantage of the silence her sudden advent had caused.

"Why is Lord Strafford in a dungeon to-day? Because, trusting your word, he obeyed your command at Hampton. Why was he put on trial? Because, faithfully, he carried out his King's behests. Why was he condemned to death? Because he stood true to the King. If he deserve death, then so do you, for you are the master and he the servant. Has God stricken you and your counsellors with blindness, that you cannot see in the destruction of

Strafford the throwing away of the shield which guards your breast, leaving you naked to your enemies? Surrender bastion, and the castle falls."

"God of Heaven!" cried the quivering Queen. "What country of the mad is this, where the meanest of subjects may so address a monarch! Strip the mantle from her back and scourge her rebellious flesh to the kennel whence she comes."

"No, no!" gasped Charles, staggering to his feet and sweeping with a gesture of his hand the documents which lay before him on the table, so that they fluttered to the floor. "Christ have mercy upon me! She speaks the truth; happy is the Prince who hears it and heeds it. I have passed my word to Strafford, and it shall be kept. I will not sign,—no, though the heavens fall. Rise, my girl! You have my promise,—the promise of a Stuart,—and it shall be fulfilled."

Charles graciously assisted the girl to her feet with the same courtesy he would have shown to the first lady of the Court.

The rage of the Queen now passed all bounds of restraint. "And this before me, your wife! You weigh the word of this bedraggled creature of the streets above that of the royal House of France, and Queen of this turbulent realm! By God, you deserve to be hooted by your loathsome mob. Who is this strumpet?" De Courcy whispered a word into her ear.

"What! The bastard of that profligate Strafford! Jesu, to what a pass this Christian Court has come!"

"Madam," said Frances with frigid dignity, "you misname me. I have the honour to be Lord Strafford's lawful daughter, acknowledged by him as such in presence of his Majesty the King."

"'T is true, 't is true," murmured Charles, visibly quailing before the increasing wrath of his wife, adding in piteous appeal, "God's wounds, have I not enough to bear without the quarreling of women."

"The quarreling of women! Dare you couple me in the same breath with such as she? Is there none in my train to whip forth this impudent wench into the wretched rabble that has spewed her into our presence. The quarreling of women! A slattern that wishes to divert, from her reputed father's head to yours, the anger of the gutter. Listen to it, my lord, listen to it."

All this was shrieked forth with gestures so rapid and amazing that the eye could scarce follow the motion of her hands. Now she flew to the window and fumbled with its fastening, too greatly excited to succeed with the opening. Several of the French gallants stumbled over each other in their haste to aid her, but the lady's impatience could not wait for them. She lifted her clenched hand and smote the diamond panes, which went shivering down beneath the fierce impact of the blow. Glass or lead or both cut the imperious hand and wrist, and the blood trickled down the fair rounded arm. The breach she made was like the letting in of waters; the roar outside became instantly articulate, and waves of meaning flooded the great apartment.

"To the block with Strafford. Death to the people's oppressor!" was the cry, and the tortured King shrank from it as from the lash of a whip.

"Harken to the wolves!" shrieked the Queen. "It is your blood or Strafford's! Which, which, which?"

Then, perhaps because of the hurt which she scarcely seemed to feel, her mood changed as quickly as her anger had risen, and she melted into tears, glided to her husband, and threw her arms about his neck.

"Oh Charles, Charles," she moaned, "it is my love for you that would coerce you. You have not been to blame, misled by an obstinate Minister who would sacrifice an indulgent master to buy his own safety. A King is not to be bound as other men. The claim of your wife and children rise superior to that of any subject, for you have sworn to protect them." Charles stood by the wall which was eight years later to be broken for his own final exit, his eyes filled with tears, caressing the woman who clung to his breast. He saw that the girl was about to address him again and said hastily,—"Go, go! You but pile distraction on distraction. Fear not; for the word of a King goes with you."

"No, no!" sobbed the Queen. "For my sake withdraw it."

Two of the bishops now stepped forward, and with gentle urgency used their persuasion on the girl to withdraw. "God keep your Majesty firm," she cried, "and so deal with you as you deal with my father." But the last sight she was to have of her ruler, as the good men pushed her to the door, was far from inspiring. His cheeks were womanishly wet, and wavering irresolution was stamped upon his brow. The twining wounded arms of his wife had reddened the white scarf at his throat with the royal, passionate blood of France.

CHAPTER VIII.—EXECUTION.

On Monday there were ever-increasing rumours through the town that Charles had signed the bill which would send his chief Minister to the block, qualified by statements equally vague that he had done nothing of the sort; but as night drew on, the rising jubilation of the crowds in the streets gave point to the more sinister report. In the evening, his usual time of calling, the sombre Vollins came to the inn, chiefly, as he said, to urge the girl to quit the turbulent city, where she could accomplish nothing, and where she might be in danger were it once guessed that she bore any relationship to the condemned man; but to this good counsel the girl would not listen. What she demanded impatiently was news, news, news, and this, with exasperating deliberation, Vollins gave forth. It was quite true that the bill was signed, not by the King's hand, but by the hands of four Commissioners whom he had appointed for that purpose. The House of Lords, and even the House of Commons, was amazed at this betrayal, said Vollins, and the effect of the announcement had been seen on the populace itself; for, after certainty came home to the people, they had dispersed quietly to their houses, and the streets were almost empty.

The girl was mute with dismay, but Vollins pointed out that the case was in reality no worse than it had been on Saturday or Sunday. By the exercise of his prerogative the King could at any moment free his Minister or mitigate the sentence, notwithstanding the fact that the Commission had signed the bill of attainder in his name. Vollins had always been distrustful of the King, but his pessimism was not increased by the hurrying events of the last few days; rather, he saw signs of encouragement where Frances found only blank despair. The signing had had the immediate effect of stilling the outcry of the public, yet it in no way increased Strafford's danger. The action was merely typical of the King's roundabout methods of accomplishing his objects. The people were notoriously fickle and could not keep up the shouting indefinitely; indeed there were already signs that they were tired of it. It was more than likely that Charles would reprieve the Earl, possibly at the last moment, and have him shipped off to France or Holland before London knew what had been done. Or, it might be, Strafford would escape when Charles saw that Lords, Commons, and people were in grim earnest. The Tower was on the waterside, and the prisoner would not be the first who had slipped away by boat the night before an intended execution. Such a plan would be peculiarly acceptable to the mind of the King, for he had given way to the expressed will of his subjects and could not be held responsible for the avolation of the convicted man. The Tower was impregnable and cared nothing for clamour.

Tuesday seemed to bear out these surmises. Frances determined to see the King once more, and learn from his own lips the fate of her father; but when she reached Whitehall she found some commotion there, for Charles was taking his departure from the palace, and people said he was on his way to the House of Lords, and that it was likely he had determined to let Strafford go. Even although this suspicion was prevalent among those assembled, there seemed to be no popular resentment of it, and the crowd loudly cheered Charles as he rode away surrounded by his jingling guards—truly a remarkable change in public sentiment since Sunday. She went from Whitehall to the Tower, viewing the stronghold from various points, but not venturing near it. At first she had some thought of asking admission that she might see her father; but she was almost certain a refusal was all she might expect, and there was ever the fear she would arouse inquiry by making any application, and so frustrate plans already formed for his rescue. Vague visions passed through her mind of prisoners escaping through the devotion of friends sacrificing themselves, or concocting ingenious schemes that resulted in liberty; but as she looked at the forbidding, strong fortress, her dreams were confronted by a very stern reality, and the conviction was impressed upon her that there was nothing to be gained in lingering about the Tower. After all, the word of the King was sufficient to open the gates, could he but pluck up courage to speak it. He was bound in honour to say the word, and Frances saw that her only chance of helpfulness lay in urging him to keep his promise.

In the evening she learned authoritatively the object of the King's visit to the House of Lords. He had pleaded earnestly for the life of his Minister, promising, if he were released, never again to employ him even in the meanest capacity. He implored them at least to grant a reprieve until Saturday, and this was so small a favour for a King to ask that Vollins was sure it would be granted, and that many things might happen in the intervening days. The confidence of a man so generally despairing as Vollins, in the certainty of a short reprieve, and in the ultimate safety of Lord Stratford, did much to bring the girl to a like belief, but she resolved, nevertheless, to see the King next day if she could win her way into Whitehall Palace.

Wednesday saw no excitement on the streets; people were going soberly about, each on his own affairs, and the reprieve had provoked no outburst, which in itself was a hopeful sign. Frances had grown to fear the hue and cry of the mob even more than she feared the indecision of the King. If he were left unterrified, all his tendency was toward mercy and the keeping of his oath.

There was no crowd to distract the attention of the guard at the palace gates opening on Whitehall, and they absolutely refused to grant her admission without an order. She turned to the captain of the guard and asked how such an order could be obtained, and that official, apparently struck by her youth and beauty, as well as her evident distress, said that if she knew any about the Court who might be sent for, and who proved willing to vouch for her, he would allow her to pass; but the rule at the gate was strict, because of past disturbances, and he had no option but refusal unless she went in under the convoy of some one in authority. Frances pondered a few moments, and hesitated, but her need was great, and she could not choose when it came to finding security. At last she said with reluctance,—"I am acquainted with Monsieur De Courcy. Is he within?"

"I do not know, but 't will be speedily ascertained." With that he invited her to a seat in the guardhouse, and sent a messenger for De Courcy, knowing there would be prompt response when the Frenchman learned that a beautiful lady awaited him, and in this he was not mistaken. De Courcy came, as debonair and as well groomed as usual, twirling his light moustache, and doffing his hat with a grand air when he saw who his petitioner was.

"I wish to see his Majesty again," said Frances, rising; "but they detain me at the gate, and I have no one to vouch for me unless you will be so kind, though I am sorry to trouble you."

"To pleasure me, Mademoiselle, you must mean. 'T is an ungallant country, as I have always said, when they keep so fair a maid a-waiting. Such a boorish act is not conceivable in France. Most honoured am I to be your sponsor, and it gratifies me to tell you that the King is at present disengaged. I beg you to accompany me."

The friend of the Queen did not even trouble to make any explanation to the captain of the guard, and he was too powerful a courtier to have anything he did questioned by the underlings. It was palpable that the officer had small liking for him, but wholesome fear of his influence in high places.

As the two crossed the yard together, the young man said with the greatest affability,—"Would you prefer to see the King alone, or in company?"

"Oh, alone, if it be possible."

"Quite possible. I shall delight in arranging a private interview, and am sure his Majesty will not refuse my request. If you do not wish to meet any of the Court, I can take you to him by a private route where we are almost certain to encounter none."

"I shall be deeply indebted to you."

They threaded their way through devious and labyrinthian passages, turning now to the right, now to the left, sometimes ascending a few steps, and sometimes a narrow stairway, until at last the guide came to a door which he pushed open.

"If you will wait here for a moment, I will go and fetch the King." He bowed gracefully as she passed through the doorway, entering a square room, the walls of which were decorated by groups of swords and rapiers of various sorts; a veritable armory. A table occupied the centre, and there were several chairs, with a lounge against the wall. A door opened upon an inner room.

De Courcy, instead of taking his departure, stepped in quickly after the girl, closed the door, and turned the key in the lock. With the grating of the key came the first suspicion to the mind of Frances that her guide was treacherous. Much as she had always distrusted him, it seemed incredible that, knowing her to be the daughter of the Earl of Strafford, anything disastrous might befall her here in the very palace of the King, the sworn protector of his people. The leer on De Courcy's face and his words speedily disillusioned her.

"If you will be seated, my dear, we may have some converse, interesting and entertaining to us both. You can scarcely imagine my joy at seeing so lovely a visitor in my poor apartments."

"Sir, you said you would bring the King. A gentleman keeps his word."

"Oh, the King in good time, my pretty one. Charles is but a doleful companion just now, and we are well quit of him. As for a man's word, the fashion seems to be the breaking of it, example being set us poor gentlemen in the highest places. For instance, our last discussion related to marriage, but times have changed since that day, and you will not be so cruel as to expect me to carry out the good domestic intentions I then expressed."

"Sir, I am very glad I shall hear no more of them."

"Truly? Then so much the better. I expected tears and reproaches, but am pleased you are not given to complaining. By my honour, I love you the more for it. So, then, I'll steal a kiss from those ripe lips to seal the new compact we are to make, and I warn you that a scream is not likely to be heard from this chamber."

"I need not your warning. You shall neither hear me scream nor see me weep."

"By Saint Denis, I like your spirit. Some scream, and some weep, but they all end by clinging."

"Sir, a warning for your warning. Approach not another step nearer me. Stand aside, rather, and allow me quittance of this place as freely as I ignorantly came hither."

"And if I cannot consent?"

"Then 't will be the worse for you."

"God's truth, but you spur an inclination already highly mettled. Still would I treat you with all courtesy. You are a nameless woman, and many of the highest dames in England are proud to call me their friend."

"That I believe to be as untrue as your saying I am a nameless woman."

"Nevertheless, one is as true as the other. Your father never acknowledged you."

"He has been burdened with more important affairs, but he will do so when he is free."

During this dialogue the participants had been constantly changing their positions, De Courcy advancing and Frances retreating, keeping the table between them. The girl's design was plain enough; she desired to hold him in conversation, gradually shifting her position, until she got between him and the door, when a sudden dash might give her freedom. But he easily fathomed this design and laughed as he checkmated it. At her last words, however, he drew himself upright, a look of genuine amazement overspreading his face.

"When he is free!" he echoed. "Powers of Heaven! Then you have not come to reproach the King, but to plead with him!"

"Why should I reproach him?"

"It would surely be useless enough, but feminine. Why? Because Gregory Brandon, with one good stroke, severed the King's word and Strafford's neck on Tower Hill this morning."

The girl's face went white as the kerchief about her throat, and, swaying half an instant, she leaned against the table for support. Something in the brutal method of the announcement convinced her of its truth more surely than if he had spoken with all the solemnity of which he might be capable. Yet she struggled not to believe.

"You are lying to me," she gasped.

"Far from it, my little lady. How could I imagine you did not know? You are surely the only person in London who is ignorant of it. Why is everything so quiet near Whitehall, where the generous citizens have been so solicitous about us of late? Merely because the centre of interest has changed to the other end of the town, and a rare show was put on the stage for all good people to see, free of cost to themselves, unless they have the brains to know of what they are bereft by Strafford's death, which is most unlikely." As he spoke he had been edging toward her, catlike, but she paid no heed to him. Then with a spring he caught her wrists, but she did not move or make any effort to free herself. She looked dully at him, as if wondering why he acted so.

"You will be pleased to withdraw yourself, sir, and let me go. My heart is broken."

She spoke with forced calmness, but there was a tremor in her tone that cast doubt on her former assertion regarding the tears.

"Your heart is not broken, and if it was I'd mend it for you. Absurd! Why, you knew the man for scarce a day, and that time is full short for the growth of any large affection."

"I shall never love any as I have loved him."

"Tush! How little you know of yourself. You are a very goddess of love, and I will——"

He released one wrist and endeavored to slip his disengaged arm about her waist. This seemed to rouse the girl from her stupor, for she suddenly thrust him back, and, taking him unaware, sent him sprawling; then she sprang for the door. But he was as nimble as she, for, quickly recovering himself, he held her tight before she could turn the key.

"Sir, you forget who I am. Release me at once, and molest me no further."

"Divinest of the fair, I swear to you——"

She whisked herself free of him, and, darting to the other side of the room, whipped down a thin rapier from the wall.

"You will be well advised to put an end to this fooling. I am now in no humour for it, and with you, never. If you have not the gift to see it, I would have you know that I detest you and despise you, and have done so since first I saw you."

"Ah, my little lady Termagant, you say as much now; but when the world knows you paid a thousand pounds for a lover there will be many envious persons who wish to be despised as much."

"You ruffian and thief! Well did Vollins estimate your honesty. But stand aside from that door, or your stealing will profit you little."

"Indeed!" cried De Courcy with a laugh, as he possessed himself of a similar weapon to that which threatened him. "'T is already squandered, and I am in sore need of a further instalment. Are you for a duel, then?"

"If you are coward enough to lift blade to a woman."

"I meet kiss with kiss, and steel with steel; always ready for either. Guard yourself, Madam."

His pretended antagonism was but a feint to throw her off the guard he advised her to maintain, for, being one of the best swordsmen of his time, he knew by her holding of the blade that she was ignorant of its practice. He brushed her sword aside, dropped his own, and sprang in upon her, grasping again her helpless wrists, her arms pinioned thus transversely across her body, her right hand still clinging to the useless hilt, with the blade extending past her shoulder and behind her. His sneering, grinning face so close to hers that his breath fanned her cheek, he pressed her back and back against the wall, the sword bending and bending behind her until the blade snapped off some six inches from the hilt and fell ringing to the floor.

"There, sweetest of Amazons, you are stingless now, and naught but the honey is to be gathered."

The very ease with which he had overcome her hoodwinked him to his danger. The proud dominant blood of the Wentworths flushed her face with an anger that steeled every nerve in her lithe body. As, with a victorious laugh, he released her wrists and slipped his arms around her, she struck him twice with lightning swiftness, first across the brow, then down the face. Nothing could well be more terrible than the weapon she had used, for the jagged iron tore his flesh like the stroke of a tiger's claw. The red cross showed for a brief moment, then was obliterated in a crimson flood.

"Cowardly poltroon, wear the brand of Cain!"

He had warned her not to scream, but now his own cries filled the room as he staggered back, his hands to his face. Yet, grievously wounded as he was, he seemed resolved she should not escape him, and, after the first shock, groped blindly for her. She flung the broken weapon to the further side of the room, and the noise of its fall turned him thither, striking against the table, and then against a chair. She tip-toed cautiously to the door, turned the key, and threw it open before he could recover himself, for he had lost all sense of direction and could see nothing. She took the immediate risk of drawing the key from the door, to ward off the greater danger of pursuit, and calmly locked him in. If screams were as ineffectual as he had insisted, he would take little good from his battering of the door for some time to come. Frances now threaded her way through the maze of passages, meeting no one, for the gloom of death pervaded the palace, at least in the direction she had taken.

She dared not hurry, in spite of the urging of her quickly beating heart, but must proceed leisurely, as if she had a perfect right to be where she was, should any inquisitive servant encounter her. At last, with a deep breath, she emerged upon the great courtyard and so came to the gate. The officer bowed to her, and she paused for a moment to thank him for his kindness to her in the earlier part of the day.

"Is it true—that—that Lord Strafford——" She could get no further.

"Yes, my lady, and grieved we all are that it should be so. This morning on Tower Hill. The Lords refused a reprieve even until Saturday." Frances bent her head and struggled with herself to repress undue emotion, but, finding that impossible, turned abruptly and walked fast down Whitehall.

"Her bright eyes, bless her!" said the officer to a comrade, "are not the only ones dimmed with tears for this morning's work."

On reaching the inn Frances thought of waiting for the faithful Vollins, but she had not the heart to meet him, nor the inclination to rest another night in the city now so hateful to her. She wrote a letter which was forwarded to him by a messenger, but said nothing of her visit to Whitehall, telling him his estimate of De Courcy had been correct, promising to send the thousand pounds to be replaced in her father's treasury as soon as she reached her home in the North, and asking pardon that his counsel had been declined.

Two hours later Frances was on her way to the North. She paused on Highgate Hill and looked back on the Babel she had left, vast and dim in the rising mist of the mild spring evening. "Oh, cruel city! Oh, faithless man! The bloodthirst of London may be whetted and not quenched, perjured King of England!" She bowed her head to her horse's mane and wept helplessly.

BOOK II.—THE MAN.

CHAPTER I.—COINCIDENCE.

William Armstrong rode his splendid black steed like one more accustomed to the polishing of saddle-leather than to the wearing out of the same material in the form of boots. Horse and man were so subtly suited, each to each, that such another pair might well have given to some early artist the first idea of a centaur. Armstrong was evidently familiar with the district he traversed, for he evinced no surprise when, coming to the crown of a height, he saw in the valley below him a one-storied stone building, whose outhouses and general surroundings proclaimed it a solitary inn, but the horse, less self-contained, and doubtless more fatigued, thrust forward his ears and gave utterance to a faint whinny of pleasure at the near prospect of rest and refreshment. The hand of the rider affectionately stroked and patted the long black mane, as if in silent corroboration of the animal's eager anticipations.

The young man was as fair as his mount was dark. A mass of yellow hair flowed out from under his Scot's bonnet and over his broad shoulders. A heavy blonde moustache gave him a semi-military air; a look of the cavalier; as if he were a remnant of that stricken band across the border which was fighting for King Charles against daily increasing odds; but something of jaunty self-confidence in Armstrong's manner betokened that the civil war raging in England was no concern of his, or that, if he took any interest in it, his sympathies inclined toward the winning side, as indeed was the case with many of his countrymen. His erect bearing, body straight as one of his native pines, enhanced the soldier-like appearance of the horseman, and it needed but a glance at his clear-skinned but resolute face and powerful frame to be convinced that he would prove a dangerous antagonist to meet in combat, while the radiant good-nature of his frank countenance indicated a merciful conqueror should victory fall to him, as seemed likely unless the odds were overwhelming.

Both prowess and geniality were on the instant of being put to the test as he approached the inn, where a wayfarer is usually certain of a welcome if he has but money in his pouch. A lanceman, his tall weapon held upright, stepped out into the road from the front of the closed door before which he had been standing, when he saw that the traveller was about to halt and dismount.

"Ye'll be fur dawnerin' on a bit faurer forret," hinted the sentinel in a cautious, insinuating manner, as if he were but giving expression to the other's unspoken intention.

"A wise man halts at the first public-house he comes to after the sun is down," replied Armstrong.

"Ah'm thinkin' a man's no verra wise that stops whaur he's least wanted, if them that's no wantin' him has good airn in their hauns."

"Aye, my lad, steel 's a bonny argument, rightly used. Whut's a' th' steer here, that a tired man, willin' to pay his way, is sent doon th' rod?"

Armstrong adopted for the moment a brogue as broad as that of his questioner. He flung his right leg across the horse, and now sat sideways in his saddle, an action which caused the sentinel suddenly to grip the shaft of his pike with both hands; but the equestrian making no further motion, conversing in an easy nonchalant tone, as if he had little personal interest in the discussion, the vigilance of the man on guard partially relaxed, probably thinking it as well not to provoke so excellently equipped an opponent by any unnecessary show of hostility.

"Weel, ye see, there's muckle folk in ben yonner that has mony a thing ta chatter aboot, an' that's a' Ah ken o't, except that Ah'm ta let nane inside ta disturb them."

"Whose man are you?"

"Ah belong ta th' Yerl o' Traquair."

"And a very good friend of mine the Earl of Traquair is. Will you just go inside and tell him William Armstrong is sitting here on his horse?"

"That wull Ah no, fur if th' King himsel' were ta ask, Ah munna let him by th' door. Sa jist tak a fule's advice fur yince, and gang awa' ta th' next botha afore it gets darker an' ye're like to lose yer rod amang th' hills."

"I must get something for my horse to eat. He's done, and should not be pushed further. I'll wait outside until their lordships have finished their council."

"Th' stalls are a' fou already, an' if not wi better nags, at least wi the nags o' noblemen, an' Ah'm thinkin' that's neither you nor me."

"The stalls may be fou, but my beast's empty, and I must get a feed of corn, noble or simple. Ye tell the Earl it's me and ye'll be thankit."

"Indeed, ma braw man, Ah tak' orders fra the Yerl himsel', an' fra nane else. Jist tickle yer beast wi' the spur, or Ah'll gie him a jab wi' th' point o' this spear."

The descent of young Armstrong was so instantaneous that the man-at-arms had no opportunity of carrying out his threat, or even of levelling the unwieldy weapon in his own defence. The horseman dropped on him as if he had fallen from the clouds, and the pike rang useless on the rough cobble-stones. The black horse showed no sign of fright, as might have been expected, but turned his intelligent head and calmly watched the fray as if accustomed to any eccentricity on the part of his master. And what the fine eyes of the quadruped saw was startling enough. The wide-spread limbs of the surprised soldier went whirling through the air like the arms of a windmill in a gale. Armstrong had grasped him by the waist and turned him end for end, revolving him, Catherine-wheel-wise, until the bewildered wits of the victim threatened to leave him through the action of centrifugal force. By the time the unfortunate sentinel lost all reckoning of the direction in which solid earth lay with regard to his own swiftly changing position, he found himself on his assailant's shoulder, gaping like a newly landed trout, and, thus hoisted aloft, he was carried to the closed door, which a kick from Armstrong's foot sent crashing inward. The intruder flung his burden into the nearest corner of the large room, as if he were a sack of corn; then, facing the startled audience, the young man cried:

"Strong orders should have a stronger guard than, you set, gentlemen. I hold to the right of every Scotsman to enter a public dram-shop when he pleases."

A dozen amazed men had sprung to their feet, oversetting a chair or a stool here and there behind them, and here and there a flagon before them. Eleven swords flashed out, but the upraised right hand of the chairman and his commanding voice caused the weapons to hang suspended.

"The very man! By God, the very man we want! In the Fiend's name, Will, where have you dropped from?"

"From the back of my horse a moment since, as your henchman here will bear witness, Traquair."

"Armstrong, your arrival at this juncture is providential; that's what it is, providential!"

"It must be, my Lord, for you did your best to prevent it. Your stout pikeman would not even let you know I was within call, so I just brought him in to give the message properly."

"Losh, if he knew you as well as I do, he would have thought twice or he stood in your way. Come to the table, man, and fill a flagon."

"I'll empty one with pleasure if the drawer will charge it."

"We have no drawer, Armstrong, but wait on ourselves, trusting the lugs of a cogie rather than the ears of a scullion. So I'll be your cup-bearer, Will."

"Thank you kindly, my lord, but I'll help myself, as my ancestor said to the Duke of Northumberland when he drove away the English cattle. The man who will not stretch an arm to slake a thirst deserves a dusty road all day with no bothy at the end of it." And, saying this, the young man drank long and well.

The sentinel had by this time got on his feet and was staring at the company like one dazed. "Where's your pike?" demanded Traquair.

"On the stanes ootside, ma lord."

"Very well, go out and lift it, and see that you hold a better grip of it when the next man comes along. Attend to Armstrong's horse, and keep an eye up and down the road."

"I'll look after my own beast, Traquair."

"No need for that, Will. We have matters of importance to discuss, and Angus here will feed the horse as well as you can do it."

"I'll eat and drink whatever's set before me, and never ask who is the cook, but I trust no man to wait on my horse. You bide by your sentry march, Angus, and I'll see to the beast."

With this Armstrong strode out of the house, the ill-used sentinel following him. As the door closed, the interrupted hum of conversation rose again.

Who the interloper might be was the burden of the inquiry.

"Armstrong's the very man for our purpose," said Traquair. "If any one can get through Old Noll's armies by craft or by force, it is Will. I had no idea he was near by, or I never have wasted thought on any other. I have known him for years, and there's none to match him, Hielan' or Lowlan'. We need seek nae farrar if Christie's Wull is wullin'."

"I have never before heard of him," said the Reverend Alexander Henderson, of Edinburgh. "What has he done?"

"What has he not done?" asked the Earl. "The Border rings with his fame, as it has rung with the fame of his ancestors these several centuries past."

"Oh, the Border!" cried the townsman, with the contempt of his class for the supposedly ignorant condition of that wild hilly belt which girded the waist of the land. "We all know what brings a man renown on the Border.

The chief requisites are a heavy sword and a thick skull. That the proposed excursion may require a ready blade at times, I admit, but a man who depends on that will not blunder through. There are too many of his kind opposed to him in Cromwell's army. It is not a wilderness like the Border that lies between here and Oxford, but a civilized country with cities, and men of brains in them. To win through and back requires skill and diplomacy, alertness of resource, as well as the qualities of riding hard and striking swift."

"William Armstrong has all these qualities, and many more," replied Traquair.

"The sample of his conduct just presented to us savors more of violence than of tact," objected Henderson. "He comes breenging in on a private conference of his betters, carrying their sentinel on his head like a shambled sheep, and flings him in a corner. This proves him a strong man, but far from a wise one, because, for all he knew, he might have been walking into an ambuscade that would have cost him his life or liberty. It was pure luck and not foreknowledge that caused him to find a friend at our board."

"You are in the wrong there, Henderson, quite in the wrong, for you all heard him say that the sentry refused to bring in his message to me. Armstrong knew I was here, and thus was well aware he was safe enough."

Henderson shook his head, stubbornly unconvinced. He was a man of talk rather than of action, and knew he spoke well, so, being a born objector to other men's proposals, his tongue was more active than his arm. When the unexpected "breenging" had occurred, every man in the room had jumped to his feet and grasped his sword, except Henderson, who sat staring, exhibiting little of that ready resource he had been commending. Now the danger was past, he apparently thought that after-eloquence made good the absence of energy in a crisis.

Traquair, ever suave so long as he carried his point, showed no signs of irritation at this line of criticism, but made comment and gave answer in a low tone and persuasive voice. The others round the table kept silence and listened to the controversy between the man of language and the man of action, ready, doubtless, to side with whichever proved the victor. The Earl leaned his elbow on the board and gazed across at his opponent.

"Look you here, Henderson. You are willing to admit there is no such city as Edinburgh between here and the King?"

"Doubtless not."

"And I need not try to convince you that Edinburgh is second to no town in the world so far as learning, judgment, and good sense are concerned?"

"Edinburgh is not in question, my Lord."

"But you'll agree with all I say regarding it?"

"Well, there are worse places than Edinburgh."

"Cautiously uttered, but true. Very good. Perhaps you will not dispute the fact that Lord Durie is one of your most enlightened citizens?"

"Durie, Lord of Sessions? Durie's Decisions are well known in law, I am told. I have nothing to say against the man."

"There you differ from me, Henderson. I have much to say against him, be his Decisions never so good. He is, and always was, a prejudiced old fool, who, if he once got a wrong notion in his head, was proof against all reason."

"Speak no ill against those in authority over us!" cried Henderson, bristling into opposition now that a definite opinion was expressed. "For twenty years he was chosen vice-president by the best men in all Scotland, none successfully opposing him, so you cannot say ill of such an one."

"Very well, very well," coincided Traquair with suspicious haste, a faint smile parting his lips. "We will take your word for it that his legal lordship is all you say. The point I wish to establish is that Edinburgh possesses an enviable shrewdness, and that Lord Durie is one of her most esteemed citizens. Other people may hold contrary opinion, but we defer to yours, Henderson. It chanced that one man holding contrary opinion so far as his lordship was concerned, and troubled with grave doubts regarding his impartiality, had a case coming before him that involved the litigant's possessions and lands. He knew that Durie was against him, and that there was no way of getting the thrawn deevil—I beg your pardon, Henderson—this upright judge—to listen to justice. This defendant slipped a word in Armstrong's ear to the effect that it would be most admirable if there was some other presiding judge at the Court of Sessions when the case was tried. The consequence was that Lord Durie, for the time being, disappeared and was accounted dead. The case was tried before his successor, and won by the contestant I have referred to, as was but right and just. Then Lord Durie came on the scene once more, to the joy of everyone but his successor, who should have been a friend of Will's if he wished the disappearance to have been permanent."

"Ah, there you overstep the bounds of probability in order to establish a false proficiency for this ranting Borderer. 'Tis well known that Armstrong had nothing to do with the kidnapping of his lordship. The judge himself admits that the powers of evil spirited him away and kept him in a warlock's castle, hoping to lure him from the path of righteousness; but, his probity proving impregnable, they could not contend against it, and were fain to let him go again unscathed, for it is written, 'Resist the Devil and he will flee from you.'"

The Earl of Traquair leaned back and laughed aloud.

"Well, you can take my word for it that he did not flee in this instance. When the judge was enjoying an airing, as was his custom, sitting his canny horse on Leith sands, Armstrong accosted him, also on horseback, and the two entered into amiable and instructive conversation. Old Durie was so charmed with his new acquaintance that he accompanied him to the unfrequented spot known as Frigate Whins, and there Will threw his cloak over the distinguished man's head, lifted him from his horse, and made off through a section of the country known better by himself than by any other, and where he was sure he was not like to meet gossiping stragglers. At last Will deposited his burden in the lonely Tower of Graham by the water of Dryfe, and there he remained for three months, not even seeing the people who fed him, for his meat was let down to him by a rope. As the judge's horse was found wandering on the sands, people came to the conclusion that his lordship had been thrown off, stunned, and drowned, the body being carried out to sea by the tide. In due time Armstrong took the gentleman back as he had come, and flattered the auld carle by telling him that, such was his learning and piety, Satan could not prevail against him. And so the learned judge just dawnered home with this idea in his head, which he speedily-got the wise city of Edinburgh to believe."

For a wonder Henderson remained silent, but one of the others spoke up.

"I remember the incident well," he said, "and if I am not mistaken the Tower of Graham at that time belonged to your lordship."

"Yes, and it does yet," replied Traquair nonchalantly. "Armstrong, being an old friend of mine, had no hesitation in using my property without my leave, for, as he explained afterward, there was no time for consultation, the case being urgent."

"It was a most suitable place for the judge's custody," continued the other drily, "because, unless a treacherous memory misleads me, a plea regarding this very property was decided in your favour by the single vote of the Lord President, who temporarily took the place of Justice Durie during his mysterious absence."

"Sir, you are quite in the right," replied Traquair, unabashed by the evident insinuation. "It was my great good luck that the case against me was heard during Durie's absence, and, as you were doubtless about to point out, this world is full of strange coincidences which our poor finite minds fail to fathom."

"A finite mind easily probes the bottom of such a shameless conspiracy," cried Alexander Henderson sternly, bringing his fist down upon the table. "What! Kidnap the Lord President of the Sessions, from the very edge of Edinburgh in broad daylight——"

"It was drawing on to the gloaming at the time," corrected Traquair soothingly, "at least so Will informed me."

"It was nevertheless an outrageous action; a foul deed that should not go unwhipt of——"

"Gentlemen," said the Earl in a tone of authority, which seemed to recall the fact that, after all, he was the chairman of the conclave, "we are wandering from the point. At this moment Lord Durie is reported to be a dying man, and whatever evil has been done against him in the long past probably troubles him less than the injustice he may himself have been the cause of. In any case we are met here together for a certain purpose, and what is said within this circle is said in confidence, for which our plighted words to each other stand sponsor. The crux of the discussion is this. Henderson objects to my man as the most fitting for our embassy, holding him to be a rude and brainless swashbuckler. That is a definite charge. I meet it by showing that this same man befooled the wise city of Edinburgh and the most learned man within its confines. A brainless bravado would have run a dirk into Lord Durie and left his body on the sands. I wish unanimous consent to tender our present dangerous mission to William Armstrong, in the hope that he may get safely to Oxford, and, what is more important, bring us with equal safety the King's written command. If any of you have some one else to propose, whom you think may accomplish his business better than Will Armstrong, I ask you to nominate the man and give reasons for your preference."

Henderson growled in his beard, but said nothing audible. Each man looked at the others as if waiting for some one else to make further suggestion; but, as the silence was prolonged, the one who had referred to the coincidence of Durie's incarceration with Traquair's case at law, cleared his throat and said that for his part it seemed that Armstrong was the proper man for the mission. With this the others agreed, and even Henderson gave an ungracious concurrence. The Earl was about to address the company when the door opened and Armstrong himself entered.

CHAPTER II.—SUSPICION.

Speak of the Devil, Wull," cried Traquair. "We have been talking of you, my man, and we have some employment for you if you are ready for it."

"Well, my Lord, there's no lack of that in these kittle times, for a fighting man gets civility and a welcome, whether in England or Scotland, whichever side he takes."

"I hope you are for law and the King, against riot and rebels?"

"Ye see, Traquair, I'm not just a faction man, but am standing clear, to give both sides fair play, as the De'il said when he was toasting the Elder on his fork, and changed his front to the fire. I suppose I am for the King, though I'm not so prejudiced but I can see something to be said for the other side. It seems to me that the King's not exactly as wise as his predecessor Solomon."

"That's treason," roared Henderson.

"Oh, not among friends who are most of them thinking the same thing," said Armstrong suavely. "But no, I shouldna say that, for it's likely you're all as loyal as my horse. Ye see, stranger, it's not to be expected that I should fling up my cap whenever the King's name is mentioned, for my family have stood the brunt of the battles on the Border this twothree hundred years, yet we got little thanks from any King for it."

"This is a fine enthusiastic messenger to send on important business," growled Henderson to Traquair.

"I would call your honour's attention to the fact that I am as yet no messenger at all, and if I am expected to be one it will be because of Earl Traquair and not on account of any sour Presbyterian that ever, thumped a pulpit in Edinburgh," said Armstrong calmly, quite accurately guessing the standing of the one who seemed to be the objecting element in the party.

"The crisis is this, William," broke in Traquair with visible impatience. "There are papers that we must get through to King Charles at Oxford. Then, what is much more important, we must get his signed warrant back to us before we can act to any real purpose in this ploy. The victorious rebels pretend that they are fighting for certain so-called liberties, but we have reason to know that their designs run much deeper, that they aim at nothing less than the dethronement and possible murder of the King. It is necessary to get proof of this to the King, and to obtain his sanction to certain action on our part; for if we move without his written commission, and our plans fail, we are like to get short shrift from Cromwell, who will deny us the right of belligerents. Whether the King believes this or not, the documents we wish to send him are less to the purpose than that you should bring back to us his commission, so you will know that your home-coming is much more vital to us than your out-going."

"I see. Still, if they kill me on the road there, it is not likely I will win my way back, so both journeys are equally vital to me."

"You will be travelling through a hostile country, but nevertheless will find many to favour you; for though the land is under the iron hand of Cromwell, he is far from pleasing all the people, although they may make a quiet mouth save a doubting head. Brave as you are, Will, it is on the smooth tongue rather than on the sharp sword that you must depend; for, however many silent friends we may have along the route, there are too many outspoken enemies for even you to fight your way through. Have you a good horse?"

"The best in the world."

"The pick of my stables is at your choice. Had you not better take a spare animal with you?"

"No. That would be advertising the importance of my journey. If I can get through at all, it must be by dawnering along as a cannie drover body, anxious to buy up cattle and turn an honest penny by selling them to those who want them worse than I do; a perfectly legitimate trade even during these exciting times. They all know the desire of a humble Scotsman to make a little money, though the Heavens and Kings be falling."

"That's an admirable idea, and you know the country well?"

"No one better. Indeed I'll trade my way to the very gates of Oxford if time is not too great an object with you."

"Time is an object, Armstrong, but you will have to do the best you can, and we shall await your return with what patience we may. You will tackle the job then?"

"It's just the kind of splore I like. Can you allow me three weeks or a month?"

"If you 're back inside of a month, Will, you 'll have done what I believe no other man in all Scotland could do. Well, that's settled then."

"Oh, bide a wee, bide a wee," cautioned Henderson, who during this colloquy had been visibly fuming under the contemptuous reference Armstrong had uttered regarding him. "This man may be brave enough, but I doubt his judgment. He may have all the wisdom he traitorously denies to the King, but it's by no means proven."

"I did not deny wisdom to the King, Mr. Pulpiteer. I said Solomon was the wisest of men, except that he was a little daft on the marrying, and in that I'm wiser than he, for whether Cromwell catch me or no, none of the lassies have caught me yet."

"You are ribald," shouted the minister angrily, "and would add blasphemy to disloyalty. I was speaking of King Charles."

"And I was speaking of King Solomon, and speaking in a lower tone of voice as well. But while we are discussing wisdom, why are you all met here in this bothy, instead of in your own castle, Traquair? This innkeeper is a treacherous, canting dog. I know him of old."

"Henderson thought it would be safer here than at my house. I'm being watched. We conceived it would be less conspicuous if the dozen of us gathered here as if by accident."

"I wish I were as sure of your messenger as I am of the innkeeper," protested Henderson, his growing dislike of Armstrong not to be concealed. "The innkeeper is a pious man who——"

"So was Judas; and he was one of the Apostles," interrupted Armstrong flippantly, unheeding the other's anger.

"He is an enemy of your friends, the cattle-thieves," insisted Henderson.

"Is he? In that case you'll know more about him than I do, and I suppose it is policy for you to stand up for him. But, Traquair, I wonder at you! Did you search the house before you sat down here?"

"No."

"I went round the steading, and there was no guard at the back."

"Angus is keeping watch, and can see up and down the road."

"The road is the last place I would set foot on if I were a spy. You have been ranting in here at a great rate. Before I came to you I could hear every word that was said. One would think it was a Presbyterian convening, agreeing on the Scriptures. I knew Henderson's opinion of me before I opened the door."

"You look like an eavesdropper," retorted the man referred to, "and that you have a libellous ungoverned tongue is proven by every word you utter."

"Tut, tut, tut!" cried Traquair, "let us have no more bickering. This is serious business and not to be settled by bandying words. Now, Armstrong, the case stands like this. Will you——"

The Earl was interrupted by a roar from the sentinel outside, which caused every man in the room to start to his feet; but before they could move, Angus came bursting in.

"Somebody dropped from the hole on the loft above the stables, an' wuz aff ta th' wood afore I could stop him."

"To horse!" cried Traquair. "Mount instantly, and let's after him."

"It's useless, my lord," said Armstrong quietly, the only unexcited man in the group. "Ye might as well look for some particular flea in all the Hielans. He'll have a horse tied to a tree, and a thousand cavalry couldn't catch him if he knows the wilds hereabout."

"It may be just some vagrant sleeping in the straw. The loft above the stables is not the loft above this room," put in Henderson; but it was plain that he was frightened. He loved a real eavesdropper as little as did any of his comrades, and knew he had talked rather loudly at times, carried away by his fondness for opposition. Traquair stood frowning and indecisive, his hand on the hilt of his sword.

"Where's the landlord?" he asked at last. "Angus, bring him in here."

The sentinel left the room and speedily reappeared with a cowering man, evidently as panic-stricken as any of his guests.

"Have there been some stragglers about to-day?" demanded Traquair.

"Not a soul, my lord, on my oath, not a soul."

"Is there connection between the room above and the loft over the stable?"

"No possibility of it, my lord."

"What did I tell you?" said Henderson, plucking up courage again. "This turmoil is utterly without foundation."

"Dash it!" cried Armstrong with a gesture of impatience. "Will you take a man's word for a thing you can prove in a moment? Get a ladder, Angus, and speel up through the hole the spy came out at. Take a torch, an' if ye drop a lowe in the straw you'll no' be blamed for it by me. See if you can win your way through from the stables to the house."

"Go at once, Angus," commanded Traquair; then to the landlord, who showed signs of wishing to be elsewhere. "No; you stay here."

"I'm feared th' man wull set fire ta the place," whined the landlord.

"Better be feared o' the rope that will be round your neck if you have lied to us," said the Earl grimly, and as he spoke they heard the tramp of the sentinel's feet overhead.

"Is that you, Angus?" asked Traquair in an ordinary tone of voice. "Can you hear what I say?"

"Perfectly, ma lord. There's a very cunnin' trap 'tween th' stable loft an' this, that one would na hev foun' in a hurry, but the thief left it open in his sudden flight."

The lips of the landlord turned white, but he remained motionless, panting like a trapped animal, for the giant form of Armstrong stood with his back against the door, the only exit.

"Very well. Come down," said Traquair quietly. When the sentinel returned, Traquair bade him get a rope and tie the innkeeper hand and foot, while the prisoner groveled for his life, his supplications meeting with no response.

"Now take him outside, Angus, and if there is any attempt on his part to move, or if there is an alarm of rescue, run him through with your pike and retreat on us. As for you, you false knave, your life will depend on your lying quiet for the moment and on what you tell us hereafter."

"Am I ta be ta'en awa', your merciful lordship?" sobbed the man, who, now that his life seemed in no immediate danger, turned his anxiety toward his property. "What'll become o' th' inn, for there's nane here to tak care o 't?"

"We'll take care o't, never fear," replied Traquair grimly.

The stalwart Angus dragged the man out, and the door was once more closed.

"I think we may venture to seat ourselves again," said Traquair, suiting the action to the word. "There's nothing more to be done, and pursuit is hopeless."

All sat down with the exception of Armstrong, who remained standing with his back to the door, gazing somewhat scornfully on the conclave.

"You will perhaps now agree with me, Henderson," continued the Earl smoothly, "that we are in no position to set up our collective wisdom as an example to William Armstrong?"

"I may at least say," returned the minister sourly, "that nothing whatever is proved. It is all surmise, suspicion, conjecture. The man who went away may well have been some lout sleeping in the straw, and no spy at all."

"There is no conjecture about the fact that the landlord lied to us. There is no surmise in my belief that he thought his trap-door was securely closed, when he lied the second time, and that the secret of the trap-door was in possession of the man who escaped. This is proof enough for me, and I think it is equally convincing to the others. Have you anything further to urge against the selection of Mr. Armstrong as our messenger?"

"Oh, very well, Traquair, have it your own way. I dare say he will do as well as another," replied Henderson with the air of one making a great concession.

"Then it's settled!" proclaimed the Earl with a sigh of relief.

But it was not.

"You will pardon me, Traquair," began Armstrong, "for you know I would be glad to forward anything you had a hand in, short of slipping my neck into a noose; but at that point I draw back. I'll not set foot on English soil now, King or no King. Henderson may go and be damned to him, for the useless, brainless clacker he is. If Cromwell hangs him, his loss will be Scotland's gain. Man, Traquair, I wonder at you! The lot of you remind me of a covey of partridges holding conference in a fox's den."

"I'm not going to defend the covey of partridges, Will; but, after all's said and done, the danger's not so much greater than it was before."

"Do you think I'm fool enough to set face south when there's a spy galloping ahead of me with full particulars of every item in my wallet? Not me! It was bad enough before, as you say; now it's impossible. That is, it is impossible for me, for the flying man knows all about me. No; the proper thing to do is to meet at your castle, or some other safe place, and choose a man whose name and description are not in the wind ahead of him."

"But I've known you to clench with quite as dangerous a task before."

"It's not the danger, Traquair, as much as the folly, that holds me back. I've been in many a foolish scramble before now, as you have hinted; but I learn wisdom with age, and thus differ from our friend Solomon."

"Will nothing change your decision?"

"Nothing; nothing in the world; not anything even you can say, my lord. I advise you to take a lad of Henderson's choosing. Any trampling ass may break an egg, but, once broken, the wisest man in the kingdom cannot place it together again. To-night's egg is smashed, Traquair."

"I cannot blame you; I cannot blame you," said the Earl dejectedly, drawing a deep sigh. Then, turning to the others, he continued, "Gentlemen, there's no more to be said. We must convene again. Would to-morrow, or the day after, be convenient for you?"

It was agreed that the meeting should take place two days from that time.

"I warn you," said the Earl to Henderson, "that I have no other candidate to propose, and will confine myself to agreeing with whatever resolution you come to."

"You are not angry with me, Traquair?" asked Armstrong.

"Not in the least, Will. I appreciate your point of view, and were I in your place I should have reached exactly the same conclusion."

"Then I must beg a bed from you to-night. I have no wish to stay in this place, and if you are bent for home, as I surmise, I'll just trot my nag alongside o' yours."

"I was this moment going to ask you, for I confess I'll ride the safer that your stout arm is near."

The company left the inn together, and in the middle of the road, before the house, they found Angus, with a torch, standing guard over a shapeless bundle huddled at his feet. The bundle was making faint pleadings to the man-at-arms, to which that warrior was listening with stolid indifference. The murmurs ceased as the group of men drew near. Traquair extended a cordial invitation to all or any to spend the night at the castle, which was the nearest house, but the others did not accept. Each man got upon his horse, and some went one direction, and some another.

"Fling your lighted torch into the loft," said Traquair to Angus, "that will prevent this woif worrying about his property. When you've done that, throw him across your horse and follow us. Has there been sign of any one else about?"

"No, ma lord," replied Angus, promptly obeying the injunction about the torch. He then tossed the howling human mass in front of his saddle, sprang into his seat, and went down the road after the two who preceded him, the flames from the burning bothy already throwing long shadows ahead.

The Earl of Traquair, chagrined at the temporary defeat of his plans, inwardly cursing the stupidity of those with whom he was compelled to act, rode moody and silent, and this reserve the young man at his side made no attempt to interrupt until they had reached a slight eminence, where the nobleman reined in his horse and looked back down the valley at the blazing steading, which now filled the hollow with its radiance.

"We will wait here till Angus overtakes us," he said. "This bonfire may collect some of the moths, and it's better travelling three than two."

"We've not far to go," said Armstrong, "and that's a blessing, for I'm on a long jaunt in the morning, and would be glad of my bed as soon as may be."

"Where are you off to?" asked the Earl indifferently, gazing anxiously down the road for a sight of his follower, who was not yet visible.

Armstrong replied with equal nonchalance, "Oh, I'm just away for Oxford, to carry a message from Lord Traquair to the King of England."

"What!" cried his lordship, nearly starting from his saddle in amazement.

"Surely my talk before these cuddies did not mislead you? I'll take your message through and bring you back an answer, if the thing's possible, but I cannot have those fools pottering and whispering in the matter. They must know nothing of my going. You will meet them two days hence, accept whomsoever they propose, and let him blunder along to a rebel gallows. It will be one blockhead out of the way, and then wise folk can do their bit travels unmolested."

"But how can I send papers with him when they'll be in your pouch?"

"Indeed, and that they will not be. This night's work compels one to a change of programme. I shall carry no papers with me. If you let me read them I'll remember every word, though they be as long as the Psalms. I'll repeat them to the King with as few slips as any man in the realm. If you have a password or sign, or if you can tell me some incident that only you and the

King know of, which will assure him that I am from you, everything else will be plain plodding. It would be folly for me, now that Cromwell's spy is on the gallop, to carry a line of writing that bears relation to politics. I'll be arrested before I'm a mile beyond the Border, so my chance of getting through will depend on the search they make. If they find nothing it is likely they'll let me go, and I must manage to get back as best I can. There's no sense in being hanged for a spy the first day I set out. I'll leave that for Henderson's man."

"You think, then, if I give the papers to him, they'll never see Oxford?"

"They'll never see Carlisle, let alone Oxford. If I were you I would give him whatever papers you wish delivered direct to Cromwell. That will put Henderson and his gang off the scent, and your information may be of much pleasure and profit to General Noll."

The Earl laughed heartily, his spirits rising surprisingly at this intimation of the young man's resolve.

"Armstrong, you're a hero. You shall read the papers to-night, and look over them again in the morning. The important matter is to get the King's commission back to us. Ah, here is Angus with his sack, so we'll say no more until we reach the castle."

CHAPTER III.—DETENTION.

The next morning, early, William Armstrong, on Bruce, his black horse, set out for the Border with the good wishes of his host. His naturally gay demeanor was subdued, and he muttered to himself with wrinkled brow as he rode along. This unwonted abstraction was not on account of the danger which he knew lay ahead of him, but because he was committing to memory the message to the King. He carried a mass of notes, which he had written the night before, and these he consulted every now and then, for his horse required no guidance, and if it had, its rider was so accustomed to the saddle that he could have directed the animal in his sleep, for Bruce needed no tug at rein, but merely a whispered word or a touch from one knee or the other.

The night after he left Traquair's castle Armstrong slept on Scottish soil, still busy with his task of memory; then he burnt the notes in the fire that cooked his supper. It was scarcely daylight when he faced the clear and rippling Esk, and after crossing the stream to "fell English ground" he halted his horse on the southern shore and cast a long look at the hills of his native country, as one who might be taking farewell of them. Then, with a sigh, he turned to his task and sent no further glance behind.

A main road lay white and deserted before him, and the country he travelled, although in general feature similar to that he left, had nevertheless a subtle difference which always appealed to his inner sense whenever he crossed the line, but it was an evasive difference, which he would have found impossible to describe in words. The same discrepancy marked the language of the northern Englisher, which to a stranger would have seemed identical with that of his neighbours, but to Armstrong's sensitive ear the speech struck alien.

Arriving at a forking of the road, both branches tending south, he paused and pondered. Which should he take? He knew them equally well. The main road led to Carlisle, and in time of peace would have been preferable; the other, less direct, would probably carry him further in these uncertain times. The country showed no sign of the devastation of civil war, unless it was the absence of a population, and a deserted condition of the thoroughfares. That he could avoid contact with the Parliamentary forces was impossible, whichever road he took, and the question now demanding solution was not so much his direction as whether it were well to bring on his inevitable encounter with the Cromwellites sooner or later. The Carlisle route promised the speedier run into the arms of the enemy, but by the other route he would have more chance of bargaining about cattle, and thereby giving colour of truth to his statement that he was an innocent Scots drover, anxious to turn an honest penny. When questioned by an officer he could then say he had endeavoured to deal with so-and-so, and later investigation would prove the fact. But to an observer he bore the attitude of a stranger who had lost his way. This was evidently the conclusion arrived at by an object hidden in the hedge which had proved his night's lodging. The object sprang out across the ditch with a suddenness that made the horse start and snort in alarm, to be soothed by the gentle pat of its rider's hand, for the imperturbable

Armstrong seemed surprised at nothing that took place. The object had the wild, unkempt appearance of one who habitually slept out of doors. His long and matted hair, emaciated face, and ragged beard, no less than his tattered clothing, or covering rather, made up of odds and ends of various costumes, formed a combination by no means attractive. He held in his hand, grasped by the middle, a long stick, somewhat taller than himself.

"My gay gentleman," he cried cheerfully, "will you pay the price of a fool?"

"Who is the fool?" asked Armstrong with a smile. "You or me?"

"There are many of us, and someone is always paying the price. That is how I get a little money now and then. England is paying the price of a fool, and has been for some years past; paying heavily too, for all fools are not as cheap as I am."

"I asked you who the fool was?"

"Ah, that is a question you may have to answer yourself," cried the object, with a cunning leer in his shining eyes. "Beware how you answer it, for if you give the wrong answer, the price you pay is your head. 'Who is the fool?' says you. That is the point, but whoever he is, we are paying for him with fire and sword and good human lives. Wherever there's strife, look for the fool that caused it, but be cautious in naming him. Which road are you going to take, my gay gentleman?"

"I was just switherin'."

"Ah, you're from Scotland. They tell me they grow a fine crop of fools there. The road on the right leads to Carlisle, and the fool's name in that direction is the King. The safest way is the one you came, and the fool's name there is like to be Cromwell, so they tell me. Am I to get the fool's price for advice?"

"You haven 't given me any so far."

"The advice all depends on what you pay for it. Let me see the coin, then I'll show you my wares. We differ in this, that I'll take whatever you give me, but you can take my advice or not, as you please."

The horseman threw him a coin, which the object clutched in mid-air with great expertness and examined eagerly.

"Thank you, gay gentleman. The advice is to turn your fine horse end for end, and get back among the fools of your own kidney. We are always safer among our own kind."

"Are there any cattle for sale hereabout? I see none in the fields."

"Everything's for sale in England, crown, cattle, opinions, swords; oh, it's a great market for cutlery. But the price is uncertain and various."

"Well, it's cattle, not cutlery, I want to buy."

"I sometimes sell cattle myself," said the object, with a cunning look.

"It does not seem a very prosperous business then. Where do you get your stock?"

"Oh, I pick it up on the roads. You'll find no cattle on the way to Carlisle. The country is swept bare in that direction. But I can lead you to a fine herd if you make it worth my while."

"In which direction?"

"Down this way. Come along. Are you after any particular breed?"

"No. Anything there's money in."

"You're just like me," said the vagrant with a laugh, as he strode off down the unfrequented road. The object walked with incredible speed, laughing to himself now and then, and Armstrong was forced to trot his horse to keep up with him. On arriving at a slight eminence the guide waved his long arm toward a steading in the valley, which looked like a deserted group of farm buildings, and said,—"There's a fine lot of cattle down yonder."

"I can see no signs of them."

"No, no! They're well stabled. Nothing lasts in the fields nowadays.

They're not such fools as that. This herdsman knows when to keep his beasts in shelter." And with this the vagabond raised a shrill shout that echoed from the opposite hills.

"What are you crying like that for?" asked Armstrong, without showing any alarm.

"Oh, just to let the farmer know we're coming. Always give friendly warning in these parts, and then you may not get something in your inside that's hard to digest. That's a fool's advice, and costs you nothing."

"Your cry meets with no response," said Armstrong, laughing at the shallow cunning of his treacherous guide, for his keen eyes noted crouching figures making way along the other side of a hedge, and he knew that if he went down the lane, at whose junction with the road the beggar stood with repressed eagerness, he would find himself surrounded. Nevertheless he followed without betraying any knowledge of the trap he was entering.

As they neared the farmhouse a voice cried sharply, "Halt!" and an armed man sprang up from behind the hedge, cutting off retreat, if such had been attempted. While the others made through the hedge to the lane, the tattered man as nimbly put the hedge between himself and his victim, as if fearing a reprisal, laughing boisterously but rather nervously.

"Brave Captain, I've brought you a fine horse and a gay gentleman, and the two are for sale."

The man who had cried "Halt!" stepped forth from the shelter of the nearest outbuilding, a drawn sword in his hand, followed by two others with primed matchlocks, stolidly ready for any emergency. Four others closed up the rear coming down the lane. There was no mistaking the fact that the man with the drawn sword was an officer, even if the object had not addressed him as Captain, a salutation to which he paid no attention; for although his uniform showed little difference from that of his men, he had in his stern face the look of one accustomed to obedience. The horseman had drawn up at the word, and sat quite nonchalantly on his steed, as if this were an affair of no particular concern to himself.

"Who are you?" asked the captain.

"My name is William Armstrong," replied the rider simply. In spite of himself, the stolid face of the leader showed some surprise at this announcement, as if he knew the name and had not expected to hear it so frankly acknowledged.

"Where are you from?"

"I came across the Border this morning. I am a Scotsman."

"Why are you here?"

"I am a cattle-dealer, and as there is little doing in my own country I thought I would just see if business was better on this side of the line. This amusing lunatic said there was cattle for sale in the valley, and led me hither, for which service I paid him a trifle."

"And so there is, and so there is," cried the lunatic; "but the price was for my advice, not for the leading hither. I must get my pay for that yet. Aye, there's cattle for sale here, and I'm the marketman."

"Peace to your folly," said the captain, scowling. Then curtly to the horseman, "Dismount."

Armstrong sprang to the ground.

"Your sword," demanded the officer.

The weapon was handed to him.

"Do cattle-dealers in your country carry arms?"

"To tell you the truth," said the young man with a laugh, "if they did not they would carry little money home with them. I not only carry arms, but know how to use them on occasion."

"I ask to see your papers giving you permission to travel in England."

"I have none. Scotland is at peace with England, and a citizen of my country should not require papers in visiting England, any more than an

Englishman would need the same to go from one end of Scotland to the other."

"Humph," growled the captain, "you are well versed in the law. I hope you are engaged in no enterprise that is contrary to it."

"I hope not, Captain. If you are King's men, you maintain that you are upholding the law. If you are Parliamentary, you swear the same thing."

"We swear not at all."

"Then I surmise you are no King's men. But in any case, until, one or other of you have declared war against Scotland, or until Scotland has declared war against either of you, or both, you meddle with a free citizen of Scotland at your peril."

"It is perhaps wisest to indulge in no threats."

"I am not indulging in any. I am stating a plain, uncontrovertible fact, that would be held by none so stoutly as by General Cromwell himself."

"Then keep your dissertations on law until you see the General, which is like to happen before we are done with you."

"Nothing would give me greater pleasure than to have a discourse with that distinguished man. He is a fighter after my own heart, and I understand he is equally powerful in controversy."

"Search him."

To this order Armstrong not only made no objection, but assisted in its fulfilment. He took off his doublet and threw it to one of the men who approached him, then held his arms outstretched that another might, with greater ease, conduct his examination. A third paid minute attention to the saddlebags, and a fourth took the saddle itself off the horse. The search brought to light some papers which the officer scanned, gaining thereby much information regarding the price of stots, stirks, and such like, but what these articles actually were, the peruser of the paper had not the slightest idea.

"What is a stot; a weapon?" asked the captain suspiciously.

"In a way it is a weapon, or at least an engine of attack," replied William genially. "A stot is a young bull."

"Be sober in your answers, sir. This business is serious."

"I see it is. There never was much humour south of the Tweed, and you folk seem to have broad-sworded away what little you had of it."

"What is a stirk? I ask you to be careful of your answers, for they are being recorded."

"I am delighted to act as schoolmaster. A stirk is a steer or heifer between one and two years old. If my answer is not taken as an imputation on any of the solemn company here, I may add that a calf grows into a stirk."

The captain glowered angrily at the unabashed prisoner, as one in doubt whether he was experiencing a display of brazen impudence or extreme simplicity. He asked no more questions concerning the papers found, but gave them to a subordinate and directed them to be tied together. He now took from his belt a folded sheet, opened it, and read its contents with care, glancing now and then at the man before him. Apparently the comparison was to his satisfaction, and he restored the document to its place with a grunt of approval.

"Is Bates ready? Tell him to come here," he said to the subordinate, who instantly disappeared, emerging from among the outhouses shortly with a young man on a fine horse, evidently a racer before that sport was abolished. The animal was impatient to be off, but the young fellow on his back curbed its eagerness with a master hand, as one born to the saddle. The captain had employed the interval in writing a brief despatch, which he now handed to the young horseman.

"Ride hard and give that to General Cromwell as soon as you can. In case you should lose it, tell him we have got our man, who crossed the Border this morning. Say we are bringing him to Corbiton Manor, as directed, and expect to reach there before dusk."

The youth, without reply or salute, pocketed the paper, shook out the reins, and was off like the wind, Armstrong watching the pair with a glow of admiration in his eyes. Although unused to the life of a camp, he was much struck by the absence of any attempt at secrecy in the proceedings. There was no effort to bewilder the prisoner or make a mystery of the affair. That his advent had been expected was perfectly clear, and that a written description of his person had been distributed along the Border was equally evident. They had been watching for him, and now they had him. There was no military fuss about the matter, and apparently very little discipline, yet instant and unquestioned obedience without accompaniment of formal deference to authority or manifestations of salute to superiors. But underneath it all was a hint of power and efficiency. Armstrong realized that he was in the clutch of an admirably constructed human machine that knew what it wanted and went straight for it. No one had spoken except the captain, yet every man was on the alert to do what was required of him instantly, capably, and in silence.

At a word from the captain a bugle-call rang out, and its effect was soon apparent. An accoutred horse was led to the captain, who sprang into his place with the ease of one accustomed to the feat, and from the buildings appeared something like a score of mounted troopers.

"Get into your saddle," commanded the captain, addressing Armstrong.

The latter tested the buckling, which a soldier had just finished, drew up the strap a point, then, with his foot in the stirrup, turned and asked:

"Am I to consider myself a prisoner, sir?"

"Whatever questions you wish to put will be answered presently by one higher in authority than I."

"I must protest against this detention, sir."

"Your protest will doubtless be considered by the officer I referred to."

"General Cromwell, I surmise?"

"Or one delegated by him. Mount, we have far to go."

Armstrong leaped into the saddle, and the troop set off, with the captain at the head, and himself in the midst of it. There was no chance of escape, even if he meditated such an attempt, which apparently he did not. The direction tended south and east, and as the sun was setting they came to Corbiton Manor, a large country house, which was seemingly the headquarters of a considerable section of the army encamped in the neighbourhood. Into a room in this mansion Armstrong was conducted and left under guard, and he was pleased to see by the spread table that there was at least no design on the part of his captors to starve him.

CHAPTER IV.—PREPARATION.

The mansion of Corbiton was a large and rambling structure, two stories in height for the most part, although in some places it rose to three, as in others it subsided into one. It was built partly of stone, partly of brick, and partly of timber and plaster, with many gables, and picturesque windows in the wide extending roof. Each of its owners had added to it as his needs required or his taste dictated, and now it was composed of many styles of architecture; but the jumble, as a whole, was beautiful rather than incongruous, as might have been expected. Time, moss, and ivy had blended the differing parts into one harmonious mass. The house faced the south, fronting a broad lawn that had once been smooth and level as a table, but was now cut up by horse's hoofs. A mutilated sun-dial leaned from the perpendicular in the centre. One gable contained a wide and tall mullioned window, which had formerly been filled with painted glass, but the soldiers, knowing nothing of art, and strenuous against idolatry, had smashed many of the pictured panes, but, finding that glass, whether colored or plain, kept out wind and rain, they had partially remedied the results of their own enthusiasm by stuffing the apertures with gaily-colored cloths, remnants of doublets or silken trousers, until the window was a gaudy display of brilliant rags, the odds and ends of a cavalier wardrobe; and thus the gay gable, from being an allegory of the days of chivalry, had become typical of the ruin that had overtaken the cause of the King.

Sir Richard Corbiton had been one of the first to fall in the Civil War, dashing with gallant recklessness against the pikes of the yeomen. Theoretically these coarsely garbed pikemen were the scum of the earth, cowardly dogs who, when they saw gentlemen bearing down upon them, should have turned and fled; but actually they stood grim and silent, and when the charge broke against this human rock, although many a lowly hut was then masterless, many a mansion was without an owner, Corbiton among the rest. Sir Richard, dying, paid the price of a fool, and in the struggle exacted the same tribute from others.

As evening drew on, the thin crescent of a new moon shed a faint mysterious light over the scene, as if it were a white sickle hung up in the sky, useless because there was no harvest in England to reap, save that of death. The dim lustre outlined the mansion, but failed to reveal the wounds it had received, and the aspect was one of peace, scarcely troubled by the footfall of a sentinel slouching along the grass in front, carelessly trailing his pike, with nothing of alert military manner about him. From one wing of the building came the somnolent drone of a hymn, but this was counterbalanced by the more intermittent hoarse chorus of a ribald song, mingled with a rattle of flagons from another part of the house, for the ale in the cellars was strong, and not all of the Parliamentary army were Praise-God-Bare-Bones. The torches within the house struck flamelike color from the remnants of the pictured glass in the great window, which gave a chromatic touch to an otherwise sombre scene unrelieved by the pallid half-light of the moon.

The sentinel stopped in his walk and stood for a moment by the battered sun-dial, listening. Faintly in the still night air came to him across the fields the beating of horses' hoofs on the hard road. Striding athwart the broken lawn to an oaken door, he smote it with the butt of his pike, crying,—"Peace within there; the General is coming." There was an instant hushing of the coarse song, then a laugh, and when some one in nasal tones raised the slow tune of a hymn the laughter became more uproarious, subsiding gradually, however, as voice after voice joined the drone. The sentinel now walked over to the main entrance, and said to some one within the hall,—"I think the General is coming."

The watchman now resumed his promenade, but he shouldered his weapon and marched more like a man on guard. Several officers came out of the hall and stood listening on the broken sward. From the darkness emerged three horsemen, two following a leader, a thickset man, who came somewhat stiffly to the ground, as if fatigued with hard riding. To the one who sprang to the bridle he said curtly,—"See the horse well rubbed down, and in half an hour feed him with corn," Then to his two followers, "Look to your horses first, and to yourselves afterward. Be ready in an hour."

The chief officer now stepped forward and said:

"You will surely stop the night, Excellency? Everything is prepared."

"No. Did my order to stay the execution of Wentworth reach you in time, Colonel Porlock?"

"Yes, Excellency. I would not have ventured to execute him without your sanction, although the death sentence was the unanimous finding of the court martial."

"The sentence was just. It may yet be carried out, or it may prove that the Lord has other use for him. Lead the way within."

General Cromwell gave no greeting to the different groups as he passed them, his heavy riding-boots swish-swashing against each other as he followed Colonel Porlock into the hall. He strode awkwardly, like a man more accustomed to a horse's back than a tiled floor. The Colonel led him into the great dining-room, one end of which was occupied by the shattered window, while the other was crossed by a gallery, and above all, very dim in the feeble illumination of two candles and some smoky torches, could be distinguished the knobs and projections of a timbered roof.

The vast room was almost completely bare of furniture, with the exception of a high-backed carved chair, which doubtless belonged to it, and a stout oaken table taken from some other part of the house, replacing the long hospitable board that had witnessed many a festive gathering, but which had been used for firewood by the troopers. The General gazed about the ample apartment for a moment, as one who had never seen it before, estimating his bearings with the shrewd eye of a practised soldier; then he pushed the table until it stood lengthwise with the room, instead of across, as before; glanced at the gallery and table, as if making some computation regarding their relative positions, drew up the chair and seated himself, setting the two

114

candles by the edge farthest from him.

"Has Captain Bent arrived with his prisoner?"

"Yes, Excellency. He came at sunset."

"Is he sure of his man?"

"He appears to be so, sir."

"Were any papers found on him?"

"Yes, Excellency."

"The other prisoner, Wentworth, is little more than a youth, I am told?"

"He is very young, Excellency."

"How came he to be set on an important outward post that night?"

"There was no danger of attack, and I placed him there of deliberate purpose. He was most reluctant to go, making one excuse and then another, saying he was ill, and what not. For more than a month he has been under suspicion of communicating with malignants, although we had no direct proof. He had been seen stealing away from the domain of Lord Rudby, the chief of the disaffected in the district. On the night in question he was watched, and as soon as he supposed himself alone he deserted his post, put spurs to his horse, and rode straight across country to Rudby Hall."

"And was arrested there?"

"No, Excellency. An unlooked-for event happened. He rode out from the grounds of the Hall, fighting his way, as it appeared, against a band of Rudby's followers, who were attacking him, and ran into the arms of our men, who were watching for him. The attacking party, seeing, as they supposed, an unknown force of rescuers, turned and fled. The night was very dark, and the account of what took place is confused, but Wentworth was carried back to Corbiton, tried, and condemned for deserting while on duty and holding commerce with the enemy."

"Umph! What version did Wentworth give of the affair?"

115

"He maintained he was no traitor, but did not give any explanation of his absence from duty."

"I thought Rudby had surrendered all arms and had taken the oath to remain neutral?"

"His men were armed with staves only, and so Wentworth, better equipped, held his own against them."

"What view did the court take of this affray?"

"They thought it merely a feint to cover the retreat of a discovered traitor. The night, as I said, was dark, and our men, being mounted, could not move silently. Knowing the house would be searched if Wentworth was hidden, this plan of seeming enmity against him was prepared beforehand, in case of discovery."

"How old a man is Rudby?"

"Nearing fifty."

"What family has he?"

"His two sons are supposed to be with the King at Oxford. There is one daughter at Rudby Hall."

"Humph! Is this the young man who is said to be a son of the late scoundrel, Strafford?"

"Yes, Excellency."

"In that very blood is hatred of the people, contumely, and all arrogance. At heart he must be a Royalist And yet—and yet——where was he brought up?"

"On the estate of Sir John Warburton, dead these some years back. Warburton was his grandfather."

"Where is the Warburton estate?"

"It adjoins the lands of Rudby."

116

"A-h! Is the boy's mother living?"

"No. His only relative is a sister who seems to be the most bitter King-hater in all the land."

"Is there not a chance the boy was on his way to see his sister?"

"It was thought not. She has been at liberty to visit him here, and has done so on various occasions."

"Has Wentworth ever been in action?"

"Oh yes, Excellency, and he acquitted himself bravely enough."

"No hanging back; no wavering in the face of the foe?"

"No, Excellency."

"Humph. Send Captain Bent to me with the papers. When he is gone, I wish you to bring me a trooper, some silent man who can be depended upon; an unerring marksman."

When Captain Bent arrived he handed to the General the papers he had taken from Armstrong. Cromwell examined them with great minuteness by the light of the candles, then set them in a bunch on the table without comment of any kind.

"Did your prisoner resist at all, or make any attempt at escape?"

"No, General."

"He made no protest then?"

"He said England and Scotland were at peace, that he therefore needed no passport; that his arrest was illegal, and that you would be the first to admit as much."

"Humph. Was he thoroughly searched? Are you sure he had no other papers than these?"

"Quite sure, General."

"Very good. Bring the man here. If the door is open, come in with him.

If it is shut, wait until you are called."

When the Captain left the room the Colonel entered with his trooper, who bore a matchlock. Cromwell dismissed Porlock, then said to the trooper,—"You will take your place in that gallery and remain there, making no sound. Keep your ears shut, and your eyes open. A man will be standing before me. If I raise my hand thus, you will shoot him dead. See that you make no mistake, and I warn you to shoot straight. Go."

The trooper, without a word, mounted to the gallery, and the General, rising, went round the table, standing on the other side. "Can you see plainly?" he cried to the man aloft.

"It would be better if both candles were at this end of the table, sir." Cromwell moved the farther candle to a place beside its fellow, then stood again on the spot his prisoner would occupy. "That is well, sir," said the man in the gallery. The General walked to the end of the room, threw open the door, and returned to his seat in the tall chair with the carved back.

CHAPTER V.—EXAMINATION.

When Captain Bent entered the galleried room with his prisoner, he found Cromwell seated at the table, his head bowed over some pages of manuscript on which he was busily writing. The General did not look up for a full minute, until he had finished the sentence he was inditing, then he raised his head and said quietly to the captain: "Go."

For one brief and lamentable instant the discipline which held the captain in its bonds relaxed, and he replied in surprise,—"And leave him unguarded, sir?"

Cromwell said nothing, but a look of such devilish ferocity came into his piercing grey eyes that the captain staggered as if he had received a blow, gasped, turned, and fled. When the Commander spoke to Armstrong there was no trace of resentment or anger in his tones.

"Will you oblige me by closing that door which Captain Bent has stupidly left open? You are nearer it than I."

Armstrong with a bow did what he was requested to do, and returned to his place beside the table.

"I fear I must begin with an apology, a form of speech to which I am unaccustomed. You have been stopped quite without just cause, and I trust you have met with no inconvenience or harsh treatment in consequence?"

"With neither, General Cromwell, if I am not at fault in so addressing you. I jalous there are not two such men as you in the army of the Parliament."

Cromwell paid no heed to the compliment, if such was intended, but although his voice was suave his keen eye searched the prisoner like an east wind.

"The stoppage may indeed save you further annoyance if you intend to travel about the country, for I will give you a pass likely to prevent such a mistake in future. You are in the cattle-trade, I am told?"

"Yes, General."

"'T is an honest occupation, and I am pleased to believe my army has ever been an upholder of it, paying for what it requires in sound money, even when the wages of the soldier were scant and in arrear. The requisitions and confiscations which have followed like a plague the track of the King's forces, devastating the country like the locusts of Scripture, are no accompaniment to the troopers of the Lord. It is perhaps your intention to deal with us rather than with the King's army, should you venture so far south?"

"Indeed I know little of English politics, and the man with money in his pouch, and a purchasing brain in his head, is the chap I'm looking for, be he Royalist or Parliamentarian."

"It is a commendable traffic with which I have no desire to interfere. You know of no reason, then, for your arrestment by my stupid captain, Ephraim Bent?"

"Truth to tell, your Honour, and I know a very good reason for it."

"Humph. And what is that?"

The General's brows contracted slightly, and the intensity of his gaze became veiled, as if a film like that of an eagle's eye temporarily obscured it.

"Some nights since, as I was making for the English line, I stopped for refreshment at an inn where I had been accustomed to halt in my travels. To my amazement I was refused admittance by a man who stood on guard. We had a bit of a debate, which ended in my overpowering him and forcing an entrance; and which was more surprised, the dozen there gathered together, or me with their sentry under my oxter, it would be difficult to tell. Swords were drawn, and I might have come badly out of the encounter had it not been that a friend of mine among the assemblage recognized me."

A look of perplexity had overspread the grim face of the General as this apparently simple tale went on. He leaned his elbow on the table, and shaded his face with his open hand from the light of the two candles, thumb under chin, and forefinger along his temple. At this point in the discourse he interrupted: "I suppose you wish to mention no names?"

"I see no objection," continued Armstrong innocently. "I take it that the men were quite within their right in gathering there, although I contended they exceeded their right in trying to keep me out of a public-house. My friend was the Earl of Traquair. The others I did not know, and I was not introduced, but in the course of the talk I gathered that the one who had the most to say was Henderson, a minister of Edinburgh, who spoke much, as was to be expected from his trade. Well, these gentlemen, finding I was for England, asked me to carry a message to the King, but I explained that I had no wish to interfere in matters which did not concern me, and they parted to meet again somewhere else."

"Do you know where?"

"I think in Lord Traquair's own castle, but of that I am not sure."

"This is interesting. We shall, of course, try to prevent any messenger reaching the King; but I do not understand why you connect the incident at the inn with your detention."

"There was a great splore about a spy that escaped, and I have no doubt, if he saw me there, and heard the proposal made to me, he might well have brought my name and description across the Border. At least that was the way I reasoned it out with myself."

"It is very like you are right. Spies, unfortunately, seem to be necessary when a country is in a state of war. Many unjustifiable acts are then committed, including the arresting of innocent men; but I am anxious nothing shall be done that will give just cause of offence to Scotland; a God-fearing country, and a friendly. When such injustice happens, as it has happened in your case, I try to make amend. How far south do you propose to travel?"

"I may go the length of Manchester or Birmingham. The distance and the time will depend on the state of trade."

"If you will tell me places you intend to visit, I will include them in the pass I shall now write for you."

"That I cannot say just at the moment. I wish to follow trade wherever it leads me."

"Then an inclusive pass, extending as far south as Manchester, will meet your needs?"

"It will more than meet them, General," said Armstrong with supreme indifference.

The Commander took up his pen, but paused, and, still shading his face, scrutinized the man before him.

"As I am unlikely to see you again, perhaps it would be as well not to limit it to Manchester. You may wish to travel farther south when you reach that town?"

"It is barely possible."

"As you carry no message from Traquair to the King, I can write Oxford on your permit as easily as Manchester."

"Thank you, General; but Manchester will be far enough."

"I may say that we are strict about those whom we allow to journey to and fro at the present time, and if you should overstep the limit of this document, you are liable to investigation and delay, and I may not be so near at hand on the next occasion."

"I quite understand, and if I wished to go farther south I would have no hesitation in begging permission of your Excellency; but I doubt if I shall even see Manchester."

"You will not be leaving Corbiton until the morning, of course?"

"No, General. I know when I am well housed."

"Then, as I have much to do, I will make out your paper later, and it will be handed to you in the morning."

"Thank you, General."

With this the Commander rose, and himself accompanied Armstrong to the door in most friendly manner. The young man, in spite of his distrust, was very favourably impressed, for there had been nothing, in Cromwell's conversation, of that cant with which he was popularly accredited. The Scot had expected to find an English Alexander Henderson; a disputatious, gruff, tyrannical leader, committing acts of oppression or cruelty, and continually appealing to his Maker for justification. But Cromwell's attitude throughout had been that of the honest soldier, with little to suggest the fervent exhorter.

After giving some laconic instructions touching the welfare of the Northerner to Captain Bent, who was hovering uneasily in the outside hall, Cromwell, bidding his enforced guest a cordial farewell, ordered Wentworth to be brought to him, and retired once more into the dim council-chamber.

With hands clasped behind him, and head bent, he strode slowly up and down the long room in deep meditation, vanishing into the gloom at the farther end, and reappearing in the limited circle of light that surrounded the two candles, for the torches had long since smoked themselves out, and there had been no replacement of them; none daring to enter that room unsummoned while the leader was within it. The watcher in the gallery felt rather than saw that there was an ominous frown on the lowered face as the

Commander waited for the second prisoner, over whom hung sentence of death.

This time a clanking of chains announced the new arrival, who was preceded by Colonel Porlock and accompanied by two soldiers, one on either side of him. The young fellow, who shuffled up to the table dragging his irons, cast an anxious look at the forbidding face of the man who was to be his final judge; in whose word lay life or death for him, and he found there little to comfort him. Cromwell seated himself once more and said gruffly: "Take off those fetters."

When the command was complied with, the General dismissed the trio and sat for some moments in silence, reading the frank open face of his opposite.

"You are to be shot at daybreak to-morrow," he began in harsh tones that echoed dismally from the raftered ceiling. This statement contained no information for the youth, but the raven's croak sent a shiver through his frame, and somehow the tidings brought a terror that had been absent before, even when sentence of death was pronounced with such solemnity by the court. There was a careless inflection in the words which showed that the speaker cared not one pin whether the human being standing before him lived or died. Allowing time to produce the impression he desired, Cromwell continued in the same strain of voice:

"I have examined the evidence, and I find your condemnation just."

The boy remembered that his father had met death bravely, asking no mercy and receiving none, and the thought nerved him. If this man had merely brought him here to make death more bitter by taunting him, it was an unworthy action; so, moistening his lips twice before they would obey his will, he spoke up.

"I have never questioned the verdict, General, nor did I make appeal."

The shaggy brows came down over Cromwell's eyes, but his face cleared perceptibly.

"You own the penalty right?"

"Sir, it is partly right and partly wrong, like most things in this world. It is right to punish me for deserting my post; it is wrong to brand me a traitor."

"Ah, you have found your voice at last, and there is some courage behind it. Desertion is an unpardonable crime. The point I press upon you is this; your life is forfeit, yet, although your fault is unpardonable, I do not say it cannot be compensated for. Even my enemies admit I am an honest trader. I will bargain with you for your life. You shall buy it of me, and I shall pay the price, even though I do not forgive the crime. We will first, if you please, clear up the charge of treachery. You were visiting your own home that night, and as it is on the farther side of Rudby Hall, your accusers naturally thought you had a rendezvous there?"

"No, General; it was my intention to have visited Rudby Hall."

"The residence of that foul malignant, Lord Rudby, so called?"

"Yes, but not to see his lordship, who is my enemy, personal as well as political."

The scowl vanished from the face of his questioner, and something almost resembling a laugh came from his firm lips.

"You are truthful, and it pleases me. Why did you make a foolish mystery of your excursions? I take the case to stand thus. Your grandfather and Rudby were neighbors, and possibly friends. You were, and are, in love with my lord's daughter, but since you belong to the cause of the people, this oppressor of the people will have naught of you. You have risked your life to see the girl, who is doubtless as silly as the rest of her class, as you will discover if I let you live. Stands the case not thus?"

"In a measure, sir, it does, saving any reflection on the lady, who——"

"Surely, surely. I know what you would say, for I was once your age and as soaked in folly. The question is, if you will risk your life for her, will you do what I ask of you to earn the girl and your life, or will you refuse, and let her go to another?"

"Sir, I will do anything for her."

"Then harken well. There was here before me, where you now stand, some moments since, the most plausible liar in the kingdom. He told me truths, which on the surface appeared to be treachery to his friend, but which he was well aware I already knew. This was to baffle me into believing him. He rides to Oxford to see the King, and in that I am willing to aid him. He may tell the King what pleases him, and those who send him,—little good will it do any of them. In return the King is to give him a commission, to be handed to certain lords in Scotland. If that commission crosses the Border, we are like to have a blaze to the north of us which I do not wish to see kindled until a year from now; then, by God———then, by God's will I shall be ready for them. We shall defeat the Scots in any case, but if this commission reaches these malcontents we cannot have the pleasure—humph!—we shall be precluded from the duty of beheading the ringleaders without bringing on ourselves the contumely of Europe. Without the King's commission they are but broilers—marauders. With this commission they will set up the claim that they are belligerents. Do you understand the position?"

"Perfectly, General."

"The commission must be intercepted at all costs. It will be your task to frustrate the intentions of the King and his Scottish nobles. But the task is more complicated than yet appears. It would be an easy matter to run this messenger through the body, and there an end. I want what he carries, but I do not wish to harm the carrier. These Scots are a clannish, troublesome, determined race. If you prick one with a sword's point, the whole nation howls. This, then, must be done quietly, so that we bring no swarm about our ears. William Armstrong is the messenger's name, and he has powerful supporters in his own country. He was stopped as soon as he crossed the Border yesterday, and brought here. He pretends to be an innocent trader in cattle, and will likely keep up that pretence. I have appeared to believe all he says, and he leaves this house to-morrow morning with a pass from my hand, giving him permission to travel as far south as Manchester, which was all he asked. I would willingly have given him safe conduct to Oxford, but he was too crafty to accept such a thing. He thinks he can make his way south from Manchester. As a matter of fact, he cannot, but I wish to make the way easy for him. Of course I could give a general order that he was not to be molested, but there are reasons against this, as we have doubtless spies in our own ranks, and a general order would excite suspicion, and would probably prove useless, because this man, south of his permit's territory, will endeavour to go surreptitiously to Oxford, and by unfrequented routes. It will be your duty to become acquainted with Armstrong and win his confidence. You will accompany him to Oxford and return with him. You will be protected by a pass so broad that it will cover any disguise either of you may care to assume. It is such a pass as I have never issued before, and am not like to issue again, so I need not warn you to guard it carefully and use it only when necessary. It reads thus:"

Here the speaker took up a sheet of paper on which he had been writing, and, holding it so that the light from the candles fell upon it, read aloud:

"'Pass the bearer and one other without question or interference from Carlisle to Oxford and return.'

"The journey south will give you the opportunity to become acquainted with your man. On the northward march you must become possessed of what he carries, and when you bring it to me you receive in its stead pardon and promotion. If you do not succeed before you reach Carlisle, then I must crush him; possibly kill him as a spy. Will you undertake it?"

"'T is an ungracious office you would bestow upon me, sir. I had rather meet him in fair fight and slay him, or have him slay me, as God willed."

"There speaks youth," cried Cromwell impatiently. "This man is a treacherous, lying spy, whose life, by all the rules of war, is already forfeit. I propose to discomfit him with his own weapons. Nay, more; I willingly save him from the destruction he merits. You are set to do him the greatest service one man can offer another. If you fail, he dies. If you succeed, he has probably a long life before him. God knows I yearn to cut no man's thread where it can be avoided, but the true interests of England stand paramount. Would you condemn thousands of innocent men to agony and the horrors of prolonged war, to save the feelings of a Border ruffian who intervenes in a quarrel that should not concern him?"

"Sir, you are in the right, and your argument is incontestable. I accept your command willingly."

A gleam of pleasure lit the rugged face of the General, for he was flattered to believe his prowess in controversy was no less potent than his genius in war. His voice softened perceptibly as he continued: "We are enjoined by the Word to unite the wisdom of the serpent with the harmlessness of the dove. Your mission combines the two attributes, wisdom and harmlessness, for you are to beguile deceit, and yet suffer the deceiver to pass on his way scathless. You save your country, and at the same time save your country's enemy, forgiving them that persecute you. What excuse will you give to Armstrong for your desire to visit Oxford?"

"My friend, the son of Lord Rudby, is there. Although we are on opposite sides, he has none of the bitterness against me shown by his father. I will say I wish to confer with him."

"That will serve. Now this pass is for two, and you can offer to Armstrong safe conduct under your guidance, giving what plea you choose for the absence of the man who was to accompany you, and who, it may be, was supposed to have procured this pass from me. Whatever difficulties arise on the journey must be met as they advance, and in so meeting them will come into play whatever gifts of ingenuity you may possess. If you show yourself worthy and diplomatic, there is scarcely limit to what you may attain in the councils of your country. The need of the future is capable men; men earnest in welldoing, energetic in action, prompt in decision, unwavering in execution. In the hope of finding you one such, I snatch you from the scaffold. The King cravenly bent your father's neck to the block, although he had shown himself to be the one strong man in his council; I arrest the order to fire at your breast, though you are yet unproven. See that you do not disappoint me."

Cromwell folded the pass and handed it to young Wentworth. "Go. This paper is your safeguard. I shall give the order that you are to be well mounted and provided with money. Send Captain Bent to me as you pass out."

Once more alone, Cromwell wrote the pass for Armstrong, giving him permission to travel between Carlisle and Manchester. When he had finished writing, Captain Bent was standing beside the table, and to him he delivered the paper.

"You will give that to your late prisoner," he said. "He is to depart to-morrow morning, not before eight o'clock, and is to travel unmolested. You have accomplished your duties well, Captain, and your services shall not be forgotten."

The silent but gratified captain left the room with straighter shoulders than had marked his previous exit. His chief looked up at the dark gallery and called out, "Come down and report yourself to the officer of the night."

For nearly ten minutes Cromwell sat at the table in silence, save for the busy scratching of his pen. Then he rose wearily, with a deep sigh, his marked face seemingly years older than when he had entered the room. Once outside, he gave Colonel Porlock the papers he had written, and said: "The finding of the court martial is approved, but the sentence is suspended. It is possible that Wentworth may render such service to the State as will annul the sentence against him. You will give him every assistance he requires of you, and the amount of money set down in this order. Bring out my horse."

"You will surely partake of some refreshment, General, before you——"

"No. My horse; my horse."

When the animal was brought to the lawn, the General mounted with some difficulty, more like an old man than a leader of cavalry. The two silent horsemen behind him, he disappeared once more into the night, as he had come.

CHAPTER VI.—INVALIDATION.

Nine o'clock of a summer's morning in rural England is an hour of delight if the weather be fine. The birds sing whether there be war or peace in the land; the trees and hedgerows and the flowers make a path to fairy-land of the narrow lanes; but the man who trusts to these winding thoroughfares, unless he know the country well, is like to find himself in an enchanted maze, and Armstrong, stopping his horse at an intersection, standing in his stirrups the better to view the landscape, wrinkled his brow in perplexity and felt inclined to change his tune to the wail of his countryman lost in the crypt of Glasgow Cathedral, and sing,

"I doot, I doot, I'll ne'er win out."

The sound of galloping hoof-beats to the rear caused him to sink into his saddle once more and wait patiently until he was overtaken. As his outlook had shown him the woods surrounding the mansion he had left an hour before in an entirely unexpected direction, and at a distance not at all proportionate to the time he had spent on horseback, the thought occurred to him that his late detainers had changed their minds regarding his liberation and were pursuing him, but he was fortified by the knowledge that he possessed a permit written by Cromwell's own hand, which no one in that part of England would dare to disregard. If the oncomer should prove a private marauder, of which the country doubtless had many, the horseman reposed a calm confidence in his own blade that gave sufficient repose to his manner. He turned his horse across the lane, completely barring the way, and with knuckles resting on his hip awaited whatever might ensue. Premising a friendly traveller with knowledge of the district, he was sure of a clew out of the labyrinth.

The hastening rider came round a corner, curbing his animal down to a walk on seeing the path blocked. The two horses neighed a greeting to each other. Armstrong was pleased to note that the stranger was a youth with a face as frank and beaming as the day; a face to which his friendly heart went out at once with sympathy, for it seemed glorified by the morning light, as if he were a lover sure of a warm greeting from his lass, which was indeed the hope that animated the boy. The hope had displaced a chilling dread, and the transformation made this daybreak very different from the one he had expected to face. He was riding out from under the shadow of death into the brightness of renewed life and promise.

Arriving as near the impeding horseman as he seemed to think safe, he came to a stand, and with a salutation of the hand made inquiry:

"Do you stop me, sir?"

This question carried neither challenge nor imputation, for, the times being troubled, no man could be certain that he met a friend on the highway until some declaration was forthcoming.

"Only so far as to beg of you some solution of the enigma of these roads. I am desirous of travelling southward, and seek a main highway, which I am grievously puzzled to find."

The other laughed cheerily.

"You could not have chanced on a better guide, for I was brought up some miles from this spot, although at the moment I am myself on a southern journey. We turn here to the right, but we have far to go before we reach the highway."

"The more lucky am I, then, that you have overtaken me. 'T would need a wizard to unravel this tangled skein of green passages."

"Indeed," cried the youth with a lightsome laugh, "I've often lost myself in their entanglements, and, what is more lasting, I lost my heart as well."

"There is one thing you have not lost, and that is time. You are just young enough for such nonsense as the latter losing. I am older than you, and have lost my way before now, as you may well bear witness, but I have kept my head clear and my heart whole."

"'Tis nothing to boast," said the boy, with an air of experience. "It simply means that you have not yet met the right woman. When you meet her you will be in as great a daze as that in which I found you at the cross-roads. You will think it strange that I make a confidant in so personal a matter of a total stranger, but, truth to tell, if I am to guide you to the highway, you must bear me company through Rudby Park, for I hope to get a glimpse of my fair one before I ride farther toward Oxford."

"Toward Oxford!" cried Armstrong, instinctively reining up his horse in his surprise. "Are you, then, making for Oxford?"

"Yes, I have been expecting a friend to come with me, but he is delayed, I suspect at Carlisle, so I must get on as best I can without him."

"I travel to Manchester," said Armstrong, more non-committal than the other appeared to be.

"Then I shall be happy to bear you company, if it so pleases you, until we come to the parting of our ways. That is, if you are not in haste and can wait until I have a word with my lass, in whose direction we are now tending."

To this invitation the Scotsman made no reply, and the other began to fear he had been too forward in his proposal. He rattled on, striving to cover his error in a flood of talk.

"She is the most winsome little lady in all the country side; the only daughter of Lord Rudby, who is——"

"Lord Rudby!" echoed Armstrong. "You fly high, my young sir."

"Why should I not? Although she is the sweetest angel that ever visited this glad earth, she makes no descent when she joins her hand to mine. I am Thomas Wentworth, eldest son to the late Earl of Strafford."

They had been travelling knee to knee in the narrow way, but now Armstrong pulled up and looked at his companion in amazement.

"Do you mean the Minister to the King of England?"

"Yes. There was no other."

"Then you are perhaps about to visit Charles at Oxford?"

"Ah, I have already told you more than was wise on so short an acquaintance," said Wentworth, trying another tack. "You yourself gave me a lesson in reticence a moment since, and you have not been so garrulous concerning yourself as I. I do not even know your name, although I suspect your native land lies north of us."

"Sir, I am William Armstrong, and Scotland is my country. As two swords are better than one, I shall be most glad to travel in your company. I may say, however, that I hold a pass from Cromwell himself, so, if you are a King's man, you may not wish to be my companion."

"Who journeys in Hades must have the devil's leave," answered

Wentworth jauntily. "I am myself abroad through Cromwell's permission, and I'll venture my pass is broader as well as longer than yours. 'Tis sometimes well to have a friend in the enemy's camp, and my friend pretends he can get anything from Old Noll. Read it, if you think I'm boasting."

Wentworth handed the document to the Scot, who read and returned it.

"Mine is but a limited permit compared with this. Where do you expect to encounter your comrade?"

"I fear there is little chance of seeing him until I reach Oxford, if indeed I find him there. I suspect he is detained at Carlisle. However, I travel on my own business, and he on his, so it makes little difference to me, save the lack of companionship. War throws together strange fellow-travellers, and I do not inquire too minutely into his affairs, nor he into mine."

"You go to Oxford alone then?"

"Part of the way with you, I hope. Yes; I'm tired of waiting, and so set out alone this morning, deviating from the main road and taking these lanes, the better to approach Rudby Hall without undue publicity."

"I see," said Armstrong thoughtfully; then, as he fell into a meditation, there was silence between them for some time. The theme of his reflection was the accomplishment of the task which lay before him. Here seemed a heaven-sent opportunity to win peacefully to Oxford, and perhaps to return as far north as Carlisle. Once in Carlisle, with Bruce beneath him, he could defy the whole Parliamentary army to catch him before he crossed into Scotland. Even at the first, the frank, honest face of the boy and his cheerful loquacity went far to disarm suspicion; then the announcement of his name and rank led Armstrong to the erroneous conclusion that the youth of necessity belonged to the Royal cause, forgetting that many of the nobles were on the side of the people, some of them active officers in the Parliamentary army. Circumstances combined to lull his natural shrewdness and conceal from him the danger of his position. He thought Cromwell was satisfied that the wrong man had been arrested, and believed the General had been thus deluded because no incriminating papers had been found on him. The spy of the inn must have reported that the messenger to the King would carry important documents to Oxford. The search had been thorough, but of course the most minute examination failed to discover what did not exist. Armstrong's prompt acknowledgment of his name, his explanation of the mission proposed to him, his reasons for refusal, must have had their weight with Cromwell, and if the spy were re-questioned he would necessarily corroborate most of the details given. Cromwell's complaisance in the proffering of an unasked passport appeared to be, in a way, compensation tendered for injury done, or at least interference, by his followers. Armstrong remembered that luck had often stood his friend, and the present encounter looked like another instance of it, so he resolved to journey with Wentworth as far south as Manchester, there to be guided by circumstances. Up to that point he need ask for no favour, for he had his own permit to lean upon. If the lad proved a true companion, he might then venture to propose that they should keep together under protection of the pass for two.

"Do you move on to Oxford at once, when you have seen this young lady?" asked Armstrong, breaking silence at last.

"Yes, and am willing to ride as hard as you like, if you are pressed for time."

"Oh, I'm in no hurry. He's a churl who would not wait while a lover and his lass whispered, and I shall do aught that I can to forward your adventure if there is any obstacle."

"I thank you, but there is like to be no obstacle at this time of the day. I hope to have the good fortune to find her walking in the garden. This would simplify my quest."

"Are you forbidden the house, then?"

"In a measure I am. I have my enemies within the walls, but my good friends also. If I get a word with one of the latter, difficulties will dissolve." Here the youth reined in his horse and sat for a moment anxiously scanning the landscape. A belt of tall trees bordered the lane, with thick undergrowth that seemed impenetrable to sight or movement. Over the tops of the bushes and between the trunks of the trees Armstrong gathered glimpses of a large mansion in the distance, extensive groups of chimneys being the most noticeable feature. Nearer was seen a carpet of green lawn, and beyond, the dappled glitter of the sunlight on a lake.

"Will you hold my horse?" asked the youth, almost in a whisper. "I must reconnoitre."

He sprang off his horse, and Armstrong grasped the rein.

"I hope they will not neigh," he said, as he disappeared into the undergrowth. It was evident the youth was well acquainted with his locality.

Armstrong sat silent, occasionally leaning over to stroke the neck of the steed he held in tether. He loved all animals, especially horses, and they reciprocated his affection. Suddenly the silence was shattered by a cry hoarse with rage.

"I have been watching your approach, perjured scoundrel! You shall not escape me this time."

"Sir, sir, I beseech you," came the entreating tones of Wentworth; "I cannot bear arms against you. Listen but a moment, sir."

"Draw, you dog, or die the death of one."

"Sir, I implore you; I cannot draw with you opposed. Sir, let me say a word——Oh!"

There was one clash of steel, then a brief cry of pain, and now silence again, all so quickly accomplished that first word and last were uttered in the time during which Armstrong leaped from saddle to earth. He searched hurriedly for the leafy tunnel through which Wentworth had passed, but before he found it the lad staggered into sight again, his left hand grasping his breast, his right dragging the sword, his face pale as chalk.

"He has killed me," he gasped.

"Nonsense. You would not now be on your feet if the wound were mortal. Who is your assailant?"

"No matter for that. Help me home."

"I shall first give the rogue a taste of his own surgery," cried Armstrong, drawing his blade.

But the other restrained his ardour, leaning heavily upon him.

"It is her father. Do not leave me; I faint. If—I——if I——I cannot direct you, take me down the lane; the high road. My home——the house to the right."

The victim collapsed in a heap on the sward, reddening the grass with his blood.

Armstrong was no stranger to the rough art of the leech. He undid the doublet and flung it open; tore away the waistcoat and shirt, disclosing an ebbing gash.

"Well pierced," he muttered. "An inch to the right would have done the job. The poor chap parried, but not enough; the onslaught was too fierce and sudden. The old man's intention was good, but the deflexion marred the thrust."

He staunched the wound with the torn shirt, and tied a sash tightly round the body. Taking a leathern flask from his pouch, he forced some fluid between the grey lips, and Wentworth, with a long sigh, opened his eyes.

"It's nothing to boast of," said Armstrong carelessly. "I've ridden twenty miles worse mangled. Can you sit your horse if I put you on him?"

"Oh God! oh God!" moaned the youth, near to weeping. "Fool that I was to risk all for the chance of a word."

"Tut, there's no risk. You'll be right as Edinburgh in three weeks."

"Three weeks. Oh, my God! Would he had killed me outright!"

"What is troubling you? Anything in which I can help? I see you are no coward, and it is not alone the wound that hurts. Is it this Oxford journey?"

The prone invalid made no reply, but, groaning, turned his face to the turf.

"Harken!" cried Armstrong earnestly. "Although our acquaintance is of the shortest, I would dearly love to do you a service. I will go to Oxford for you, and do there whatever you wish done."

The speaker reddened as he said this, and his conscience reproved him for thus making use of the other's infirmity, although he maintained stoutly to himself that he was honest in his proclamation.

The stricken youth was no less troubled in mind than in body, feeling himself a treacherous wretch, accidentally well punished; but he, too, inwardly braced his weakening purpose by the thought that he acted for the good of his country, an action tending toward the speedy return of peace.

"Help me to my horse," he pleaded, ignoring the proffer just made to him. "I must get home and learn whether this hurt is serious or not."

"It is far from serious, I tell you, and it means only a month's idleness. Lean you on me. There; make no exertion. I will lift you to your saddle."

The powerful Scot raised him as if he were a child, and, with a woman's tenderness, set him gently on his horse. He got into his own seat so promptly that his steadying hand was on his comrade's shoulder before the swaying body could do more than threaten a fall.

"This way, you say?"

Wentworth nodded wearily, and the two set out slowly for the high road. Despite their awkward going, the edifice they sought was soon in sight, situated in a park, to which a winding lane led from the main thoroughfare. The place seemed deserted, and as they neared it Wentworth showed a faint anxiety that he might reach his room unobserved.

"My sister must be told, of course, and a doctor brought; but I wish to avoid a rabble of gossiping servants if I can."

"I will carry you wherever you direct, and if we meet anyone we must enjoin silence. Can you indicate the position of a private door through which we may enter."

"The most private door is the most public door. The front entrance will likely be deserted. I would walk, but that we must hurry or be seen. Take me up the stair and to the second room on your right. That is always ready for me."

The Scot took the youth again in his arms and speedily laid him on his own bed. The jolting, despite the care taken, had shifted the rude bandaging, and the wound bled afresh. Armstrong, anxious for the safety of his burden, had not noticed that his own doublet was smeared with blood. With the better appliances now at hand, he did what was immediately necessary, and revived the lad's ebbing strength with a second draught from the leathern bottle. A sound of singing came to them as he finished his ministrations.

"That is Frances——my sister," breathed Wentworth with closed eyes. "Break it gently to her, and say I am not dangerously hurt. She will know what to do."

CHAPTER VII.—DETERMINATION.

Armstrong stepped out into the hall, closing the door softly behind him. The melody was coming from the broad stairway, and ceased as the singer seemed to pause on the landing. He remembered that landing as he came up with his burden. Its whole length was lit by a row of mullioned windows, and one of these, being open, gave a view upon the green lawn in front of the house. He stood hesitating, undecided whether to advance as far as the head of the stair or await the coming of the girl where he was. Then he heard her voice evidently calling through the open window: "John, there are two saddled horses under the trees. See who has come."

Armstrong strode forward to the stairhead.

"Your pardon, madam," he said. "One of the horses is mine; the other belongs to your brother. May I ask the man to look after them?"

The girl turned quickly, her dark eyes wide with alarm. Into the mind of the intruder, looking down upon her from his elevation, flashed the words of her brother,—"It simply means you have not yet met the right woman. When you meet her, you will be in as great a daze as that in which I found you at the cross-roads."

"She is magnificent," he said to himself. With her mass of black hair falling in wavy cascade over her shoulders, her midnight eyes appealing and dashed with a fear that swept the colour from her cheeks, she looked a pallid goddess standing against the pictured panes.

"My brother!" she cried at last. "What of him?" Then, noticing the blood on Armstrong's coat, she gave utterance to a startled exclamation, moving a step forward and checking herself. "Is he wounded? Has there been a battle? Where is he?"

"He is wounded, but not seriously. I brought him to his own room."

Without another word she sprang up the stair, past her interlocutor, and flew along the hall, disappearing into the invalid's chamber. Armstrong thought it best not to intrude at the moment of their meeting, so passed on down the stair and out to the horses, where he found an old servitor standing guard over them, apparently at a loss what to do or how to account for their presence.

"Are you John?" asked the Scot.

"Yes, zur."

"Who is the doctor that attends on this family when any of them are ill?"

"'E be Doctor Marsden, zur, down t' th' village."

"How far away is the village?"

"'Bout dhree mile, zur."

"Very good. Get on that horse, which belongs to your master, ride to the village, and bring Doctor Marsden here as quickly as you can."

"Be Marster Tom ill, zur?"

"Yes, he is; but mind you say nothing to any one about it. Away with you."

Armstrong led his own horse to a stall in the stables, took off saddle and bridle, then went to the well and removed the stains from his clothing as well as water would do it. Going toward the house he met the girl.

"My brother says you tell him the wound is not dangerous. Is that true?" she asked.

"Quite true. I've had a dozen worse myself," he replied, with encouraging exaggeration. "But he will have to lie still for a month or more under your care."

"He says that is impossible, but I told him he shall do as the doctor orders, duty or no duty. I am going to send for Doctor Marsden, so pray pardon me."

"I have already sent for Doctor Marsden. I took that liberty, for it is better in such a case to lose no time."

"Oh, thank you!"

The girl turned and walked to the house with him. He found the patient restless and irritable. The wan whiteness of his face had given place to rising fever. His eyes were unnaturally bright, and they followed Armstrong with a haunted look in them. His visitor said nothing, but wished the doctor would make haste.

When Doctor Marsden arrived he went about his work in businesslike fashion. A physician of that day had ample experience with either gunshot or sword wounds, each being plentiful enough to arouse little curiosity respecting their origin. He brusquely turned Armstrong and the sister out of the room, after having requisitioned what materials he needed, and the two stood together in anxious and somewhat embarrassed silence on the landing, within call if either were needed. The girl was the first to speak.

"I fear my brother's case is more dangerous than you would have me suppose," she said in tremulous voice.

"Not from the wound," he answered.

"From what, then?" she asked in surprise.

"I do not know. He has something on his mind. I saw that from the moment he was hurt. He is very brave, and this accident of itself would make little impression on him. My acquaintance with him is but a few hours old, yet I know he is a fearless youth. Are you aware of a mission that takes him to Oxford?"

"I have not the least knowledge of it. I heard no hint of his going, and he said nothing of his journey when we spoke together."

"He told me he had expected a comrade who had failed him. Cromwell himself gave him a pass for two. He said he was to see the brother of his sweetheart, who is with the King in Oxford."

"That is very likely. The two were great friends always, even when they took opposite sides in this deplorable contest which is rending our distracted country."

"There must be more than friendship in this journey, otherwise Cromwell would not have given him such a pass as he holds. Then for an unknown, un-vouched-for man to enter Oxford at this moment is highly perilous, an action not to be undertaken lightly. If he go in disguise, and such a pass be found on him, not all Cromwell's army could save him. It may be he is commissioned to treat for peace, but that is unlikely. Such proposals should come from the defeated force. Depend upon it, something important hangs on this Oxford excursion, and if anything can be done to relieve his mind regarding it, this will do more toward his speedy recovery than all the leech's phlebotomy. If I can render service to him in Oxford, I shall be glad to undertake his commission."

"Do you, then, go to Oxford?" asked the girl innocently, turning her disquiet and disquieting eyes full upon him.

"I——I had no such intention when I set out," stammered Armstrong, abashed that for once his natural caution had forsaken him. "It matters little how far south I go, and I am willing to do an errand for a friend. I took him for a Royalist at first, and so saw no danger in his purpose, but if he be a Parliamentarian, then Oxford is a place to avoid."

140

"Did he not tell you he was a Parliamentarian?" questioned the girl, now alarmed in her turn.

"No. You told me so."

"I? You must be mistaken, sir; I gave you no information about my brother."

"You said his friend in the King's forces had not thought the less of him because he took the other side."

"I am distraught with anxiety about him, and gave but little heed to my words. I would have you remember only what my brother himself told you."

"You need have no fear, madam. Anything said by either of you will never be used to your hurt. I am a Scot, and have nothing to do with English strife."

Their conversation was interrupted by the opening of the door and the reappearance of the doctor. The girl could not conceal her trepidation, for the nontechnical stranger's assurances had slight weight with her.

"Thomas is doing very well; very well indeed," said the old man. "You have no cause for alarm, not the slightest, if he can but be kept quiet for some days, and rest where he is for a few weeks. You attended to him, sir, and I take it that you possess a smattering of our art."

"I have need of that knowledge, Doctor," replied Armstrong, "for those who have done me the honour to run me through rarely had the consideration to make their attack within easy call of a surgeon."

"Royal; or Parliament, sir? One likes to know before opening one's mouth."

"Neither, Doctor, I'm a Scotsman."

"Ah, that accounts for it." Then, turning to the girl, he said, "Your brother wishes to speak with you, and I have reluctantly given my consent. You will stay with him as short a time as may be, and I will be here to see that you do not overstep a reasonable limit. One word more. Do not argue with him, or dispute anything he says, no matter how absurd it may seem. Agree to any proposal he makes, even if you know it cannot be carried out. He is evidently disturbed about his duty. Soothe him, soothe him and concur. There is little use in telling a lad in his condition that duty must wait till wounds are healed, but he will recognize that fact when he is well again. Meanwhile humour him, humour him. Away, and I'll count the minutes till you are out again. I will find John and send him for a competent nurse."

Frances opened the door gently and met her brother's hungry eyes. She sat down beside him, taking his fevered hand between her cool palms.

"Oh, I'm a doomed man; a doomed man!" he groaned.

"Nonsense, Tom; the doctor quite agrees with the stranger that your wound is not dangerous."

"I was not thinking of the wound; that does not matter."

"What does, then, dear?"

"Sister, this morning at daylight I was to have been taken out and shot." The girl's hands tightened on his. "Cromwell himself reprieved me last night, but on conditions. The sentence still hangs over me, and now I'm helpless to avert it, and all through my own folly. Oh, I have been a heedless fool! With every incentive not to take risk, I have walked blindly——"

"Yes, dear, yes; but tell me how I can aid you. The stranger says he will do anything you want done in Oxford, going there specially on your errand, and he looks like a man to be trusted."

The lad drew away his hand, turned his face to the wall, and groaned again.

"Cannot you trust him?"

"Trust him!" he cried impatiently, "Frances, Frances, it is against him I am going to Oxford! The man is a spy carrying a message to the King. He is interfering in a quarrel that should be no concern of his, and his life is already forfeit, as indeed is the case with my own. But the price of my life is

142

the thwarting of him. The King will give him a commission to be taken to the Scottish nobles. It is that document I was to rend from him, by force if necessary, by cunning if possible. I was to give him every aid to reach Oxford, but on the way back I was to gain possession of this commission and ride to Cromwell with it; then life and promotion were mine, and now I lie here helpless as a trussed fowl."

"A loathesome, treacherous task for a man to put upon the shoulders of a boy."

"But look you, Frances, 'tis but meeting treachery with treachery. Armstrong has no right in this contest, and his success means a new blaze of war with the loss of thousands of innocent lives. It means the possible triumph of the King who murdered our father and broke his pledged word to him and to you. And seeming trickery may be real mercy, as in this case it is, for if Cromwell cannot obtain the King's letter by stealthy means he will crush this Armstrong as ruthlessly as he would crush a gnat. By no possibility can this Scot ever see his land again if he holds that fatal instrument, for the whole army is watching him. But once bereft of it, he is free to go as he pleases. The simpleton thinks he has deluded Cromwell, and is blundering on through a fool's paradise that bristles with unseen swords. If I were his dearest friend I could do him no greater service than to purloin the document of doom he will carry when he turns his face north again."

"What do you wish me to do?" asked the girl in a low voice, her eyes staring into space, her hand trembling with apprehension at what she knew intuitively was to be required of her.

"Frances, dear, you once took a journey alone to London, to see our father. Again you went the same road, to aid him if you could, and failed, to our lasting grief, through the supineness of a thrice-perjured monarch. Will you refuse to set out on a shorter expedition, not for my sake only, although the saving of my worthless life will be one effect of your success, but to overturn what is perhaps the final plot of our father's slayer, who has already deluged the land with blood. Will you not help to bring more speedily that peace the kingdom yearns for, and the only peace now possible?"

"I'll do it," she said quietly, rising, stooping over, and kissing him.

He clung to her hand with the tenacity of the weak and helpless.

"Frances," he said hurriedly, "remember you are protected by Cromwell's own pass, so have no fear. In case of need the army or any part of it must stand ready to aid you if you call upon it. Old John will ride behind and look after you. Although the pass mentions two only, it is so sweeping that they will doubtless take it to include a servant. Any subordinate will hesitate before he delays one carrying so broad a permit from Cromwell himself."

"Yes, yes. I shall meet with no difficulty, you may be sure. You have already talked too much, and the doctor will censure me. Good-bye, Tom. Get speedily well, and that will be my reward, for I swear to you, by our father's memory, that my hand shall give into Cromwell's the King's parchment." Kissing him again she tore herself away from him.

"Send Armstrong to me," were his parting words to her.

Armstrong entered the room shortly after Frances had left it.

"This will never do," cried the Scot cheerily. "The doctor is in despair over the time your sister spent with you, and he is at this moment chiding her. Me he has threatened with direst penalties if I exceed a scant minute. So I shall just have to bid you farewell and be off, wishing you quick recovery."

"Armstrong," said the boy huskily. "My sister must take to the Oxford road and remedy my default. Will you be her comrade there and back?"

"As faithfully as ever belted knight attended fair lady," replied Armstrong, his eyes suddenly ablaze with joy.

"John will attend her, and I am sure your good sword will protect her if need be."

"You may take oath on that."

"I give you the pass which is safe-conduct for you both, and I think it will serve to cover John as well. If not, your own might shield him as far as Manchester."

144

"My own will shield me as far as Manchester, and this will, more appropriately, convey your sister and her servant."

"Yes, yes! That of course, as it should be. My head is spinning, and my thoughts are astray."

"After Manchester we will manage some way. Be not uneasy about that. I give you the word of a Scottish gentleman I will care for your sister as if she were my own."

Armstrong took the pass, which was now ominously stained red. He grasped his supposed friend by the hand, bade him farewell, and wished him quick healing. Wentworth's throat choked, for a feeling of strong liking for the man almost overpowered him, but a stinging sense of his own perfidiousness held him silent. Remorse was already biting worse than the wound in his side. The stranger turned for a moment at the door, waved his hand, and called to him to be of good cheer. A sob broke from the lad's throat, and weakly he cursed the exigiencies of war.

BOOK III.—THE JOURNEY.

CHAPTER I.—DISAGREEMENT.

When Armstrong left the room where the wounded boy lay he found Doctor Marsden alone, pacing up and down the long hall, visibly impatient. However, he appeared gratified that the stranger had contented himself with so short an interview.

"I think," said the Scot, "I have soothed his mind as successfully as you administered to his body. I undertook the duty which troubles him, and now he has nothing to do but get well, which I am sure will be the speedier that he is in your skilful care."

"You are very complimentary, sir, and I thank you. If you succeeded in putting his mind at ease you have taken a great weight from mine, for I like to treat corporal wounds uncomplicated by mental worry. I am expecting the nurse every moment and will just step inside until she comes."

Armstrong bade the practitioner farewell, and this proved the last he was to see of him. The young man went to the stables to feed and water Bruce, not knowing how soon he might have need of him.

Horse and man were glad to greet each other. Armstrong examined the animal with care, and was pleased to note that he was none the worse for his long and toilsome journey of the day before. The Scot found himself wondering into what part of the land he had got. Cumberland he knew, and Northumberland very thoroughly, but this district was strange to him. As a rule he was able to estimate with some exactitude the distance a horse travelled in a day, but the journey with Captain Bent had been over a rough country, in continually changing directions that had ended in bewildering him. High passes had been crossed, and deep valleys traversed with a speed that said much for the mobility of the' Parliamentary troopers. They had avoided villages, keeping through barren lands, uninhabited for the most part, until they reached the fertile and cultivated region in whose outskirts was situated the estate of Corbiton Manor. The questions he asked of his captors had invariably gone unanswered, either because the men were silent from nature or from command, or because they knew as little of the road as he did. The trend of the present morning's journey had been southeast, the country becoming more and more populous as he proceeded.

Returning to the house, he met Frances Wentworth evidently in search of him. It seemed to him she had been weeping, and there was a perceptible change in the cordiality of her manner toward him. He feared this was perhaps to be accounted for by the admiration of her beauty which his glances might have betrayed, and he resolved to be more careful in future, although it was difficult to repress the exaltation he felt at the prospect of being her companion on a long and possibly dangerous expedition.

"Has my brother spoken to you of my visit to Oxford?" she asked.

"Yes."

"Are you in great haste?"

"Not in the least."

"Would it be as convenient to you to set out tomorrow morning as this afternoon?"

"Quite. It would be better, in fact, for my horse had a hard day of it yesterday, travelling I don't know how many miles. Perhaps you can tell me where I am. I could get no information from my surly gaolers."

"You are in the southern part of Durham, near the Yorkshire border."

"We have come even farther than I thought. A day's rest will do no harm to the horse, for he little knows what is before him."

The girl seemed at a loss for a reply.

"I thank you," she said at last, somewhat primly, as she turned away. Then, pausing and hesitating a moment, she continued with face half averted,

"My brother and I are twins and perhaps the more devoted to each other on that account. I would do anything for him. I wish to stay and see the nurse installed. There are many things to think of at such an unexpected crisis, and no one to think of them but me."

"I thoroughly understand the situation, and I wish I were able to tell you how completely I sympathize with you. Although I know your brother so short a time, I am only too glad to be of the slightest assistance to him."

This gracious avowal did not appear to have the effect it merited. Some trace of a frown marred the smoothness of the girl's brow, and her lips became compressed. If a stranger is to be robbed and thwarted, it is embarrassing to hear friendly protestations from him, especially when there is no doubt about their truth. This man was evidently the soul of honest candour, and the repulsion which had sickened the girl's mind at the revolting task fate had assigned to her was increased by the genuineness of his good will.

"I thank you," she murmured again, and left him abruptly.

It was very early next morning when Armstrong stood by his black horse in the lane under the trees, waiting for his fair charge, who seemed to exercise the privilege of her sex in being late. Old John was already mounted on an animal that, besides carrying him, was pack-horse for the luggage required by the young lady on her travels. When the girl appeared, Armstrong stepped forward to offer his assistance; but he was a fraction of a second too late, for, ignoring him, she was in her saddle and away before he could utter a word. He admired the light ease with which she accomplished this act, and saw at once she was a practical horsewoman on as good terms with her steed as he was with his own. She rode down the lane to the main road, then turned south, never looking again toward the home she was leaving; hurrying, indeed, as if it were her purpose to get out of sight as soon as possible. The undulating nature of the country soon concealed Warburton Park mansion, and the trio rode on steadily, the girl in front, Armstrong following close, and Old John lagging somewhere in the rear, as if he knew that, after all, his heavily laden nag must set the pace, however briskly the more metalled cattle ahead of him started off.

After an hour of this Armstrong began to wonder where he was going. Nothing had been said to him regarding the route to be taken, and the girl went on as confidently, never turning her head, as if she and not he were to be the leader of the expedition. He laughed quietly at this, then, gathering rein, Bruce, requiring no other hint, stepped out and overtook the horse in front.

"Have you any plan marked out with reference to the roads we may take, or the towns we are to pass through or avoid?" he asked.

"Yes. We will reach York to-night, then follow the London road as far as Stamford. After that we branch southwest through Northampton to Oxford."

"It is all settled then," he said, smiling.

"I know the way well, and you told me you were a stranger. I have passed between York and London four times," she answered seriously, and with a chilling tone of finality which seemed to indicate that further discussion was unnecessary. The inflexion may have been too subtle to impress itself upon the young man, for he continued with obvious geniality,—"You have wandered far afield for one so young." To this remark the girl made no reply. Her eyes were fixed on the road ahead, and Armstrong, being at a loss to continue a one-sided conversation, found nothing further to say. He was vaguely conscious of the constraint that had come between them, for she had talked with him freely enough the day before; but he could not account for the change. He had always been accustomed to the free-spoken communion of men, and knew little of the vagaries of the other sex, whom he had ever regarded as the more talkative. He feared he had offended her by some thoughtless observation, and racked his brain trying to remember what it might have been. If it were her brother who rode beside him he would have asked him plainly where the offence lay, and would have fought him joyfully if the answer was not to his mind; but he was afraid of this dainty lady and anxious not to displease her. He began to see that he ran risk of disappointment in his anticipation of pleasure through a companionship which the other party plainly regarded as enforced and not at all to her liking.

They approached a declivity which disclosed a small hamlet at the foot of which flowed a stream.

"Do you know the name of this river?" he asked. "It is the Tees," she answered shortly.

"Then that will be Yorkshire beyond?"

"Yes."

Again he could think of nothing further to say, and inwardly chafed at his own awkwardness. He sympathized deeply with his companion, compelled to leave her only brother lying helpless from a serious wound, and thought her taciturnity arose from brooding on his peril, which in part it did. He wished he could call to his tongue some consolatory phrase, but his usually ready wit seemed to have deserted him. Yet he thought it impossible that they should journey thus gloomily the length of the land. Perhaps to-morrow would prove an amendment on to-day. And so through Yorkshire the silent progress continued.

The road was better than that to the north of the Tees, and also less deserted. They passed long trains of pack-horses travelling toward York, and occasionally met an equestrian, sometimes alone, but more often attended by one or more servants. So far they had seen nothing to show that civil war cursed the country, and no soldier had stepped forward to question their purpose in being abroad.

"This is not unlike some parts of Scotland," he said at last, in an ill-fated attempt to revive a conversation which he did not recognize as dead and beyond his power to resuscitate. The girl reined in her horse, and Bruce stopped through sympathy, old John halting, that the respectful distance he kept might not be decreased. Frances held her head high, and there was a sparkle of determination in her eye. It was best to begin right, and she would put this persistent man in his place, a task already too long delayed. And perhaps the putting of him in his place would lessen the clamour of her own conscience.

"Sir, who are you?" was her amazing inquiry.

"Me?" gasped Armstrong. "I'm a Scotsman."

"Perhaps I should have said, what are you?"

"You mean——Oh, I'm a drover—a dealer in cattle."

"Did my brother tell you who I am?"

"He told me his father was the late Earl of Strafford."

"Yesterday I was grateful to you for the aid you afforded my brother, as I should have been grateful to my servant if he had occupied your place; but I should not have forgotten the distance between that servant and myself. Strafford's daughter does not recognize a drover as her social equal. I ask you to take the position I set for you when I began this journey."

Armstrong's face became very red, and then all colour left it as this pronouncement went on. His back stiffened, and, although he spoke with measured calmness, there was a thrill of cold anger in his words.

"Do you mean, madam, that I am to ride with your servant?"

"That is what I mean."

"I have no objection in the least. From the conversations we had together he shows himself a man of knowledge and a lover of horses, which is an easy passport to my liking."

"I am glad his company is so much to your taste, and I shall be obliged to you if you fall back with him, as I wish to ride alone."

"That will I not do under command; for, although I may cherish old John's conversation, I cannot admit the claim of superiority you set up. I am a drover, I said, and so your ancient King Alfred might with equal truth have dubbed himself a baker, if old tales are true. I am William Armstrong of Gilnochie Towers, Lord of the Lands of Langholm, Dalbetht, Stapil-Gortown, Shield, and Dalblane. I can trace my lineage as far back as any noble in England, and come to my ancestral thieves as soon as they. In courtesy we Armstrongs are the equals of any Englander, and in battle we have never turned our backs on them. The castles of my clan line the river Liddel, and when I ride with my friend, the Earl of Traquair, I ride by his side and not with his followers."

"Sir, you overwhelm me with your grandeur," said the girl loftily, rejoiced to find herself in what promised to be a quarrel. She was human, and thought it would prove easier to rob an enemy than a friend. "I thought the crowns of England and Scotland were united, but I see I was mistaken. I travel with the king of Scotland, and he is doubtless on his way to Oxford to confer with his brother the king of England."

"Madam, I go to greet his Majesty, Charles, and if he dare to address me as you have done I will tell him I am more king of the Border than he is king of England, and my saying will be true."

Frances Wentworth bowed low in mock humility.

"Your Highness of the Border, will you permit me to ride in your train? I know I am not worthy, but I ask the boon that I may seek consolation in communion with my servitor."

"Madam, you may ride where you please," gruffly replied the thoroughly angered Scot, tingling with wounded pride.

"Sir, I thank you," replied the maiden, bowing again, "and I am delighted that you should exhibit to one so lowly as I, an example of that courtesy of which you just now boasted."

To this the indignant man made no reply, thus changing his former relations as regarded conversation. He urged on his horse, and she, after pausing awhile and seeing that John would approach no nearer, also went on, and thus the three kept for the day their new relative positions.

When the excitement of this verbal encounter had passed, the gratification at bringing about a rupture between them proved short-lived. Suddenly she was on the verge of tears, but strenuously repressed them, fearing he would look back, which he never did. That mood vanished, and hot anger replaced it, the more intense as she knew herself the aggressor. Nevertheless he had been boorish, she said to herself; almost brutal in his insolence. If he were a tithe of the gentleman he so blatantly proclaimed himself, he would have turned round and apologized for his rudeness, even if his anger at first had been justified. But there he rode in front of her, hand on hip and head held high, as if he were lord of the land. A beggarly Scot, proud and poor, from whose tongue flowed glibly a list of barren acres which civilized men would disdain to live upon, like the stunted lands to the north of her own home. Never turned his back indeed! If her father had been allowed a free hand, he would have chased all such braggarts home to their kennels. Even now, with his pretended independence, this Scot was travelling on his traitorous mission under the safe-conduct of the man he would betray. It was no treachery to outwit a spy, but a patriotic duty, and she would bid adieu to all qualms of conscience. And yet—and yet, he had told her brother he would treat her as his own sister, and it was they who had begged his convoy! Still, he may have eagerly seized the opportunity of the pass to get himself scathless to Oxford and back to Carlisle. Thus varying emotions surged through her heart, to be followed by anxious questionings and at last deep depression, during which her head hung and her dimmed eyes saw nothing of the road. Unheeded, the sun passed the meridian, and at last she was roused to a sense of her surroundings by the stopping of her unguided horse before a roadside inn. Armstrong, his black steed brought to a standstill across the highway, sat rigidly upright, and he said, when she thus unexpectedly looked at him with something of startled appeal in her eyes,—"We stop here for rest and refreshment."

"I need neither rest nor refreshment," she answered wearily.

"I was not thinking of you, madam, but of the horses. They have already gone too far without food, but in this benighted land there has been no opportunity of baiting them till now."

"Yes, you said it was like Scotland," she answered sharply, whipped to fresh anger again that she should have imagined he thought of her when he did not.

She sprang lightly from her horse to the ground, and, without a look at the faithful animal that had carried her so far, walked very straight to the door of the hostelry and disappeared within it.

When the time of waiting had ticked itself out on the old clock of the inn, Armstrong ordered the horses on the road again, and sent old John to warn his mistress that the way was still long to York. She came out promptly, mounting proudly without a word, and the expedition set forth as before, old John contentedly bringing up the rear. All afternoon they made their progress along the very direct road, no utterance from any one of the three. Frances grew more and more tired of this doleful journey, so woefully begun, placing the blame on her own weary shoulders for the most part, but now and then filled with a growing hatred of the stolid figure in front, who never once turned round; never once slackened the pace; never once made inquiry of any kind. What brutes men were, after all! The horses they bestrode were the better animals!

At last the nearly level rays of the evening sun glorified the towers of the grey minster, transforming them for the moment into piles of rosy marble, and the walled town was spread out before them. They came to Bootham Bar, and here, for the first time, a man-at-arms questioned their right of way. Armstrong silently presented to him the blood-stained pass, bearing the signature of the Man of Iron.

"Is he on the pack-horse of your company?"

"Yes."

"Enter."

The man-at-arms stood aside, and the trio went up the clattering street until they came to a house of entertainment once called "The King's Head," with a picture of Charles on the swaying sign, now slightly changed to represent Fairfax, a good Yorkshireman, while the lettering had been obliterated and "The Fairfax Arms" painted over it. The leader of the expedition ordered the best apartment in the house for the lady, and sat where he was while the bustling landlord assisted the fatigued traveller to dismount. Armstrong and old John saw to the disposal of the horses, then the young man walked to the minster and round it, noticing everywhere the ravages of the late siege. The town had not yet recovered its arrested prosperity, and most of the people he met were heavy-footed soldiers and citizens in sombre dress. York had been Royalist to the core, and now calamity seemed to brood over it. Armstrong made his way to a mercer's shop in the main street.

"My garments," he said to the obsequious proprietor, "are somewhat stained, and I would renew them."

"There are many changing their coats nowadays," replied the man, "and we must even cut them of the cloth most popular."

He whipped out a measuring-tape and deftly took the dimensions of his customer, muttering the numbers as he stretched his arms.

"I have no time to spare for the making of a costume, but must content myself with what lies on your shelves."

"Sir, I took you for a traveller, and am but estimating what will best become you. Your inches are just on the large side, sir, but I shall pleasure you, never fear."

He spread out on the long table some apparel in dejected brown, which, as it seemed to Armstrong, was but clumsily cut.

"You would garb me as a shepherd, I see. I come from the North, where we are not tailor's models, perhaps, but we scorn such duds as you exhibit. Cannot you furnish me with something more like what I wear?"

The mercer looked at him, hesitating for a moment, then led the way to an inner room.

"I can show you goods there is little call for, and if you are satisfied with them you take them at your own price and risk."

He closed the door and brought out from their concealment rich garments of the Cavalier fashion, which he handled gingerly, as if afraid of them.

"Ah, that's more like. Now I shall set myself out from top to toe in something suitable for riding. My horse and I are two sections of the same thing."

In the privacy of the back room the change was effected, and presently William Armstrong stood as gay and comely a man as could be found in all England, superbly attired, with filmy lace fluttering at neck and wrists. The mercer hovered before him, rubbing one hand over the other, with an artist's appreciation of the result his efforts had produced, and indeed something more glimmering behind in the depths of his appraising eye.

"You will make many a heart beat faster if you pass through the streets of York in that fashion," said the mercer.

"I doubt it. I was never one to be popular with the lasses."

"I was not thinking of women, sir, but of men who have fought and lost."

"Oh, all's not lost because York is taken! There will be a King in England for many a day yet, never you fear."

The mercer cast a timorous glance about him, then suddenly thrust forth his hand.

"You are a brave man. God make your prophecy true. I thought you came in to change your coat with the times, like the rest of us."

"Coats matter little if the heart is right," replied the Northerner, returning the proffered clasp. "You will do what you like with this discarded shell of mine, for I travel light and cannot be bothered with it. So, good-bye."

"'Ca cannie,' as your countrymen say, when once you reach the street. Avoid the soldiery and get free of York as soon as you can."

The gloom of evening was on the town when Armstrong emerged, yet he had not gone twenty steps before a stern officer planted himself square in his path.

"Who are you?" came the curt demand.

"A friend who has been looking for you. The shops are closing, and I am purposing to buy a pair of pistols like the one whose butt I can see in your belt. I may need your help to open a gunner's booth for me."

"You speak lightly."

"There is need of that when it grows dark."

"Fellow, you shall come with me and explain yourself."

"Not so. You shall come with me and do my explaining. And as the day is fading, read that while it still holds." Armstrong handed him the pass and the officer scanned it suspiciously.

"To Oxford," he muttered. "If you are not on the road between Carlisle and Oxford, you are at least in the costume for the latter sink of iniquity."

"Yes, and I have the pass to bring me there. Do you dispute it?"

"No."

"I am glad of that, for you would come into collision with Oliver Cromwell if you did. Now give me your aid toward firearms."

The officer turned with him and walked down the street, beat at the door of the gunshop, and saw the desires of the stranger fulfilled. Then he accompanied him to the door of the inn, bidding him good-night, and disappearing down the unlighted street.

The young lady was partaking of the repast prepared for her in the private parlour set aside for her use, said the landlord in answer to his guest's inquiry. On being shown to the door Armstrong knocked on the panels, and was admitted by old John, who was in attendance.

The girl sat at a table and looked up with surprise, not recognizing her visitor in his new finery, thinking some stranger had mistaken the room; but, seeing who it was as he advanced, she turned her gaze away from him and gave no greeting. If he came to apologize now, it was too late, she said to herself, and his first words showed that this was indeed his purpose.

"Madam," he said with a courtly inclination of his head, which obeisance, it flashed across the girl's mind, had been purchased with his fresh accoutering, a thought that almost brought a smile to her lips, which she hoped to keep firm. "Madam, I crave your pardon for my unseemliness of temper to-day. I am at best an uncouth person, travelling at the head of my own men, who question neither words nor acts of mine, and so have led me into the gruff habit of expecting obedience and not censure. I am no squire of dames, as there is little need to tell you, for already you know it from this day's experience of my ways; but I am deeply grieved that I fell so far short of the courtesy which is your due, and I trust you will forgive my lapse of manners."

Here was an apology indeed, that might well have called forth a generous response, and undoubtedly would have done so from a woman of the world; but Frances had been too sorely hurt by his long incivility toward her. Ladies in the romances she had read were always treated with the utmost chivalry, and, if truth must be told, she was tired and cross, so she hardened her heart, bent her proud eyes on the latticed window before her, and made no reply.

There was a few moments' silence in the room; then her punishment came in his next words.

"I had hoped we might part good friends."

"Part!" she cried in sharp terror, and those wide black eyes of hers quickly deserted the blank panes to fall upon him. She had never anticipated such an outcome of their quarrel as this, nor dreamed that it was easily possible for him to circumvent all her plans by withdrawing himself from her company. Instantly the dread consequences of such a determination on his part—and she had had a glimpse of his resoluteness—loomed up before her, every little disagreement between them sinking into nothingness before this fearful alternative. She dared not lose sight of him until her mission was accomplished, or her brother's life and her country's ruin paid the penalty of her foolishness. She must cast herself at his feet, if necessary, to retain him, and here she had jeopardized everything in an outburst of temper. A chilling fear crept into her heart that any complacency she might show him would be too late. Secretly she had rather admired his sturdy independence and pride of race, comparing it with her own vacillating purpose, ready one moment to forgive and the next to ban; but now this lofty self-respect might prove her undoing.

"I fear I overrated my power of serving you," he continued, "and I forgot for the moment how slight was my acquaintance with your family. Manchester, and not Oxford, is my destination, and I shall make for that town to-morrow before you are astir. The country is not nearly so disturbed as I expected to find it, and the roads are perfectly safe; indeed you know the route better than I. This pass is a most potent document and will open every gate. I leave it with you." He placed the paper on the table before her. "If I might venture to counsel you, I should advise you not to take it into Oxford unless you have some satisfactory plea to account for its possession."

"Have you had anything to eat since you came into York?" Her voice was as sweet as the note of a nightingale.

"No," said Armstrong with a laugh. "I had forgotten about that; a most unusual trick of memory."

"I was too angry with you at the wayside inn, and I could not touch a morsel, so I thus came famished into York. John, see if Mr. Armstrong's meal is prepared, and ask them to serve it here. I think you Scottish people possess a proverb that it is unfair, or something like that, to speak with a hungry man."

"Yes, many of our sayings pertain to eating. We are an uncouth folk, I fear."

"Indeed you are far from uncouth to-night, Mr. Armstrong. I thought it was we ladies who hurried to the mercers when we came to town, but you lost no time in the delightful quest. That was why I was so deeply offended with you when you came in. You are most ungallant not to have invited me to go with you. I could not have visited shops alone."

"You had no need to visit the shops. Nothing they sell could improve you."

"Am I so hopeless as that?" said the girl, with the sigh of the accomplished coquette, leaning back in her chair and entrancing him with her eyes.

Armstrong blushed to the roots of his flaxen hair and stammered,—"I——I meant you are perfect as it is."

She laughed merrily at his confusion, and her mirth came the heartier as she saw she was to accomplish her object; then the laugh was checked as a sudden wave of pity for him surged over her. For all his size he was a very boy in lack of guile, and a shiver ran over her as she pictured what he must think of her when he knew. The sudden tension was relieved by the arrival of old John and the servants carrying a meal hot and savoury, whose incense was a delight to the starving man.

"There," she cried, "sit down opposite me. Put this pass in safe keeping until I seek for it. You will surely not be so cruel as to desert me on the first stage of our journey?"

"Madam," said the bewitched man, "I shall do with eagerness whatever it is your pleasure to ask of me."

CHAPTER II.—RECONCILIATION.

Another glorious summer morning greeted the pilgrims at York; a morning so clear and splendid that it seemed to have lifted the gloom which covered the captured city, as the sun might dissipate a veil of mist. In spite of her fatigue of the day before, Frances was the first afoot, and at this setting forth Armstrong and old John were the laggards, as she blithely informed them when they appeared.

As they rode away from the ancient town the girl could scarcely refrain from joining the larks in their matin song, such a strange feeling of elation filled her being. She had had her first intoxicating taste of power; the supreme power of a beautiful woman over a strong, determined man. He had come to her the night before with resolution stamped on his masterful face; came of set purpose, a course of action well marked out for himself in the long dreary ride to York, and he announced that purpose to her, catching her entirely unaware. She was without experience in the ways of men, knowing nothing of them save such enlightenment as a sister might gather from a brother, and this knowledge she saw instinctively would be of no service in the contest that so unexpectedly confronted her. As boy and girl the arguments with her brother had been of the rough-and-tumble order, where the best man won and the other sat down and cried. Armstrong had said in effect, "I leave your company," and a glance at his face left no doubt but he meant it. What instinct of heredity had placed her potent weapons silently before her; what unsuspected latent spirit of coquetry had taught her on the instant how to use them? A melting glance of the eyes; a low, lingering tone of voice; and this stubborn man was as wax in her hands. She had shorn him of his fixed intention, as Delilah had shorn Sampson of his locks; and as this simile occurred to her the spectre of her mission rose before her, and she remembered with a shudder that the parallel of Delilah held true in more senses than one. She glanced sideways at her Samson riding so easily on his splendid horse. What a noble-looking youth he was, and how well his new attire became him. Not any of the courtiers she had seen in the gay entourage of Charles in London could be compared with him. And what an ill-flavoured task was hers: to baffle him; to humiliate and defeat him; to send him crestfallen and undone to his own land! Delilah indeed! "The Philistines be upon thee, Samson!" Poor Samson! She had always been sorry for him, as she read, and now—now—hers was the role to wreck him! Again she glanced at him, and thus caught his gaze bent upon her. He smiled at her; was smiling when she turned her head.

"I can read your thoughts in your face," he said.

"Can you?" she asked in alarm.

"Yes. At first the pure sweet beauty of the morning appealed to you. You were glad to leave the shut-in streets of the town and be once more in the fresh open country. The song of the birds charmed you, and had there been no listeners your voice would have joined theirs. When first I saw you, you were singing, and that was the morning of the day before yesterday; yet it seems ages past, and I have known you all my life. It was my ill-omened fate to break upon you with evil tidings, and a remembrance of my news disturbed you a moment since. The thought of your brother came to you, and the sunshine of your face died out in sorrow for him, wishing you had news of him. Do not be concerned for him. I have seen many a wound deeper than his, and they were of small account with youth and health to contend against them."

The girl sighed and turned her face away, making no comment upon his conjectures, which were so far astray from accuracy. Why had she given no thought to her brother, whose welfare had never before been absent from her mind, yet who never before was in such danger as now? Why had a stranger's image come between them, so monopolizing her mental vision that all her pity had been for him? Delilah was the stronger woman, with no qualms of conscience to unnerve her steady hand. She remembered her kin and wasted no thought on the stranger who fell in love with her in the valley of Sorek. "And when Delilah saw that he had told her all his heart, she sent and called for the lords of the Philistines saying, 'Come up this once, for he hath shewed me all his heart.' Then the lords of the Philistines came up unto her, and brought money in their hand." Money in their hand! The price of a trusting man! Was there anything so baleful as that in all Scripture? When she presented Cromwell with the locks of Samson she would quote that sinister verse to him. Well this lord of the Philistines knew that her brother was not guilty of the treason for which he had been condemned. Cromwell came, not with money in his hand, but with life to be given or withheld, as foul play was successfully accomplished or the reverse. A helpless rage at the part assigned to her filled her heart with bitterness, and her eyes with tears.

"I wonder what valley this is we are descending?" said Armstrong.

"The valley of Sorek," said her lips before her reason could check them.

"What?" cried the young man, amazed, although the reply gave him no hint of its inner meaning. Then he saw that some strong emotion had overpowered her, against which all her struggles were in vain. Instant sympathy with her sorrow manifested itself in his action. He brought his horse close beside her, reached out and touched her hand.

"Dear heart, do not grieve," he said tenderly. "I pledge my faith your brother is better already. Would I had thought of it in time, and there might have been a horseman travelling all night to York, bringing you later tidings of him; but I am ever behindhand with my purposing, and remember a project when it is too late to put it into action. Many a fight that same backhandedness has led me into. I am for ever trusting the wrong man and laying myself open to his craft, yet am I hail-well-met with the next, learning no lesson from experience. Talking of this thrust your brother got, I remember well, two years ago, when three men who bore me no good will came to me and said the Earl of Traquair had bade them make peace with me. I was very willing and struck hands with them. So off we set together, at their behest, to Traquair's Castle, that we might ratify our compact, for the Earl was a good friend of mine. We had gone near on five miles, and were chatting pleasantly together, when in the twinkling of an eye the three set on me. Three to one is no odds for an active man to grumble at if he can face them and has a rock or a tree at his back, but we were on the open plain, and I had a blade in my ribs before I could put hand to hilt. I drove Bruce at the first assailant and, ran him through as he went down. Then I cut for it till the followers were separated; so I turned on the one nearest me, gave him his dose, and chased the third man until I began to sway in my saddle. If he had but known and halted, he would have won an easy victory. Well, there were three good honest, satisfying wounds on three men,—each, I venture to say, worse than the one your brother got, and no doctor within thirty miles; yet the three of us are as hearty to-day as if we didn't know what a sword was made for. So have no fear about your brother. He'll be out and about by the time you are home again."

"Your story reminds me of the Roman tale. It was a cowardly act of your three enemies."

"I think it was rather that way. I did not heed their onslaught so much as their pretence of friendliness beforehand. Still, we mustn't be too critical when a feud is forward. Things are done then that we are sorry for afterward."

"I judge from what you say that you have forgiven the three?"

"Oh, as for that, I had forgotten all about them; it was your brother's case brought them to mind. I suppose I have forgiven them; but if I met them on the road here I'd loosen the sword in its scabbard and be prepared for blade or hand, whichever they offered. But come, we have now a level road before us. Let us gallop. There's nothing so cheers the mind as a charge on a good horse. We will make old John stir his stumps."

They set off together, and old John did his best to keep them in sight. Some fourteen miles from York they baited their horses, then pushed on through Bawtry until Tuxford came in sight more than an hour and a half after noontide, a longer stretch than Armstrong thought good for either man or beast. It was not yet five in the morning when they left York, and with the exception of a bite and sup at their only halting-place they had nothing to eat until two o'clock. Many of the numerous inns along the road were deserted and in ruins; the farther south the journey was prolonged the more evident became the traces of war, and Armstrong found that he had scant choice as to resting-places.

"I hope," said the girl, who knew the road, "that 'The Crown at Tuxford has not been blown down again. It was a good inn."

"More chance of its being blown up," replied Armstrong, flippantly. "Was it blown down once?"

"Yes, about half a century since, in a tempest, but it was rebuilt. You should have a kindly feeling for it."

"Why?"

"The Princess Margaret Tudor rested there in 1503, when she went to Scotland to marry your king."

"By my forefathers, then, the 'Crown' is a place of evil omen for me. Would that the fair Margaret had slept in it on the night of the storm."

"And now I ask, why?"

"Because her son, James V, came down to the Border, and by treachery collected the head of my clan, with about forty or more of his retainers, and hanged them, denying either trial or appeal. Jamie missed those twoscore men later in life, when his cowardly crew deserted him. We Armstrongs seem ever to have been a confiding race of simpletons, believing each man's word to be true as the steel at his side. Margaret was as false as fair, and a poor Queen for Scotland, yet here am I now risking life or liberty for one of her breed, the descendant of those fell Stuarts who never honoured woman or kept faith with man."

"Sir, what are you saying?" cried the girl, aghast at the unheeding confession into which his impetuosity had carried him.

"God! You may well ask!" said the young man, startled in his turn at the length he had gone. "Still, it does not matter, for you would be the last to betray me. I'll tell you all about it some day, and we will laugh over our march together, if you forget what I said just now. The end of our expedition is not to be the end of our acquaintance, I hope, and you live but a day's march from the Border. Will you let me take the day's march in your direction, now that I know the way?"

"I make no promise until we reach home again. Then you may not wish to make the journey."

"Little fear of that. I must see you again, if only to tell you of my luck in cattle-dealing, at which you showed such scorn yesterday."

"Do not let us speak of that. There is 'The Crown' inn; and even if the shade of the Princess Margaret does not haunt it, I am pleased to see there are people more substantial around its doors. It is not deserted."

"It is level with the times. The crown is blotted from the signboard, although some of the old gilding shines through the new paint."

It was late in the afternoon before they were on horse again, and they jogged down the road at an easy amble. Newark was passed, but they did not stop there longer than was necessary to show their permission to travel, for Newark had been a Royal town garrisoned for the King and besieged more than once. Armstrong had intended to stay the night there; but the authorities showed some reluctance in accepting a pass for two as convoy for three, and it needed all the young man's eloquence and insistance on respect for Cromwell's signature to get old John past the barriers, so when once this permission was granted he thought it well to push on clear of the place and risk the danger of camping out beside the road.

His luck still stood his friend, and at Grantham, some ten miles farther on, as the sun was setting, they came to the ancient archway of "The Angel" inn, a house that gave every indication of furnishing the best of cheer.

"At last," cried Armstrong, "we have shaken off the omens, and I find a lodging fit for you. 'The Angel' for an angel, say I, and here it is. No haunting Margaret of the past, nor inquisitive Roundhead of the present to molest us."

"I am not so sure," laughed Frances. "If ghosts walk these planks, you may wish the graceful Margaret in their stead. In one of the rooms of this house Richard III signed the death-warrant of the Duke of Buckingham. The place hints the fall of kings."

"Lord, lassie, you know too much history and too many legends of this gloomy land. I wish we were safe back in the North again."

"So do I," she said with a sigh, as he helped her down from her horse.

CHAPTER III.—COMPANIONSHIP.

The buxom landlady of "The Angel" remembered Frances and her four former visits to the inn, so she took charge of the girl in the most motherly way, fussing over her and seeing to her comfort.

"No, nothing is changed here," she said, "though dear knows there's trouble enough in the land, and strife and what not; good men going away and never coming home again, or coming back broken and torn. I'm sure I don't know who's in the right, but somebody's deeply in the wrong, and God's heavy hand is on us all. England will never be England again, I'm thinking. I waited on the King my own self in these rooms when he went north not so long ago, and kind and gentle he was to all about him. I'm sure I don't know what he has done that his own folk should rise against him and pen him up in Oxford, as if God's Providence had ended on earth, and His anointed was no more than Jack Lorimer the sweep. And the name of God is always on their lips, but I'm thinking if they talked less of Him and were kinder to His creatures they would be fitter to meet Him when their time came. But, dearie, I must n't run on like this, for there are listening ears all about us, and a poor old body like me has been warned more than once. I fear it is not the King that is to blame, but them foreign people that's ever at his ear, and I thought little of them when they were here. There must be something fell wrong when the nobility themselves turn against him. Well I mind when the great Earl of Strafford himself came south and stayed the night here. If he had lived things would have been different, for he looked more the King than the King himself. Ah, he was a man for you! There, there, dearie, you're tired, and I go chattering along. But don't you cry again, dearie, for it's all long past and done with, and doubtless for the best, though our finite sight may not see that. What a babbling, thoughtless old wife I am; for I remember now, when you were here last, and I showed you the oriel window where Strafford sat, and told you the glint of your eye and the hold of your head reminded me of him, you sat there and wept and wept as if your heart would break. Kind-hearted you were, dearie, and I often thought of you and wondered how you were getting on. But now is not the time for tears, but for joy if ever you are to have it. I knew so comely a lass would not wander long alone, and that's a fine man you've got. I saw how it was the moment you came, for the light in his face when he helped you down from your horse comes but once in a man's lifetime and your own."

"No, no, no, no! You are wrong. He is almost a stranger to me, but is a friend of my brother. He is nothing to me."

"Do you tell me that? Well, well, we never know what the future holds for us, dearie, and unless I'm very much——"

"He was travelling this way, and my brother asked him to give me company. My brother was wounded and could not come."

"Wounded? Oh, I am grieved at that. Many a brave lad——is it dangerous?"

"They say it is not, but it frightens me."

"Yes, yes, dearie; but them that know are like to be right, and we must always hope for the best. Now here's the meal for you, and you will not get a better between York and London. Your man—ah, there I go again—the stranger is looking to his horse, no doubt, as a careful traveller should, and we will see to him when he comes in, so do not you wait."

It was late when Armstrong returned from the stables, for old John's pack-horse showed signs of distress from travelling between seventy and eighty miles that day, and as the slowest horse in the party sets the pace, the animal had to be seen to and cared for.

After his bounteous supper the young man strolled about the rambling inn, and to his surprise came upon a lonely figure in a dim alcove.

"Dear lass!" he cried, "you should have been at your rest long ago. This will never do,"—but he sat down beside her. The place was narrow and very cosy, as if the oriel window recess had been constructed for two lovers.

"I am not tired," she said, "and have much to think of, so I knew I could not sleep."

"You should sleep well after so long a day in the open air. Deep thinking is the enemy of rest, and rather useless in the main. I'll wager you're wishing for news from the North."

"Yes, I was."

"Well, see the uselessness of that."

"I know it, but how can one guide one's thoughts?"

"Oh, it can be done. They say Cromwell has the power of dropping to sleep the instant he gets half an hour to himself. He has plenty to think of, and yet he must be able to guide his thoughts or abolish them for the moment, or he could not do that."

"They say also that he has some secret power by which he gets news before any one else, and thus appears where he is most needed at the time he is least expected."

"I doubt that. He has well-trained men in his service, which is the whole secret. Do you like Cromwell?"

"I do not."

"You surprise me. I thought you were a partizan of his. You remember what I said when we were approaching this inn?"

"You said many things."

"Aye. But I said one in particular that I would have wished recalled if it had been said to any one but you. I promised to let you know all about it some day, but I've thought over the matter and I'm going to tell you now."

"No, no! I do not wish to hear."

"But listen a moment———"

"No! I have been trying to forget what you said."

"It is not fair to you that you should be exposed to an unknown scath. This did not occur to me when I set out, but your journey may be jeopardized because of my being deeper in dangerous projects than you have any suspicion of. So I have need to tell you my real errand in the South."

"Mr. Armstrong, I refuse to hear you. I will not be burdened with what does not concern me. Is your memory so short that you forget what has befallen yourself and your kin by trusting to strangers? I warn you to beware of me, and to treat me as if I were an enemy."

"As if I could!"

"As if you must. I have no patience with a confiding man, who needs ever to be kneeling at the confessional. I wish to know nothing of your affairs."

"At the confessional? Indeed, and you are right about that. But I have no desire to confess for confession's sake. I wished but to warn you."

"Very well; I turn the tables and warn you. I ask you to think of the injustice of what you were about to do. If you are on some secret mission, there are others besides yourself involved. It is most unfair to them that you should make a confidant of any person without their consent."

"You say sooth. If you take my hint and promptly disown me should I become involved, I am satisfied."

"I can the more readily disown you if I know nothing of the traffic you are engaged in."

"True, true!"

"They say this inn is part of what was once the monastery of the Templars, and I think the influence of these warrior priests remain in it; for I, too, was tempted to confession when you came. But we must have none of that."

"My lady, you would find me a more eager listener to a penitent than you proved to be. This alcove is like a niche in a temple, and doubtless has heard many a confidence since the Templars built it."

"It shows us a good example; it keeps silent about them."

The two were startled by a deep voice that broke in upon their discourse. They had heard no one approach, but now there stood before them at the outlet of the recess a tall, gaunt figure in the sombre garb of the Parliamentarian, as if he were the spirit of some forgotten Templar of whom they had just been speaking; indeed he seemed the modern embodiment of one of that fanatic, sinister band, for while his bearing betokened the fervid exhorter, a sword by his side indicated that he used the physical as well as the spiritual arm. His cheeks were sunken, and a two-days stubble on his chin emphasized not only the emaciation of his face, but the unhealthy clay colour of his skin.

"A word with you. Who are you? Whence come you? Whither are you bound, and to what purpose?"

"Egad!" muttered Armstrong under his breath, "here's a father-confessor indeed, and right willing to take on the task with no misgiving."

The girl wondered how long the apparition had been standing there, and rapidly ran over in her mind what had been said between herself and her companion since he came. Armstrong spoke up, and, while speaking, proffered his pass to the interloper.

"Sir, that document will possibly satisfy all your questionings." The stranger, taking it, held it near the lamp and read its brief wording.

"This answers none of my questions, except, and then by inference only, that you are perchance destined for Oxford."

"Is not the signature sufficient passport, so long as you do not find us south of Oxford or north of Carlisle? We are within the region over which the passport extends."

"For the second time I propound my inquiries."

"Then for the first time I return them to you. Who are you? Whence come you? Whither are you bound, and to what purpose?"

The man answered without the slightest show of resentment against what he must have known to be an intended impertinence.

"I am Hezekiah Benton, an humble preacher of the Word, and, if need be, a wielder of the sword. I came from Newark, and purpose returning thither, God willing, with more knowledge concerning you than you gave when you passed the gate."

"Very well, Mr. Benton, I will be equally frank, pausing to note with surprise that the signature of his Excellency General Cromwell is invalid south of Newark——"

"I said not so," interrupted the preacher.

"You imply as much by questioning after it has been shown to you."

"If you are entitled to hold this pass, you will meet no obstruction within its limits. As no persons are named upon this paper, it is my duty to satisfy my superiors that it is not misused."

"Pardon me, Mr. Benton, but has it not occurred to your superiors that if General Cromwell had wished the names known he would have set them down as fully as his own?"

Hezekiah thoughtfully scratched his stubbly chin, and was evidently nonplussed by the view so calmly presented to him. After turning the problem in his mind for a few moments, he replied: "Nevertheless you are travelling on the London road. This pass reads Carlisle to Oxford. Newark is not on the highway between these two towns."

"Admirably reasoned, Mr. Benton, and I envy those who have opportunity of hearing your discourses. They listen to good logic, I stand warrant. But the apparent mystery is soon dissolved. This paper was written by his Excellency at Corbiton Manor, in the county of Durham, at about this hour of the night three days ago, what time, if I may so put it, I was the guest of his Excellency at that place. If you will bear the county of Durham instead of the county of Northumberland in mind, you will observe I have taken the quickest route to Oxford, when the state of cross-country roads is considered. So far as the London direction is concerned, we deflect from it to-morrow at Stamford, and will rest, God permitting us, at Northampton to-morrow night. Any further questions will be as cheerfully answered, for I know you would not ask them without authority and a full explanation to give to General Cromwell, should he chance to dislike the uncovering of that which he was at some pains to conceal."

Hezekiah Benton made haste in returning the passport to the suave and eloquent man from whom he had obtained it.

"Sir, your disquisition is most complete and satisfactory. If but a tithe of it had been given at Newark I would have been saved a hurried journey, and you a cross-examination. I give you good-night, and God be with you."

"May he see you safe in Newark again, and grant you length of days to expound His Word," responded Armstrong devoutly, as he rose from his seat and bowed.

Frances rose also when their visitor had taken himself off.

"You are something of a diplomatist, Mr. Armstrong, but I fear diplomacy requires a touch of hypocrisy. Could you not have dismissed him without the benediction?"

"Why? I meant it thoroughly. I am a religious man with a creed as grim as his own; a Presbyterian. I meant every word of it. He is a good man; notice how mildly he answered my scoffing return of his own questions. He made me ashamed of my frivolity."

"A religious man, are you?"

"Yes, why not?"

"I don't know. I had not thought of you as such. Your account of another man's pass did not seem strictly accurate."

"It was true nevertheless. Every word I said was true. I never even hinted the pass belonged to me."

172

The girl laughed and held out her hand.

"Yet you cannot deny that he gathered a wrong impression."

"Ah, that was his fault, not mine. Hezekiah himself would tell you to possess the wisdom of the serpent as well as the harmlessness of the dove. But do not let me be too self-righteous. I will be honest with you, and admit at once that had a direct falsehood been necessary I would have used it. I was determined not to give him any name, for the pass I hold from Cromwell set Manchester as the limit, and we are now south of Manchester. I would have given the good Benton my name at York, but not at Grantham."

"You think, then, that where great events are at stake,—a man's life let us say, or a country's welfare,—one is justified in using deception?"

"Most assuredly. I should have no hesitation in trying any ruse to save my friend or serve my country. Do you not agree with me?"

"I am trying to. Yes, I do agree with you. I do! I do! I do!" she cried with a sudden fervour that surprised him, for it seemed out of proportion to the importance of the ethical question they had been discussing. He had been holding her hand all this time, and she seemed to become newly aware of that fact and hastily withdrew it, blushing as she did so. She spoke rapidly, as if to cover her confusion:

"I use the words furnished me by our visitor. I give you good-night, and God be with you,"—and she was gone before his unreadiness could frame a response.

CHAPTER IV.—FRIENDSHIP.

Next day the three were not as early beginning their march, because Northampton was barely fifty miles distant, and the day was longer than the way. The good landlady of "The Angel," bustling and voluble, saw them off with many blessings, and wishings that God would speed them. Stamford furnished bait for their horses and a short rest for themselves. Then they took the deflecting road for Northampton, but their pack-horse limped and their progress was slow. Frances was in better spirits than was the case since the pilgrimage began, for she had now persuaded her mind, which eagerly wished to be convinced, that her future action would save the lives of two men,—Armstrong's not less than her brother's,—and so she had come to look upon her unsuspecting companion as her beneficiary rather than her victim. He himself had unknowingly been advocate against himself, and she was surprised to note how much influence his argument exerted, thinking it was because she was so anxious to be confirmed that the deed which circumstances compelled her to do had more of right than wrong in it. If he was indeed a Presbyterian, as he had said, his sympathies must, after all, lean toward the Parliamentary side rather than toward the Royal cause, and disappointment at the failure of his mission could not be very severe. She had heard him say nothing which showed enthusiasm or even concern for the King; in truth the remark which had inadvertently escaped him was to the effect that it was folly for one of his name to do service for the line of Stuart, and he had characterized the race as fair and false. Whatever motive, then, had sent him on this dangerous mission, it was neither love for the King nor loyalty toward his cause. Armstrong always spoke of himself as an outsider, having little interest in the quarrels of the English, whom he quite evidently regarded as an inferior race, easily overcome if fronted by real fighters. She smiled as she recollected his embarrassment once or twice in the midst of a diatribe against them, when he remembered just too late that he was talking to an Englishwoman. One fact, however, she failed to recognize, which was that in the intervals of conversation her mind was entirely filled with this blond Scot, to the exclusion of everything else.

The day passed pleasantly enough, even if progress was slow. Armstrong related many interesting or amusing anecdotes of the Border, and the girl came to the conclusion that life must be anything but dull in that hilly district. They partook of their noontide meal at a hospitable farm-house, for inns were few and mostly untenanted. They learned that it would probably be dark by the time they reached Northampton, but there was a new moon to light their way. They were off the main line of travel and had the road practically to themselves. At about five in the afternoon they heard the tramping of a squadron behind them, coming on at a rapid walk. Armstrong suggested that it would be well to draw into the hedge while the troopers passed, and this they did. The Scot sat easily on his horse, watching the somewhat imposing oncoming, the breastplates of the men scintillating in the declining sun, which shone full upon them. Suddenly Armstrong straightened and, unconsciously perhaps, his hand grasped that of the girl beside him.

"Have you ever seen Cromwell?" he asked.

"No."

"That is he at the head of the cavalry."

She drew away her hand, and sat there, scarcely breathing, fearful of the approaching encounter, which now could not be avoided. If Armstrong were equally perturbed he showed no sign of it, and she admired his nonchalance as she glanced momentarily at him. But her eyes turned instinctively again to the leader of the troops. There was something masterful in his very bulk; he seemed a massive man on his huge horse; power personified were horse and man. His unblinking eye faced the sun like an eagle's, and he came stolidly past them, looking neither to the right nor the left. The firm face was as inscrutable and as ruthless as that of the Sphinx.

Four and four came the men behind him; some old, but erect; the majority middle-aged; all cast in the same mould as their leader. They sat like him, and looked straight ahead like him. Polished steel on head and front, but nothing ornamental in their outfitting. No drums, no flags, no trumpets; a shining, yellow bugle at the hip of the foremost,—that was all. Everything for use, nothing for display.. Clanking past they came, four and four, four and four, in seeming endless procession; weapons, and chains at the horse's bits, jingling the only music of their march. Not a word was spoken, not a glance to one side or the other. At last the final four went by, and Frances drew a breath of relief that a menace was past and done with.

"Do you think he saw us?" she whispered, not yet daring to speak aloud,—a precaution rather absurd, for she might have shouted while they were within arm's length of her, and she would not have been heard in the trampling of the horses.

"Saw us!" echoed Armstrong, "yes, every thread of our garments. What a man! God of war, how I should like to fight him!"

"I thought you admired him."

"So I do, more than any other on earth. If I had seen him before, I doubt if I had been here."

"I understood you to say you met him at Corbiton."

"Met him, yes, by dim candle-light, smooth and courteous. But I never really saw him until now. You cannot rightly judge a man—a fighter, that is—until you have looked at him on horseback. That man knows my business. For the first time since I set out I doubt my success."

"Will you turn back?" she asked, her voice quavering.

"Oh, no! I'm his Roland. If we do not cross swords, we'll run a race, and may the best man win. But I feel strangely uncomfortable about the neck, and I think of my ancestor Johnnie and the Scottish king."

He raised his chin and moved his head from side to side, as if the rope already throttled him. Then he laughed, and she gazed at him in fascinated terror, wondering he could jest on a subject so gruesome.

"That man is likely to defeat me," he continued. "His plans are all laid, and already I feel the toils tightening around me. I am satisfied he knows every move I have made since I left him. The unseen spy is on my track, and, by my sword, I'd rather circumvent him than rule the kingdom. Wull, whaur's yer wits? Now's the time ye need them, my lad. In the first place, I dare not go through Northampton; that's clear."

"Why?"

"In my soul I'm certain a crisis awaits me there. I'll be nabbed in Northampton. Then the question, 'Why did you refuse a pass to Oxford'?"

"Did he offer you one?"

"Yes. The next question will be,' Why are you south of the limit set by yourself, travelling to Oxford on another's pass?' To that query there's no answer. I'm a self-convicted spy, and then the scaffold, according to all the rules of war."

"Pardon me if I do not follow your argument. If he has tracked you, as you think, there is no more reason he should stop you at Northampton than at Newark or Grantham. Aside from that, why did he not hold you when he had you?"

"Oh, I had not put my neck into the noose then. As for arresting me at Newark or at Grantham, I see now that such was his intention, but our friend Hezekiah failed him. It was undoubtedly Cromwell's purpose that we should have gone back with Benton."

"Still, I do not believe you. If Cromwell is as crafty as you seem to believe, it is likely he wishes you to reach Oxford. Unless that was the case, why should he have offered you the pass?"

"My lass, there are several sides to this problem, and what you say has the stamp of probability on it. Nevertheless, I'll overset his arrangements. I am the only one of us three who cannot give good excuses for being in these parts. Here is the pass which protects you and old John," he said, giving her the document. "You and he will to Oxford at your leisure. I shall gallop across country, will evade the Parliamentary lines as best I may, and will be in Oxford to-morrow morning. That will throw Old Noll a day out of his count."

"Then you leave me to meet Cromwell alone?"

"You have no need to fear the meeting. Your plea is perfect. Your brother was wounded, and you have undertaken his task. Of me or my plans you know nothing, and I was with you merely because I happened to be travelling this way, and had brought your wounded brother to his home. And here is a great warning to us all. Happy is the person who can abide by the truth; who has no secret designs to conceal. My lady, I envy you."

Frances made no reply, but sat there, bending her eyes on the ground. There could be no doubt that his new resolve was the best move in the circumstances, and she was not in a position to inform him that his night march was unnecessary, and that he would be wise to husband his horse's power until he left Oxford, for then would come his time of need.

"Well, let us get on," he cried. "I'll take the first by-road south."

Cautious old John, with his limping horse, had gone forward while they stood talking together, and now they cantered to overtake him. Frances was glad of the cessation of conversation that she might have opportunity of meditating on some argument that would retain him by her side. If he left her, she was resolved to seek out Cromwell at Northampton, tell him of her brother's disaster, and explain her own effort to make good his absence. When Cromwell was convinced that both her brother and herself had faithfully endeavoured to carry out the Commander's wishes, he might then heed her pleading that sentence be annulled, or at least suspended, until the boy had another chance of proving his loyalty to his party. She thought she should succeed in this appeal for mercy, as she was sure Cromwell himself must know her brother was not a traitor. Her meditations were interrupted by Armstrong suddenly drawing in his horse and standing up in his stirrups. She also stopped and looked inquiringly at him. A high hedge bordered the road, and he was endeavouring to peer beyond it.

"What is it?" she asked.

"I thought I caught a glint of a helmet over yonder."

They went on at a walk, and shortly after passed a road that crossed their own. Up this cross-road to the north, two troopers sat on their horses; down the road to the south were two others. As Armstrong and his companion continued west, the four troopers came out of their concealment and followed them.

"By St. Andrew, trapped! I'm trapped as completely as ever was Englishman in Tarras Moss!" muttered Armstrong.

CHAPTER V.—AFFECTION.

The four troopers allowed the distance between themselves and the forward party neither to increase nor diminish until darkness set in, when they closed up, but said nothing. There was no further conversation between Frances and the young man. He held himself erect, and beyond the first exclamation gave no intimation that he was disturbed by the prospect before him. She was victim to the most profound dejection, and was relieved when the gathering gloom allowed her pent-up tears to fall unseen. The universal silence made the situation the more impressive. The sun had gone down in a bank of cloud which now overspread the heavens, threatening a storm and obscuring the moon.

At last the lights of Northampton glimmered ahead, and shortly after a guard in front summoned them to stand. The troopers behind them also stood, but took no part in what followed. An officer examined their pass by the light of a lantern, but did not return it to them. His words seemed reassuring enough.

"You are stopping the night at Northampton?"

"Yes," replied Armstrong, although the pass had been given up by Frances, and the officer's inquiry was addressed to her.

"Have you any particular lodging in view?"

"No."

"You may meet trouble in finding a suitable abiding-place," said the officer, "more especially for the lady. Northampton is little better than a barracks at the moment. I will take you to 'The Red Lion.'" Saying this, but without waiting for any reply, he led the way with the swinging lantern. "The Red Lion" proved a much less attractive hostelry than the hospitable "Angel" at Grantham. It seemed occupied chiefly by armed men, and resembled military headquarters more than an inn.

"You will perhaps wish to see to your horses yourself," suggested the officer to Armstrong.

"Yes, after I am assured that the lady is——"

"Have no anxiety on that score. I will place her in the guardianship of the hostess, and will wait here for you."

The assurance had all the definiteness of a command, and Armstrong, without further parley, led away his own horse and hers, followed by old John.

"Come this way, madam," said the officer to Frances.

He escorted her up a stairway, and at the top turned to her and said in a low voice: "General Cromwell's commands were that you should be brought to him as soon as you arrived."

"Very well. I am ready."

He knocked at a door, and a gruff voice from within told him to enter. He opened the door and went in, followed by his prisoner.

"I have brought the woman, General. The man is under guard below." Saying this, and receiving no reply, the officer laid the pass on the table and withdrew, closing the door behind him.

Cromwell stood at the window, looking down on the dark street below, dotted with moving lights. His broad back was toward his visitor, and he did not turn round even when he addressed her. On a chair rested his polished breast-plate and steel cap, otherwise he was accoutred as he had been when she saw him on the road. His voice was hoarse.

"Who are you, wench, and what are you to this man, that you range the land brazenly together under a pass written for neither of you?"

With some difficulty the girl found her voice after two or three ineffectual attempts to speak, and said: "I am Frances Wentworth, sister to Lieutenant Wentworth of General Cromwell's army."

The General's ponderous head turned slowly, and he bent his sullen eyes upon her. She wondered Armstrong had not seen the brutal power of that countenance even by candle-light.

"Why is your brother not in your place?"

"My brother was sorely wounded the morning he set out, and now lies between life and death in our home."

"How came he wounded?"

"He met Lord Rudby, who attacked him. My brother would not defend himself, and so was thrust through the body. Armstrong brought him to our house, and the doctor says he cannot be moved for a month at least."

"Why was I not informed of this?"

"I did not know where to find you."

"You, wench, surely did not know where to find me; but your brother knew that a message to his nearest superior would find me."

"My brother, I have told you, was dangerously wounded, and had but one thing in his mind."

"What was that? Lord Rudby's daughter, most like."

The rich colour mounted in the cheeks of Frances, but she answered slowly: "It was to have done with the task you had set upon him."

"He committed it to your hands then?"

"He did."

"What was the task I set him?"

"It was to steal from Armstrong the King's commission, and to deliver the result of that theft to General Cromwell, the receiver."

"Wench, your tongue is over-sharp; a grievous fault. I pray you amend it."

"Not until I have told you I am no wench, but a lady."

"We have had too much of lady's meddling in England, and will have less of it in days to come. A wench, if she be honest, is better than a lady, who is seldom honest. Your meddling in this matter has come near to causing a serious disarrangement of great affairs. How was I to know who you were or why you travelled? Has that foolish head of yours so little understanding that, though you stopped at York, at Newark, at Grantham, you gave no officer of mine a clue to your vagabondage?"

"A woman can fulfil her duty without so much babbling of it. My foolish head never thought a great general wished his designs published from one end of England to the other."

The shaggy brows of Cromwell drew down over eyes that shot forth dull fire. He turned completely around, seemed about to speak, but did not. The flame of his glance died out, and he advanced to the table, picked up the pass, examining it critically, back and front. Then he handed it to her, saying slowly,—"If your brother had your brain without your tongue, he would advance faster than he does."

"Am I, then, to go on with this adventure?"

"Yes. You will reach Oxford to-morrow. The King will delay, and shuffle, and suspect, until our Scot is in a fine fume of impatience. For three days more I shall be in Northampton. After that for a week I shall be at Broughton Castle, some few miles west of Banbury. If you should be delayed longer in Oxford, I shall let you know where I am by means of De Courcy, who——"

"De Courcy!" exclaimed the girl.

"Yes; what do you know of him?"

"If he is the same man who was in the entourage of the King in London,—a Frenchman of that name,—I know nothing good of him."

"You cannot look for every virtue in the character of a spy, and we who are doing the Lord's work must use the tools the Lord places in our hands."

"The Lord has naught to do with De Courcy. He is a devil's man, body and soul."

Cromwell scowled at her. "What mean you by that, hussy?" he asked shortly.

"I mean that De Courcy would sell you as readily as he would the King, if there was gold to be made of the bargaining. The Philistines come with money in their hands, and they always find a De Courcy, male or female."

At this Biblical allusion the face of Cromwell cleared like magic, and she had a glimpse of another facet of his character. A certain exaltation which had nothing of hypocrisy in it radiated from his countenance, and his voice rang clear when he spoke.

"Aye, my girl, and when there is a Samson of sin to be bound and blinded, the Philistines do right to accomplish the act as best they may. Judge not, that ye be not judged. Perchance this work to which your hand is now set is not done for either God or your country."

"It will be done for my brother's life."

"Aye, truly; and that is your Philistine's wage. De Courcey toils not for the life of another, but for gold, and let him that is without sin cast the first stone. I give the wage demanded, and care nothing so that God's work be done. God's work is the one thing important, so scorn not De Courcy or any other, but seek his aid in Oxford if it be necessary to communicate with me."

"That shall I never do," muttered the girl under her breath; and if Cromwell heard he paid no heed.

"Have you given thought to your purpose?" he asked.

"I have thought of nothing else; it has never been absent from my mind."

"How do you hope to accomplish possession?"

"I expect to enact the scriptural part of the 'thief in the night,' somewhere between Oxford and Carlisle."

He had seated himself at the table, leaving her still standing before him. At these words the frown came again to his brow, and anger to his eyes.

"I do not like your iteration; it is not to the purpose, and is but womanish."

"I am a woman, and must bear the disadvantages of being so. As you have said, that matters little so that the good work be done."

"Between Oxford and Carlisle is vague. I cannot trust to a scheme so lacking in definiteness. I shall have Armstrong laid by the heels long before he reaches Carlisle. If the wench's hand fail, then comes the rough paw of the trooper immediately after. Your chance will be in Banbury, where you must contrive to have him stop for the night."

"If we leave Oxford early in the morning he will not be content to stop in Banbury, which is less than twenty-five miles away, and even on the coming hither we have covered more than double that distance each day. He will be urgent on his return."

"True, but there lies your task in management; you may fall ill, and I question if he will leave you. I can order your pass taken from you at Banbury, and a night's delay caused. You will go to the inn called 'The Banbury Arms,' at the sign of the blazoned sun. The inn-keeper will ask for your pass, and when he sees it he will place you in adjoining rooms which are fitted for your purpose. There is a communicating door, bolted on your side, invisible, except by close scrutiny, on the other. What follows will depend on your skill and quietness. Has the man any suspicion of your intention toward him?"

"None in the least. He is honest and kind."

"Ah! Do not dwell too much on his kindness in your thoughts, nor trust anything to his honesty. Make it your business to know where he keeps the King's letter, and when it is once in your possession speed at once to Broughton Castle and deliver it into my hands. I will exchange for it full pardon and a Captain's commission for your brother, and if you have further to ask my ear will be inclined toward you."

"I shall have nothing to ask except that this Scot be allowed to pass unscathed to his home."

Cromwell gazed intently at her for a moment, and she returned his look clear-eyed and unabashed. He replied slowly: "If I were willing to harm the Scot the case would be much simpler than it is. You left your home thinking only of your brother, but now the stranger occupies at least a part of your mind."

"It is natural we should feel compassion for those we injure."

A short time before the General had intimated that her tongue was an unruly member, and for a moment it seemed that her impulsive inexperience in dealing with men was about to wreck her plans, for now even the girl was shrewd enough to see that she was sowing distrust of herself in her opponent's mind by incautious utterances. Cromwell leaned back in his chair, and a look of rapt meditation crept over his features. The girl saw she had vanished from his vision, and that the grim man was alone with himself, inwardly questioning his thoughts and demanding an answer. She realized intuitively that once this answer were given, nothing she could say or do would turn him from the purpose decided upon.

"O Youth, Youth!" he murmured, "how unstable thou art! A broken reed; undependable! Give me the middle-aged; the steadfast. Youth is the flash of the burning flax; middle age the steady flame of a consuming fire. Is it not better to imprison this man secretly or hang him openly? He is a convicted spy; every law of war will uphold me. If I grasp the thistle it may sting me, but I shall uproot it. Yet——yet, why at this time bring upon me the brawling Scots? Could I be but sure——the brother risks all at the supreme moment and falls as the fool falleth. Why should she be more firm? Were I sure of her——"

"Sir, you can be sure of me," cried the girl in a panic, terror-stricken at the sight his muttered phrases conjured before her.

"What! What! What! What say you?" Cromwell shook himself as a man rudely awakened from sleep.

"I say you can be sure of me. I shall not falter."

"You will bring me this document?"

"I swear to God I will."

"Nay, nay, swear not at all. If a man's word bear him not up, he will sink when his oath alone buoys him. Wench, I will trust you; but remember this: if I am compelled to take this man through force of arms, to surround him with a troop and publicly wrench his burden from him, I must as publicly hang him, to warn the next Scot who would make the essay on Oxford. If you succeed, you save not only your brother's life, but this man's as well. Now go. Let there be no turning back from the plough to which your hand is set."

Frances retreated and let herself out of the room. On the stair-head at the end of the passage, well out of possible earshot, two soldiers stood on guard, and between them an elderly woman, who immediately advanced when she saw the girl leave the General's room.

"I am the landlady," she said. "Will you come with me?"

"I wish a word with my friend," replied Frances. The woman appeared nonplussed, and stood hesitating; but at that moment the officer who had conducted her came up the stair and approached. "I wish to speak with Mr. Armstrong," she said to him. "Where is he?"

"One moment, madam, if you please," replied the officer, knocking at the General's door. He was not bade to enter, but the single word, "Oxford," uttered in a deep voice, came from within. The subordinate appeared to understand, and with a bow to the lady said: "Mr. Armstrong is waiting below. Will you come down, or shall I ask him to come up?"

"You may tell him I wish to see him."

She walked to the head of the stair and saw Armstrong alone in the lower hall, pacing up and down with a fine swagger of Scottish indifference, which he must have been far from feeling, while the doorway was blocked by two guards holding grounded pikes. The moment the young man saw her he came bounding up the stair two steps at a time. All the guards, above and below, seemed struck with simultaneous alertness, and made a motion which, if continued, would have brought their weapons to bear on the prisoner, but a slight signal from the officer's hand brought back their former stolidity.

"Oh, Mr. Armstrong, I merely wished to know at what hour we set out to-morrow."

"Do we set out to-morrow?" he asked in a whisper. "Yes, there is no obstacle between here and Oxford. I was up so late last night, and that, with this long, dragging journey to-day, has tired me. All I wished to know was the hour for to-morrow."

"But you will have supper with me?"

"No. I can eat nothing. I am too tired."

"Now, that's strange. I'm as hungry as the Tweed at flood time. Let me persuade you."

"Thank you, but I would rest. Good-night."

In all his life he never forgot that picture of the girl at the stair-head looking down upon him. There was a pathetic droop in her attitude which was usually so firm and erect, as if the gloom of this fortress-inn oppressed her. Childlike and forlorn she seemed, and a great wave of pity surged up in his heart for her, while his arms thrilled with a yearning to enclasp and comfort her.

"Good-night!" he cried, impulsively thrusting forth his hand to her. She did not appear to notice the extended hand, and he almost imagined she shrank from it. As she went away he had one more lingering look from her, over her shoulder. A smile, sad and weary, but inexpressibly sweet, lingered on her lips.

"Good-night," she whispered.

CHAPTER VI.—REJECTION.

There had been a lashing of rain and a clatter of thunder over Northampton in the night, as if the town were again besieged; but morning broke clear and beautiful, and when the pilgrims got out into the country again, the freshness of the air, the sparkle of the rain-drops on the trees, caused the world to seem newly made. The girl rode silent and thoughtful, but the young man was bubbling over with high spirits.

"What a wonderful magician is the morning after a rain in midsummer!" he cried. "It transforms everything and glorifies the commonest object, and it transmutes our thoughts from lead to silver. Last night, with the sky overcast and the coming storm growling in the west, when the air hung heavy and the gloom settled down upon us, every man was a lurking enemy, and that innocent tavern a place of dungeons instead of ale-cellars. This morning, hey, presto! a wave of the conjurer's wand, and every soldier is a jolly fellow and a well-wisher. I'm ashamed to confess it in this bright light, but last night I was in a panic, like a lad passing through a graveyard. Never before did my spirits sink to so low an ebb. Those kindly men bustling round to be of help to me with the horses seemed, to my distorted brain, on the watch lest I should give them the slip, and when the guards were set at the door after I had entered and was waiting for you, I thought they were so placed to keep me prisoner, and when the polite officer told me they were there every night, I actually disbelieved him. Even his own actions seemed suspicious, but now, as I look back on it, he was merely one of the few courteous persons in the Parliamentary army."

Armstrong suddenly threw back his head and laughed aloud, as if some humourous recollection had come to him.

"That poor officer must have thought me mad. When I came in from the stables I called for the landlady and asked where you were. She said you were in your room. I then requested her to find out if you would see me for a moment, and without reply she disappeared up the stair. I waited and waited, but she did not return. The officer was now by my side, chattering away about something to which I gave no attention. All at once the absurd idea struck me that you were with Cromwell, taken there by the officer, and that Old Noll was brow-beating you and threatening you, to learn something of me and what I was about."

"No one asked me anything about you or your business," said the girl.

"Of course not. I see that plainly now, but I give you my word it was real enough then. Without a word of warning I broke in on the amazed officer and shouted, 'Where is General Cromwell?' The man looked dumbfounded, as well he might; then he answered quietly enough, 'The General is in the Castle, half a mile from here.' Even then a glimmer of sense came to me, and I explained that the General had passed us that afternoon, and I wondered if he had stopped at Northampton. The officer said he had, and next moment the landlady appeared at the stair-head, and you a moment or two after. What tricks imagination can play with a man!"

"I was as anxious as you were last night, and shall always think of Northampton as the gloomiest town I ever saw."

"I am glad to be quit of it. I wonder if that officer has given us the right direction? It seems to me that we should be bearing further south for Oxford. But perhaps the road takes a turn presently."

"The road is right for the way we are going. We pass through Banbury, which is not much longer than the direct route. I intend to leave Old John at Banbury, and with him this permit, which will be a danger to carry until we turn north again. Banbury is on the straight road to Scotland, which I suppose will be the way you go on your return."

"You are right in that. I'll travel north as the crow flies if I can."

"Then what say you to making Banbury our first stop on the homeward run, after we leave Oxford, taking early to the road the next morning."

"How far is Banbury from Oxford?"

"Less than thirty miles, I think."

"Oh, we can do better than that. I must make from seventy to one hundred miles a day on my road home."

"There is sometimes real speed in apparent slowness."

"True. We shall be guided by circumstances, of course. Much will depend on the hour of the day we are done with Oxford."

Frances said nothing more, for she saw that the stop at Banbury would have to be managed from Oxford, and that it would require some tact on her part to arrange it. The ever-increasing moon was against her, for if there was much delay at Oxford, not only would Armstrong be the more impatient to get north, but night would soon be almost as light as day, and therefore travel would only be limited by the endurance of themselves and their horses. She wished Cromwell had selected some spot at least fifty miles farther away than Banbury, but, with a sigh, accepted the conditions presented to her and resolved to do her best.

At Banbury she had no difficulty in leading her unsuspicious comrade to "The Banbury Arms," and there they left Old John with his crippled horse. The landlord was a quiet, furtive-looking man, with a manner that suggested an intermittent glancing over the shoulder. Frances resolved to say nothing to him at this time, believing they had come so quickly from Northampton that she was in advance of any instructions he was to receive, but in this she was mistaken. With Cromwell to decide was to act, and some one had evidently come through in the night. While they halted, waiting the preparation of a meal, the soft-footed innkeeper, watching his opportunity, drew the girl aside and asked her if she possessed a pass; if so he would like to see it. He was very apologetic, saying all public-house keepers so near to Oxford were compelled by the military charge of the town to assure themselves that travellers who stopped with them were properly vouched for, otherwise it would be his duty to detain them and report to the local commandant. She presented the pass to him without a word, and he read it in silence, then looked at her as if he expected some comment. At last he said:

"Perhaps you intend to stop here on your return?"

"Yes. Have you received instructions already?"

"I have, and everything is prepared. Would you come up now and look at the room? Then, if for any reason I am not here when you come back, you will see that no mistake is made."

He took her to an upper room and explained to her the action of the concealed door, which moved without a sound on well-oiled hinges.

"During the night you occupy this room. I shall have a horse ready, and will be in waiting for you myself until morning. I am to show you the way to the Castle. When you see the General, perhaps you would do me the kindness to tell him that this room was prepared within two hours after I received his commands. He likes prompt service."

"I shall tell him of your promptness if I remember to do so."

"Thank you. Perhaps you will let me remind you of it when you ride to the Castle?"

190

"Very well."

"You will find the road to Oxford without impediment until you reach the lines of the King. I hope you will have a safe sojourn there and a speedy return."

The girl thanked him for his good wishes with what courtesy she could call to her aid, for at heart she loathed him; his smooth, oily, ingratiating manner, and his shifty glance making her shiver with repulsion. Yet, she said to herself, conscience accusing, this man was merely an assistant in a deed where she herself acted the leading part. He was a mercenary, doubtless, doing what he was bid, but against a stranger and an enemy, while she plotted against a friend and a man who trusted her. Fervently she prayed that Providence might intervene between the resolution and its accomplishment, in some way rendering her project unnecessary. There was a slight hope that the suspicious King might not receive Armstrong as the envoy of the Scots. He carried no credentials, and Charles, if he employed him, must accept the Borderer's unsupported word that he was what he declared himself to be. She feared that Charles was in such straits that he would clutch at any straw, but hoped his natural distrust would come into play, so that Armstrong might return empty-handed to Scotland, while she would be relieved of this fell betrayal, from which, as events stood, she saw no way of escape.

Glad was she to leave Banbury behind her, but tremblingly did she dread the time when she should see it again. The road, as the innkeeper had predicted, was clear, and now for the first time during that journey she was alone with her fellow traveller, Old John pottering over his lame horse in the stables of the Banbury inn.

The spirits of the young man were as high as those of the girl were low. He saw that for some reason unknown to him she was depressed, and he tried to banter her into a more cheerful frame of mind; but, this effort bringing with it indifferent success, he broke out into song, and carolled to her some of the Border ballads, both sentimental and humourous, varying his chanting with explanatory excursions into the legends that had given rise to the verses. This was more successful, for few can withstand the magic of a sympathetic voice and a good song, especially when the summer afternoon was perfect, as all the days of their march had been. The birds on either hand warbled an accompaniment; the landscape was empty of humanity, and they had the fair world to themselves. If tormenting thought would but have left her unmolested, the girl knew she would have delighted in this irresponsible outing as thoroughly as her companion enjoyed it. To all outward appearance they were in a very elysium of peace, yet they were approaching the storm centre of the most distracted country on earth, and this seemed typical of her own situation, for although an enforced calm characterized her demeanour, despair was raging in her heart.

Several times the obedient Bruce, guided by an unseen touch, edged close to her, but Armstrong could not fail to perceive that the girl shrank from his proximity, and this abashed him, silencing his song and jocularity. But a lover must be bold if he would prosper. Here was a Heaven-sent opportunity, and what more can a man ask than that? In an hour or two they would be in the midst of a thronged city, where she would meet the friends she expected to see. Who could predict what might happen? It was possible she would elect to remain in Oxford. One or more of her friends might accompany her back to Durham. Now or never was the motto. Yet he had not the least notion how he ought to begin, but thought that in such a crisis a great deal must depend on the presentation of the case. Why had he let slip so many chances of getting information on a subject that now loomed with new importance before him? There was her own brother, to take the latest instance, who would have been glad to find a confidant, and needed but the slightest encouragement that morning in the lane to dissipate all the mystery surrounding a proposal. Thomas Wentworth had solved the problem, yet he was no older than this slip of a girl riding by his side. They had gone a mile or two in silence; a silence in marked contrast to his soniferous setting out. Frances feared that her seemingly sullen indifference had offended him, and, glancing surreptitiously at him from under her long lashes, met his own eyes fixed upon her. She smiled a little and said: "Have you no more songs?"

"I have one more," he answered, speaking hurriedly, "but I have never sung it before, and am just a little in doubt how to begin. I think if I got the measure of it I could carry it on, but am not sure."

"Is it that you have been thinking about so long?"

"Yes. There is a chorus to it, and there you must help me."

"How can I if I don't know it?"

"If I can sing a song I never tried before, perhaps you could do the same with the chorus."

"Very well, let me hear the song. Is it one of those fighting ballads?"

"No. It is a love song, pure and simple."

"I like the others better. Brave and noble actions are the only deeds worthy of poetry."

"I used to think that myself, but I have come to change my mind. It seems to me now that true love is the only theme for either song or story."

"Oh!" said the girl, with a coldness that froze instantly his budding enthusiasm. She sat up straighter on her horse, and turned her face resolutely toward Oxford, as if she did not approve the tendency of the conversation. Armstrong was stricken dumb at finding his indirect course thus blocked before him. The girl was the first to speak.

"I wonder how soon we will be in sight of Oxford," she said.

"Not for a long time, I hope."

"Why do you say that? Are you not as eager as I to reach Oxford?"

"There are some important matters to be settled before we come to the end of our journey."

Frances directed upon him a look of troubled resolution. Intuitively she knew that they were come to the edge of a declaration which she had hoped might be avoided. Several times on the way the danger seemed to approach and vanish, but now the glow of his luminous eyes were not to be mistaken. In them she read a consuming love of herself which was not to be balked, yet which must be balked, and so it became now or never with her, as it was with him. Whatever words he found would be less eloquent than the glances he had before now cast upon her, and it was well to have the event over and done with.

"What important matters are to be settled?" she asked firmly.

All courage seemed to desert him under the intensity of her survey, but with the dourness of his race he urged himself forward, yet not in a direct line. Something of the military strategy with which he would approach a fortress insinuated itself into his love-making.

"We must decide in what guise you are to enter Oxford."

This remark certainly had the effect of throwing the holder of the fortress off her guard. It swept away the tribulation from her brow. After all, the case might not be so serious as she had thought, and jubilantly she welcomed the respite, for she had no wish to add a humiliation to the wrong which fate had decreed she should work upon him. She breathed a sigh of relief and said:

"What guise? I'm afraid I do not understand."

"You see, hitherto we have been shielded by a pass. Its wording was such that little inquiry was made about either of us. Now, for the first time we have no protection, and what we say to those who accost us must prove our safeguard. I shall be asked who you are. I told your brother that I would treat you as if you were my own sister, but I cannot call you my sister at Oxford."

"Why not."

"For one reason, because you go to meet friends who know that I am not your brother, and if inquiry is made we are at a disadvantage."

"True, true! I had forgotten."

"Another reason is that if we claimed such relationship no one would believe us, for your hair is as black as the raven's wing, and mine is like the yellow corn."

For the first time that day the girl laughed outright and lifted her eyes to the locks that so well became him. The simile of Samson again flashed upon her and checked her mirth, but she put the thought resolutely away from her. Armstrong laughed also, well pleased with his progress.

"I had not thought of that," she said.

"But I thought of it, and also of a way to circumvent it. If they ask who the lady is, I shall tell them she is my betrothed."

"No, no, no!" gasped the girl.

"Why not? as you asked a moment since. All's fair in love——and war. The country is at war, and we may make true the rest of the adage."

"No, no!" she repeated.

He was now close by her side and endeavoured to take her hand, but she held it from him.

"You say no because you will not act a lie, and I honour you for your truth. You are robed in truth, my beloved, as an angel is——"

"Oh, cease, cease, I beg of you!"

"Frances, this is the song that bubbles in my heart, and if my lips could worthily fulfil their prompting, I would put it to such words and such music as woman never listened to before. But, lacking eloquence, I can only say, My lady, I love you."

"And I can only say I am sorry if this be so."

"If! Why do you say if? Do you not know it to be true?"

"I know it now that you tell it to me."

"Must a man speak ere he can convey to the woman he loves the fact that he loves her?"

"If the woman love him not, he must speak, and still she finds his preference unaccountable."

"You do not love me?"

"No."

"And cannot?"

"And cannot."

"You would even rob me of all hope, the lover's guiding star?"

"If you call it robbing to take from you what should never have been possessed."

"Why should I not have possessed that hope? Is it because I am untitled, while you are the daughter of the man who was the proudest peer in England?"

"Titles have naught to do with it."

"Titles are but a breath; still, men have intrigued for them, have sold their souls for them, as others have bartered for gold. That shall I do. I thought never to beg from any man, yet for this King I stake my life, and it is but fair he should cover my wager. I will say to him, I go to Scotland on your behest, through an enemy's country. Death or treachery dog every footstep I take. I may win or lose, but if I win, then I demand the stakes, which will not take a silver penny from your depleted treasury. Make me Earl of the Southern Marches."

"You ask a just reward, but 'twould be useless as assistant to the quest you now pursue."

"Frances, no lover truly entitled to bear that dear name, thinks himself worthy of her on whom his heart is set, and I do not plead my own worthiness when I sue for your favour. But I am buoyed up by the thought that every day we live some woman marries some man, therefore are women to be persuaded, and there are none on earth but us to persuade them. Why should my fortune be worse than that of my fellows?"

"Sir, you forget or ignore that every day of our lives some woman refuses some man, and never marries him. Why should your fortune differ from that of so many of your fellows?"

"You have pierced the armour there, my girl, so I own my simile defective, and fall back on my own unworthiness, to beseech your pity on it, and point the way to that amendment which will make me deserving in your eyes."

"Sir, you force me unduly. You drive me toward confession. Pitying God is my witness that I hold naught against you."

"Then, Frances, all is well with us. An English princess, as you told me, journeyed north to marry a Scottish king. Let us furnish a quid pro quo, for the King of the Border rides south to win an English princess. Here we are on the march together to meet the descendant of Scottish prince and English princess, so we cannot do better than follow the example of his forebears."

"Sir, your precedent is unfortunate. The English princess made but a foolish wife for the royal Scot, and their descendant is a man whose word is a frail dependence. Indeed you said their house had exercised a fatal influence on yours, so beware the omens. Put not your trust in princesses, English or other."

"I put my trust on one as on an altar, and kneel before it."

"That I warn you not to do. Many a man has lost his trust through such blind folly."

"So shall not I."

"Sir, you are confident, and are likely to meet with confidence betrayed. You must accept my answer as final, and let us have an end of this fruitless and embarrassing conversation. I can never marry you."

"There is but one circumstance to prevent it."

"Then believe that circumstance exists."

"You love another?"

"I do not."

The young man laughed joyously, but no corresponding smile disturbed the set lips of the girl. He should have seen how painful this dialogue had been to her, but with a lover's selfishness he had eyes for nothing but the object of pursuit; ears for nothing but the words he hoped to compel her to say; pursuing her thus from one point of refuge to another, each abandoned in turn, with no thought but that of capture. Her face was white with dread, a whiteness made the more striking by the jet framing of her hair. Never during the conference had she looked at him since the first direct gaze when she took the resolution to have this disturbing business put at rest forever. The horses walked on unguided, her eyes on the road immediately before her. When he accused her of loving another she glanced up at him for one brief moment, and answered before she thought, wishing her reply recalled as soon as it was uttered, for if she had agreed with him, he himself had said it was at an end. Bitterly did she regret her heedless destruction of the barrier which would have separated them. Now she must erect another, more terrible, more complete, be the consequences what they may.

"Sir, you laugh. I am glad your heart is light, for mine is heavy enough. If I loved another, 't were a small matter, for the man were not likely so estimable in a woman's eyes as you are. As I have said, you drive me toward confession, and here is one bold enough for a maiden to make. I admit you please me well, and if I had loved another—a woman's affection is fickle— you were like to benefit by its transference. But there is an obstacle between us more serious than the one you proclaimed sufficient. Take that as truth, and ask me no more."

"I must be the judge of the obstacle. What is it?"

"I dare not tell you."

"Will you never tell me?"

"I shall make full confession when this war is finished, if you ask me."

"What have we to do with the war?"

"You speak as a Scot. 'T is an unnecessary question, for you know all in England are entangled in its meshes."

"But it can have nothing to do with your feeling toward me, or my adoration of you."

"You shall judge when you hear."

"Then let me hear now."

"No. Your persistence, when you see how distraught I am, dims your title of gentleman. A lady should not be coerced."

"Your censure is just; but oh, pity my despair if this obstacle be real! It cannot be real. Whatever it is it shall dissolve before my burning love as mist before the sun. Tell it to me now, that I may show you that it is the fabric of a vision."

The girl remained silent, her impetuous lover fiercely questioning her bowed head with his eyes. But as if in the interval of stillness a spectre intervened between them and brought a startled expression into his eyes, their intensity sharpened suddenly, and he said in a low voice: "Do not tell me you are already married?"

"And what if I am?" asked the girl hopelessly. "Would the knowledge that such were the case end this useless discussion?"

"No, by my salvation, it would not. If you admit but the slightest esteem for me, I will carry you to my castle in the North and hold it safe for you against the world. Are you, then, wedded?"

"I am wedded to deceit. Sir, I am not worthy your love, or that of any other honest man. If you knew what it costs me to say this, you would let these words be the last we speak in this painful debate."

"Deceit? Not worthy of any honest man? Lord save you, child of sweet innocence, if this is all that troubles you, there is nothing in our way to the church. Your eyes are limpid wells of honesty. You could not harbour a deceitful thought if you tried. I would trust my life, my honour, my very soul to your keeping, assured that———"

"O God of mercy! why do you torture me?" cried the girl in a burst of anguish, bending her head over the horse's mane. The astonished young man placed his hand affectionately on her shoulder, and felt her shudder beneath his touch.

"My dearest lass," he began, but never finished the sentence.

"Halt!" came a sharp command. Armstrong looked up like a man awakening from a dream.

"'Fore God!" he cried, wonder-stricken, "we're on the outposts of Oxford."

A ragged soldier barred the way, with musket held horizontally. An officer in a uniform that had once been gaudy, but now showed signs of hard usage, came out from the cabin at the side of the road when he heard the sentinel's challenge. Though his costume was so threadbare, he carried it with a swagger that had almost a touch of insolence in it, but this bearing melted to a debonair deference when he saw a handsome young woman before him. He lifted his hat and addressed her companion.

"Pardon me. Have you the pass-word?"

"No. I am from Scotland and bear a message to his Majesty the King."

"From Scotland? May I glance at your credentials?"

"I carry none. I have come through a hostile country; have been searched once or twice and arrested as often. Had there been writing on me I should not now be standing at the doorstep of Oxford."

"I shall do myself the honour of conducting you to the Chamberlain of his Majesty. And the lady?"

Armstrong took the girl's hand, this time without opposition on the part of its owner; it was cold as ice.

"The lady is my wife," he said boldly; then added, in a whisper heard only by herself,—"that is to be."

The officer bowed and led the way to the town.

"I wish we were in Scotland," said the young man very quietly.

"So do I," sighed the girl.

"Because what I said at the outworks would then have constituted a marriage between us, if you had replied yes."

The girl withdrew her hand from his and turned away her head.

CHAPTER VII.—CHECKMATED.

The one on foot and the two on horseback entered the fortress which had hitherto proved impregnable, and traversed its streets until they came to "The Crown" inn. Oxford was no longer the home of learning for any art save that of war. A few students still strolled its thoroughfares, but the military man was everywhere. The colleges had been turned into barracks and arsenals; the King himself lived in Christ Church, over the towers of which floated the royal standard, now almost the only red spot in all England.

As the party came to a halt the officer turned to Armstrong. "A propitious meeting," he said, "here comes the Lord Great Chamberlain himself."

Armstrong noted the approach of a man with a countenance so remarkable that it might have been taken as typical of war. From brow to chin was drawn a long red scar, while another ran transversely across the forehead just over the eyes, so that there flamed from his face an angry cross that gave a most sinister expression to a visage which, lacking these time-healed wounds, would have been handsome. The Chamberlain stopped abruptly in his advance, his gaze riveted upon the girl, and there came into his eyes a look of such malignity that Armstrong instantly turned his glance upon his travelling companion. The girl's cheeks had gone deathly white, and she swayed blindly in her saddle, perilously near to falling. The young man sprang from his horse and caught her just in time. Bitterly he blamed himself for this unexpected collapse, cursing his persistence on the road, when he had plainly seen that some strong emotion tormented her. This mental perturbation, combined with the physical strain she had undergone during their long journey, fully accounted for the prostration of the moment at the end.

"My poor lass," he said regretfully, "I am to blame. I am a thoughtless, selfish hound to have so sorely troubled you with my insistence."

"It is not that," she whispered faintly, leaning heavily on him with the pathetic helplessness of a tired child, a dependence which sent a thrill of pity and love for her tingling to his finger-ends. "Take me in; take me in quickly. I am ill."

Now the Lord Great Chamberlain, all smiles and courtesy, stepped forward and said with authority to the innkeeper:

"The chief rooms in the house for the lady. Turn out whoever occupies them, whatever their quality."

The landlord called his wife, and Frances was given into her care.

The officer introduced the traveller to the high official: "My Lord Chamberlain, this gentleman says he has come from the Scottish nobles with a message for his Majesty. Sir, Monsieur de Courcy, Lord Great Chamberlain to the King."

Frenchman and Scot bowed to each other, the grace of the gesture being almost entirely in favour of the former, despite his marred face.

"Sir," said Armstrong to the officer, "I thank you for your guidance; and you, my lord," to De Courcy, "for your kind and prompt command with respect to the lady. She has had a long and tiring journey through a dangerous country, under continual fear of arrest, and so it is not to be wondered that a woman should succumb to the strain at the last."

"Our countries have ever been friends and allies," said De Courcy with the utmost amiability, "and I trust that we, meeting on what is to each of us foreign soil, may be animated by a like regard."

"I thank you, my lord, and, speaking for myself, admit that I have always looked with affection upon France and her brave and gallant sons."

Again De Courcy graciously inclined his head, and replied: "And believe me, sir, if you were acquainted with her daughters, your affection for the fair land would not be diminished. I regret that I have never set foot in Scotland, but hope some day that such will be my privilege. The officer who has left us did not give me your name."

202

"I am William Armstrong, somewhat known on the Border, a Scottish gentleman, and a loyal subject of his Majesty the King."

"Then you are very welcome in Oxford, and I am sure his Majesty wishes there were more like you in the environs thereof and the regions beyond. It is now too late to see the King to-day, and probably you are not loath to meet a night's rest after a hard day's riding. I will arrange a conference for you with his Majesty as soon as possible."

"Thank you. If I may hint that every day is of value, you will perhaps urge upon the King the danger of delay."

"I shall not fail to do so. Good-night."

For the first time in his life Armstrong left his horse to the care of others and entered the inn to inquire after the welfare of the lady who absorbed his thoughts. She sent word that she was quite recovered, but would see no one until the morrow. With this he was fain to be content, and he wandered about the town in the gathering dusk, hoping to do her a service by discovering the whereabouts of Lord Rudby's son, to whom he supposed she carried some message from her brother. He learned that this young man, who was a captain in the King's army, had been sent, it was supposed, to London, but nothing had been heard of him for a month or more, and whether he was prisoner or not, none could say. This intelligence depressed Armstrong, who feared that the girl had taken her long journey for nothing, and that the failing to find the one she sought might entail serious consequences upon her brother or herself, for each in turn had manifested great concern touching the mission she had undertaken.

Next morning his first visitor was the Lord Chamberlain, who expressed deep regret that the King was indisposed and could not see any emissary from the Scots that day. The high official spoke feelingly of the disappointment the monarch had been called upon to endure through the unmerited success of his rebellious subjects, and this statement seemed to the traveller only what was to have been expected.

During the day Armstrong was privileged in securing one brief interview with Frances. The landlord had placed two rooms at her disposal, and in the scantily furnished parlour the young man had called upon her. The improvement she had affirmed the evening before was scarcely borne out by her appearance, for she was wan and dispirited, so much so that when Armstrong announced the disappearance of Captain Rudby, the tidings did not seem to depress her more than was already the case. However, the news clung to her mind; for, as he was telling her that the King could not see him that day, she suddenly said, in a tone which showed she had not been listening, that as Captain Rudby was not in Oxford, there was no reason why she should stay. She would go on at once to Banbury, and there await the coming of Armstrong. But the young man would not hear of such a course. It was impossible, he said, that an unprotected lady in the disturbed state of the country should travel alone between Oxford and Banbury. It was not likely that he would be held from the King more than another day, and then they would both set out together. Besides, she needed all the rest she could obtain before they turned north again. The girl was too deeply dejected even to argue the question, when he so strenuously opposed her desire. It seemed that a contrary fate was tightening the coils around her, and all struggle against it was fruitless. There were unshed tears in her eyes as she glanced timidly up at him, and she had the haunted look of one who was trapped. The unforeseen meeting with De Courcy, although Cromwell's words should have prepared her for it, had completely unnerved her; that nightmare face of his confronting her whenever she closed her eyes. The past had come up before her in its most abhorrent guise. She remembered striking him fiercely with the jagged iron she happened to hold in her hand, and thought anything was justified that enabled her to escape his clutches, but that he would carry so fearful a disfiguration to his grave chilled her with fear of his vengeance; for if ever murder shone from a man's eyes it glared in his when she caught his first glance the evening before. All during the night the terrifying vision drove sleep from her couch, and she pondered on some possible method of escape, but without result. How gladly she would have confided her peril to Armstrong, did she stand in honest relation to him, but she could not bring herself to ask help from a man whom she had just rejected and whom she would shortly rob. When Armstrong mentioned the absence of Rudby, she had utterly forgotten that the ostensible reason for this Oxford journey was to see him, and for a moment it appeared that here lay a loophole of escape, but Armstrong's outspoken opposition to her plan left her with no adequate excuse for persisting in it. All force of purpose had deserted her, and it seemed impossible that it could have been she who for the sake of a father she had seen but once had braved the rage-mad Queen of England and threatened the monarch himself in his own court in the height of his power. What subtle change had come over her imperious will? What alchemy had converted the strong wine of her resolve to vapid water? It was not personal fear. She had met De Courcy before, and even when he had her at his mercy, lured into his private room, her high courage never faltered. But now her whole impulse was to call for aid from another; to have that other protect her, and to obey his slightest wish. Here was a mutability indeed for the daughter of the strenuous Strafford! This feeling was something new, something strange, something unaccountable. And that other stood before her, anxious to heal her hurt, but diagnosing wrongly, powerless to apply the soothing balm. She wished him there, for his strong presence calmed her; yet she also wished him gone, that she might collect her scattered thoughts. Absent or present, he disturbed her, and she wondered if this could be love, which she had imagined brought peace and joyous content.

During this unsatisfactory coming together, little was said by either. The girl sat in a chair by a small table, and he stood on the other side. Most of the time her head rested on her hand, and he saw she was near to tears. He censured himself again for his ill-timed avowal of the day before, but saw no method by which he could annul its consequences save by saying nothing more.

On the third day of his stay in Oxford the suave De Courcy was compelled to bewail the continued indisposition of the King. There were various important matters awaiting his Majesty's attention, he said, but nothing could be done until his recovery. Meanwhile, to pass time that must be hanging heavily on the visitor's hands, the thoughtful Frenchman suggested that Armstrong should indulge in a stroll around the fortifications. Oxford was believed to be unassailable, but De Courcy would be pleased to hear any criticisms the new-comer cared to pass upon the defences. Armstrong expressed his concurrence with this proposal, and thought at first that the obliging foreigner was to be his guide; but shortly after they set out, De Courcy introduced him to an officer who was to be his cicerone, and excused himself because of the King's illness, which had placed on his shoulders many duties that had heretofore been absent from them. As soon as the two were out of sight, De Courcy hastened back to the inn, passed up the stair, and knocked at the door of the room occupied by Frances Wentworth. On receiving permission to enter, he went in and closed the door behind him. The girl, who had expected a different caller, rose from her chair and stood silent.

"Madam, this is a meeting which I have long looked forward to with pleasant anticipation."

"Sir, I regret that I have no share in your felicity."

"Perhaps you prefer that we should meet as enemies."

"I prefer that we should not meet at all, and, knowing this, you may be good enough to make your visit as short as possible."

"I cannot find words to express my sorrow, on learning I am so unwelcome. I am sure that when last we met, I did my best to make your visit as long as I could, so why should you wish to shorten mine?"

It seemed to the girl that there was something unnecessarily shameless in his allusion to a circumstance that had so disfigured him. As she made no reply, he went on with airy nonchalance: "Will you excuse me if I lock the door, and, showing that experience is a proficient schoolmaster, I ask the extension of your forgiveness to cover the act of putting the key in my pocket. We live and learn, you know. Not that I fear any interruption, for the innocent and excellent Scot is at this moment investigating our battlements under the care of a shrewd guide, and will not return this three hours or more." The polite intruder locked the door and put the key in his pocket; then advanced toward her. She retreated to the other room, and for a moment he thought she was about to barricade herself within, but she reappeared on the instant with a jewelled dagger in her hand.

"I warn you, sir, that if you approach within striking distance I will pierce you to the heart."

The Frenchman smiled and waved his fine white hands with a gesture of inimitable grace.

"Fairest of the Wentworths," he said, "the glances of those lustrous eyes have already pierced that sensitive organ. Alas, that it is my fate they should beam upon me in anger. Well, my Lady Wentworth, you see I do not approach you, but grant my bravery the justice to believe that it is not fear of the sting that prevents my sipping the honey. May I sit down, and if I place this table between us, will you feel safer?"

"You will be safer so long as it remains between us."

"I assure you my own safety weighs but lightly with me. I implore you to be seated, for I cannot converse at ease with a lady who is standing."

"I prefer to stand. Your ingrained courtesy will then cause you to make our conference brief."

"It distresses me to say that you are prolonging the conference by standing. We have grave particulars of state policy to discuss, and I cannot begin while you are so cruel as to put me in the light——"

"Oh, very well!" cried Frances, impatiently, taking her own chair; whereupon he, elegantly gracious, seated himself opposite her, with the table between them.

"How ideally charming you look! I swear there is none to compare with you, even in that land of loveliness to which I have the honour to belong. Will you believe me when I say that there has not been a day since I last saw you, that I have not thought of you. I was angry at first, as you may well imagine, but at last I saw that I had been to blame, although I think the punishment must have obliterated my crime."

He paused for a few moments, but, she making no reply, he continued:

"Grief for the loss of you filled my heart. You think I come here as an enemy, but I come as a suppliant. In the folly of that time at Whitehall I refused you marriage, and I do not wonder you were wroth at me. I wish to atone for what you justly considered an insult, and am willing to marry you in the face of the world."

"I thank you."

"I shall ask no questions anent this awkward Scot who has been your courier, for I am sure you can have thought nothing of him."

"I thank you."

"You return thanks coldly, but I know that is the English nature. The fire of France is not to be expected in this northern clime, but if you say yes to my pleading, I am satisfied."

"If I wished for fire I would go down and not abroad for it. I had sooner wed the fiend from the pit than you."

De Courcy laughed lightly.

"That were a sulphurous mating indeed! Still you see how I adore you when I restate my determination to occupy the devil's place at your side before the altar. You but whet my expectation, for I should dearly love to tame you as your Shakespeare tamed his shrew."

"That you shall never do while a hand's breadth of steel will rid me of you, or myself of the world. Escape is too easy."

"Not from an Oxford dungeon, my dear. This mediaeval town furnishes us with dark pits in which there is no fire, and consequently they have a cooling effect on the hottest temperament. These are pits of which I am the fiend. My dear, you underrate my power, or overrate my patience."

"There are English gentlemen in Oxford. On what plea could you induce them to think that an English lady should be placed in a dungeon?"

"Yes, there are English gentlemen here, and some French gentlemen as well. They are unanimous in their detestation of a spy, male or female. Your man we shall hang out of hand, and there will be little difficulty about the pleasing task. I shall myself plead that your life be spared, and they will agree. Everything will be done with that beautiful legality which the English so much admire, but even from this moment you are entirely in my power, and a sensible woman should not need so much argument to convince her that the situation is hopeless."

"Armstrong is no spy."

"He may have difficulty in proving he is not. I am glad to note that you admit by inference that you are a spy."

"I can prove he is not a spy."

"Your evidence would be tainted. You are an accomplice. Besides, you could not clear him without condemning yourself."

"Such will I gladly do. I glory in that I would sacrifice myself with joy to save William Armstrong, the awkward Scot, as you called him. What would you give to hear me say this of you?"

"Much, my dear, much. Oh, I delight in you! You know how to sting without using your poniard. But I am not of a jealous nature, and love conquest for its own sake. I have told you I care nothing for the Scot, and you might easily have had him journey for the North again if you had not been so impetuous. Now I shall hang him, merely as the first step in breaking the stubborn pride which adds such zest to your overcoming."

"One word from me to Armstrong will transfer the danger to you. He will break you like a reed."

"Indeed, my dear, you do yourself injustice in threatening me. You shall have no opportunity of speaking your one word, for when next we meet, if we part now without coming to amicable arrangement, you will be on your knees to me pleading for his life."

"That will I not. I shall go to the King."

"Frances, you dishearten me, and cast grave doubts on the possession of that sound sense with which I credited you. Was your first appeal to the King for a man's life so successful that you build hopes on a second?"

"If Charles had kept his word with me then, he would not now be encaged in Oxford. He abandoned my father and clung to such as you, and not a foot of English ground remains to him but what he stands on."

"What would have happened had Strafford lived, neither you nor I can tell, and all discussion thereon is aside from our present purpose. Will you make terms with me?"

"I will not."

"You prefer the dungeon?"

"You dare not imprison me."

"Why?"

"Your master will not allow you."

The Frenchman leaned upon the table, a patient beneficent expression on his scarred features, and spoke to her gently, as one who must deal with a petulant, unreasonable child.

"My dear, let me put a quietus for ever upon your mad idea that any help is to be expected from the King. I beg you to believe that I speak the exact truth. Do you know what the King thinks of you?"

"He does not think of me at all. He has forgotten me."

"Pardon me. There you are mistaken. He thinks you came to Whitehall the day of your father's death to assassinate him. He believes that I imperilled my life to save his. The scars of your claws, however repulsive they may be to others, are to him a constant reminder of his supposed debt to me. Judge you then, my dear, what your position in Oxford would be did the King but dream you had crept surreptitiously into his stronghold. Need I say more?"

"No. But you should have paid better heed to what I said."

"What did you say?"

"I said your master would not permit you to injure me."

"But I have shown you that the King——"

"I am not speaking of the King. Your master is Oliver Cromwell."

Either the cross on his face became redder, or the sudden pallor of his other features made it appear so. Slowly he withdrew his elbows from the table and leaned back in his chair, moistening his lips, gazing on the girl with the intensity of a new-born fear. She sat motionless, returning his look without flinching.

For some moments the room was as silent as if it were deserted. At last he spoke huskily:

"What do you expect to gain by making so absurd a statement?"

The girl rose with a gesture of impatience, walked to the window and back; then to the window again, and unfastened a latch that let free a latticed sash, as if the room stifled her and she wanted air. Then she exclaimed: "Oh, let us have a truce to this fooling; I am tired of it. You say I shall beg on my knees to you, but you have mistaken your own attitude for mine. Why do I make such a statement? Because Cromwell told me in Northampton that if I met difficulty in Oxford, you, his spy, would assist me."

"Good God!"

"Aye! Good God! You did not think such a man would blab out secrets of death to a woman, but there is this to say on his behalf, that he was merely recommending one spy to another. He thought mutual safety would be their bond of union, and he was right."

"Then you knew you would meet me in Oxford? Why did you seem so distraught when the event happened? That was acting, I suppose, to fall the easier into the arms of the Scot."

"I had no need to act to bring that about. I hoped to avoid you, and would have done so but for the chance encounter. And now you see, sir, that my peril is as nothing to yours. My countrymen will not injure me; I know them better than you do, but even if it were otherwise, I have but to bend my strength to the pillars and crush you and myself in the ruins of the falling house,—an enactment, I assure you, that fits my nature better than the part of Delilah into which I am cast."

"They would not believe one self-convicted."

"Would not believe me? I dare you to put it to the test. Believe me?" She stood by the window and held up her hand. "I have but to strike open this leaded pane and cry to the officers passing in the street, 'I am the daughter of Lord Strafford, help me, for here I am caged with a French spy, a creature who has sold King and comrades for Cromwell's gold.'"

"In God's name, woman, do not speak so loud. There is no need for frenzy. I did but jest when I spoke of molesting you."

"I am in no jesting mood."

"You do not need to tell me that. I am quite willing to further your behests, if you but trust me and tell me what you want."

"Can you expect me to trust you?" asked the girl, coming back to the table.

He was now standing on the other side, all self-confidence gone from his attitude, speaking almost in a whisper, so anxious was he that she should have no excuse for raising her voice again.

"I suppose I have not earned your trust."

"Oh, but you have. I trust you implicitly because you stand under the shadow of the scaffold, and at a word from me the bolt is drawn. You will postpone all thought of revenge until your neck is out of the noose; of that I am very well convinced. I refuse to make terms with you, but I give my commands which you must rigidly follow unless you court calamity. You will take Armstrong to the King, and cease to block his way. You will see that we are free to leave Oxford, and are unmolested while we are within these walls. One false move and you bring your doom upon you. While we are in Oxford the rope is round your throat, so pray to the demon who aids you that we may make speedy and easy exit. Shudder to think that your fate hangs on the action of a woman, wholly unstrung, and that even a suspicious look from any officer in this garrison may instantly precipitate the disaster you apprehend."

"I implore you to be calm, madam. I swear I will carry out your orders to the letter. Do not, I beg of you, take panic at any chance word by another."

"Unlock the door and leave me. See that you do not come again."

CHAPTER VIII.—DESTINY.

On the morning of the fourth day Armstrong was delighted to learn from De Courcy that the King had recovered and would see him at noon. The foreigner engaged the envoy in a long conversation, the object of which was to discover whether or not the girl had said anything to him of the excited conference of the day before. The unsuspecting Scot, entirely off his guard, thinking he spoke with a friend, was read by the other like an open book, and De Courcy was speedily convinced that Frances Wentworth had kept her own counsel. This gave the spy renewed confidence, and as they walked down the street together De Courcy held his head higher than had been the case when he last turned his back upon "The Crown" inn. His buoyant nature was quick to recover from depression, and his malice, fed anew from his late rebuff, set his alert mind at work to contrive some plan whereby he might salve his wounded pride and avenge himself on the girl and his favoured rival, even at some slight risk to himself. Although the danger of exposure seemed imminent enough when he was with her, he knew that as she grew calmer and reflected upon the situation she would be more and more reluctant to wreck everything in order to bring punishment upon him. He would get them out of Oxford that day if possible, but he would instill a poison in the young lover's mind that would take all sweetness from the journey.

De Courcy had offered to show Armstrong the way to the King's rooms, so that there should be no delay when the Scot set out for his appointment at twelve o'clock, and they had now entered the quadrangle of Christ Church, which was deserted save for the guards at the gate. Armstrong thanked him for his guidance, and was turning away, when the other, who seemed about to speak, glanced at the soldiers on duty, then, thinking the spot ill chosen for what he had to say, invited the Scot to his room. They went up a stair together, and entered De Courcy's apartment, the host setting out wine and asking his guest to seat himself.

"Has the lady who accompanied you quite recovered from her fatigue?" asked De Courcy, indifferently.

"Well, as I told you, I met her yesterday for a few moments only, and I am sorry she was not in the highest spirits, but she will be the better for seeing the green fields again. Like myself, she is of the country, and does not thrive within the walls of a town."

"Yes, I noticed that when she was in London."

"In London? Did you know her in London?"

"Oh, hasn't she told you of our relationship? Perhaps I should not have mentioned it."

"What do you mean by your relationship? You are French; she is pure English."

De Courcy threw back his head and laughed, unheeding and indeed unnoticing the angry colour mounting in a face that had grown suddenly stern.

"My dear comrade, there are other relationships between a young man and a handsome woman than the ties of kinship. But those days are long past, and I should never have recalled them had it not been that you two have been travelling about the country together, I make no doubt, with an innocence that recalls the sylvan days of yore."

Armstrong pushed back his chair and rose to his feet.

"Sir, the lady took her brother's place, he being unexpectedly and grievously wounded. My position has been that of true comrade to her."

"That is precisely what I have said. I said your journey was one of Arcadian innocence."

214

"Those were your words, but your tone bears a meaning I resent."

"You are quite in error. I will say no more about her."

"You have already said too much or too little. Tell me in plain words what this relationship was to which you have referred."

"First answer me a question. Are you betrothed to Frances Wentworth?"

"No. I told you I acted the brother's part toward her in this journey."

"Oh, we all say that; but I am not in the least curious. If you intended to marry her, then were my mouth sealed. Very well; since you will have it, and I take your word as a gentleman pledged that you will say nothing to the girl of this until you are clear of Oxford, know that I was once her betrothed. She was to have been my wife, and would have been my wife to-day had her father not fallen."

"Your wife!"

"Yes. Her father gave me permission to pay my court to her. She could not have been much more than sixteen then, and I was her first lover, a personage that a girl never forgets. At first she was frightened, but that stage did not last long. Her father's ruin changed my plans, and I refused to marry her. I announced this refusal to her in the seclusion of my own room in Whitehall and——"

"Sir, you lie!"

Armstrong's sword seemed to spring of its own will from the scabbard, and his hand drew it a-swish through the air with the hiss of a deadly serpent. The Frenchman shrugged his shoulders, but did not move. The three words of his opponent had been spoken very quietly, despite his impulsive action. De Courcy did not raise his voice as he asked: "Which of my statements do you question?"

"No matter for that. We fight on this phrase in Scotland. No man ever called me liar and lived."

"'T is a coarse phrase, I admit, and did I not represent my King—were

I as free as you—you should have had my response in steel ere this. But I cannot wreck the King in a private quarrel of my own. Whether you killed me, or I you, 't would be equally disastrous to his Majesty."

"I care nothing for the King. Draw, you poltroon, or I shall kill you where you sit."

"My dear Armstrong, I refuse to be murdered under a misapprehension on your part. I have said nothing against the girl. 'T is all your own hot blood. And indeed your brawling is the girl's greatest danger; she might well tremble if she knew your present occupation. If you run your nimble sword through me, you give the girl to the fate that befel her father."

At the first word of danger to Frances the point of Armstrongs blade sank to the floor, and he stood hesitating. A gleam of triumph glinted and died in the eye of the Frenchman. He knew he was the victor, although the chance he had run at one stage of the game almost made his heart stop beating.

"How can any action of mine jeopardize Lady Frances Wentworth?"

"If the King knew this girl was within his jurisdiction, she would be instantly arrested, tried, and condemned. She entered Whitehall the day her father was executed, for the sole purpose of murdering Charles. I prevented the carrying out of that purpose, and these scars on my face are the results of my interference with a maddened woman."

"Again, you lie, yet if she had killed you both she would have accomplished but the justice of God."

"As to the truth or falsity of my statements, regarding which you make comments of unseemly terseness, you may ask the King when you see him, or you may ask the lady herself when you get her out of Oxford. If you precipitate a turmoil here, you are like to tumble her pretty head in the basket. When this war is done with, I will go far to teach you the correct method of addressing a gentleman."

Armstrong's sword dropped into scabbard again, and he drew a breath that was a sigh. The poison was already at work. He remembered the distress of the girl on the road, and her wail, "I am not worthy the love of any honest man."

"I shall never question her or any other, but will believe her lightest word against the world when she condescends to tell me. Meanwhile I shall get her out of this thieves' den as soon as may be, and by God when I meet you——"

De Courcy had risen, and now bowed slightly to his perturbed guest.

"Sir, you shall meet me at twelve, and it will be my privilege to conduct you to his Majesty. Good morning."

He stood by the window overlooking the quadrangle and watched his late visitor cross it, staggering once as if he had partaken freely of the wine which remained untasted on the table. As the Scot disappeared under the archway De Courcy laughed.

"My fine, strutting cockerel," he muttered, "I'll lay you by the heels before two days are past. Cromwell's at Broughton, curse his tattling tongue. How many more has he told of me? Never mind. He's the coming man. The King's game is up, and I shake the dust of Oxford from my feet to-night. Saint Denis, if she had only known! Every man in Oxford distrusts me except the King."

When Armstrong was brought before Charles, a great pity filled him as he gazed for the first time on that gaunt, haggard face, the face of a beaten man with his back to the wall. He found no difficulty in convincing the King that he was a well-accredited envoy, and his Majesty inquired eagerly about the disposition of the Scottish people toward him, the number likely to take the field in his behalf, who their probable leaders were, and how soon they would be ready for the fray. All these questions Armstrong answered as hopefully as he could, in deep commiseration for a defeated man. The King commanded one of his secretaries to write out the required commission, and while this was being done Armstrong related to him the purport of the papers which he had not dared to bring with him. The names of the nobles were inserted in the document from the dictation of the Scot; then the King's seal was affixed, and Charles signed the parchment. He seemed in feverish haste to get the business done with, as if every moment lost was irreparable. When the ink was dried, and the parchment folded, Armstrong placed it in safe keeping within his vest. While thus engaged the King said a word to the secretary, who handed him a light rapier, then whispered to the messenger the single word "Kneel." The Scot flushed to think he had been wanting in the etiquette of the court, his kind heart yearning to proffer any deference which should be rendered to a monarch, more especially that he was no longer in a position to enforce homage. He dropped on one knee and bowed his head. Charles, rising, touched the rapier blade lightly upon the shoulder of the kneeling man, saying: "Rise, Sir William Armstrong, and be assured that if you bring this poor signature of mine to Scotland, there is no title in my gift you may not demand of me."

Armstrong rose, awkward as a school boy, not knowing where to look or what to say until he caught the cynical smile of De Courcy standing at the right hand of the King.

"I congratulate you, Sir William," said the Frenchman. The sight of the smile aroused the new hatred against the man which was smoldering in his heart, and he made no reply to the greeting, but said to the King: "Sire, the only thanks I can tender you is haste to the North, and may God make my arm as strong to defend this signature as my heart is true to your Majesty."

With that he turned his back upon royalty, a grievous breach in the eyes of courtiers, and fled.

"God grant it," said the King, with a sigh, as he sank once more in the seat from whence he had risen.

"There is no doubt of it," said De Courcy, softly.

"Doubt of what?" asked the King.

"The oath he took will sit lightly on his conscience. He prayed that his arm's strength might equal his heart's fealty. I distrust those who talk glibly of their hearts, and his was a most ambiguous prayer. If his heart be not true, and he made no assertion that it was, his strong arm will avail us little."

218

"Surely if ever honesty beamed from a man's face it was from Armstrong's. The Scots are trustworthy men."

"Some of them, your Majesty."

Uneasy suspicion came into the sunken eyes of the King as he turned them on his Chamberlain.

"What do you fear, De Courcy?"

"I have been studying the man these three days past. I accepted without question his assurances, and threw him off his guard. Cromwell loves an honest-looking envoy, and from what Armstrong said I am sure he saw Cromwell no farther away than Northampton. He was very ready with his account of his own country people, but he told us nothing about the marvellous luck that brought him safely through a hostile land, which we know to our cost is admirably patrolled. There is young Rudby, gone this month and more to Edinburgh, and yet no word of him. And this stranger expects us to believe he came over the same ground unscathed and unquestioned in less than a week."

"O God! O God! In whom can I place dependence," cried the tortured King, burying his head in his hands. Then he raised it and said with a trace of anger in his voice: "If you knew this man to be a traitor, or an emissary of that rebel, why did you bring him into our presence?"

"I could not be sure of him, your Majesty, and there was always a chance that he was loyal and might get through."

"To raise my hopes like this and then dash them to the ground!"

"Not so, your Majesty, if you will pardon me. Do you place importance on this commission?"

"The utmost importance. I know Traquair, and he will raise all Scotland for me if this commission reach him."

"Then we will mak siccar, as a famous Scot once said."

"Ah, De Courcy, that was said when a treacherous murder was intended. How will you make sure that Armstrong is honest?"

"I should trouble no more about Armstrong, but if you will issue a duplicate of that commission I will guarantee that it reaches the hand of Traquair. I am a Frenchman, and a subject of the French king. I carry my passport to that effect. Even if I am stopped, I shall resist search on the ground of my nationality, and Cromwell is too greatly in awe of the power of France to risk its might being thrown in the scale against him. Indeed I doubt if I could offer a greater service to your Majesty than to be captured and appeal to Louis."

The King's face cleared.

"You would not stop Armstrong then?"

"Assuredly not. If his copy gets into Cromwell's hands he may slacken his alertness and not be on the outlook for a duplicate. As I said before, there is a chance the Scot plays fair, but two commissions in the hands of Traquair will do no harm, and we mak siccar."

"You are in the right, and your advice is always of the best. How soon will you be ready to leave?"

"This very moment, your Majesty. There is no time to be lost."

"True! True! True!" Then to the secretary, "Write another. Do you remember the names?"

"Yes, your Majesty. I have them here on a slip."

De Courcy bade farewell to the King, who urged him to return as soon as horse could bring him, and went to his room to prepare for his journey, the duplicate commission following him there.

Armstrong strode to the inn, sped up the stair, and knocked at the door by the landing. Frances herself opened it, the determination on her face to refuse admission to any other than he melting into a welcome as she greeted him.

"My girl, are you ready for the North?"

"Yes, yes, ready and eager. Have you seen the King?"

"I have, and his royal signature rests over my heart."

The joy fled from the girl's face; she turned and walked with uncertain steps to the table. A hope had arisen that the venomous De Courcy would have prejudiced the King against the young man, and that the hateful task of robbery would not be required. But now this last refuge had failed. She strove not to weep.

"If you would rather not go until to-morrow," said Armstrong, "I can wait, but, lassie, I'm desperate anxious to leave Oxford as soon as possible. We will not travel farther than Banbury to-night."

"I am ready," she replied with forced firmness.

BOOK IV.—THE RETURN

CHAPTER I.—TENSION.

The road between Oxford and Banbury is the most peaceful of thoroughfares, laid with reasonable directness, gently undulating in parts, passing through quiet villages and a sweet country, mildly beautiful, yet to the mind of Frances Wentworth this innocent highway ever remained, as it were, a section of the broad path to perdition. In after life she never thought of it but with a creepy sensation of horror. She was compelled to traverse ground that was the scene of her lover's proposal, with the lover whom she had rejected. The futile incident, she thought, must be constantly recurring to his mind as it recurred to hers, now that they rode side by side once more along this ill-favoured highway. Even though he sat silent on his horse, more gloomy than was his wont, she guessed what he was thinking. In Oxford, God be thanked they were quit of it! a grave danger was left behind, but in Banbury awaited the cruel test. There the stage was prepared for her enactment of the part of a midnight Lady Macbeth, to rob the sleeping Scot, not of his life, but of that for which he had staked his life and for the preservation of which he stood willing to give up his life. Heretofore she had lulled an accusing conscience by telling it that her deed would preserve his life, but now that she knew him better, such solace was withdrawn from her. There was little likelihood that he would travel far beyond Banbury without discovering his loss, and, while he would never suspect her of the theft, it needed no seer to predict his course of action. He would return instantly to Oxford, and when next he was baffled it would be by Cromwell's troopers, and then, she had the General's own word for it, came condemnation and the noose.

Despondency seemed to be the portion of William Armstrong as well as of his fair companion. She surmised that he was pondering on the events which had happened when their faces were set south over this course, and in part she was right; but the thoughts which rankled in his mind were those implanted by De Courcy, and the wily Frenchman had been accurate enough in his belief that the young man's pleasure in the northward journey would be spoiled. He could not bring himself to ask any explanation from the girl, nor even tell her what De Courcy had said, for he saw that already a weight of woe oppressed her, and to that burden he would not add a pressure of the slightest word. He possessed a supreme confidence in her, and only feared that she had loved this runagate once, and that some remnant of this long-ago affection still remained. Her own words before they reached Oxford, her own action during the encounter fronting "The Crown" inn, disturbed him far more than the insinuations of the Frenchman. He strove to rid himself of these thoughts, but they were very intrusive and persistent. At last with an effort he roused himself and cried with feigned hilarity,—"Frances, we travel like two mutes. The influence of saddened Oxford is still upon us both. We are long out of sight of the town, so let us be done with all remembrance of it. The meeting with the King this morning has stirred me up to a great pity for him, but vexed meditations on his case are no help either to him or to us. The spur is the only weapon I can wield for him now, so let us gallop and cry, 'God save the King!'"

With that they raced together for a time and were the better of it. He had become almost cheerful again when the spires of Banbury came into view, and thanked fortune that the first stage of their march was safely over.

They found Old John and his pack horse both ready for the road again, and Armstrong was plainly loath to let such a fine evening slip by without further progress, but Frances seemed so wan and worn that he had not the heart to propose a more distant stopping-place, and, with a sigh, he put up his horse for the night.

While he was gone the innkeeper came furtively to Frances, and, after seeing the pass, led her to the prepared room and showed her the door.

Much against her will, Armstrong insisted upon her coming to supper with him, although she protested she had no appetite, and indeed sat opposite him most forlorn and could not touch a morsel. In vain he urged her to eat, but she shook her head, avoiding his glance and keeping her eyes downcast.

"My girl," he said anxiously, "you are completely tired. I see that you are on the point of being ill if better care is not taken. Rest here a few days, I beg of you. Eager as I am to be forward, I will stay if you wish to have me near you. Or I will push on and come back for you."

"I shall be well enough in the morning, most like. I am tired to-night."

"And dispirited too."

"Yes, and dispirited. You will excuse me, I know."

"Frances rose to her feet, but seemed so faint that she leaned against the table for support. He was by her side at once.

"My sweet lass, I am so sorry for you. Tell me what I can do for you, and on my soul, my life is yours if you require it."

"No, no! God grant you take no hurt for my sake."

He slipped his arm about her waist and would have drawn her toward him, but with more strength than he had expected her to possess she held away. His great love for her almost overcame him, and all the prudence he had gathered was scattered suddenly to the winds. "Dear, dear lass, one touch of our lips and see if all doubts do not dissolve before the contact."

Now she wrenched herself free, and would have escaped but that he sprang forward and caught her by the wrists, a grip she was to remember later in the night. In spite of this prisoning, her hands were raised to the sides of her face, and a look of such terror shot from her eyes that he feared some madness had come upon her.

"Not that! Not that!" she shrieked. "The kiss of Judas! It would kill me!"

His arms dropped paralyzed to his sides, and he stepped back a pace, amazed at the expression she had used and the terror of her utterance. Next instant he was alone, and the closed door between them. Still he stood where she had left him.

"The kiss of Judas!" he muttered. "The kiss of Judas! She loves him, thinks me his friend, trying to take Judas advantage of him because we are alone together. De Courcy spoke truth. Wae is me, she loves him, and I, blind fool——Oh God! pity that poor girl, and this insanity of passion wasted on so rank a cur!"

Frances fled to her room and threw herself on the bed in an agony of tears. This storm subsided into a gentle rain of subdued weeping, and finally ceased as she heard the heavy tramp of riding-boots in the adjoining room. She sat up in the darkness, listening intently. He closed the wooden shutters of the window, shaking them to be sure that their fastenings were secure. Then the bolts of the outer door were thrust in their places, but, this apparently failing to satisfy the doubts of the inmate, there was a sound of some heavy article of furniture being dragged across the room; then the tramping ceased and all was still. She sat there thinking of nothing; her mind seemed to be dulled by the ordeal awaiting her and the fear of it, but there was no thought of turning back or trying to avoid it. Dimly she was sorry for herself and for him, sleeping in his fancied security, yet in a set trap; but on her action this night depended her brother's life, and that outweighed all other considerations, even if her brain were alert enough to cast them in the opposite scales. Unheeding she had heard the clock in a neighbouring tower toll the hour; now it struck again and she counted the notes. Eleven! It was still too early. People slept heavier as the night wore on. She thought of their journey; of the halt at York; of their talk in the niche in the hotel of the Templars; of various incidents along the road; the march past of Cromwell's troopers, four and four, all looking straight ahead, and as she remembered them they seemed to be passing her now; passing, passing, passing; then Cromwell stopped and smote his steel breastplate with resounding clang. She lifted her head with a start, and the clang of the breastplate changed to the toll of the bell in the tower. Heavens, she had been asleep; her brother's life hanging on her drooping eyelids! One, two, three four, five, six, seven! It must be midnight, and the first five strokes had been on Cromwell's breastplate. She roused herself and attempted to take off her shoes, but her hands were trembling so she was forced to desist. She sat up again, telling herself it was better to wait until all effect of the long chiming had ceased, for the striking of twelve sometimes disturbed or awakened the soundest sleeper. The clock tower seemed dangerously near, as if it were approaching her hour by hour. At last the shoes came off, and in stockinged feet she stood by the secret door, waiting till the frightfully rapid beating of her heart should moderate. It threatened to choke her. Then she slid back the bar and drew open the door, all so smoothly oiled that there was not the whisper of a creak. She tiptoed into the cavern of blackness and silence, holding her spread hands in front of her, moving slowly with the utmost caution, step by step. In her mind she had estimated, from her earlier survey of the room, that nine steps would take her to the bed; now she realized she had taken a dozen and yet had not come to it. She stood bewildered and listened. The helplessness of a person in the pitch dark thrilled her with a new fear, upsetting all her calculations. The panic of pulsation in her throat and in her ears at first rendered any attempt at listening futile; but at last she heard his regular breathing, as peaceful as that of an infant, and it came from the other side of the room. For a moment this terrified her, and she wondered if she were really awake, or in the mazes of some baffling nightmare; but the solution came to her mind and quieted the growing agitation. It had been his bed that he dragged across the floor, and he was now sleeping against the outside door. And all his preparations were as naught, because of this midnight spectre, moving upon him! She changed her direction and, with her former stealth, came ghost-like to the edge of the couch.

His doublet was open at the throat; that was so much to the good. Like a snowflake in its coldness and its lightness, her hand stole down underneath his vest, fluttered by the slow, steady, subdued beating of his heart, running no such wild race as her own at that moment. It seemed incredible that at last her fingers closed on the parchment; but there it lay, and gently she drew it forth. Was the robbery to be so easily accomplished after all? Ah, she had congratulated herself too soon. It stuck fast; either the silken cord that bound it was caught, or the document was secured to the vest,—a contingency she had never thought of, and yet what more natural? Twice she tugged it gently, then a third time more strenuously, when it came unexpectedly away and her knuckles struck the sleeper under the chin. Instantly, like the snap of a steel trap, his fingers closed upon her wrist, and his voice rang out as wideawake and clear as ever he had spoken to her: "Frances!"

226

Now the racing heart stopped dead. Lucky for her that at this supreme moment all action was impossible, and that she was stricken into frozen marble. She imagined he was awake and knew her, and then the cold horror of her situation numbed thought at its source.

"Frances!" The voice came more sleepily this time, and he repeated thrice very rapidly, "Frances, Frances, Frances!" Feebly her heart had taken up its work again. She was not to die as she had feared. Sodden with drowsiness, his voice rambled on, and came to an indefinite conclusion.

"My darling, you are in danger. We must get out of Oxford. Everything, every——your safety, my dear. The King——" Then the words became indistinct and died away; but alas! the grip of iron remained on her wrist. For a long time she stood there motionless; then tried to disengage his fingers gently; but at the first movement the grasp tightened again. One o'clock struck. He slept so silently that it began to appear to her agitated brain that she was a prisoner of the dead. She came near to sinking from very weariness. Two o'clock tolled from the tower. Sometimes she fancied she slept standing there, but her five jailors did not sleep. She kept wondering in which direction lay the open door, for at times the room seemed to swim around her, thus disturbing all sense of locality. She almost laughed aloud when she thought of herself free, but groping helplessly for the open door, failing to find it, and she shuddered that even the remembrance of laughter should come to her at such a time; surely a sign of approaching frenzy. Then it seemed the fingers loosened; but hand and wrist had lost all feeling, and she could not be sure. She tottered and nearly fell; when she stood upright again she was free; he muttering to himself, and his hand slashing undirected on the mattress, as if it missed something it sought drunkenly to recover. The girl could scarce repress a cry of joy at her release. She moved eagerly in the path that should lead her to the door, but, hurrying too much, came upon his jack-boots on the floor, and fell helplessly, so overwrought that even when her feet touched them she could not draw back.

"Who's there? Who's in this room?" cried Armstrong. She was standing again, fully expecting to hear his feet on the floor; but the bell struck three, and he counted dreamily, and all was still again. When she reached her room, she closed and barred the door as silently as she had opened it. The tension relaxed, she felt she was going to swoon. Blindly she groped for her shoes, murmuring, "O God! not yet,—not yet. Give me a moment more." Finding her foot-gear at last, she dared not wait to put them on, but stole softly down the stair, steadying herself against the wall. The cool air outside struck her like the blessing of God, and soothed her whirling head. She heard a horse champing his bit, then a whisper came out of the darkness: "Is that you at last, madam?"

"Yes," she said, sinking on the doorstep, and leaning her head against the lintel, the cold stone grateful to her hot forehead.

"You are not hurt, madam?" inquired the man anxiously.

"No, no," she gasped; then, with an eldritch little laugh, "I want to put on my shoes, that's all."

CHAPTER II.—ACQUITTANCE.

Either the moon had set, or lay behind a cloud; for the night was very dark, with no trace of morning yet visible in the east. Frances buckled on her shoes and stood up. The innkeeper led forward his horse, and would doubtless have proffered his assistance, but when she spoke he learned she was already in the saddle.

"Set me on the road to Broughton, if you please?"

"The word for to-night is 'Broughton,'" he whispered, then took the horse by the bridle and led him down the street. The girl became aware that the town was alive with unseen men; for at every corner the innkeeper breathed the word "Broughton" to some one who had challenged his progress. She realized then that Cromwell had surrounded Armstrong with a ring of flesh; a living clasp, as her own wrist had been circled earlier in the night. At last they came suddenly from the shadow of the houses into the open country, and the night seemed lighter.

"Straight on for about a league," said the innkeeper. "You will be challenged by a sentinel before you reach the castle, and he will lead you there. Remember that the word, going and returning, is 'Broughton.' Do not forget, I beg of you, to tell the General that all preparations were made to your liking;" and with that the honest man let go the rein, smote the horse on the flank, and bade her goodnight.

In spite of herself the girl experienced that exhilaration which comes of the morning air, the freshness of the country, and the movement of a spirited horse. She breathed deeply and felt as one brought newly to life again. If it were not for her upbraiding conscience and her distress of mind, she could have sung for the joy of living. But the Biblical phrase, "A thief in the night," haunted her, and brought a choking sensation to her throat. Once or twice she wavered and almost turned back; for there was still time to undo; but reflection showed her the uselessness of retreat, as the town she had left was man-environed, and, until Cromwell gave the word of release, Armstrong could no more reach its outer boundary than she could have escaped when his fingers closed upon her wrist. Her sacrifice must be complete, or all she loved were involved in common ruin. So, with the phrase ringing in her ears, "Thief in the night, Thief in the night," through the night she galloped, until her horse suddenly placed his fore feet rigid, and came to a stop so abrupt that the shock nearly unseated her.

"Who goes?" came the sharp challenge from under the trees that overshadowed the highway.

"Broughton," she answered automatically.

"Are you the woman from Banbury?"

"Yes."

"This is Broughton Castle. I will lead your horse."

They descended a slight depression and came to a drawbridge, passed under an arch in the wall, then across a level lawn, on the further edge of which stood the broad eastern front of the castle with its numerous mullioned windows, a mysterious half-light in the horizon playing on the blank panes, which recalled the staring, open eyes of a blind man. The house seemed high and sombre, with no sign of light within. The sentinel beat against the door, and it was opened at once. Muffled as had been the knocking on the oak, it awoke the alert General; for when Frances had dismounted and followed her guide into the ample hall, Cromwell stood at the head of the stair, a candle in his hand. Less mindful of his comfort than Armstrong, he had evidently slept in his boots; and, as Frances looked up at him, his strong face seemed older than when she last saw him, although but a few days had passed. The swaying flame of the candle, held on a level with his head, made the shadows come and go on his rugged features, and emphasized the deep furrows in his face. His hair was tousled, and he had the unkempt appearance of a man who had slept in his clothes. But his eyes burned down upon her, as if their fire had never been extinguished even for a moment.

"Come up," he commanded, and, as she ascended the stair, cried impatiently, "Well!"

"There is the King's commission," she said quietly, presenting the document to him. He took it without a word, turned, and entered the room; she following him. He placed the candle on a table, did not take the time to untie the silken cord that bound the royal communication, but ripped it asunder, and spread open the crinkling parchment, holding it up to the light. He read it through to the end, then cast it contemptuously on the table, muttering:

"Charles Rex! A wreck you have made of life and opportunity and country." Then to the girl. "Wench, you have done well. Would you were a man."

"The pardon for my brother, sir, if it please you."

"It is ready, and the commission as captain also. You see I trusted you."

"So did another, and through his faith he now lies undone in Banbury."

"You have not killed him?" cried Cromwell sharply, looking with something almost like alarm at the uncanny apparition. All beauty had deserted her, and her face seemed pinched and small, white as the parchment on the table, and rendered unearthly in its hue by the mass of cavern-black hair that surrounded it.

"Killed him? No! But I have killed his faith in woman, cozened him, lied to him, robbed him, to buy from you, with the name of your Maker on your lips, a life that you know was not forfeited, but which you had the power to destroy."

"Ah, yes, yes, yes! I remember your tongue of old; but it may wag harmless now, for all of me. His life was forfeited; aye, and this Scot's as well. But no matter now."

He threw before her the pardon for her brother and his commission as captain, then strode out of the room to the head of the stair again, and she heard his strenuous voice:

"Hobson!"

"Here, Excellency."

"Ride at once to the commandant at Banbury. Tell him the Scot goes free. Tell him to send word north, and see that he is not molested; but should he turn in his tracks and attempt to reach Oxford again, hold him and send word to me."

"Yes, Excellency."

"Send up a stoup of wine."

He waited at the stair-head until the wine was brought, then took it into the room and placed it on the table before her.

"Drink," he said.

"I cannot," she cried.

"Drink, drink," he shouted in a voice so harsh that it made her tremble. She lifted the flagon to her lips, and barely sipped the liquid.

"Drink!" he roared, bringing his clenched fist down on the oaken table with a force that made the very room quiver. The word had all the brutal coarseness of an oath, and it beat down her weak resolution as the storm levels the sapling. She drank deep, then let the flagon drop, raised her hands to her face, and burst into a helpless wail of weeping. Cromwell's face softened, now

231

that he was obeyed, and he looked at this passion-swayed human flower with the air of a puzzled man. Then his huge hand patted her heaving shoulders with some attempt at gentleness.

"There, there," he said, in tones not unkindly, "do not distress yourself. You are a brave wench, and the wine will do you good, though you take it as it were a leech's draught. I meant no harshness toward you; indeed you remind me of my own daughter, who thinks her father criminal, and will shout for this foolish King in my very ears. Aye, and is as ready with the tears as any one of you, to the bewilderment of straight-going folk. I have a younger daughter who is your namesake, and I love her well. You will rest here in Broughton."

"No, no!" sobbed the girl. "I must at once to Banbury. Give me, I beg of you, a pass for my servant to the county of Durham. I would send him on to my brother without delay, so that your release may reach him as soon as may be."

"But you? You do not purpose travelling further with this Scot?"

"I have done the crime; I must not shirk the punishment."

"Tut, tut, this is woman's talk. There is no punishment. He dare not place a hand on you. You may have an escort of twenty men, who will see you safe for all the Scots that ever depredated their neighbours."

The girl dolefully shook her head.

"My punishment will take the shape of no harshness from him. It will come to me when I see his face, knowing me a thief in the night. This punishment is with me now and will be with me always."

"Woman, I do not like your bearing, touching what you have done. You did your duty by your country, God aiding you. Neither do I like your attitude towards this meddler in affairs of state. What is your relationship to him?"

"Merely that of the highwayman toward his victim."

"Sharp words again; hollow-sounding brass, and the tinkling of cymbals.

I ask you if there has been any foolish talk between you?"

"If 't were so, 't is not an affair of state, and I shall follow the example of General Cromwell and allow no meddlers in it."

A wry smile came to the lips of her questioner, and he remarked drily:

"I told you the wine would do you good."

He sat down by the table and wrote the pass for John, the servant, tying the three papers together with the discarded silk cord that had wrapped the parchment of the King. Giving her the package, he accompanied her to the head of the stair, and stood there while she descended. He did not offer her his hand, nor say any word of farewell. They needed now no candle, for the early daylight was coming through the broad eastern window. Half way down the stair she turned, and looked up at him.

"The innkeeper at Banbury did everything that was possible for a man to do in aiding me."

Cromwell made no comment on this piece of information, standing there as if he were a carven, wooden statue, part of the decoration of the hall. She completed her descent, passed outside without looking back, and mounted the horse which a soldier was holding for her. The birds were twittering in the trees, and the still water of the moat lay like molten silver in the new light. She rode up the aclivity, then galloped for Banbury, reaching the town before anyone was astir. The streets were entirely deserted, Cromwell's command having cleared them, and the invisible guards of a few hours before, whom the magic pass-word stilled, seemed as nonexistent as if they had been phantoms of a vision.

The sleepy innkeeper received the horse, and she crept up the stair of Old John's room and knocked upon it until he responded. She gave him his pass, and the two documents for her brother, and told him to set off for Durham as soon as he got his breakfast, making what haste he could to Warburton Park, he was to tell her brother that she was well and would follow shortly. Then she went to her own room, threw herself on the bed, dressed as she was, and, certain she would never enjoy innocent sleep again, slept instantly.

CHAPTER III.—ENLIGHTENMENT.

When William Armstrong awoke, he thought he had overslept himself, for the trampling of horses sounded in the paved courtyard below. The one window of his room, over which he had drawn and fastened heavy wooden shutters the night before, let in a thread of light which showed him a new day had come, and the activity in the yard made him fear he had lain longer abed than was his custom. He was the more convinced of this in that he remembered hazily the clattering hoofs of a horse some time before, and then later, another being led out; now there appeared to be a third, and the hum of talk came up to him. His window overlooked the stable yard, and he recognized the mumble of the hostler who had assisted him yesterday. He lay still, half drowsed, the mattress most alluring to him, when suddenly he was startled wide awake by a voice he knew.

"Then I turn to the left for Broughton?"

"Yes, sir," muttered the hostler.

Armstrong leaped from his bed, placed his eye at the chink in the shutters, and peered down into the stable yard. The voice had not misled him. De Courcy, sitting on a horse, was just gathering up the reins and departing. The Scot lost no time in pulling on his boots, pushing aside the bed, unbolting the door, and making his way down the stair. What did this gaily plumaged bird of ill-omen here in the country of the Parliament, when his place was beside the King? Was there treachery afoot? It looked like it. Once outside, he saw it was still early, with the sun scarcely risen. He accosted the yawning hostler.

"Who was that man you were directing to Broughton?"

"I don't know, sir."

"When did he arrive?"

"Last night, sir, after dark."

"Did he stop in this house?"

"Yes, sir. I thought he was a friend of yours, for he knew your horse when I was putting up his own. He asked if you were here, and I told him you were in the room over the yard."

"What is Broughton; a hamlet?"

"It is a castle, sir. Lord Say's castle, about three miles from here. General Cromwell is there now; it is his headquarters in this district."

"Cromwell!"

The young man stood stock still, his eyes gazing into vacancy. What traffic had this King's Chamberlain with Cromwell? How dared he come within the Parliamentary lines, undisguised, unless—unless——Like inspiration the whole situation flashed upon him. De Courcy knew the burden he carried, and had seen where it was placed. He was on his way to sell his secret and set the troops on the track of the messenger. He must be off at once and outride the traitor. Before De Courcy had gone his three miles, he would have traversed a dozen, and from then on it would be a race to the Scottish border.

"Is my horse fed?"

"Yes, sir."

"Get him out at once. I will arouse the others." He took three steps toward the inn, then stopped as if shot, his hand clutching his breast.

"By God, he's got the thing itself. Robbed, as I'm a sinner!"

Now the disturbance in the night stood out clear in his memory, but he wasted not a thought over it. In upon the astonished hostler he swept.

"Never mind the saddle, fellow. Spring up behind me and show me the road to Broughton. Up, I say, the horse can carry a dozen like us. Here are two gold pieces for you; guidance and a still tongue in your head is what I want."

Armstrong grasped the two pistols from the holsters, flung the hesitating hostler upon the animal's back, and leaped up in front of him.

"Which way, which way, which way?"

"Straight down the street, sir," gasped the terrified man, clasping the rider round the waist. "Now to the right, sir, and next to the left. That's it, sir. Up the hill. Ah, there's your man, jogging on ahead, leisurely enough, if it's him you seek."

"Right! Slip off; I can't stop. God be with you!"

The hostler rolled in a heap along the ditch, staggered to his feet, feeling his limbs for broken bones, thinking his gold pieces hardly earned in such usage; then, satisfying himself that the damage was not great, hobbled back to Banbury.

De Courcy, riding easily, as the man had said, wholly unsuspicious of pursuit or any reason for it, had disappeared into a hollow when Bruce, like a thunder-cloud, came over the crest, and charged down upon him with the irresistible force of a troop of dragoons. The Frenchman, hearing too late the rumble of the hoofs, partly turned his horse across the road, the worst movement he could have made, for Bruce, with a war-neigh, came breast on, maddened with the delight of battle, and whirled opposing horse and rider over and over like a cart-wheel flung along the road from the hand of a smith. De Courcy lay partly stunned at the roadside, while his frightened steed staggered to its feet, leaped the hedge with a scream of fear, and scampered across the field to its farthest extremity. Armstrong swung himself to the ground with a quieting word to Bruce, who stood still, panting, and watching every movement of his master. A pistol in each hand, Armstrong strode over to his victim.

"You halter-dog, traitor, and scullion, give me the King's commission."

"Sir, you have killed me," moaned De Courcy faintly.

"You bribed thief, the rope is your end. You'll take no scath through honourable warfare. Disgorge!"

De Courcy, vaguely wondering how the other knew he carried it, drew from within his torn doublet the second commission signed by the King, and handed it up with a groan to the conqueror. As it was an exact duplicate of the one he had lost, even to the silken cord, the honest Scot had not the slightest doubt he had come by his own again, and the prone man was equally convinced that some one had betrayed to Armstrong his secret mission, yet for the life of him could not guess how this were possible. The young man placed the document where its predecessor had been, then said to his victim: "Had I a rope and a hangman with me, you would end your life on yonder tree. When first I learned your character, you were in some danger from my sword; a moment since you stood in jeopardy from my pistols; beware our third meeting, for if you cross my path again, I will strangle you with my naked hands, if need be."

De Courcy made no reply. He realized that this was not a time for controversy. A standing man well armed has manifest advantages over an enemy bruised and on the ground, and some thought of this came to the mind of the generous victor now that his anger was cooling. He felt that it was rather undignified to threaten a helpless adversary, and if he were a traitor to the King, let the King deal with him. So, whistling to his horse, he sprang on his back, and rode to Banbury at a slower pace than he had traversed the same highway some minutes before.

The hostler made grievous pretence that he had been all but murdered by his fall, and Armstrong examined him minutely, as he would have done with a favourite horse, pronouncing him none the worse for his tumbling, but rather the better, as he was now more supple than he had been for years. He rewarded the man lavishly, nevertheless, and gave him the recipe for a liniment good for man and beast, should after-complications ensue.

"I hope, sir," whined the man, "that you did not treat the gentleman you were in such haste to meet, as roughly as you did me."

"Very much the same," cried Armstrong, with a laugh, "but you are the better off, because I left him neither gold nor medicine; taking from him rather than bestowing."

"Ah, is that your game?" whispered the hostler, a glint of admiration lighting up his eyes. "Dang me, if I did not take thee for a gentleman of the road when first I clapped eyes on thee. Be sure I'll say naught, for I've cut a purse myself in younger days. Those times were better than now. There's too many soldiers and too few gentlemen with fat purses travelling the roads nowadays for our trade."

Again William laughed, and shook hands with the old man, as one highwayman in a good way of business might condescend to another less prosperous, and the veteran hostler boasted of his intimacy with a noted freebooter for the rest of his days.

"Rub down my horse well, while I am at breakfast," said Armstrong, and, receiving every assurance that the beast of so excellent a highwayman should get earnest attention, he went to the inn and there found Frances awaiting him.

The girl was standing by the window, which was low and long, with a valance of crimpled spotted muslin running athwart the lower half of it. A bench was fixed beneath the window, and on this bench the girl had rested a knee, while her cheek was placed against the diamond panes. The light struck her face and illuminated it strongly, and she stood so still that she seemed to form part of a tableau which might have been entitled "Watching." On the table placed in the centre of the room, breakfast was spread.

It was a jubilant man who disturbed this quiet picture by his abrupt in-coming. The early morning gallop, the excitement of contest, the flush of victory, all had their effect on his bearing, and he came in with the mien of a Saxon prince, his yellow hair almost touching the beams of the low ceiling. The two formed a striking contrast when the embodiment of elation approached the embodiment of dejection. There was a new furtiveness in the brief glance she cast upon him, and after her first startled cognizance she looked beyond him, on either side of him, over his head, or at his feet, but never turned her eyes full upon him as of yore.

"Ah, my girl," he cried, "you have not slept well. I can see that at once. This will never do; never do at all. But you are certainly looking better this morning than you did last night. Is that not so?"

"You are looking very well," she said, avoiding his question.

"Oh I've had a morning gallop already."

"What! With the ride to Scotland still before you. Is not a merciful man

238

merciful to his horse?"

"He should be, but I may say this for Bruce; he enjoyed the ride quite as much as I did. And now I am ravenous for breakfast, and eager for the road again." He tinkled a little hand-bell that rested on the table. "We have another splendid day for it. The sunrise this morning was positively inspiring. Come, lass, and sit you down. We must get the roses back into those cheeks, and I think the ride to-day will do it; for we will be nearing the North, ever nearing the North, and you are just like me, you are yearning for the Northland, where all the men are brave and all the women fair."

"Fair and false, perhaps you would add. That was your phrase, I think."

William laughed heartily, drawing in his chair.

"Yes, about our Stuarts, not about our ladies. They are ever leal and true. And indeed many of them are dark as well as fair, and they are the best. Dark hair, fair face, and a loyal heart; there is a combination to cherish when God is good to a man and allows him to meet it."

The servant had now answered the tinkling bell, and Frances was too busy acting the housewife to make any comment on his enthusiastic description of what was to be found in the North. Her pale cheeks reddened as he spoke, and he took this for a promising sign. She was convinced that he had as yet no knowledge of his loss, and wondered when and where such knowledge would come to him. She hoped the enlightenment would be delayed until they were near the Scottish line or across it. Then she must tell him the truth at whatever cost to herself, and persuade him, if she could, not to return. When she made her confession, she would be in a position to relate all Cromwell had said to her; show him that the General had given orders which would block any backward move, and reveal his determination to hang the Scot should he entangle himself further with English politics. Yet she had the gravest doubts that these dangers would influence him. She knew him well enough to be aware that his own personal safety weighed but lightly with him, and the very opposition would determine him to try conclusions with it, unabashed by the overwhelming odds against him.

These reflections troubled her until the time they were on their horses once more, when Armstrong interrupted them by crying out:

"Where's old John?"

"I sent him on ahead long since," replied Frances.

"Good. We shall soon overtake him. Good bye, pirate!" he cried to the grinning hostler. "May I meet you on the road next time with a thousand pounds on you, and if you whisper 'Banbury' to me, I will not lift a penny of it."

"Good luck to you and your fair lady, sir," replied the enriched old man, raising his cap in salute. He wished more travellers like the brawny Scot came that way.

"Why do you call the poor man a pirate?" asked Frances.

"Oh, we're comrades!" laughed Armstrong. "He thinks me a capable, prompt, and energetic highwayman, and admitted on the quiet that he had cut a purse himself upon occasion in the days of his youth."

"And why does he think you a highwayman?"

"Ah, that would be telling. Suppose it is because I escort the fairest lady in the land? The sex have ever favoured the biggest rascals. No, I shall not incriminate myself, but shall maintain my pose of the amiable hypocrite. Here rides Will Armstrong, the honest man, if you take his own word for it. But the hostler knows better. He sees secret comings and goings, and draws his sage conclusions. Banbury! O Lord, I shall never forget Banbury! It is a place of mystery, the keeper of dark secrets and sudden rides, of midnight theft and of treachery. Ask the Broughton road, where Cromwell lies, to reveal what it knows. Things happen along that track which the King knows nothing of, and his royal signature takes journeys that he never counted upon."

"Heaven's pity! What do you mean?" moaned the girl, whitening to the lips. He laughed joyously, but checked himself when he saw the terrifying effect of his words on his companion. They were now clear of Banbury and trotting along the Coventry road. Their departure had met with no opposition, and they had seen not even a single soldier. The open country lay

240

before them, the turrets of the town sinking in the rear.

"My foolish words have frightened you. Forget them! I am accumulating experiences that will interest you to hear when the time comes for the telling of them, but of one thing I am assured, the good Lord stands by his own, and He has shielded me since yesterday morning broke. Come, Frances, let us gallop. That, and a trust in the Lord, will remedy all the ills of man or woman."

She was glad of the respite and they set off at full speed, nevertheless her mind was sorely troubled. "What did he know, what did he know?" beat through her brain in unison with the clatter of the horse's hoofs. It was not possible that chance had brought him thus to the very centre of her guilty secret. Cromwell, treachery, midnight stealth, the Broughton road, these words and phrases tortured her. Was this, then, the line of his revenge? Did he know all, and did he purpose to keep her thus in suspense, hinting, soothing her fears, then reviving them, making her black crime the subject of jest and laughter? She cast a glance over her shoulder. Banbury had disappeared; they were alone, flying over the land. The doubt was unbearable; she would endure it no longer. Impetuously she reined her horse to a stand. "Stop!" she cried, and at the word her own horse and Bruce halted and stood. The young man turned with alarm to her agitated face.

"What do you mean by your talk of Broughton and Cromwell?"

"Oh, that is a secret! I did not intend to tell you until our journey was ended, when we could laugh over it together."

"It is no laughing matter. I must know what you mean."

"All dangers are laughable once they are past. An unknown, unsuspected danger threatened me at Banbury. It is now past and done with, and the person who plotted against me can harm me no more. There are reasons why I do not wish to mention this person's name. Barring that, I may tell you now as well as another time, if you care to listen."

"Do I know the person?"

"Oh, yes! You knew the person long before I did. It was a person I trusted, but not know to be a traitor and a thief."

It was some moments before Frances could speak, but at last she said very quietly, looking down at her horse's mane,—"Tell me the story, and I will tell you the name of the thief."

"You slept badly last night Did you hear anything?"

"I—I———-I heard the clock strike the hours."

"I heard it strike three, but lay so locked in drowsiness that I knew not the Lord was calling to me. If the Seven Sleepers were melted into one, I would outsleep that one. Well, to get on, I was robbed in the night. It must have been at that hour, for I remember dimly some sort of disturbance. But Providence stood my friend. By the merest chance, it might seem, but not by chance as I believe, I saw the creature make for Broughton. 'So, here's for Broughton,' cried I, 'on the bare back of Bruce, and see if my good pistols would win back what had been stolen from me.' The Broughton road it was, and the pistols did the business." Saying this, he whisked from his pocket the King's commission, waving it triumphantly aloft. Her wide eyes drank in the amazing sight of it, slowly brimming with superstitious fear, and then she asked a duplicate of the question that had been asked of her a few hours before.

"Did you kill Cromwell?"

"Cromwell! I never saw him."

"From whom, then, did you wrench that parchment?"

"From the thief, of course. He never reached Cromwell."

"Oh, I am going mad! Who is the thief, who is the thief?"

"De Courcy, if you must know. Why does this trivial matter so disturb you? De Courcy followed us from Oxford last night, and was lodged at our inn. By some means he penetrated into my room, stole this from me, and I never missed it until I saw him ride for Broughton, and not even then, to tell the exact truth. But I remembered that he had seen me place this paper in the inside pocket of my vest, in the King's own presence, and then the whole plot came to me. Before he saw Broughton, Bruce and I were down upon him like a Highland storm on the Lowlands. 'My sword! you should have seen us! For a minute there was one whirligig of horse's legs and Frenchman, like a raree-show of acrobats struck by a whirlwind. If I had not been so angry I would have had the best laugh of my life,"—and the genial William threw back his head and made the wood echo with his merriment at the recollection. But the girl was sober enough.

"This is not the King's commission," she said quickly.

"Oh, but it is!"

"It is not. Have you read it?"

"No, but that's soon done."

He untied the cord and unfolded the sheepskin.

She leaned eagerly forward and scanned the writing, while Armstrong read it aloud.

"You see," he cried gleefully. "Of course it is the commission. There are the names of Traquair, and all the rest, just as I gave them to the secretary, and there is 'Charles Rex' in the King's own hand."

"It is a duplicate. Cromwell has the original. You never left De Courcy alive within a mile of Broughton Castle?"

"I did that very thing. Not as lively as I have seen him, yet alive nevertheless."

"Then ride, ride for the North. We have stood too long chattering here."

"All in good time, Frances. There is no more hurry than ever there was; less, indeed, for it seems to me that Cromwell, for some reason, wants to come at this by fraud and not by force. But now that De Courcy's name is mentioned between us, I ask you what you know against him more than I have told you?"

"Against him? I know everything against him. Would that you had killed him. He would sell his soul, if he has one. He robbed my dying father, and on the day of his death, when I was the only one in London who did not know he was executed, De Courcy lured me to his apartments at Whitehall under pretense of leading me to the King that I might plead for my father's life. There he attempted to entrap me, snapped in my hand the sword which I had clutched from the wall to defend myself, and I struck him twice in the face, and blinded him with his own false blood, and so escaped. Judge, then, my fear when I saw him there at Oxford."

"The truth! The truth! At last the truth!" shouted Armstrong, as if a weight had fallen from his shoulders. "The truth has a ring like honest steel, and cannot be mistaken when once you hear it. He lied to me about you in Oxford, and I called him liar, and would have proven it on him, but that he told me you were in danger. I should have killed the whelp this morning, but that he could not defend himself."

"The truth! Yes, but only part of it. He did not rob you last night."

"Nonsense! He did."

"I robbed you. I stole into your room and robbed you. I carried the original of that document to Cromwell himself, and it is now in his hands. It was the price of my brother's life. My brother was set on your track by Cromwell, and, being wounded, I took up his task. Do you understand? That was my mission to Oxford. To delude you, to rob you, and I have done it."

"Girl, you are distraught!"

"I am not. Every word I tell you is true."

"You are saying that to shield some one."

"Look, William Armstrong! For two hours and more, last night, you held me by the wrist. There is the bracelet with which you presented me,— black proof of the black guilt I confess to you."

She held her hand aloft, and the sleeve fell away from the white and rounded arm, marred only by the dark circles where his fingers had pressed.

"Do you say I did that?"

"Yes. If still you do not believe me, measure your fingers with the shadow they have cast."

She reached out her hand to him, and he took it in his left, stroking the bruised wrist with his right, but looking into her eyes all the while.

"Frances, is it this secret that stood between us?"

"Yes."

"Is this all that stood between us?"

"All! Is it not enough? All! It is a mountain of sin that bears me to the very ground."

"Why, dear lass, did you not tell me?"

"Tell you? It was from you, of all the world, I must conceal it until now."

He laughed very quietly, fondling her hand.

"Bless me, how little you know! What is quarreling King or rebellious country to me compared with you? No wonder my beating heart did not awaken me with your hand upon it, for it was co-conspirator with you, and wholly your own. Heaven mend my broken patriotism!—but if you had asked me, I would have ridden myself to Cromwell with the King's signature."

"Do you———can you forgive me, then?"

"Forgive you? You are the bravest lass in all the land,"—and with that, before she was aware or could ward off his attack if she had wished to do so, he reached impulsively forward, caught her off her horse, and held her in his arms as if she were a child, kissing her wounded wrist, her eyes, her hair, her lips. "And now, do you forgive me, Frances?"

"Oh, willingly, willingly! Trespass for trespass. 'As we forgive them that trespass against us.' But set me on my horse again, I beg of you."

"I can hardly believe you are here yet."

"Cease, cease, I beg of you! The moments are too precious for it."

"Precious they are and most preciously employed."

"Will, Will, I implore you. Do you not understand? You are jesting on the brink of the grave. De Courcy has crawled to Cromwell ere this, and that grim man is lighting the North against us. They are now on our track."

"The way is clear. There is no one in sight, and we can outride them when they come."

"They are riding across country to intercept us. Oh, let not my arms hold you back for destruction. Cromwell himself told me he would hang you if he had to take you openly."

"He dare not. Have no fear!"

"He dares anything. You do not know that man, and your condemnation, this document, rests now on the heart it would still. Cromwell will move the world to tear it from you. If you love me as you say, let us to the North at once."

Well he knew the truth of her warning, now that he understood the case, but was reluctant to let her go. The last appeal had its effect, and he placed her once more on her horse. Together they set off again, through a land that seemed silent and at peace; but it was only seeming.

CHAPTER IV.—ENTANGLED.

There was some delay at Warwick, and the authorities proved reluctant to let them proceed farther with the journey. It was evident that the commandant had received instructions regarding the very pass they presented to him for their safe conduct, because he retired with it to the guard-house, where he remained for a time that seemed perilously long, and even when at last he came out with it he was plainly still suspicious, and in doubt regarding what action he should take. It was Frances who turned the scale in her own favour and that of her companion.

"Where did you get this pass?" the commandant asked.

"At Corbiton Manor, in the county of Durham."

"Who gave it to you?"

"It was given to me by General Cromwell's direction, and written almost in my own presence, I might say, or at least a few moments after I had been speaking with him."

"You went from Durham to Oxford?"

"Yes."

"And have come from Oxford here?"

"Yes."

"Did you travel through Banbury?"

"We stopped the night at Banbury; at 'The Banbury Arms'."

"Stopping there by the direction of General Cromwell himself," put in the girl, much to the surprise of William Armstrong. The officer looked up at her with interest.

"When did the General give you such instructions?"

"Several days ago, at Northampton."

"You saw him at Northampton?"

"Yes, and I saw him again this morning before daybreak."

"Really. And where was that?"

"At Broughton Castle, three miles west of Banbury. In my presence he told his aid to ride to Banbury, and send word North that this pass was to be honored. Has the commander at Banbury not obeyed his General's instructions?"

"Yes, he has," admitted the officer, looking with admiration on the young woman who spoke so straightforwardly; "but the communication came to me by way of Coventry, and it was somewhat vague. The messenger reached here but a scant half hour since, and he spoke of one person, not of two. May I ask your name?" he continued to the man.

"William Armstrong."

"That is right, my orders are to pass William Armstrong, holding a permit from the General, but say nothing of a lady."

"That is doubtless the messenger's mistake," said Frances confidently. "My brother is, or was, up to this morning, Lieutenant Wentworth of the Parliamentary forces in Durham. This morning General Cromwell wrote out his commission as captain, and that I brought away with me from Broughton and sent it direct to Durham by my servant. But you may detain me if you wish, or send an escort with me back to the General. It will be a more serious matter if you detain Mr. Armstrong, who is a Scotsman, and whom the General has been at some pains to further."

"Indeed, madam, I shall detain neither of you. My only excuse is that the messenger was not as clear as he might have been, and you come so close on his heels. Besides, I have had disquieting news from Birmingham. There is a rising of some sort forward. Birmingham has already been smitten sore by the King's troops, so there is little fear that the citizens have risen in his favour, but I surmise that there has been some sort of Royalist outbreak elsewhere in the North. Something is afoot, for messengers have been galloping through Alcaster to the east of us for Birmingham. You heard nothing of that further south?"

"No," said Armstrong, who nevertheless had a shrewd suspicion where the trouble lay. "If there is any Royalist rising in Birmingham I would like to avoid the place. I have no wish to get among the Royalists. Are there roads by which we can win east of Birmingham?"

"Oh, yes! I will sketch out a route for you, whereby you may reach the main highway some seven miles north of Birmingham, at Sutton Coldfield."

"I shall be much indebted to you, if you will be so good."

The officer retired to the guard-house and brought out a rude map of the district, which he gave to Armstrong after explaining it. He sent a soldier to set them on the right way when they had left the village. When the soldier had departed, and the two were once more alone, Armstrong turned in his saddle and looked back at the frowning towers of Warwick Castle, looming up through the trees, very suggestive of a prison.

"That was a narrow shave," he said, "and I have to thank you, Frances, that we have squeezed through."

The girl shook her head.

"Alas, circumstances are proving too strong for me," she said sorrowfully, "and all my old ideas of right and wrong are being flouted day and night. Just now I have used truth for the purposes of falsehood, a fault which I chided in you earlier in our journey. I wish we were free of the entanglements and might be honest once more."

"You have done well. Have no fear, and I still insist that the Lord stands by us. We cannot meet force with force, and must use what craft we are possessed of. Cromwell uses it, and so does the King. Why should we be debarred? I think we are well out of that trap, and I am wondering how many hours will elapse before the commander is sorry he let us go."

They lunched on bread and cheese at a wayside hut, and once, when they reached the top of a hill, they saw what they took to be Birmingham away to the west. The by-roads they were traversing proved to be deserted, and they resolved to keep to them rather than seek the main highway at Sutton Coldfield or elsewhere, for they considered that their comparative slowness would be more than compensated for by greater safety. This course soon proved of doubtful wisdom. Without a guide the intricate lanes were puzzling, and often came to an end without any apparent reason. When they took to the fields the soil was heavy in many cases, and fatigued their horses, besides entangling them sometimes in low-lying lands that were almost marshes. To add to their difficulties the sun became obscured in a haze, and the temperature dropped sharply, condensing the moisture in the air about them, involving them in a mist that was worse than the darkest night. Still they struggled on, leaving the direction entirely to their horses. At last they came on what appeared to be a cart track, and, following it, they arrived at a labourer's hut which faced a lane. Armstrong, without dismounting, knocked at the door with his sword, and a frightened woman, holding it ajar, answered the summons.

"We have lost our way," said the young man, throwing her a coin to bespeak good will; "can you tell us where we are?"

"Where are you going?" asked the woman, which proved a somewhat difficult question to answer.

"What is the nearest town to the north of us?"

"Lichfield."

"And how do we get to Lichfield from here?"

"Follow this lane to the cross-road, then take the lane to the left for two miles, and it will lead you into the main road. Turn to the right, and Lichfield is five or six miles further on."

"If, instead of going to the main road, we keep to this lane, where will it lead us?"

"It stops at the cross-road."

"Where will the lane turning to the right lead us?"

"I don't know."

"Is there any way to the North except by the main road?"

"I don't know."

"How long have you lived in this cottage?"

"Twenty-three years, sir."

"And you know only the way to Lichfield?"

"Yes, sir."

He thanked the woman, and they rode on through the fog. The limited knowledge of the English peasantry regarding the geography of their own district had baffled him more than once during their journey, and this was but a fair example of the ignorance he had to contend against. He resolved to take the turn to the right in preference to the leftward lane. He feared

Lichfield or any other place of similar size, and he dreaded the main road. It was impossible for Cromwell to patrol the whole country at a moment's notice, so the by-ways would be safer if less direct. Their progress had been so slow that there was ample time for a hard rider with relays of horses to have spread a warning far ahead of them, and now caution, rather than speed, was their game. These points he discussed with his companion as they rode along in the fog, and she agreed with his conclusions. Each tried to cheer the other, but both were undeniably discouraged by the conditions that surrounded them.

About a mile from the hut they came to the end of their road, with the horizontal lane at its head, extending east and west. As they turned to the right, some object loomed in the fog ahead, and there came a sharp cry:

"Who goes there?"

"To the left," whispered Armstrong, turning his horse. Frances obeyed instantly, but the man in front fired his musket into the air and raised a shout, whereupon four others sprang from the dripping bushes, and two of them seized the reins of the startled horses.

"Resistance is useless," said the soldier hanging to the rein of the plunging Bruce, "there are a hundred men along this lane."

"I have no need to resist," cried Armstrong with affected indignation, although none realized so well as he that the game was up. "We are peaceful travellers under safe-conduct from General Cromwell himself."

"The lieutenant will be here directly," said the man, and as he spoke a party of horsemen came galloping down the lane.

"Who fired that shot?" cried the officer in charge. Before an answer could be given he came upon the two captives. "Who are you?" he demanded.

"Travellers to Carlisle, who have lost their way in the mist and are seeking the high road."

"If you have a pass, let me see it."

"Here it is!"

"Your name is Armstrong, perhaps?"

"The pass does not say so."

"Do you deny it?"

"No."

"You are prisoners. Where is the bugler?"

"Here, sir."

"Sound the recall."

The man placed the bugle to his lips, and the merry notes rang out into the obscurity. All remained silent, then, like an echo from east and west, almost in unison, came a similar call; and faintly in the further distance another. The company seemed to increase mysteriously, as if pikemen were being distilled out of the fog, and after a roll-call, every name being answered, the lieutenant gave the word to march, and horse and foot set out for the west, the two prisoners in the centre of the phalanx. The head of Frances drooped, and Will rode close by her side as cheerful as ever, trying to comfort her.

"Clever man, this Cromwell," he whispered with admiration in his tones. "You see what he has done? He has run thin lines across the country as fast as horses could gallop, stringing out the local men as they went along. We have probably blundered through one or two of these lines, but were bound to be caught sooner or later, unless we made for the coast on either side, and that would but have delayed things a bit, for there was little chance of us getting ship with all ports in his hands. It serves me right. I should have killed De Courcy and then galloped for it. However, the Lord stands by us, Frances; never forget that."

"It doesn't look much like it," said the girl despondently.

"Oh, well, nothing looks like itself in this accursed fog. Why could n't we have had this mist on the road from York? Still, I don't think it would have made any difference, once Cromwell's riders got to the north of us. Resourceful man, Oliver. I like him."

"And I don't. Yet you are supposed to be against him, and I am supposed to be for him. I fear him; I fear him."

"Oh, there's no danger; not the slightest for either of us. You have done your task, and have done it well. I am the blunderer. But I stand on my status as a Scot, and I will argue the matter out with him. The man I tumbled into the ditch was the King's Chamberlain, and not a Parliamentarian, and a foreigner at that. The document I am supposed to carry was not given to me by the King, but taken by force from a minion of the King, and a Frenchman. I have assaulted no Englishman, and Cromwell knew I was travelling on this pass. He cannot deny that he wrote it, and for exactly the purpose it has served. Oh, I shall have a beautiful legal argument with Old Noll, and will upset him with his own law. I'm in no danger; neither are you."

"I trust it will appear so."

"It cannot appear otherwise. He was trying to frighten you when he said he would hang me. He is a sly, capable dog, who will be satisfied with having beaten me, and will not court trouble with my countrymen by hanging even a Borderer. It cost one of our Kings his throne to do the like of that."

This conversation, with which there was no interference on the part of their captors, was brought to a conclusion by their arrival at the main road. Here a halt was called and the bugle was sounded, again to be answered, as before, from different directions. "Dismount," said the officer to Armstrong, whereupon the latter, without a word, sprang to the ground. Against the next move he protested, but his opposition was unavailing and indeed unreplied to. The officer gave the lady and the two horses in charge of a party of six, with orders to take them to Lichfield and install them in the cathedral. A guard was to be set at the door, and no communication was to be allowed with any one outside. Orders from headquarters were to the effect that the lady was to be treated with every deference, and these orders were impressed upon the six men. The detached squad disappeared down the road in the fog, and Armstrong stood disconsolate and angry, but helpless, surrounded by troopers.

The monotony of waiting was relieved by the frequent arrival of companies from the east and from the west, who did not stay at the cross-roads, however, but marched south toward Sutton Coldfield and Birmingham. Thus the little company standing at arms was continually augmented, and continually reduced to its original size. It was waiting for some one higher in command than the mild lieutenant, and nearly two hours passed before this man, set in authority, arrived. Armstrong heard the trampling of horse to the south, and presently the sound of voices became quite audible through the fog. There seemed to be a dispute going forward, which was something unusual in the Parliamentary forces, where, if discipline appeared lax, instant obedience was invariably required.

"I tell you, Colonel, I am to take charge of the lady and escort her to Cromwell."

"I have no orders to that effect."

"I have come direct from Cromwell, and those were his orders."

"I do not take orders from you. I hold written instructions relating to both the man and the woman, and these I shall carry out."

"You will be wise to hang the man on the nearest tree, and take his papers to Cromwell."

To this there was no reply, and Armstrong now knew that De Courcy had not been so badly hurt as he had pretended, for he had taken a long ride to the North since then. The prisoner recognized his voice long before his cavalier costume emerged from the mist. De Courcy had not changed his apparel, and it formed a strange contrast to the Parliamentary uniform, as indeed did Armstrong's own dress.

"Ah, my young friend," cried De Courcy, the moment he recognized the prisoner, "you had your laugh in the morning, and I have mine in the evening."

"There is a time for everything," replied Armstrong indifferently, "and my time for laughing is in the morning. It is brighter then."

"Yes, it looks rather dark for you at the moment, and you seem less merry than when I met you earlier."

"Oh, there were more amusing things happening then, that's all. How's your horse?"

"We are neither of us the worse for our encounter. Do n't you wish you could say the same for yourself?"

"I do, and I thank you for your sympathy."

"Have you sent the woman to Lichfield?" asked the officer-in-chief of his subordinate.

"Yes, Colonel; some two hours ago."

"Very well. We will relieve you of your prisoner. Take your men to Birmingham."

"Is there any truth in the Royalist rising there, Colonel?"

"None in the least. Have you heard anything?"

"Nothing but a rumor that there was an outbreak of some sort. I heard that a detachment from Lichfield was to leave for Birmingham."

"We will turn it back if we meet it. Good night!" At the word the lieutenant and his men marched off to the south, and Armstrong was taken in charge by the squadron of horse. A trooper was dismounted and his steed given to Armstrong, of whom no questions were asked, as he had expected. They seemed very sure of their man. The cavalry set off to the North, and De Courcy rode close beside his enemy, taking a delight in taunting him. To this enforced companionship the Scot objected and made appeal to the colonel.

"Sir, am I your prisoner, or do I belong to this renegade King's man? Who is in authority here,—you, or this Frenchman?"

To this the colonel made no reply, nor did he order De Courcy to the rear, probably not wishing to offend one who seemed to be a friend of Cromwell's. The angry Scot was forced to make the best of it in silence, while the Frenchman, very polite and jocular, pressed ironic services upon him, asked after the girl, and said he would use his influence with Cromwell to have a silken rope used at the coming execution of so distinguished a spy. It is ill to tamper with a Border temper, as the Frenchman soon discovered. Armstrong slipped his knife from his belt and held it in readiness, when his attention was drawn to the trampling of an approaching host in front of them, and he remembered that here was coming the troop from Lichfield, which expected to meet a body of the King's men if the rumour from Birmingham were true. The rumour had no doubt been started by the riding North in hot haste of this courtier now at his side, at a time when such costume was not seen outside Oxford. Besides, the country was in a constant state of alarm, and the wildest tales were current, whose constant contradiction by afterevents did nothing to allay ever-recurring panic. Armstrong quietly gathered up his reins, watched his opportunity, and, instead of running his blade between the ribs of De Courcy, jabbed the point into the flank of the Frenchman's horse.

CHAPTER V.—SANCTUARY.

However graceful the Frenchman might be on foot, and no one denied his elegance of bearing, he was but an amateur on horseback, and when his steed unexpectedly plunged forward he relinquished the reins and grasped the mane. For one brief moment the attention of the troop was diverted toward the unexplained antics of the maddened horse and the imminent overthrow of its rider. It is one of the defects of human nature that man is prone to laugh when he sees a fellow creature in some predicament from which his own superior skill leaves him free. Every man in the company was a faultless rider, and nothing their horses could do would have been any embarrassment to them. To see this dandified foreigner, whom at heart they despised in any case, crouching like a gaudily dressed monkey on a frolicsome dog, and screaming for help, was too much for even the saddest of them, and a roar of laughter went up which did nothing toward quieting the injured and frightened quadruped. If it had been the horse of Armstrong that had begun these dancings, his guards would have been instantly on the alert for an attempted escape, but at the very moment their eyes should have been on the Scot their attention was withdrawn. Armstrong did not laugh, but, thrusting back his knife, whipped out his sword, and struck De Courcy's horse twice with the broad of it. His own steed leaped forward under the prick of the spur, and before the colonel could give a word of command the two had disappeared in the fog ahead. Even then the colonel, who was the only man that had his wits about him, did not think there was the least chance of escape, for he had heard the troop coming toward him, and Armstrong must run directly into it. He rose in his stirrups to give the alarm to those ahead, when all heard a ringing shout: "Charge, cavaliers! God save the King! To hell with the Roundheads! Charge!"

Out of the fog came a spattering fire, then a volley. Two horses and three men went down, while the other troopers hastily unslung their carbines and fired down the street without waiting for the word of command.

"Stop, you fools!" yelled the colonel, "you are shooting your own men." Then to the oncomers he roared a like warning, which was drowned in another volley. The Lichfield men were not to be taken in, even if they had heard the warning. With their own eyes they had seen two cavaliers burst upon them out of the fog with a strident cry for the King. De Courcy, coming first, they concentrated upon him, and he went down before them. Armstrong, swinging his sword, smiting right and left, bellowing like a fiend in true cavalier style, a very Prince Rupert come again, dashed at the weakest spot, and his impetuosity carried all before him.

"Never mind him," cried the leader, as some would have pursued. "Fire, and break their charge," and fire they did right stoutly, until a maddened officer, with a bravery that scorned the bullets around him, galloped along their front, waving his sword and commanding them to stop.

"You are killing your own men! There are no Royalists, but an interfering fool of a Frenchman and an escaped Scot. Back to Lichfield!" Nevertheless, a battle is not quelled at a word, and the brave colonel pressed through among them and galloped in pursuit of his late prisoner.

Once clear of the clash, Armstrong was not sparing of a horse that belonged to someone else. At great risk to his neck he raced through the blind fog, sword in hand, ready for further opposition should he meet it. He emerged from the fog with a suddenness that startled him. The sun had set, and there, barely a mile away, stood out against the darkening sky the great red bulk of the cathedral with its war-broken towers, and the little town huddled at its feet. At the same moment he became aware that some one was thundering after him, and again he dug the cruel spurs into the labouring horse. A glance over his shoulder showed him the colonel breaking through the bank of fog, and he thought of turning and fighting him on the run, but the sound of firing had ceased, and he knew the colonel would prove a stouter combatant than the Frenchman, so he hurried on. Aside from this, Lichfield had been roused by the sound of the guns, and he saw the long narrow street that lay between him and the cathedral becoming alive with pikemen, and knew he would have his work cut out for him if he was to get safely through the town. As soon as he came within earshot he shouted to them: "Barricade the street! The King is upon us. I have just escaped. Our men are on the retreat. Defend the town to the south. Barricade! Barricade!" Thus he clattered through Lichfield, shouting.

Soldiers are so accustomed to the word of command that they obey first and think after, if at all. Seeing a rider in the costume of a cavalier come tearing down upon them, they made hasty preparation for stopping him; but his tone of authority was so well assumed that they gave way before him, and began the running out of carts and whatever other obstructions they could lay their hands upon, to make the way difficult for the oncoming colonel, who swore as loudly at their stupidity as if he were the King's own.

"What are you about, you accursed clodhoppers? Don't you know a King's man when you see one? Leave that rubbish and follow me to the cathedral."

Armstrong's horse, nearly done, staggered over the bridge and up the slight incline that led to the cathedral precincts. Across the grounds surrounding the church had been raised a great earthwork, and the battered west front of the sacred building showed that war had been no respecter of sculptured beauty. A lone pikeman paced up and down before the cathedral door, but paused as he saw this impetuous rider, whose horse had stumbled and fallen at the top of the rubbish heap.

"What do you there?" shouted Armstrong, springing nimbly from his fallen horse. "Did n't you hear the firing? Down to the street and help your comrades; the town is attacked! Run!"

"I was told to stand here," objected the bewildered guard.

"Run, confound you! Do you question the word of an officer?"

The man, trailing his pike, ran, and disappeared down the street.

"Frances, Frances, are you within? Open the small door; it is I, Armstrong."

"Yes, yes, I knew you would come," he heard her say, and then followed the welcome rattle of the bolts. But they must be speedily drawn if they were to clear the way for a man hard pressed. Over the barricade surged a wave of pikemen, twoscore or more, the mounted colonel behind them, urging them on with pungent oaths.

"Sanctuary! Sanctuary!" shouted Armstrong, raising his sword aloft, standing under the arched doorway, steadfast as one of the stone knights beside him.

"Sanctuary be damned!" cried the colonel, urging his horse up the embankment. "Down on him, you dogs, and take him dead or alive!"

In spite of the cursing of the colonel; in spite of the battered condition of the great church; in spite of the deadening influence of the war, the cry of "Sanctuary" struck home to many of the hearts there opposed to the fugitive, and the pike-topped crest of the human wave paused for one brief instant, yet it was enough. Before the wave broke and fell, the small door gave and swung inward. As the pikes rattled against it, Armstrong had the bars and bolts in their places again.

"Break down that door!" he heard the colonel roar outside, while the impetuous William clasped the girl in his arms and kissed her.

"Lord, lassie, I'm glad to meet you again, although it's just dark enough in this place for the seeing of any one."

The young woman shook herself free.

"We wasted too much time at that before. Let it be a lesson to us. This place is a stable. Our horses are well fed, and the saddles are still on them."

"But is there a way out?"

"Yes, a small door in the northeast corner. Come."

"It will be guarded, surely."

"No. I think they wanted me to escape, for they went out that way after barring the front door. But they did n't think you would be with me when I took my leave. Come quickly, or they will be round to it from the front."

"I doubt it. The colonel is a Birmingham man and a powerful swearer, who knows nothing of this church—or any other, I think. The men will not remember the back door until it is too late, and then I pity them; they will hear language from the colonel."

The two made their way to the farther end of the cathedral, where the horses were stalled. The vast nave was dark and would soon be black as a cellar until the moon rose. It was used as a military storehouse, as a stable, and as a dormitory for troops when the accommodation in the town was overtaxed. As Armstrong and his companion stumbled over obstructions toward the horses, the spacious chamber rang with the impact of timber against the stubborn doors. Frances, knowing the geography of the place, led the way with her horse, and Armstrong followed with his. Once outside, there was more light than he wished for, but their way to the rear was clear, and, mounting, he took the lead, crossing an alpine ridge which had done duty during the siege, and taking a somewhat terrifying leap down to the greensward of the field at the back of the cathedral. Then they ran north through a slight valley, and, for the moment, were safe from observation.

"The moon will be up soon," said the young man, "and I do n't know whether to welcome it or fear it."

"We shall do neither, as we have no influence one way or another, and must bear its disadvantages or the reverse, as chance wills. Now tell me what happened. How did you escape?"

The tale was soon told, half humorously, as if it were an escapade rather than an escape, and the narrator wound up with a determination to avoid the main road in future.

"There I do not agree with you," she said. "I have been alone in that cathedral some three hours or more, and have had time to think. You said we blundered into the ambuscade, and so we did. You have hewn your way out by a marvellous combination of luck and prowess, but such exploits are not to be depended upon. You must use your mind, as well as your right arm and the swiftness of your horse, if you are to win Scotland."

"Frances, you discourage me: I looked upon my escape rather as a triumph of wit than of muscle. The setting of the Roundheads at each other's throats in the mist seemed an inspiration, and the cry of 'Sanctuary' gave me just the moment of time that was needed. Your estimate of me is that of the Reverend Henderson of Edinburgh, who held I had barely sense enough to direct a stout blow."

"No, no, I give you full credit for great ingenuity, but we stumbled upon, the Parliamentarians with no plans made. Everything has been done on the spur of the moment, and has not been thought out before the crisis came. A few chance remarks got us clear at Warwick; while inspiration and a fog were your safety at Lichfield, and even then by one brief instant of time. The recurrence of such strokes of luck and good management are not to be looked for. Some time the moment needed will go against us, and then all is lost."

"True enough. What do you propose?"

"I propose we take to the main road again, which must be near at hand on our left."

"You forget we have no pass from Cromwell now. The lieutenant has it."

"You will have a pass for yourself the moment you are north of Manchester, which cannot be more than fifty miles away. We must get over those miles as speedily as possible; therefore the main road is our route."

"Yes, if it were practicable; surely danger lies thick along the main road."

"I do not think so. While in the cathedral I heard troop after troop of men going northward. They will carry the news of your capture, but not of your escape. Until they beat in the door of the cathedral and search the place thoroughly, no messenger will be sent North. We are ahead of them once more, with the news of your capture travelling in front of us. We will keep ahead so long as we ride fast and until we stop somewhere for the night; then they having relays of horses, while we have only our own, will pass us. We cannot ride all night, or we shall kill our horses; but We can cover a good deal of the ground between here and Manchester. Once north of Manchester I think you are fairly safe. So I propose we ride now for the main road, and keep going as long as our horses are able to travel."

"Agreed; but, following your own instructions, what are we to say when we are stopped? We have no pass, so how am I to account for myself?"

"You are a Roundhead soldier, sent on to Manchester by the colonel at Lichfield."

"I look like a Roundhead soldier!" cried William, with a laugh.

"You will. It is always well to have some one in a travelling party who can think. Have you not noticed the load you carry behind your saddle?" Armstrong turned. The rising moon displayed a steel cap that looked like an overturned pot and a bundle of cloth, all neatly strapped on.

"The cathedral is a storehouse for uniforms and accoutrements enough to fit out a regiment. I selected the largest suit I could find, with cloak and cap, and belted them to your saddle. Now I shall hold your horse while you go into the thicket and change your raiment. Conceal your cavalier costume as well as you can, so that, if they trace us over this fog-sodden turf, which is likely, they will get no hint of your new appearance. It might be well to climb a tree and tie your discarded shell among the leaves, with the straps that bind the bundle to your horse, and be careful to leave neither the King's message nor your purse with your finery."

It was a happy omen for future domestic peace that the huge man did at once and without question what the comparatively fragile young woman bade him, she holding his horse while he made the rapid change. When he emerged, the horse plunged, and she had some ado to hold him until he heard his master's voice and laugh.

"Yea, verily, this is a transformation indeed," cried Armstrong, looking at himself in the moonlight. "My name is Hezekiah, and the steel cap is a thought on the small side, but the rest o' the duds are not so bad."

"The cap was the largest I could find," laughed the girl, "and will fit closely enough when your locks are shorn."

"Oh. Must I sacrifice this vanity of Absalom as well?"

"Surely. If I am to be your Delilah, I must fulfill my duty. I searched the whole cathedral for that which would do the work of shears, but could find nothing. However, the first cottage we come to will supply us with a suitable instrument. Now mount, and let us away."

They speedily came upon the main road, and cantered on through the beautiful night, determined to put fifty miles, or thereabout, between themselves and Lichfield, but before they had accomplished half that distance Armstrong saw that the girl was completely exhausted in spite of her disclaimers, for, aside from the tiresome day's travel, she had had little sleep the night before. It was most tempting to push on, for the night was perfect and the road was good. Even though they passed through several villages they were not questioned. Soldiers in drab cloaks and steel caps were too common on the road to cause comment, and they were, as yet, in advance of any news of escape.

At last they came to a farmhouse near the roadside, and Armstrong beat up the inmates, bringing a woman's head to an opened window. At first she would admit no one at that hour of the night, but the moon shining on the steel cap and the long cloak apparently gave her confidence. Her husband was in the south with Cromwell, she said. She could make a place in the house for the lady, but the soldier would find better accommodation than he was accustomed to in an outhouse. With this Armstrong expressed himself as amply satisfied. They dismounted, and he led away the horses. He found a place for them in a shed, examined them, and rubbed them down with care. Having satisfied himself that they were none the worse for their long journey, he attended to their wants and flung down some bundles of straw for his own night's lodging. He began to think he must go supperless, or run the risk of foraging in an unknown pantry, if he could find entrance, when he saw Frances approach from the house with a loaf of bread and a lump of cheese on a trencher, and a measure of ale. He met her half way and relieved her of the load. Under her arm she carried some cumbrous weapon, which she brought out when he assumed the burden of the provender.

"It is a pair of sheep-shears, which the woman tells me is all she has, but I assured her they were most suitable for my purpose. Now sit on this stone here in the moonlight and be shorn; for we must set out in the daylight without those long locks of yours. You look too much like the King, even with your cloak and steel cap."

The girl laughed softly as she said this, and snapped the big shears menacingly. He sat on the stone like the obedient young man he was, shook out his lion's mane, and in a few moments was bereft of it. The girl stood back and surveyed her work, laughing, but nevertheless with a tinge of regret in her laughter.

"Oh, it's a pity!" she cried. "All the King's horses and all the King's men are not worth the sacrifice. I hope it will grow again, for, if not, the Philistines be upon thee, Samson. Your dearest friend would n 't know you now."

Armstrong smiled ruefully and passed his hand in anxious doubt over his cropped head.

"I suppose it will grow again, unless my dearest friend refuses to acknowledge me with this curtailment, when I shall become bald through grief at her defection."

"I make no promises, if you mean me. I shall very likely reconsider. You are never the man who cast a glamour over me at Oxford and elsewhere. I fear I am no true Parliamentarian after all, but I shall not come to a decision until I see you in the daylight. Perhaps the cap will be an improvement, but

I doubt it."

He squeezed on the cap, which was still too small.

"By the bones of my ancestors, it will need Peter, the blacksmith of Gilnockie, to get this off again!"

"That is worse and worse," urged his tormentor. "I cannot bear the sight any longer, or it will drive sleep away from me. Good night, my poor, shorn Samson,"—and she was off before he could spring up and intercept her.

CHAPTER VI.—EXPEDIENCE.

Great is the recuperative power of youth, and shortly after sunrise the two were on the road again, refreshed and with high courage, to face the outcome of another long ride. They had travelled farther than their estimate of the night before, and so found themselves but little more than twenty miles south of Manchester. In the night the weather had undergone another change, and the sun was hidden, while now and then a scurry of rain passed over them. To the North the outlook was black and lowering. They were approaching the land of storm.

"I have made up my mind," said Frances, "that we must part. No, it is not on account of that cropped head of yours, but rather to save it."

"I have been thinking myself that it is wrong you should share my danger, when there is nothing to hinder you from going across country to your own home."

"I shall not go across my country until I have seen you safely into your own. But, as you know, the swearing colonel and his men are not looking for me. Perhaps they think I took the opportunity left open to get away from the cathedral; but on the other hand, if wise, they must have looked for our horses' tracks, and then they learned we left Lichfield together. I propose to act as your scout. I shall ride a mile or two ahead, and if I am stopped, you will strike to the right or to the left, and avoid the danger if you can. On every elevation I reach I will stand for a few moments. If my horse faces west, the way between us is safe; if he faces east, there is danger."

"Frances, I would rather run the risk and have your company."

"I am sure you would, but"—and she laughed—"now that you are clipped, you are the one who is beautiful, and I the one who is wise. It is really to your advantage that I should see as little of my Roundhead lover as possible, and you would be foolish to detain me, for I cannot help glancing at you now and then, and whenever I do, I sigh for the cavalier who wooed me yesterday. Women are not so changeable as they say, and I am constant to my first adorer."

To this William made no reply, gazing somewhat gloomily at the storm away on the horizon.

"There, there," she cried, riding alongside and touching his hand. "I have offended his vanity, and he doesn't like to be laughed at. Poor boy, you little know what is in store for you. Don't you understand you will have enough of my company in the days to come, and may well spare some of it now? I shall not disown my promise if you remind me of it when your love-locks are over your shoulders again. But, seriously, my plan is a good one unless you have a better to propose. We must quit the main road now, and avoid Manchester as we avoided Birmingham, but we should have a care that we do not ride into another ambuscade, and if I go first that may be prevented."

"When I see you interfered with, I will just gallop to your assistance."

"You shall do nothing so foolish. No one in England is going to injure me; but you are not safe until you are over the Scottish line. We shall be north of Manchester in three or four hours, and then you have your own pass. You are really a most creditable Roundhead. After Manchester we can travel in company again, if you wish. Have you anything better to propose?"

"Yes. I propose we stay together and take our chances."

"Good bye," she cried gaily, touching up her horse, then, over her shoulder as she galloped off, "Remember. West, safety; east, danger."

Armstrong had not only to curb his own inclination, but his horse as well, who viewed with evident disapproval the departure of his mate. At the summit of the first hill the girl turned her horse across the road facing west, waved her hand to him, and disappeared over the crest. And thus the journey went on; sometimes two miles between them, sometimes less. Manchester was seen and left in the rear. He now tried to catch up with her, but she kept valorously ahead, as if she were some fabled siren luring the poor man on. For a time he lost sight of her, then, as he mounted a hill, saw her standing on a crest a mile away, like an equestrian statue against an inky sky; but this time her horse faced the east, and he thought she was motioning with her handkerchief in that direction. She stood there until he sent his horse over the hedge and made in the direction of a forest, then the darkness seemed to swallow her up. He skirted the edge of the wood. Rain was now coming down heavily, but before it blotted out the landscape he passed the head of a valley and saw dimly through the downpour a large encampment of white tents. A man in drab on a black charger stood little chance of being seen against the dark forest from the encampment, but he moved on as rapidly as he could, knowing that if a lull came in the deluge he ran great risk of detection by the outposts. Some distance on he stood for a time under the trees, blessing the long cloak, which formerly he had maligned for its ugliness, for now it proved of good material and waterproof. The girl had evidently gone directly down into the camp, and he was at a loss what to do. Duty called him to press forward to the North, but duty is often an ill-favoured jade whose strident voice is outdistanced by the soft whisper of a beautiful woman. Armstrong dared not shout, and the deluge formed an impenetrable curtain whichever way he turned. He skirted the wood for some time, then crossed the fields to the west until he came to the road which trended North from the camp. Here he stood in the rain, and wondered whether she was detained, or whether she had already passed the spot he now occupied. They had made no arrangement for meeting again in case they should lose sight of each other, and he blamed himself for his negligence on this important point. One thing was certain. It was useless to stand here until he was dissolved. Even his stout-hearted horse had assumed an attitude of the utmost dejection, with drooping head, the water pouring off every part of him. Should the weather clear, which he was compelled to confess there seemed little likelihood of it doing, he was in danger so near the camp. He resolved to turn North, go on until he reached some place of shelter, and there wait. Progress was slow, for the lane had become a quagmire. The forest which he had skirted extended now to the west, and the road became a woodland track, but just where it began to penetrate into the wilderness there shone upon him a ray of hope. From an overhanging branch of the first tree hung a limp and dripping white rag, tied by one on horseback in such a position that it might brush the face of a rider passing that way. He took it down, and it proved to be a lady's handkerchief. If he had followed the edge of the wood, he could hardly have missed it; if he came along the lane he was almost certain to see it. He thrust this token under his cloak and chirruped to his discouraged horse. When something like a mile had been cast behind him, his horse neighed, and was answered by another further ahead. Then he came to a forester's hut, and in an open shed, sheltered from the storm, stood the companion of Bruce, who showed lively pleasure at the encounter.

Inside the hut a cheerful sight met his eyes. A fire of faggots blazed on the hearth, and before it stood a radiant young woman, arranging the brands to their better burning with the tip of her boot. On a high stool was spread her steaming cloak. In a far corner sat the old forester and his wife, frowning on their visitor and their newly arrived guest; for strangers were viewed with universal suspicion by high and low, little good ever coming of them in the minds of the peasantry, while the chance of danger was always present; danger whether hospitality was proffered or withheld. There was more likelihood of entertaining devils unaware than angels, and well the afflicted poor knew it.

However, less risk lay in succoring a steel cap than a feathered hat, so the moment the dripping horseman shoved in the door, the old woman rose and began to set out a meal of dark bread and swine's flesh, boiled and cold.

"Ah, here you are at last," cried the girl. "I was beginning to fear I should have to go back to the camp for you. Did you find my token?"

"Yes."

"Give it to me."

"Not so. Findings are keepings. You cannot prove your right to the property."

"Alas, honest travellers are few, as these good people seem to think.

268

Throw off your cloak. Here is a wooden hook by the fire that I have kept for it. Draw up your stool and eat. I was so hungry that I didn't wait. You see what it is to possess a good conscience once more."

"I possess a good appetite any way."

"Then sit down, and I shall be your waiting-maid."

"What news have you?"

"Hush! Great news, for I am the very princess of scouts. One thing at a time, however, and the one thing now is this black bread, which is like the old woman here, better than it looks. We can get nothing for our horses at this place, so must set out again as soon as possible, in spite of the rain."

When he had finished his meal and stood again with her before the fire, she whispered to him: "You must not pay these people too lavishly. They are somewhat near the camp, and although they do not seem over talkative it is better to run no risks. Bargain with them; be as a very Jew in computation."

"I'll do better than that. I'll be a very Scot, and so save money."

Once on the road again, she gave him her budget of news.

"You are a hero, William Armstrong. England is ringing with your exploits, and I never dreamed with what a valorous knight of old I travelled. It seems you stormed Warwick Castle and took it. You passed unseen through cordons of troops, and it is suspected you have dealings with the Devil, who travels beside you in the guise of a female, as is right and proper, and who appears and disappears at her will. Single-handed, you scattered two armies at Lichfield——"

"Oh, give the Devil her due!"

"With her aid, of course; that is always understood. You attacked Lichfield cathedral and captured it, and there is much disapproval among the peasantry that Cromwell had formerly dismantled it, for they think that if this had not been done the holy belongings of the place would have baffled you. The cathedral now reeks of sulphur, and you escaped in a whirl of flame amid a storm of bullets. They know that nothing will prevail against you but a silver pellet, and even that must be well aimed. So I am not sure but I have been mistaken in disguising you, for if any Cavalier shows himself in the North, the inhabitants are like to take him for Satan and fly from him."

"Then they are not good Christians, for they are told to resist the Devil and he will flee from them. You think, then, that my fiendish character will protect me?"

"Not so; but you have nothing to fear between here and Carlisle. I thought you said De Courcy had been killed?"

"He went down, and I supposed him shot, but was in too much of a hurry to inquire."

"He and others rode to the North last night, and they are now between us and Carlisle."

"He has as many lives as a cat. If that is the case, why do you say the road to Carlisle is clear?"

"Because from Carlisle to Newcastle, right across England, the cordon is to be stretched, and from Carlisle west to the coast. Before we can reach there; a line of men, almost within touching distance of each other, will extend from sea to sea, and all traffic North will be stopped. A thousand pounds is on your head, and Cromwell thinks to stay you, not with silver, but with gold. The General himself is on his way North, to see that you are trapped, or to be ready for any outbreak of the Scots should you win through."

"I fear I have been unable to convince Oliver that I am the devil, since he takes such excellent human means of frustrating me. A thousand pounds! And yet you held that first day I was of slight value!"

"I have confessed my error since. The camp I visited is breaking up to-day, and moving on to Carlisle. Twenty-three thousand men, I was told, but, being mostly foot, there is no chance of their overtaking us."

"Well, the North looks black with more than rain, though goodness knows there is enough of that. I wish I were in Glasgow."

"What do you propose to do?"

"You are the plan-maker of this foray. What do you propose to do, or have you thought of that yet?"

"I have not only thought of it, but have received instructions on it. I have heard the officers discuss what should be done, but I want to hear your conclusions first."

"Very well. The line runs from the west coast to Newcastle. At Newcastle I am more than forty miles from Scotland at the nearest point, while at Carlisle I am less than ten. Every step east I go, I am placing myself more and more at a disadvantage, yet I might go east simply because of this, and because they know that I know that they know I am on the road to Carlisle. Having fallen into one ambush, they will imagine me on the constant outlook for another. Going free for so long, they might even count on my increasing carelessness, but shrewd men would not lippen to that Knowing I am singlehanded and can make no stand, they will expect me to creep through at night, either east or west of Carlisle, and as near as may be to that place, trusting to the short distance and the fleetness of my horse in a race for the Scottish Border. I am a hillsman, accustomed to threading my way through a wild country, with a keen eye for an enemy. I have avoided all the big towns, Birmingham, Manchester, and the like, so they will not expect me to risk either Newcastle or Carlisle. Night will be the time when they are greatly on the alert, especially if this storm continues. Very well again. Who am I, if questioned? I am a trooper of Cromwell's own horse, sent North from Warwick, having seen this escaped devil of a Scot, and therefore the more likely to identify him. I have become detached from my company in the storm. I will ride into Carlisle in broad daylight, and ask where the Warwick horse are to be found. They were ordered to Carlisle, I shall say. I shall not avoid the commander, but will seek for him. Then, if I can saunter over the bridge, it's 'Hoorah for Scotland,' and may the best hoofs win."

"Good," cried the girl, "and well reasoned. They all agreed that Carlisle was the weakest link in the chain."

"Did they so? Then that makes me hesitate. If those in Carlisle think it the weakest link, they will strengthen it."

"The officer's plan was not so bold as yours. Of course they did not know you were travelling in the likeness of one of themselves. They thought you would abandon your horse before you came to Carlisle, creep into that town after dark, avoid the bridge, which is sure to be well guarded, swim the Eden, and be across the Scottish border by daylight. There are two defects in your own proposal; your accent is not that of Warwickshire, and De Courcy is sure to be in Carlisle and may recognize you. Besides this, you may meet some one who knows the Warwick regiments, and you are not even acquainted with the name of the captain of your supposed company. I think the night attempt more like to prosper."

"In the night every one is on the alert, and a Roundhead cannot be distinguished from a cavalier, so there is closer scrutiny. I can enact the stupid trooper to perfection, having natural gifts toward stupidity. There is a risk, of course, but this is a risky journey at best. If I once get over the bridge at Carlisle, I'll beat all England in a race for the Border."

"I hope you will. I said I would see you across into Scotland, but I am convinced that purpose is futile, and I shall prove but a danger to you. A Warwick trooper on duty does not wander over the country a-squiring of dames. I have given you good advice and a Roundhead's equipment, and have acted as your scout, so I must not imperil your mission by hanging to the skirt of that sopping cloak. To-night we shall likely reach Yorkshire, and to-morrow I bid you God speed and make across the county to my own home."

"Indeed, lass, I have come so to depend on you, I shall be but a lost sheep, shorn at that, if you leave me."

"The wind is tempered to all such, and if you depend on your own wit you are likely to prosper. But you should have some care for me. It is my own safety I am thinking of."

Although the day was far from being one that incited toward hilarity, Armstrong laughed, and turned his dripping face up to the storm. The girl joined him, but with less of merriment in her tones.

"You will never persuade me," he said, "that there is a tinge of selfishness about you, or that you ever think of yourself when there is a friend to think of."

"There is worse to come," she went on. "I must beg of you to sacrifice that moustache. You will never get through Carlisle with that on your lip. Anyone who has ever seen you before would recognize you now, in spite of cloak and cap."

"Madam, you ask too much. The kingdom of England may fall, but this moustache, never."

"Really," laughed the girl. "If you saw it at this moment you would not be so proud of it. It has drooped and wilted in the rain like a faded flower. 'Twere better done away with, for it will mark you out from the smooth-faced troopers who throng Carlisle."

William somewhat wistfully wrung the water from it, and attempted to draw it out across his cheeks.

"Madam, I suspect your design. One by one you have depleted me of what goes to make up a Borderer, and gradually you have reduced me to the commonplace level of those crop-eared villains who are fighting against their King. Then, when I come to you and say, 'I beseech you to fulfill your promise to me,' you will reply, 'Away, Hezekiah, I know you not.'"

"'T is near to that point now, and a little more or less will make slight difference with me, while it will greatly aid your passage through Carlisle."

"Would it not be well to have my ears cropped also?"

"They are somewhat prominent, now that your locks are gone. I wish I had brought those shears with me. You see now why I must leave you. Oh, the vanity of man! The self-conceit of woman is a molehill compared with a mountain. But take courage, William. I shall not be near you when the deed is done, and the moustache sacrificed, and you will wait in Scotland until it grows again. Perhaps by that time our English troubles will be finished, and thus Armstrong and England will be their true selves at the same moment."

They had long since reached the main road and were making way as well as they could through the mud. The rain had not ceased, nor did it show any sign of ceasing. It needed frivolous talk to keep the spirits up in such weather. The young woman was earnest enough in her resolve to further his disguise by the means she had suggested, but to this she could not get Armstrong to say either yea or nay. He changed the subject.

"You never told me how you managed to get so much information in the camp. Did they let you pass unquestioned?"

"It happened that I knew the officer in charge, and he knew me, and was rather apologetic in his demeanour toward me, for he was one of those of the court-martial who condemned my brother. I told him, truly enough, that I had been to see Cromwell and had obtained his complete pardon. That I had seen the General at Northampton, where he had made me a promise, and again at Broughton Castle, where he had redeemed it. I was now on my way home; that was all. The officer was very glad indeed to hear of my success, and said, what was also true, that he had deeply regretted the condemnation, but that the court could not do otherwise with the evidence before it. He had no suspicion that I was the female fiend who accompanied the man they sought, and as the talk was all of this man I could not help but hear, and was indeed very glad to listen."

As evening drew on, conversation lagged, and they rode silently together, keeping doggedly to the work in hand, in spite of the flagging energies of their horses and their own bedraggled weariness. The rain fell with pitiless steadiness, and darkness came on early, with no chance of a moon being visible that night. The welcome light of a town twinkled ahead at last, and they resolved to stop there unless the risk threatened to be overwhelming. At the outskirts they learned that they had reached Clitheroe, and that "The Star" inn offered fair accommodation for man and beast. They were not to reach Yorkshire that night, and had accomplished less than thirty miles from Manchester. They dismounted at "The Star," two very water-soaked persons, and their reception was far from being particularly cordial.

"Are you one of the troopers billeted here tonight?" asked the host, who appeared not over pleased to welcome such enforced guests.

"No, I pay for my accommodation. I am an officer of the Warwick horse."

"I was warned this morning to keep all the room I had for a company from Manchester."

"Then that need not trouble you. They will not be here to-night. They did not strike camp until this afternoon, later than they expected. Should any arrive who have a better right here than I, I will turn out, at whatever time of the night it is necessary. I want two rooms, and a sitting-room with a big fire. And get us a hot supper as soon as you can. There is good stabling for the horses, I hope?"

"The best in Lancashire. You are on this hide-and-seek business, I suppose?"

The landlord had become wonderfully genial, now that there was the prospect of good orders and gold ahead.

"What hide-and-seek business?"

"This slippery Scot. Have you got him yet?"

"No. It is thought he has made for the coast."

"Never you fear, sir. I know that kind of cattle, and have had them staying with me many's the time. He'll take to the hills, and you mark my word, unless you hold hands across England, you'll not catch him, and even then you'll have to look well to your feet, or he'll slip through between them."

"I hardly, see how a man on horseback can do that."

"You mark my word, they'll be looking for a man on horseback, and he'll be sneaking through the grass; then they'll be looking in the grass, and he's whistled to his horse and is off over the hills. I know they chaps, and have played blind man's buff with them myself. You mark my word, that lad is in Scotland before to-morrow night, and laughing at you all."

"Oh, I hope not!"

"You try to catch an eel by diving after it, and all you get is a wetting."

"Well, I'm wet enough now, landlord, and have caught no eel yet, so if you'll order a brisk fire going, we will see what we can do in the way of eels tomorrow."

It proved that Armstrong was quite right about the non-arrival of the Manchester contingent, and his deep slumber was not disturbed by any notice to quit. All night long the rain lashed down, but at daybreak it ceased, although the heavy clouds hung low in the sky. After a good breakfast the two set out, and were not molested or questioned as they passed from under the shadow of the castle at Clitheroe.

CHAPTER VII.—VICTORY.

Despite the night's rest, the horses were stiff after the long struggle with rain and mud the day before. If the situation was to be saved by a race, there seemed little chance of success with animals so tired and discouraged. With the exception of the departure from Oxford, the riders were more silent and melancholy than at any other time during their journey together. They had discussed the case in all its bearings the previous night, before the blazing fire, and had come to the conclusion that it would be safer to part. Armstrong was now in a country that he knew reasonably well, and he had no need to ask his direction from any chance comer, which was an advantage to a fugitive. They had agreed to deflect toward the east and bid good-bye to each other at Kirby Stephen, he striking northwest to Penrith, and she taking the main road east, entering Durham at Barnard Castle. There was no blinking the fact that while a Parliamentarian trooper might pass through this land unquestioned, especially as so many soldiers were making their way North, a trooper with a beautiful young woman of aristocratic appearance would certainly cause comment and excite curiosity. The nearer they came to Carlisle, the greater would be the danger of embarrassing questions. They had a wild country to traverse, bleak hills and moorland, and the roads as bad as they could be; but although they left Clitheroe at five o'clock it was past noontide before they reached Kirby Stephen, a distance of less than forty miles. They had met no one, and so far as the morning section of the journey was concerned, the road to Scotland was clear enough. At the squalid inn of Kirby Stephen they partook of what each thought was their last meal together for a long time to come, and then, in spite of her protests, he accompanied her east out of the town and into the lonely hill country. At last she pulled up her horse, and impetuously thrust out her right hand, dashing away some tear-drops from her long lashes with her left.

"Good bye," she cried, the broken voice belieing the assumed cheerfulness of the tone. "I cannot allow you to come farther. You must now bid farewell to your scout."

"Dear lass, it breaks my heart to part with you in this way," stammered William, engulphing her small hand in both of his, then drawing her to him. "It shames my manhood to let you go this wild road alone. I must see you to your own door, in spite of all the Cromwells that ever broke their country's laws."

"No, no!" she pleaded. "We went over all that last night, and settled it. I am safe enough. It is you who are in danger. You will come to me when this trouble is passed and done with."

"By Saint Andrew, I'll come to you as soon as this letter is in Traquair's hands."

"Again, no, no! Cromwell is a hard man, and if you steal through his cordon you must not come within his power in a hurry."

"No fear, lass, he dare not touch me. Once my foot's in Scotland, I'm like that ancient chap you told me of; I draw virtue from the soil and am unassailable. Cromwell wants nothing of me when this packet escapes him. I'll turn back from Traquair the moment I give it to him."

"I do not permit such folly; remember that." She wept a little, then laughed a little. "I do not wish to see you until your hair is grown again. My Scottish Samson, you must come to me with flowing locks, as when I first saw you, so that I may forget I have been your Delilah."

For answer he kissed her protesting lips again and again, then she hid her face in his sombre cloak and sobbed quietly. The patient horses, now accustomed to any vagaries on the part of their owners, stood quietly close together.

"Good-bye, good-bye, good-bye," she cried breathlessly, then whisked herself from him and was gone, never looking back, but waving her hand as she rode. He sat motionless as she had left him. At the top of the distant hill, outlined against the dark sky, she drew in and stood. Dimly he saw the flutter of something white in her waving hand, and he drew from his breast her own handkerchief and waved in return. He pressed his hand across his eyes, and, when he saw more clearly, only the blank sky and the bare hilltop confronted him.

"Now curse the man who tries to stop me," growled Armstrong through his set teeth. "I have been too mild with these ruffians. I'll break him across the pommel of my saddle as if he were a rotten spear."

The rain began to fall once more as he passed again through Kirby Stephen, but he paid slight heed to it and pushed on to Penrith, where he bought a day's provender, so that he would have no need to make request for food as he neared the danger spot. Just before darkness set in, the sky cleared somewhat, and he saw ahead of him the gloomy bulk of Carlisle castle. He turned aside from the main road, and before the night became black found quarters for himself in a barn that contained some fodder for his horse. He threw himself down on the fragrant hay and slept peacefully.

In the morning the rain was again falling steadily. He reconnoitered his position. There was no dwelling near, and he determined to let his horse rest all that day and the next night, so that he should be in trim for anything that might happen when the pinch came. A day more or less could make little difference with the effectual guarding of the bridge, which was now doubtless held as strongly as it could be. He was convinced that success must depend ultimately on the speed of his horse, and he could not enter the contest with an exhausted animal. Bruce was never so carefully tended as on the day before the crisis, and as his intelligent head turned toward his master, he seemed to know that something unusual was afoot. On the second day Armstrong thought it best not to enter Carlisle too early in the morning. He wished to mingle with a crowd and not to ride the streets alone. The second night in the barn, with the rest of the day and night before, had left both himself and his horse fit to face anything that might ensue. The day was fine; the clouds had cleared away, and the sun was shining on the sodden ground. When he came in sight of the main road he saw what appeared to be an army marching North. He halted at the cross-road, in doubt regarding his next move. The men, in a long line, were on foot, trudging sullenly, wearily forward, water-soaked and mud-covered. No man looked up or seemed to take an interest in anything but the dismal work in hand. Far on toward the gates of Carlisle rode a group of horsemen, and at the rear another squad of mounted men encouraged the laggards to keep up for a little longer. Armstrong sat on his horse until the latter company was abreast of him.

"That is Carlisle ahead, I hope," said one of the officers.

"Yes," answered Armstrong. "Is this the Manchester contingent?"

"Yes. Brutal weather we've had," growled the officer.

"It was that," assented William, cheerfully, falling into line with them, "but it seems on the mend."

"Aye, now that our march is finished."

"Oh, you are likely to go farther afield, across country, when you reach Carlisle."

"I suppose so," replied the officer, gruffly, not too good-natured over the prospect. No one asked Armstrong who he was, and the elaborate fiction he had prepared to account for himself was not called for. The troopers were worn out by their contest with the elements and the roads, and all curiosity was dead in them. There stood Carlisle in front, and that was enough. The foot soldiers struggled on, in no definite order of formation, each doing the best he could. The officers rode silent behind them. Thus they all marched into Carlisle without question, and in their company the man the army was seeking. After a slight delay and pause in the streets the new troops moved on to the castle. Armstrong found no difficulty in falling behind, being thus free of the town. He knew every turn of every street and lane in the place as well as he knew the inside of his own pocket. He resolved to ride leisurely to the bridge, cut through the guard, if it did not prove too strong, and then trust to the spur. The town was thronged with military, but no one paid the slightest attention to him. As he jogged along very nonchalantly, more contented with the prospect than a few days before he would have thought possible, Bruce awoke the echoes by neighing loudly.

"Now, old man, what did you that for?" whispered William.

He looked ahead and was stricken speechless for the moment by seeing Frances Wentworth on her horse, without doubt a prisoner, two troopers riding on either side of her, and a young officer in front. She had unquestionably seen him, for her brow was wrinkled with anxiety; but her eyes gazed steadily past him into the distance. As he made toward the party they flashed one look of appeal upon him, which said as plainly as words, "For Heaven's sake, ride on and do not recognize me!"—but the young man was oblivious to everything except the fact that she was in some trouble.

"Where are you going with this lady?" he demanded of the officer.

"You may well ask," said the man, in no accent of pleasure. "We have come across country to Carlisle under orders from one in authority, and now we must hale her back to Durham, where General Cromwell is stationed; and those are the orders of some one else."

"But it is all a mistake," cried William.

"That's what I'm telling you," said the man, with a short laugh.

"This lady is the sister of Captain Wentworth of our army."

"So she says. Others say she is the woman who was with the Scotch renegade. I know nothing of it and care less. I obey orders."

"Sir," said Frances, coldly, "I beg you not to interfere. It is a mistake that will be explained in due time, but these men must do as they are told. That much you should know."

Although her words were spoken harshly enough, her eloquent eyes were bringing him to his senses and a realization of the unwisdom and futility of his behaviour. Before he could speak again, a sharp voice behind him rang out: "Why are you loitering there? Get on with you!"

Without turning, he knew who the speaker was, and if he had not, the gleam of fear in the girl's eyes might have warned him of peril.

"This man questions my orders," said the officer.

"No man has a right to question your orders. Who is he?"

Armstrong was edging away, but De Courcy spurred the horse he rode in a semicircle to cut off his retreat. Instantly the Frenchman raised a shout that echoed through the streets of the town, and arrested every foot within hearing.

"The Scot! The Scot!" he roared. "Stop that man; never mind the woman. After him. Sound the signal and close the bridge. The thousand pounds are mine, by God!"

Now Bruce was doing his best down the main street of Carlisle. A dozen shots spattered fire harmlessly, and a big bell began to toll. Armstrong was well ahead of the troopers who followed him, and he gained ground at every stride. The pursuers were continually augmented from each lane and alley, and came thundering after the flying man like a charge of cavalry. A turn in the road brought the bridge in sight, and Armstrong saw it was guarded only at the end nearest him, and that merely by two lone pikemen. He would mow them down like grass, he said to himself, as he drew his sword.

"Stand aside," he yelled. "The Scot is loose, and we're after him."

The men jumped aside, glad they were not called upon to arrest such a progress as they beheld coming down upon them. It was apparently one of their own officers who commanded them, and there was neither time to think or question. As the horse's hoofs struck the bridge, the deep crash of a cannon boomed from the castle, and before the fugitive reached the centre there arose at the other end of the bridge—he could not guess from whence they came—a troop of horse, as if the thunder of the gun had called the company magically from the earth. Bruce stopped on the crown of the bridge, at a touch of the rein, quivering with excitement, raised his head, and gave a snort of defiance at the blockade ahead of him. Armstrong glanced back; the bridge had closed on him like a trap, both ends stopped by forces impossible for one man to contend against.

"That cannon-shot did it. Well planned," he growled to himself, his horse now drawn across the bridge, alert for the word of command whatever it might be. Below, the swollen Eden, lipping full from bank to bank, rolled yellow and surly to the sea. Right and left, at either end of the bridge, stood a mass of steel-clad men, impregnable as the walls of the castle itself. De Courcy sprang off his horse and advanced with a valour which Armstrong, sitting there, apparently calm, had not given him credit for.

"He's my man," he cried. "Shoot him dead if he raises his hand." Then to the Scot. "Surrender quietly. You have no chance. A score of muskets are turned on you."

"If they shoot, some of them will wing you. Better warn them not to fire," replied Armstrong mildly, as if proffering to a friend advice which did not concern himself.

"Do you surrender?"

"Come and take me, if you are anxious for the thousand pounds. It's worth the money."

The Frenchman hesitated, edging cautiously along the parapet, so that if his friends shot he would be as much as possible aside from the line of fire. Seemingly his confidence in their marksmanship had not been augmented by Armstrong's warning.

"If you raise your hand to a weapon," said De Courcy, "they will fire on you, and I cannot stop them. They will not wait my word."

"I know. I shall not raise my hand."

The Frenchman dashed forward and seized the bridle of Bruce.

"Come quietly," he shouted.

"I will," said Armstrong. He leaned forward; said sharply to his horse, "Over, my lad!" and smote him a rising blow on the shoulder with his open hand. The horse raised his powerful front, and stood poised for a moment like a statue, then launched himself into space. As De Courcy felt his feet leave the stones, he let go the rein and fell sprawling on the parapet, but Armstrong leaned over and grasped him by the loose folds of his doublet.

"Come down with me, you traitor!" he cried. There was a scream of terror, and the next instant the river roared in Armstrong's ears. When he came to the surface he shook his head like a spaniel, swept the water from his eyes, and looked aloft at the great bridge. The parapet was lined with troopers, all stricken motionless, as if they had been transformed to stone. De Courcy, one moment afloat, shrieked for help, then sank again. Armstrong knew that the paralysis on the bridge would not last long, and he turned his horse toward the bank of raw clay.

"No one in command up there, apparently," he muttered. "We must make the most of it, old man."

The panting horse, breathing laboriously, essayed the bank and slipped back. Armstrong let loose his sodden cloak and flung it on the flood, turning the horse that he might take the ascent at an angle. The crowd still stared at him as if it were a show they had come out to see. Bruce, his feet once more on firm ground, shook his mane and gave forth a wild whinny of delight. Now the voice of command came in a blast of anger from the bridge.

"After him, you fools! What are you staring at?"

"Too late, my lads, I think," ventured William, as he leaped his horse across the ditch that divided the fields from the road. Once the followers came near him, and he turned in his saddle, threatening them with his pistols, and they, forgetting that his powder was water-soaked, fell back.

The troopers found no difficulty in believing that a man who jumped his horse over Carlisle bridge into the Eden was directly aided by the devil, as had been rumoured, and they made no doubt the powder would soon dry on such a pit-scorched favourite as he. They felt sure he could put the pistols to deadly use in case of need.

From the moment Bruce struck his hoofs on the road the horses behind had no chance of overtaking him. They fell farther and farther to the rear, and at last the silvery Esk gleamed ahead, while all along, since pursuit grew hopeless, William had been feasting his eyes on the blue hills of Scotland. He walked his horse through the Esk, but it, too, had been swollen by the rains, and Bruce again had to swim for it before he reached the other side. William sprang to the ground, flung his arms round the neck of his sterling companion, laying his cheek against that of the horse.

"You've won the race, my boy. All the credit is to you, and Bruce, my lad, poets will sing of you." Then, with a choking in his throat, he knelt down and kissed the soil, the sensible horse looking on in wonder. As the young man rose to his feet and saw, on the other side of the Esk, the troopers lining up, his mood changed, and he laughed aloud. Drawing forth his leathern bottle, he held it aloft and shouted to them: "Come over, lads, and I'll give you a drink. Don't be feared; none o' the water got into this."

But the officer dared not cross the boundary, Cromwell's orders had been strict, so he and his men stood glum, making no response to the generous invitation.

"Well, here's to us a'," cried William, raising the bottle to his lips.

"And now, my friends," he continued, replacing the flask and springing into the saddle, "don't be so down in the mouth. You've seen a Scotchman run, which was more than your ancestors saw at Bannockburn."

And with that he rode for Traquair Castle.

CHAPTER VIII.—ACCOMPLISHMENT.

As evening drew on, the old warder of Traquair Castle beheld a sight that caused him to rub his eyes in the fear that they were misleading him. A horseman bearing the guise of a Roundhead trooper, his steel cap glittering, approached the ancient stronghold. That such a man dared set foot on Scottish soil and ride thus boldly to the home of the most noted Royalist on the Border seemed incredible, but the warder was not to be caught napping, and he gave orders that the gates be closed and guarded, for the Border was ever a land of surprises, and one must take all precaution. Doubtless this lone trooper had a company concealed somewhere, and was advancing to parley, although he carried no flag of truce. He came on with a fine air of indifference, and stopped when he found his way barred, sitting carelessly on his horse with an amused smile on his lips.

"What's yer wull, surr?" demanded the warder from the wall.

"That's it," replied the horseman.

"Whut's it? I dinna unnerstaun' ye."

"Wull's ma name," said the rider with an accent as broad as that of his questioner. "Wuz that no' whut ye were spierin'? Dinna staun glowerin' there, Jock Tamson, like an oolet or a gowk. Can ye no' see Ah'm English? Gang awa' and tell yer maister that a freen o' Crummle's at th' door an' craves a word wi' him."

"Dod!" cried the Bewildered warder, scratching his head, "if ye hae a tongue like that on ye since ye crossed the Border, ye've made the maist o' yer time."

"Is the Yerl o' Traquair in?"

"He's jist that."

"Then rin awa' an' gi'e ma message, for Ah'm wet an' tired an' hungry."

The warder sought Traquair in his library, where he sat, an anxious man, with many documents spread out on a table before him.

"Yer lordship, there's a soldier in the uniform of the English rebels at th' gates, wha says he's a freen o' Crummle's, and begs a word wi' ye."

"Ah!" said the Earl, frowning, "they've caught poor Armstrong, then, and now, in addition to our troubles, we'll need to bargain with that fiend Noll to save his neck. Everything is against us."

"He may be an Englisher, but he's got a Scotch accent as broad as th'

Tweed."

"He's one of our countrymen fighting for Cromwell, and therefore thought by that shrewd villain the better emissary. Bring him in."

"There may be others o' his like in hiding, ma Lord."

"Close the gates after him, then, and keep a strict watch. There's no danger on that score yet, but lippen to nothing. This man's just come to strike a bargain, an' I'm afraid we must dance to the tune he pipes. Bring him in."

When William and the warder came in together, a moment or two passed before the Earl recognized his visitor, then he sprang forward and held out both his hands.

"In God's name, Armstrong, is this you?" he cried. "What have they done to you? Save us all! Who has shorn and accoutred you like this?"

"The necessities of the chase, Traquair. This is a disguise, and although you saw through it, I'm happy to think I deluded Jock Tamson there."

"Losh!" cried Tamson, peering forward, "ye'll never threep doon ma throat that this is Wull Armstrong."

"Sir William, if you please, Tamson," corrected the new knight. "The title was bestowed upon me by his Majesty himself, and I shall expect that deference from the lower orders, Tamson, which the designation calls for. Still, Jock, I'll forgive your familiarity if you'll help me off with this helmet, that seems glued to my skull."

The old man grasped the edges of the steel cap with both his hands when Armstrong bent his head. He braced his foot against that of the helmet-wearer, and pulled with all his might, but his strength was unequal to the task.

"Lord pity us!" growled Will, "catch me ever putting my head in a trap like this again. I'll have to take it off with a boot-jack."

"Bring in Angus," laughed the Earl, "he'll pull either the helmet or the head off you."

The huge Angus came lumbering in after the warder, who went in search of him.

"Have you had your supper, Angus?" asked the Earl.

"Yes, ma lord."

"Then let us see what strength it's given you. Tug this iron pot from Armstrong's head."

Angus, bracing himself as the warder had done, jerked ineffectually several times.

"Pull, ye deevil," cried Armstrong. "Ye've no more strength than a three-year-old wean."

"Ah'm feart to thraw yer neck," protested Angus.

"Never mind the neck. Being hanged by Cromwell is as nothing to this. Pull, ye gomeral! Am I to go about with my head in a metal bucket all my life? Pull!"

Angus put forth his strength, and the helmet gave way with unexpected suddenness, whereupon Angus sat down on the floor with a thud like an earthquake, the steel cap in his lap. Traquair slapped his thigh and roared till the rafters rang.

"Will, you'll be an inch taller after that. I never saw the like of it. I've heard that a man's head grows with new honors placed upon him, but I had no idea it was so bad as that. Man, where's your hair? And did they chop it off with a battle-axe? If that's a fair example of barber's work in England, I'm glad I live in Scotland."

Armstrong rubbed his shorn head slowly with his open palm.

"A barber may have other qualities than expertness with the shears," he said.

"The trick of the shears is surely the chief equipment for the trade."

"Yes. You're in the right. My hair was cut in a stable-yard under the moonlight, with great haste and blunt blades. We will see what your own poll-man can do in still shortening the result. I have been hotly chased, Traquair, and hair-cutting was the least drawback that troubled me. I think my tailoring is even worse than my barbering, and there, also, you must stand my friend. Is the Castle tailor out of work?"

"My whole wardrobe is at your disposal, Will."

"Nothing in it would fit me, and I am a thought particular about a new dress, as I have lost all self-respect in this one. I may borrow a hat from you, if you have one of the latest fashion, with a fine feather on it."

"Aha! What's come over you, Will? Some lady in the Court of Charles? You didn't fash much over your clothes in the old days."

"I don't fash much now, as you may see by my array. Still, it is n't duds, but food that is the first necessity. I've had nothing all day but a hurried drink out of the Eden. It was as thick as brose, and about the same colour, but not so sustaining."

"They're preparing supper for you now, and I'll bear you company when it's ready. I'm eager to hear what befell. So the King knighted you. Deed, he might have gone farther than that and made you a marquis or a duke at the same cost."

"Oh, he offered me anything in his gift if I brought the commission safely through to you,—a promise that I'm thinking I'll never trouble him to redeem. Nevertheless, here's the packet, a little damp, but none the worse for that."

He placed the cause of all the trouble on the table, and Traquair turned it over and over in his hands, with no great delight in its possession, as the messenger thought. The Earl sighed as he opened it at last and slowly perused its contents in silence, laying it on the table again when he had finished.

"You're a wonderful man, William," he said. "If every one in Scotland did his duty as thoroughly as you do it, we would soon place the King on his throne again."

"Is there more trouble brewing?"

"More trouble, and the old trouble, and the new trouble. Every one pulling his own way, and in all directions, thinking only of himself, and never by any chance of the interests of the whole."

"May I tell Cromwell that? He seemed at some pains to intercept a billet that you receive but lightly."

"Tell Cromwell! You're never going to write to that scoundrel?"

"I intend to see him before the week is past."

"What! You're not such a fool as to put yourself in Cromwell's clutch again?"

"Just that."

"Will, I wonder at you. Angus got the steel bonnet off you with some work, but no man in Scotland can get Cromwell's rope off your neck if once you thrust your head through the noose."

"Cromwell's not such a fool as to hang me. If he did, it would but unite your wavering hosts like an invasion of Scotland."

"It would be a heavy price to pay for union, Will."

"The price will never be paid. Cromwell knows what he wants, and he does n't want me now, however anxious he was for my company this morning."

"Have you actually seen him?"

"I met him the first day I crossed the Border. I saw him once again, and I travelled over most of England on a pass from his own hand. Cromwell and I have a mutual respect for each other by this time, but there are some matters of difference between us that I think will best be settled by word of mouth, so I'm off day after to-morrow to foregather with him. I cannot go sooner, because my new gear will not be ready, and I want to give the General time to withdraw his troops from across the country, so that I may come on him in other fettle than as a prisoner."

"Who is the woman, Will? I knew you would go clean daft when you met her."

"Never you mind. As the Border is a land of nobility and romance, we will call her an Earl's daughter to please you."

"More like some peasant girl who assisted you to escape from your enemies."

"Well, whoever she is, Traquair, I'll make her Mrs. Armstrong when I get the chance."

"Lady Armstrong, you mean. You're forgetting your new dignity. Surely if the case stands thus you will ask the King to fulfill his promise and make you a baron at the least."

"That will I not. I'll trouble the badgered man no further."

"I know the ways of the sex better than you do, and I warrant you the lady will give you no rest until the title's yours, whenever she knows you have earned it and have had the offer of it."

"She thinks less of these things than I do, even."

"Then she is no peasant lass."

"I never said she was."

At this point, greatly to the delight of Armstrong, whose answers were becoming more and more short, his supper was announced, and Traquair with his arm over the shoulder of his guest, led him to the dining-room.

The tailor came when supper was finished, and measured his new customer, received minute directions concerning the garments, and retired protesting he would do his best in the limited time allowed him. The barber operated as well as he could on a head that began to nod in spite of the efforts of its owner. Sleep laid its heavy hand on Armstrong, and the voice of Traquair sounded distant and meaningless, something resembling the rush of Eden water in his ears, whereupon William nearly got those useful members cropped in earnest. At last he found himself in his room, and, for the first time since he left that hospitable mansion, enjoyed the luxury of lying between clean sheets with his clothes off. Then he slept as dreamlessly as his ancestors.

CHAPTER IX.—MATRIMONY.

A night, and a day, and a night rejuvenated the tired man and his horse. Clothed and in his right mind he was once more the gallant Borderer, ready to face whatever fortune had in store for him; on this occasion, so Traquair said, more superbly attired than ever had been the case before; but Armstrong held that this was merely interested praise of the Castle tailor. Traquair endeavoured to persuade him not to trust himself again on English soil, but his advice was unheeded, as is usually the fate of unasked counsel. Traquair wished him to take a bodyguard of a score or more, but Armstrong pointed out that unless he had an army at his back able to defeat Cromwell's forces all other assistance was useless. He risked everything upon his belief in Cromwell's common sense, and from this position nothing Traquair said could turn him. The Earl rode with him as far as the Esk, and there bade him good luck and God speed.

When Armstrong had once gone over a road, he needed no other guide than his own memory and instinct of direction. He made directly for the farmsteading where first he had been arrested, and found it deserted; then took the route over which his captors had conducted him, expecting to reach Corbiton Manor before darkness set in. This plan was frustrated by the fact that he had allowed too scant time for the cordon across the country to be withdrawn. Cromwell was indeed calling in his men, and massing them at Carlisle, Newcastle, and Hexham, which latter town Armstrong's own ancestors had frequently pillaged. He learned of this movement from chance wayfarers, and was on the alert not to fall within the scope of any marching company. There was evidently no secret about Cromwell's intentions, and the Scot surmised that the General wished his plans to be well spread over the land, and thus overawe the Northerners in any hostile projects they might think of undertaking, showing his readiness to crush them if they ventured to set foot across the Border.

About mid-day Armstrong caught sight of the first large body of men, and he was compelled to hide for several hours in a depression on the moor until they and the danger were past. This delay retarded his arrival at Corbiton Manor until after nightfall, when the full moon shone upon the ancient mansion, instead of the silver crescent which hung in the western sky when last he visited the place. It seemed incredible that the space of time could have been so short, for the events of a life were crowded into the interval. As he approached the ancient house, the challenge of a sentinel brought him to a stand, and called from the hall several officers.

"Is Cromwell here?" asked the newcomer.

"This is the headquarters of his Excellency, General Cromwell," said one of the officers, with some severity in his tone, a rebuke to the questioner's off-hand method of designation.

"That's the man I mean," replied Armstrong. "I never heard there were two of the name or the kind. Well; tell him that William Armstrong, who carried the commission from the King to Scotland, is here, and requires a private conference with him."

The strong moonlight was shining on the back of the horseman, and in the faces of the officers. The latter did not obey the injunction laid upon them, but their leader gave, instead, a brief command, and in a moment two dozen pikemen surrounded the rider, who laughed heartily and said: "My lads, you are too late. You should have done that trick several days since. Oliver will give you no thanks for it now. Go in and tell him I am here, and send some one to take charge of my horse while I talk with him."

The chief officer hesitated for a moment, then turned and disappeared within the mansion, while Armstrong dismounted and gave to the soldier who took his horse minute instructions touching the treatment of the animal.

"You are all good horsemen," said the visitor, in his most genial accents, "and will doubtless respect Bruce here, whatever you think of his master; for this is the charger that louped over the parapet of Carlisle bridge, and, after that, beat the best you had in your cavalry in a race for the Border. If your chief should come to a disagreement with me, take care of the horse at least, for you have n't another like him."

The horse was led away, palpably admired by all the men, for some of them stroked and patted his flank, speaking soothingly to him. William stood with his hands in his pockets, the centre of a ring of armed men, his gay dress in striking contrast to the more sober uniform of his guards. Cromwell was taking his time making up his mind, and the young man thought this delay was not an encouraging sign. He had thrust his head between the lion's jaws, and the minutes that passed before he could know whether the brute was going to bite or not were irksome to him especially as there was now nothing to do but await the issue. At last the officer reappeared, dismissed the guard, and said curtly to the prisoner: "Follow me."

Armstrong was ushered into the huge room which he remembered so well, and found Cromwell sitting alone at the table, as if he had never left it. Even the two candles stood where they had been placed before, but the face of the seated man seemed more inscrutable, more stern, than he recollected it. This was the leader of the Ironsides on the Northampton road, rather than the urbane man who had pretended to believe the story of the search for cattle.

Armstrong swept off his feathered hat most courteously as he approached the table, bowed, and, standing at ease on the spot he had formerly occupied, said: "Good evening, General!" The General lifted his heavy eyes to the cropped head, now glistening in the light, and although his firm mouth remained immobile, the slightest suspicion of a twinkle scintillated for one brief moment in his searching glance.

"Good evening. You wished to see me?"

"Yes, General, and have come from Scotland this very day for no other purpose."

"You are out of employment, perhaps, and are looking for re-engagement?"

"Well, General, if I was, you are the man I should come to for a recommendation. In a manner of speaking, you are in the right. I have been riding hard this while back for other folk, and now I have taken a bit of journey on my own account. You see my case is——"

"I will state the case," interrupted Cromwell, menacingly. "You stood here and lied to me."

"You sat there and did the same by me."

"You stood here and lied to me. You came as a spy, mixing with affairs that did not concern you."

"Pardon me, General. I took service for my King, and you will be good enough to remember that Charles is King of Scotland, even if it pleases you to forget that he is King of England, and that he will be, till he dies, your King as well as mine."

"He is King of Oxford solely."

"Very well. Let me tell you, you'll find that same Oxford a very hard nut to crack if you attempt to take it by assault. I went carefully around the fortifications, and would seek no better job than to hold it against you and your whole army. There would be many a cropped head low before you got mine in your clutches," and William passed his hand sympathetically over his denuded crown, as had become a custom with him. His questioner bent forward with more of eagerness than he had hitherto shown, all thought of the indictment he was heaping up seeming to pass from his mind.

"Where is its weakest spot?" he said, as one expert might seek counsel from another who had personal experience of the subject.

"That is the beauty of it. There is no weakest spot."

"Is there not? We shall never need to take it by assault, but if that were thought best, it might be attacked from the south."

Armstrong raised his eyes to the ceiling and meditated for a moment.

"I think you're right," he said, "but it would cost a'wheen o' men."

"Yes; better men than are within its walls, and they shall not be sacrificed. I can wait, and the King cannot. You delivered the King's message to Traquair?"

"Yes. That's what I went for."

"And you have the impudence to come to me, thinking I will allow you to return?"

"Say confidence, rather. I am very sure you will allow me to return."

"Yes, confidence is the word, but with a mixture of impudence as well; the malt and the hops. It never crossed your mind that it was a dungeon you were approaching?"

"I thought if you did anything, it would be hanging."

"And why not?"

"Because my death by rope would be just the little fillip that Scotland needs at the present moment. You thraw my neck, and the Scots are at yours before I am fairly happit in the ground."

"You look upon yourself as important to your countrymen, then?"

"I do nothing of the kind. Man, I wonder at both you and the King. Neither of you understand the Scottish nature in the least. If the King had any comprehension, he would have had the heather afire years since. A man may dawner about Scotland all his life, hungry and athirst, cold and in rags, getting fewer kickshaws than kicks, none paying heed or anything else to him, but let him die the death of a martyr, and his tired bones are more potent than ten thousand live men. Ma sang! I'd like to see ye hang me! There's poor Traquair, at his wit's end for discouragement through dissension among the people and their leaders. You hang me, and you've done the trick for him."

Cromwell leaned back in his chair, his lids partially closed, but they could not veil the look of admiration he cast upon the man standing before him, who spoke enthusiastically of his own execution as if it were rather a good joke on his opponent. For some moments the General kept silence, then he said abruptly:

"Will you take a commission in my army?"

"I will not."

"I thought you were a fighter."

"I am, but I prefer to engage under Traquair's banner if he raises it."

"Against me?"

"Just that."

"And you think I will let you go?"

"I'll take my oath on it."

"You are right. The way is clear to Scotland, to Oxford, or where you please. What have you come to me for?"

"For Frances Wentworth."

"I thought as much. In this I cannot oblige you. With you I have nothing to do, and you are at liberty. That wench of Wentworth's stands on a different footing, inasmuch as she has proved traitor to her own. I shall do nothing to injure her, but she shall taste captivity until she confesses her error."

"She is no traitor, but did well the work you set for her."

"I set no work for her. 'Twas given to her brother, and his folly brought her into the business."

"You gave your consent at Northampton; thus I say you set her to the task, and well she performed it. If your men had done your bidding as faithfully, I had never crossed the Esk."

"She connived at your escape from Lichfield, and elsewhere."

"True, but she was a free woman then, having fulfilled her duty to you."

"You are quibbling. She is a traitor, and more honest than you; she admits it."

"I say she is a true woman," cried Armstrong, red anger flushing his brow. The hot Border blood sprang into mastery for the first time during their controversy, and he failed to note that Cromwell remained cold as at the beginning, and might be negotiated with, if he had remembered the commander's resolve to enlist the Scot in his service. But before the General could give hint of a bargain, the impetuosity of the younger man left him only the choice of killing the Scot where he stood, or apparently succumbing to him, a most dangerous alternative had Armstrong to deal with one less schooled in the repression of his feelings than Cromwell. The ill-advised Borderer dropped his hat silently to the floor, flashed forth his sword, and presented it at his opponent's throat.

"They tell me you wear concealed armour,"—his voice was quiet in its intensity, almost a whisper,—"but that will not help you. No human power can avail you at this moment, for if you cry out my blade advances, and a bit of your backbone sticks to the point of it. You see I cannot help myself, but must kill you unless I get your promise."

Cromwell sat rigid, not a muscle of face or body moving. The sword was held as steady as a beam of the roof.

"I implore you to heed me," continued the young man, seeing the other did not intend to speak. "I implore you, as if I were on my bended knees before you, and my life in your hands, instead of yours in mine. Will you let the great affairs of state be jeopardized to thwart two lovers? With you slain, the King wins, for there is none in England can fill your place. Have you sons and daughters of your own that your heart goes out to? Think of them, and be kind to us."

"Will you marry the girl?"

"Surely, surely."

"Here, before you depart together?"

"Here and now, if there is one to knot us."

"You know that a promise given under coercion does not hold?"

"I know it well, but the word of General Cromwell is enough for me, once it is passed, however given."

"Then take down your sword; I promise, and am well rid of you both."

With a deep sigh of relief Armstrong sheathed his sword and lifted his hat from the floor. Cromwell rose from his chair and paced twice up and down the long room between the great moonlit windows and the table. He paused in his march, looked up at the dim gallery, and said: "Cobb, come down."

To Armstrong's amazement, who thought he had been alone with the General, he heard lurching heavy steps come clumping down the wooden stair, and a trooper, with primed musket in his hand, stood before his master.

"Cobb, why did you not shoot this man dead when you saw him draw his sword?"

"Because, Excellency, you did not give the signal."

"If I had, what then?"

"He was a dead man before he could move an arm, or your finger was on the table again."

"You have done well. That is what I like; exact obedience, and no panic. Keep your lips closed. Go and tell your colonel to come here."

The man withdrew, and Cromwell resumed his walk, making no comment on the brief dialogue. William blew a long whistle, then he laughed a little.

When the colonel came in, Cromwell turned to him and said: "Is that malignant brawler, chaplain to Lord Rudby, in the cells yet?"

"Yes, Excellency."

"Tell your men to clear out the chapel at once and light it. There are some stores in it, I think, and bring the reverend greybeard to me."

In a few moments the colonel returned, accompanied by an aged clergyman, who, despite his haggard and careworn look and bent shoulders, cast a glance of hatred at the General, which seemed to entitle him to the epithet Cromwell had bestowed upon him. To this silent defiance Cromwell paid no attention, but said to him:

"Sir, you may earn your liberty to-night by marrying two young people in the chapel."

"That will I not," returned the clergyman stoutly, "and all your tyranny cannot compel me to do so."

"The wench," continued Cromwell, unmoved, "you already know. She is Frances Wentworth, daughter of the late Earl of Strafford. The groom stands here before you; William Armstrong, a Scot, who has but lately carried a message from the man Charles, at Oxford, to Traquair on the Border. I should hang him, but he prefers the noose you can tie to the one my hands might prepare."

The old clergyman looked at Armstrong with an interest he had not displayed on entering the room.

"Have you, then, seen his gracious Majesty, the King?"

"Yes, reverend sir, and but a few days ago."

"And carried his message safe through these rebellious hordes now desecrating the land?"

"There was some opposition, but I won through, thanks to my horse."

"And thanks, no doubt, to your own loyal courage. God bless you, sir, and God save the King. The lady you have chosen is worthy of you, as you of her. In God's shattered temple, I will marry you, if its walls remain."

When the colonel came in with Frances, the girl turned a frightened look upon the group as she saw who stood there.

"Oh," she cried impulsively, "I told you not to come."

"'Tis you who are to obey, not he," said Cromwell harshly. "He has come for you. Will you marry him?"

The girl allowed her eyes to seek the floor, and did not answer him. Even in the candle-light her cheeks burned rosy red.

"Come, come," cried Cromwell impatiently, "yes, or no, wench."

"I will not have her so addressed by any," spoke up Armstrong, stoutly stepping forward; but the girl flashed a glance from her dark eyes on the commander.

"Yes," she said, with decision, then directed her look on her lover, and so to the floor again.

"Are there candles in the chapel?"

"Yes, Excellency," replied the colonel.

"Bring some of the officers,—I think witnesses are needed,—and your regimental book, if there is signing to be done. 'Twill hold them as fast as the parish register, I warrant." Then to the clergyman, "Follow me, sir, and the rest of you."

With that Cromwell strode out and led the way to the chapel, so hastily converted from a storehouse to its former purpose. The old divine took his place with the young people before him, the group of officers in the dimness near the door. Cromwell, however, stood near the girl.

"Slip off one of your rings and give it to this pastor," he whispered to her. "We are short of such gear here, and I doubt if your man ever thought of it."

Frances, without a word, selected from the number on her fingers that which had been her mother's wedding-ring, and handed it to the clergyman.

"Dearly beloved, we are gathered together here in the sight of God, and in the face of this congregation, to join together this Man and this Woman in holy Matrimony; which is an honourable estate, instituted of God in the time of man's innocency, signifying unto us the mystical union that is betwixt Christ and his Church; which holy estate Christ adorned and beautified with his presence, and first miracle that he wrought in Cana of Galilee."

As the sonorous words resounded in the ancient chapel, the old man straightened himself, the former anger in his face gave way to a benignant expression, and his attitude took on all the grave dignity of his calling. He went on with the service until he came to the words:

"Who giveth this woman to be married to this man?"

Cromwell stepped forward and said brusquely, "I do."

The clergyman seemed to have forgotten the Commander's presence, and now paused when it was recalled to him; then he went on to the end, and added, in a voice trembling with emotion: "God bless you, my children, sworn to love and cherish each other in this time of hatred and war. May you live to see what my aged eyes may never behold,—peace upon this distracted land, and the King upon an unchallenged throne."

"Amen, and amen!" said the deep voice of Cromwell, "provided the word 'righteous' is placed before the word 'King'."

Once more on horseback, and clear of Corbiton Manor, her hand stole into his.

"Well," he said, "which way?"

"If you are willing, I will take the way known to me, and lead you to my home; to-morrow you may take the way known to you, and lead me to yours."

"Frances, I am ready to follow wherever you lead." And so they went forth together in the glamour of the moonlight.

THE END

YOUNG LORD
STRANLEIGH

CHAPTER I—THE KING'S MOVE IN THE CITY

IT was shortly after nine o'clock in the morning that young Lord Stranleigh of Wychwood, in a most leisurely fashion, descended the front steps of his town house into the street. The young man was almost too perfectly dressed. Every article of his costume, from his shiny hat to the polished boots, was so exactly what it should he, that he ran some danger of being regarded as a model for one of those beautiful engravings of well-dressed mankind which decorate the shops of Bond-Street tailors. He was evidently one who did no useful work in the world, and as a practical person might remark, why should he, when his income was more than thirty thousand pounds a year? The slightly bored expression of his countenance, the languid droop of his eyelids, the easy but indifferent grace of motion that distinguished him, might have proclaimed to a keen observer that the young man had tested all things, and found there was nothing worth getting excited about. He was evidently a person without enthusiasm, for even the sweet perfection of his attire might be attributed to the thought and care of his tailor, rather than to any active meditation on his own part. Indeed, his indolence of attitude made the very words "active" or "energetic" seem superfluous in our language. His friends found it difficult, if not impossible, to interest Lord Stranleigh in anything, even in a horse race, or the fling of the dice, for he possessed so much more money than he needed, that gain or loss failed to excite a passing flutter of emotion. If he was equipped with brains, as some of his more intimate friends darkly hinted, he had hitherto given no evidence of the fact. Although well set up, he was not an athlete. He shot a little, hunted a little, came to town during the season, went to the Continent when the continental exodus took place, always doing the conventional thing, but not doing it well enough or bad enough to excite comment. He was the human embodiment of the sentiment: "There is nothing really worth while."

In marked contrast to him stood, undecided, a man of his own age, with one foot on the lower stone step which led up to the front door of his lordship's town house. His clothes, of undistinguished cut, were worn so carelessly that they almost gave the impression of being ready-made. His flung-on, black slouch hat suggested Western America or Southern Africa. His boots were coarse and clumsy.

But if the attire was uninspiring, the face merited, and usually received, a second glance. It was smooth-shaven, massive and strong, tanned to a slight mahogany tinge by a more eager sun than ever shines on England. The eyes were deep, penetrating, determined, masterful.

Lord Stranleigh's delicate upper lip supported a silken mustache carefully tended; his eyes were languid and tired, capable of no such gleam of intensity as was now turned upon him from the eyes of the other.

"I beg your pardon, sir, but are you Lord Stranleigh of Wychwood?"

His lordship paused on the upper steps, and drawled the one word "Yes."

"My name is Peter Mackeller, and the Honorable John Hazel gave me a letter of introduction to you, saying I should probably catch you in at this hour. It seems he underestimated your energy, for you are already abroad."

There was an undercurrent of resentment in the impatient tone Mackeller had used. He was manifestly impressed unfavorably by this modern representative of a very ancient family, but the purpose he had in view caused him to curb his dislike, although he had not been tactful enough to prevent a hint of it appearing in his words. If the other had gathered any impression of that hint, he was too perfectly trained to betray his knowledge, either in phrase or expression of countenance. The opinion of his fellows was a matter of complete indifference to him. A rather engaging smile stirred the silken mustache.

"Oh, Jack always underestimates my good qualities, so we won't trouble about his note of introduction. Besides, a man cannot read a letter in the street, can he?"

"I see no reason against it," replied the other sharply.

"Don't you really? Well, I am going across to my club, and perhaps as we walk along together, you will be good enough to say why you wish to see me."

306

Lord Stranleigh was about to proceed down another step when the other answered "No" so brusquely that his lordship paused once more, with a scarcely perceptible elevation of the eyebrows, for, as a rule, people did not say "No" to Lord Stranleigh of Wychwood, who was known to enjoy thirty thousand pounds a year.

"Then what do you propose?" asked his lordship, as though his own suggestion had exhausted all the possibilities of action.

"I propose that you open the door, invite me in, and give me ten minutes of your valuable time."

The smile on his lordship's countenance visibly increased.

"That's not a bad idea," he said, with the air of one listening to unexpected originality. "Won't you come in, Mr. Mackeller?" and with his latchkey he opened the door, politely motioning the other to precede him.

Young Mackeller was ushered into a small room to the left of the hall. It was most severely plain, paneled somberly in old oak, lit by one window, and furnished with several heavy leather-covered chairs. In the center stood a small table, carrying a huge bottle of ink, like a great dab of black metal which had been flung while soft on its surface, and now, hardened, sat broad and squat as if it were part of the table itself. On a mat lay several pens, and at one end of the table stood a rack such as holds paper and envelopes, but in this case of most minute proportions, displaying three tiers, one above the other, of what appeared to be visiting cards; twelve minute compact packs all in all, four in each row.

"This," said Lord Stranleigh, with almost an air of geniality, "is my business office."

The visitor looked around him. There were no desks; no pillars of drawers; no japanned-metal boxes that held documents; no cupboards; no books; no pictures.

"Pray be seated, Mr. Mackeller," and when the young man had accepted the invitation, Lord Stranleigh drew up opposite to him at the small table with the packets of cards close to his right hand.

"And now, if you will oblige me with Jack's letter, I will glance over it, though he rarely writes anything worth reading."

Mackeller handed him the letter in an open envelope. His lordship slowly withdrew the document, adjusted an eyeglass, and read it; then he returned it to the envelope, and passed it back to its owner.

"Would it be too much if I asked you to replace it in your pocket, as there is no waste-paper basket in this room?"

Mackeller acted as requested, but the frown on his broad brow deepened. This butterfly seemed to annoy him with his imperturbable manner, and his trifling, finicky, childish insincerity. Confronted with a real man, Mackeller felt he might succeed, but he had already begun to fear that this bit of mental thistle-down would evade him, so instead of going on with his recital, he sat there glowering at Lord Stranleigh, who proved even more of a nonentity than the Honorable John Hazel had led him to believe. He had been prepared to meet some measure of irresponsible inanity, but not quite so much as this. It was Lord Stranleigh himself who broke the silence.

"What do you want?" he asked, almost as if some of his opponent's churlishness had hypnotically permeated into his own being.

"Money," snapped the other shortly.

"Ah, they all do," sighed his lordship, once more a picture of indolent nonchalance.

He selected from the rack beside him four cards, one from each of the little packs in the lower range. These he spread face upward on the table before him.

"I never trouble about money," said his lordship, smiling.

"You probably don't need to, with thirty thousand a year," suggested Mackeller.

"Ah, that's exaggerated," explained his lordship. "You forget the beastly income tax. Still, I was not referring to the amount; I merely wished to explain my methods of dealing with it. Here are the names and addresses of four eminent solicitor persons in the city. There is little use of my keeping four dogs and barking myself, is there? I've really twelve dogs altogether, as represented in this cardcase, but one or other of these four will doubtless suit our purpose. Now, this firm of solicitors attends to one form of charity."

"I don't want charity," growled Mackeller.

"Quite so. I am merely explaining. This firm attends to all the charities that are recognized in our set; the hospitals, the—well whatever they happen to be. When applied to personally in these matters, I write my name on the card of these solicitors, and forward it. Application is then made to them. They look into the matter, and save me the fatigue of investigation. The next firm"—holding up a second card—"deals with charities that are our of our purview; halfdays at the seaside, and that sort of thing. Now I come to business. This firm"—showing the third card—"looks after permanent investments, while this"—lifting the fourth—"takes charge of anything which is speculative in its nature. The applicant receives the particular card which pertains to his particular line of desire. He calls upon the estimable firm of solicitors, and either convinces them, or fails: gets his money, or doesn't. So you see, my affairs are competently transacted, and I avoid the emotional strain of listening to explanations which probably I have not the mental grasp of business to understand. Now, which of these four cards may I have the pleasure of autographing for you?"

"Not one of them, my lord," replied Mackeller. "The Honorable John Hazel said that if you would listen to me, he thought I might interest you."

"Oh, impossible," drawled his lordship, sitting back languidly in his chair.

"Yes, he said it would be a hard task, but I am accustomed to difficulties. I asked you, as we came in, to give me ten minutes. Will you do it?"

"Why," protested his lordship, "we have already spent ten minutes at least."

"Yes, fooling with cards."

"Ah, I'm more accustomed to handling cards than listening to a financial conversation; not these kind of cards, either."

"Will you, for the sake of John Hazel, who tells me he is a friend of yours, give me ten minutes more of your time?"

"What has Jack Hazel to do with this? Are you going to share with him? Is he setting you on to me for loot, and then do you retire into a dark corner, and divide? Jack Hazel's always short of money."

"No, we don't divide, my lord. Mr. Hazel has been speculating in the city, and he stands to win a bit if I can pull off what I'm trying to do. So, if you agree to my proposal, he will prove a winner, so will I, so will you, for you will share in the profits."

"Oh, but I don't need the money."

"Well, we do."

"So I understand. Why doesn't Jack confine himself to the comparative honesty of the dice? What does he want to muddle about in the city for?"

"I suppose because he hasn't got thirty thousand a year."

"Very likely; very likely. Yes, that strikes me as a sufficient explanation. All right, Mr. Mac-keller, take your ten minutes, and try to make your statement as simple as possible. I hope statistics do not come into it. I've no head for figures."

"My father," began the young man, with blunt directness, "is a stockbroker in the city. The firm is Mackeller and Son. I am the son."

"You don't look to me like a stockbroker. That is, what I've always expected such a person to be: I've never met one."

"No, I'm in reality a mining engineer."

"But, my dear sir, you have just said you were a stockbroker."

"I said my father was."

310

"You said Mackeller and Son, and that you were the son."

"Yes, I am a partner in the firm, but, nevertheless, a mining engineer."

"Do stockbrokers make mining engineers of their sons?"

"One of them did. My father is a rigidly honest man, and preferred me to be an engineer." His lordship's eyebrows again elevated themselves.

"An honest man and a stockbroker? Ah, you do interest me, in spite of my pessimism."

"The great difficulty," went on Mackeller, unheeding, "is to obtain an honest estimate of the real value of any distant mining property which is offered for sale in London. There has never been a mining swindle floated on the public which has not had engineer's reports by men of high standing, showing it to possess a value which after events proved quite unreliable. So my father made me a mining engineer, and before he touches any property of this nature, or advises his clients to invest, he compels the promoters to send me out to the mine, and investigate."

"I see," said his lordship, with almost a glimmer of comprehension in his eyes. "Rather a shrewd old man, I take it. He protects himself and his customers, provides a good livelihood for you, his son, and that at the expense of the promoters. Excellent. Go on."

For the first time young Peter Mackeller smiled. "Yes," he said, "my father is very shrewd. He comes from the North, but for once he has got nipped, and the next few hours will decide whether the accumulations of a lifetime are swept away or not. Indeed," he continued, glancing at his watch, "that will be decided within eight minutes, depending on whether I interest you or not."

"Continue," commanded his lordship.

"Early in the year a property called the Red Shallows, situated in West Africa, was brought to him by a syndicate of seven men, able, but somewhat unscrupulous financiers. Their story appeared incredible on its face, for it was no less than that the gold was on the surface, in estimated value a thousand times the amount for which they wished the company formed. They wished my father to underwrite the company for a hundred thousand pounds, and they stipulated that the shares should be sold, not by public subscription, but taken up privately among my father's clients. Afterwards, when the value of the property was fully proved, there would be an immense flotation running into millions, and the profit of this my father was to share."

"Pardon my interruption," said his lordship.

"If what these men stated was true, why didn't they send some one with a basket, and gather the gold they needed, without going to any stockbroker and sharing with him."

"That, my lord, is practically what my father thought, although, of course, he did not believe a word of their story. Still, he understood that these men were not mine magnates in the proper sense of the word; they were merely financiers, speculators, who did not wish to wait for the full development of their property, but simply intended, so they said, to go as far as was necessary to convince the public that this was an even bigger thing than the wealthiest mine of the Rand, and so loot their gold, not from the bosom of the earth, but from the pockets of the British public; but, as I have said, he did not believe a word of their story. However, he made the usual proviso that they should send me out there, and the seven men instantly placed in his hands the necessary amount for my expenses, and I sailed away."

"Why should sane financiers spend good money when they knew they would be found out if they were not telling the truth?"

"Well, my lord, that thought occurred to both my father and myself. I reasoned it out in this way. These seven men had acquired the goldfields from a party of explorers, or from a single explorer, who had discovered it. They probably paid very little money to the discoverer, perhaps not buying it outright, but merely securing an option. Whoever had parted with his rights had evidently succeeded in convincing the syndicate that he spoke the truth. Whether the syndicate hadn't sufficient capital to develop the property, or preferred to risk other people's cash in opening the mine, I do not know, but they evidently thought it worth while to spend some of their own money and send me out there, that they might receive an independent and presumably honest opinion on its value. Be that as it may, there was no exposure forthcoming. The property proved even richer than they had stated. It so seldom happens in the city that anything offered for sale greatly exceeds in value the price asked for it, that the members of the syndicate were themselves surprised when they read my report. It had been arranged, and the document signed before I left England, that my father should get for them not less than fifty thousand pounds nor more than a hundred thousand, for working capital to send out an expedition, buy machinery, and so forth. Now, however, the syndicate proposed that the company should be formed for something like a million pounds. My father pointed out to them the impossibility of getting this sum, for the property was in a locality not hitherto known as a gold-bearing region. Then again, my own standing as a mining engineer carried no particular weight. Although my father believed implicitly in my reports, I was so lacking in celebrity in my profession, it would be folly to attempt to raise any considerable sum on my unsupported word, and rather unsafe to make this discovery public by sending out more eminent engineers. Besides, as I have said, the papers were all signed and stamped, and my father, having a good deal of northern stubbornness in his nature, insisted on the project being carried out as originally projected, so the syndicate was compelled to postpone its onslaught upon the purse of the public.

"My father's compensation was to be a large allotment of paid-up shares in the company, but in addition to this, so great was his faith in my report he himself subscribed, and paid for stock to an extent that rather narrowed his resources. However, his bank agreed, the manager knowing him well, to advance money on his Red Shallows as soon as they had received a quotation on the Stock Exchange.

"The flotation was carried out successfully, my father's friends subscribing largely on his mere word that Red Shallows was a good thing. Only fifty thousand pounds' worth of shares were sold, that being considered enough to purchase the machinery, and send out men in a chartered steamer, with materials for the erection of whatever buildings and appliances as were supposed to be necessary. The rest of the stock was held by the syndicate,

313

with the exception of the amount allotted to my father as compensation for his work. I was to have been appointed engineer of the mine, and had gone to Southampton to charter a suitable steamer, when suddenly an attack was opened upon the new company. Several of the financial papers led this attack, saying that the public had been grossly misled; that there was no gold or other minerals within hundreds of miles of the spot, and that all who had invested in the venture would lose their money. Immediately after this the syndicate dumped its shares on the market, and their price went down with a run."

"Wait a moment," interrupted his lordship. "I think I have given you more than the promised ten minutes, but I believe I have been able to follow you up to the present point. Now, I should like to ask a question or two. Didn't the seven men know that throwing their shares on the market would lower the price?"

"Oh, they knew it perfectly well."

"Then why should they wish to disparage their own property?"

"To freeze out my father and his friends."

"How could they do that if your father and his friends refused to sell?"

"As a matter of fact many of my father's friends have sold. They became frightened, and preferred to lose part rather than the whole. You see, my father had placed every security he possessed into the bank, but with the persistent pounding down of the stock it's going lower and lower every day; in fact, it is unsalable at the present moment. The bank has called upon him to put in further securities, or cash, otherwise it will sell all his possessions for what they will bring."

"But in ruining your father, does not this syndicate ruin itself?"

"No. The financiers have held their annual meeting, appointed a president, board of directors, and all that, and this board is securely in office for a year. As soon as my father and his friends are wiped out the syndicate will quietly buy back the stock at a much lower price than that at which they sold it, and even in crushing my father they will have made a pot of money for themselves."

"Killing two birds with one stone, eh? Isn't there such a thing as gratitude in the City at all?"

"I fear, my lord, there isn't very much of it."

"What amount of money do you need to protect your father's stock?"

"I think five thousand pounds would do."

"I don't pretend to know much about business, Mr. Mackeller, but it seems to me that would merely be the thin end of the wedge. Suppose they keep on, and lower the price of stock still further? Should not I need to put a second five thousand pounds into your hands to protect the first?"

"That is true, Lord Stranleigh, but I don't see how the shares can go much lower than they are. They closed yesterday at two and nine per one-pound share. But in any case the bank will stand by my father if it can. The manager believes in him, although this official, of course, must look after his own employers, but the very fact that my father can put in five thousand pounds this morning will do much to maintain his credit with the manager, and within a very few days we will have time to turn round. I have already seen one or two financiers, and told them what the property is, but they are city-wise, and shake their heads at what they regard as an attempt to unload upon them. So I went to Mr. Hazel, and asked him for an introduction to some one who was rich, and who knew nothing of the ways of the city."

For the first time during the interview, his lordship leaned back and laughed a little.

"You are playing on my ignorance, then?"

"No, I thought perhaps I could get you to believe me."

His lordship did not say whether he believed him or not, but he pressed a button underneath the desk, and there entered to him a solemn-faced man, who stood like a statue, awaiting orders.

"Perkins, will you bring me four check books?"

"Yes, my lord."

"And, Perkins, tell Henri to be at the door with my red automobile within six minutes."

"Yes, my lord."

The man departed, and returned a few moments later, placing on the desk four very thin check books, finally retiring as noiselessly as he had entered.

"An ordinary check book," said his lordship to Mackeller, "does so distort one's coat when placed in an inside pocket, that I cause my books to be made with only one check each inside. I shall now write you out one for five thousand pounds, so that I shall not need to carry its cover with me."

With great leisureliness the young man wrote out a check, tore it from its attachment, and handed it to Mackeller.

"I lend this to you, but I don't think it will be of the slightest use, you know."

"I am quite positive it will protect my father's stock, my lord, and as I am sure that stock will be worth a hundred sovereigns on the pound, if you will accept half my father's holding for this check, I can promise you this will be the biggest day's work you've ever done."

"Ah, that wouldn't be saying very much. Of course, as I told you, I don't pretend to understand business, but where the weak point in your defense lies seems to be in this. Your seven wise men have a year to play about in. I think you said the president and board of directors had been elected only the other day?"

"Yes, my lord, that is so."

"Very well, don't you see they have nearly twelve months during which they can still further press down your stock. The bank will tire of holding what they consider worthless securities, and unless your father can get enough money to redeem all that he has placed in the bank, this five thousand will not even prove a stop-gap."

"I don't agree with your lordship. You see, I shall now keep hammering away on my side. I shall print my report, and post it to every big financier in the city. I shall tell the whole sordid story of this syndicate's action."

"People won't believe you, Mackeller."

"A great many will not, but several may, and these will say 'The stock is so cheap, we might as well take a flutter on a quantity of it.' Then the members of the syndicate are shrewd enough to know that they will excite curiosity, and that some other engineer may be sent out to the property. No, I am convinced that if they do not manage to ruin my father before the end of next week, they will never risk what they now know to be a valuable property by letting its shares lie round loose for anyone to pick up."

"Ah, you are optimistic, I see. That's because you have been out in the open so much, instead of haunting your father's office."

At this moment the arrival of the automobile was announced, and his lordship rose slowly to his feet.

"I'm going to give you a lift as far as your father's office, and I want you to introduce him to me. I have been looking at this question merely from the mining engineer's standpoint. I should like to know what the city point of view is, and that I shall get from your father, if he is the honest man you say he is. So we will run down into the city together. I suppose the sooner my check is in your bank the better."

"Yes, the bank opens at ten, and it is past that hour now."

"We have taken a little more than our ten minutes," said his lordship, beaming on his guest with that inane smile of his, as they stepped together into the tonneau of a very large red automobile, which was soon humming eastward.

Into the private room of the stockbroker, Mac-keller ushered Lord Stranleigh of Wychwood, and there they found at his desk a rugged-faced, white-haired, haggard-looking man, who glanced up at them with lowering brows.

"I've got five thousand pounds," said the son at once.

"Then run with it to the bank."

"I will, as soon as I have introduced to you Lord Stranleigh of Wychwood. Your lordship will excuse me, I am sure."

"Oh, yes. I stipulated for your absence, you remember, because I do not in the least rely upon your plan," but the young man had departed before his lordship's sentence was finished.

The elder Mackeller looked intently at the newcomer. Being offered a chair, his lordship sat down.

"Is it from you that my son got the money?"

"Yes."

"If you did not believe in his plan, why did you give him the cash?"

"Well, Mr. Mackeller, that is just the question I have been asking myself. I suppose I rather took to him, and in spite of my determination not to, I became interested in the story he told me. I think your seven syndicate men must be rather exceptional, are they not?"

"No. I am exceptional in allowing myself to be caught like a schoolboy."

"I am quite unversed in the ways of the city, Mr. Mackeller, and I should like to know the modus operandi of a case like this. Are your seven men personally selling their stock?"

"How do you mean personally? They don't go on the market and trade, of course."

"Then they must employ some one else?"

"Oh, they are employing a score of brokers, all offering the shares with no takers."

"Do you know these brokers, Mr. Mackeller?"

318

"Every man jack of them."

"Are they enemies of yours?"

"There is neither enmity nor friendship in the city, Lord Stranleigh."

"Your most intimate acquaintance, then, would smash you up all in the way of business?"

"Of course."

"What a den of wild beasts you are!"

"Yes, I have long thought so, and, indeed, with this transaction I had intended to withdraw from the business and settle on my farm. You see, I did not bring up my son—he's the only boy I have—to this business, but unluckily I got nipped just at the moment I intended to stop, as is so often the case. I expected that my holding in this mine would leave me not only well off, but rich, for I have the utmost confidence in my son's report, and my certainty of a fortune caused me to relax my natural caution at exactly the moment when I should have been most wide awake."

"Do you think the five thousand pounds will clear you?"

"I don't know. There's been a panic among those whom I induced to go in with me on this deal, but if I say it myself, my reputation is good, and I think if I can hold on for a week or two longer, the tide will turn. All my life I have endeavored to conduct this business strictly on a truth-telling plan, and that is bound to tell in my favor the moment the panic ceases."

"Do you mean, then, Mr. Mackeller, that the hammering of this mine has caused a financial panic in the city?"

"Oh, no, no! When I refer to a panic, I mean only among those few that have gone in with me; that believed me when I told them this was one of the best things I ever had offered to me. The Red Shallows flotation is too small an affair to cause even a flutter in the city, yet it threatens to grind me to pieces."

"There are, you say, twenty stockbrokers selling these shares, and you know their names. Where do they offer the shares?"

"On the Stock Exchange, in their offices, in the street, anywhere."

"Is there another twenty stockbrokers whom you could trust?"

"Yes."

"Suppose at twelve o'clock to-day, exactly to the minute, your twenty went to the offices of the other twenty, would they find in those offices some one to sell them this stock?"

"Yes."

"Even if the principal were absent?"

"Yes."

"Before selling, would the syndicate score of stockbrokers communicate with each other, or with their principals?"

"I don't know. It would depend on their instructions."

"Suppose they refused to sell when a bona fide offer was made?"

"Then the stock would instantly rise, and your five thousand pounds would not be needed. I see what you mean, Lord Stranleigh. You are going to make what they call a bluff. But, you see, they'd instantly unload the stock on you. They wouldn't refuse to sell."

"Ah, I was afraid they would. Very well, Mr. Mackeller, take this commission from me, the first I have ever given in the city. I am more accustomed to gambling in my club, or at Monte Carlo, so I must depend on you to look after the details. Quietly but quickly select your twenty men; give them carte blanche, but make it a sure proviso that they each attack the stockbroker you direct them to, at exactly the same moment. Let there be no intercommunication if possible, and tell your twenty to buy everything in sight so far as the Red Shallows are concerned."

"But, my lord, that may take a fortune, and the sellers will insist on immediate payment."

"They will get it, Mr. Mackeller. I am naturally a plunger, and this game fascinates me, because I don't understand it."

"I think you understand it a great deal better than you pretend, my lord, but this may require half a million of money."

"Very well. Get whatever papers ready that are necessary to protect you. I'll place the money at your disposal, and we ought to have all the stock that's for sale by ten minutes after twelve. Your son and I have been doing business on a ten-minutes' basis, but in this case we'll allow half an hour, and see what happens."

The elder Mackeller looked sternly at this dapper young man of the bandbox, so beautiful, so neat, so debonair, so well-groomed, and the young man became so uncomfortable under the fierce scrutiny of those hawklike eyes, that his own drooped modestly like those of a girl, and with the thin, elegant glove which he held loosely in his right hand Stranleigh flicked an invisible particle of dust from his trouser leg.

One need not be deeply versed in human nature to understand the temptation which now assailed the gray-haired stockbroker. It was as if a fawn-colored dove had made an appeal to a bald eagle that had swooped down from its eyrie in the crags where its young lay starving. It was as if a bleating lamb, all alone, were making courteous suggestions to a hungry wolf. Here was reproduced the situation of which city men dream when they enjoy a good night. Here, into the den of a stockbroker had innocently walked a West-end clubman, a titled person, almost shamefully rich, concealing beneath the culture of the colleges an arrogance and an ignorance equally colossal. Here was a fowl to be plucked, and its feathers were not only abundant but of the most costly eiderdown nature, and here the astute Mackeller had the victim entirely to himself, with none to protect or interfere. The aged stockbroker, wise in the ways of the city, and yet but now entrapped by them, drew a long breath and heaved a deep sigh ere he spoke.

"Lord Stranleigh," he said at last, with severity, "it is my duty to warn you that you are putting your foot into a quagmire which may be so bottomless that it will overwhelm you. No man can say what this syndicate has up its sleeve, and once you involve yourself, you may be drawn in and stripped of all your possessions, great as I am told they are. You have given a check for five thousand pounds to my boy, and you say it is because you believed in him. That expression touches my flinty heart. I believe in him, and this belief is about everything of value I retain in the world to-day. Now, if you wish to protect that five thousand, do it by giving him another five, or another. My boy is all I've got left. I'm fighting for him more than for myself. Now here are you, about his own age, yet completely inexperienced in financial trickery, so I cannot allow you to walk blindly into this financial turmoil."

The young man looked up at the speaker, and his smile was singularly winning. The usual vacant expression of his countenance had given place to pleasurable animation.

"But you are experienced, Mr. Mackeller?"

"Yes, and see where my experience has landed me. I'm up to the neck, yes, to the very lips, in this foul quagmire; a bankrupt at a word from my banker."

"Are you a college man, Mr. Mackeller?"

"No."

"Perhaps you have little faith in a college training?"

"I have none at all for a practical man. It is the worst training in the world for a person who is to be engaged in business."

"In that case, Mr. Mackeller, I hesitate to cite a historical instance which occurred to my mind when your son was talking to me of your syndicate of seven. As the incident is six hundred years old, it is unlikely to impress a modern city man. Nevertheless, there was once upon this earth a syndicate of seven much more powerful and important than your johnnies. The chief of this syndicate was Jaques de Molay, Grand Master of the Templars, and the other six were his powerful, pious officers. They were arrogant people, and their wealth was enormous. Kings and noblemen had deposited their treasures with the Templars, the bankers of that time, and the Order was so rich it had become a menace to the world. Why, your seven nonentities, with which you try to frighten me, are mere helpless puppets compared with those seven giants of finance, and besides money this notable seven had an armed force of veterans at their back before whom even a king with his army might tremble. But Philippe le Bel, King of France, did not tremble. He worked in on the seven the twelve-o'clock rule that I am recommending to you. At high noon, on the 13th October, 1307 (please note the fatal conjunction of the two thirteens) every Templar in France was arrested. He gave them no chance of communicating with each other. The army of the Templars lay helpless and officerless. The wealth of the Templars was at the mercy of the king. The syndicated seven were burned at the stake in Paris.

"I imagine that your son thought my attention wandered two or three times during his narrative. I saw him set his jaw as one who says 'I will interest this man in spite of his brainlessness.' But I was thinking of the magnificent simultaneousness of the king's action, and I have no doubt the Mackeller of his day warned him of his danger in meddling with the Templars. An unholy desire filled me to try this six-century-old method, the king's move, as we would say at chess, on our modern and alert city. I have some loose cash in the bank, and don't need to sell any securities. For the last ten years my income has been thirty thousand pounds annually, and very seldom have I spent more than five thousand of that sum in one twelvemonth. My automobile is at your door, and at your disposal. You and I will drive first to my bankers, and arrange that there will be no hitch so far as cash is concerned; then I shall take a cab to my club. Telephone number, 15760 Mayfair. Just note that down, please. Now what are the shares of Red Shallows selling for this morning?"

"They opened at two shillings and sevenpence on the pound share, but have dropped several points since."

"Ah, well, a few hundred thousand pounds will buy quite a quantity of half-crown shares, and if we act simultaneously, as the king struck, we will acquire everything in sight before the stuff has time to rise. Come along, Mr. Mackeller, there's not a moment to lose. If you organize this sortie in silence and effectively, you will show the savage seven there's life in the old dog yet."

At ten minutes after one that day a large red automobile drew up in front of the Camperdown Club on Pall Mall, and Mackeller with his son stepped out of it. Lord Stranleigh met them in the hall apparently cool and unexcited, but he was coming away from the tape machine, which was recording that Red Shallows were leaping up toward par. Lord Stranleigh led his visitors in to the Strangers' Room, which was empty, and closed the door.

"Well, my lord," said Mackeller, "those fools have sold some fifty thousand shares more of stock than there is in existence."

"It seems to me," drawled his lordship, "although I know nothing of city ways, that such overselling is injudicious."

"Injudicious!" shouted young Mackeller, "why, you've got them like that," and he raised his huge fist into the air and clenched it with a force resembling hydraulic pressure. "You can smash them. They can't deliver. They've not only lost the mine, but you can ruin them by placing any price you please on the shares they've sold and cannot produce."

"That's true," corroborated old Mackeller, nodding his head, "and the bank didn't use your five-thousand-pound check after all."

"Here it is," said the young man, producing it.

"Ah, well," said Lord Stranleigh, slipping the paper into his waistcoat pocket. "Let us be thankful you two are just in time to join me at an excellent meal. I've been expecting you, and I've ordered a French lunch in honor of the late Philippe le Bel. He burned his syndicate of seven at the stake, but we'll merely burn our syndicate's fingers."

CHAPTER II—THE PREMATURE COMPROMISE

THE Camperdown Club in Pall Mall is famous for its cuisine, and young Lord Stranleigh of Wychwood provided a lunch on the day of the great coup that was notable even in the Camperdown. The elder Mackeller did justice to the prime vintage which his lordship shared with him, but young Mackeller proved to be a water drinker. After lunch they retired to a small private smoking room, where they could review the situation without being interrupted, and here coffee, liquors, cigars, and cigarettes were set out, and the waiter retired.

"It would seem, then," began his lordship, "that you and I, Mr. Mackeller, are owners of a property situated somewhere along the west coast of Africa, a dozen miles or so up a river whose name I do not remember, and which I could not pronounce if I did."

"The Paramakaboo," interjected Mackeller, junior.

"Thanks," drawled Lord Stranleigh. "The property is known as the Red Shallows: I suppose because gold is red and the deposit is on the surface."

The two Mackellers nodded.

"I hope I am not unduly confident when I take it for granted that there are no 'buses running to Para-what-you-call-it, nor steam launches either?"

"No," said Peter Mackeller, "it is several hundred miles from the nearest port of call by any of the regular liners, or even tramp steamers. Once there, you must charter whatever kind of sailing craft is available, for the mouth of the Paramakaboo."

"I see. Now, I presume, Mr. Mackeller, that, being an adept at this sort of thing, you have made your purchases of shares strictly according to the rules of the game. No hole is left for this syndicate of seven to crawl out, is there?"

"No," said the elder Mackeller.

"They will probably try to wriggle away," suggested Stranleigh, "as soon as they learn they are trapped."

"Undoubtedly," replied Angus Mackeller, "but I see no way of escape except through the court of bankruptcy, which is a road these men won't want to travel, and even if they did, they have lost all this property, at any rate. They've done themselves out of Red Shallows, whatever happens."

"How many shares did you buy, Mr. Mackeller?"

"In round numbers, three hundred thousand."

"And how much did that cost me?"

"Again in round numbers, thirty-seven thousand, five hundred pounds. Some of the stock was bought as low as two-and-four, the bulk at half a crown, and a quantity of shares at two-and-seven and two-and-eight. I'm reckoning the lot to average half a crown a share."

"How many shares does the company possess?"

"The authorized capital of the company is £250,000 in shares of one pound each. Fifty thousand shares were sold to provide working capital, and ten thousand allotted to me for forming the company, and securing the fifty thousand pounds without publicity."

"Well, Mr. Mackeller, my head is useless so far as figures are concerned, but it seems to me, speaking heedlessly, that these men have promised to deliver to me sixty thousand shares, the bulk of which does not exist, while the rest is in our possession."

"More than that, Lord Stranleigh," replied Mackeller, "because I bought a quantity of shares in addition to the ten thousand allotted me; then three or four of my colleagues have not sold, including your friend, the Honorable John Hazel."

"Well, then, it would appear that these syndicate johnnies have bitten off more than they can chew, as they say out West. How soon will they discover the particulars of the situation?"

"They doubtless know it now, my lord."

"And what will be their first move?"

"They will probably endeavor to compromise."

"Which means they will try to see you, for of course they know nothing of me in this transaction."

"It is very likely they will approach me."

"What will you do, Mr. Mackeller?"

"I shall await your instructions."

"Oh, my instructions are of no value. I'm a mere amateur, you know, whose dependence is on you. What is your advice, Mr. Mackeller?"

"I should compromise if I were you."

"Yes, an Englishman dearly loves a compromise, doesn't he? But if I thought these fellows would put up a decent and interesting fight, I should like to see them squirm."

"That isn't business, my lord."

"Isn't it? Well, what would the city call business in this instance?"

"Strip them of everything they possess, short of making them bankrupt."

"Oh, that's a beastly sort of compromise! That's the city's idea of fair play, is it? Well, I'm blest! They'd surely fight if confronted with such a prospect as that."

"How can they fight? They've undertaken to turn over to you anywhere from sixty to seventy thousand shares of Red Shallows, which they do not possess, and cannot obtain. You're the only man in the world from whom they can buy this material which they have sold. There is no competition in this deal. They must pay the price you ask. If you say these shares you bought for two-and-sixpence are now worth ten pounds, they must pay the difference, or go broke."

"Well, Mr. Mackeller, that seems simple enough, doesn't it? The only information I need is how much money these fellows possess. How shall I set about finding out?"

"Your bank could give you a pretty close estimate, and I'll inquire at mine."

"Then that's all settled. I'm cast for the hardhearted villain in the piece, I suppose?"

"Yes, you may be hard-hearted or the reverse, just which you choose."

"Will their women and children come and plead with me, on their knees, with tears in their eyes?"

"I've known that done, my lord, but I've never heard that it has had any effect in the city."

"I think I'll turn that job over to you, Mr. Mac-keller. You'll be my plea-receiver. I dislike having my emotions worked upon. They tell me that a harrowing of the emotions causes wrinkles and sallowness, and I'm particularly careful of my complexion. Both you and your son seem to have neglected these simple precautions, for your complexions are irretrievably ruined; yours through leading a hard-hearted life in the city, and his by yachting on the river Paraboola."

"Paramakaboo," corrected young Mackeller.

"Thanks, so it is. How should we make the first move toward gathering in those shares which do not exist?"

"I suggest," replied the elder man, "that you should formally demand that the president of the company and the board of directors turn over to you all the papers and belongings of the company, also its balance at the bank, also the resignations of the president and each of the directors. Give them legal notice that no check is to be drawn upon the bank account."

"How much money do you suppose is left in the bank?"

The younger man answered.

"They have chartered the tramp steamer Rajah, which now lies at Southampton. I was in charge of its fitting out. A few thousand pounds have been spent in surface-mining machinery, in provisions, and in corrugated iron for the building of shelters for the engineering staff and workmen. It was not the intention at first to erect a smelting furnace at the mine, but to load the ship with ore, and send her back to England. I returned to London from Southampton, when my father telegraphed to me about the crisis in the affairs of the company. I had spent less than five thousand pounds, so there should be forty or forty-five thousand pounds in the bank."

"I suppose," suggested his lordship, in a tone of supreme indifference, "that they have probably drawn the whole amount out by this time, and perhaps have divided it among the immaculate seven."

"In that case," replied the elder, "they will be forced to account for every penny of it."

The conference was here interrupted by a gentle knock at the door, and one of the club servants, entering, presented a card to Lord Stran-leigh, which bore the words, "Jacob Hahn; Hahn and Lewishon, Solicitors, Frankfort Buildings, Bucklersbury."

"I don't know this man," said his lordship, looking at the servant. "Are you sure he asked for me?"

"Yes, my lord."

"Perhaps it's you he wishes to see, Mr. Mac-keller. Do you know Jacob Hahn, solicitor?"

"Oh, yes, Hahn and Lewishon. They are solicitors for the syndicate, and also solicitors for your Red Shallows company."

"Ah, quite so! Had I better see him, or shall I refer him to you at your office?"

"As this is a private room, my lord, and as there are three of us present, while he will be alone, I think it would do no harm to hear what he has to say."

"Very good. Bring him in."

Jacob Hahn proved to be a big, genial-looking man, with a cast of countenance that gave but a very slight hint of Hebraic origin. Despite the air of confidence with which he advanced, he seemed to be somewhat taken aback at seeing Mackeller and his son seated there. He nodded to them with a smile of good fellowship, nevertheless, and said to the elder man:

"Perhaps, Mr. Mackeller, you will introduce me to Lord Stranleigh of Wychwood."

"That is as his lordship says," commented Mackeller grimly, but Lord Stranleigh rose to his feet with a smile as engaging as that of the solicitor.

"I think no introduction is necessary, Mr. Hahn, for I understand you and your partner represent me, temporarily, at least, so far as the Red Shallows property is concerned. Pray, take a chair, Mr. Hahn. May I offer you some coffee, and what liquor do you prefer?"

"No liquor, if your lordship pleases. Thanks for the coffee."

"Then help yourself, Mr. Hahn, to cigars and cigarettes, whichever you prefer. You'll find them not half bad."

"Thank you."

"How did you know I was interested in the gold mine, Mr. Hahn?"

"Ah, your lordship, it is our business to make these little discoveries. I called at Mackeller's office, but no one knew where he was. I realized, however, that he had not been the financier of this rather startling incursion, and it was not long before I learned the facts of the matter. Oh, not at your office, Mr. Mackeller! There was no one there but that most discreet old man who is even more difficult to pump than you are yourself. I've tried it with both of you on various occasions, so I am quite competent to make a comparison," and with this, the good-natured man laughed. "I then drove to your residence, my lord, and finally to this club, on the chance of finding you."

"Ah, you city chaps are so clever, Mr. Hahn, that it is easy for you to catch us less alert people of the West End."

The solicitor laughed heartily, as if he greatly admired Lord Stranleigh's remark. He was a very friendly person, and beamed upon the young nobleman in a most ingratiating manner.

"I'm afraid it's the other way about, my lord. I happen to know several stockbrokers who within the past few hours have come to the conclusion that the West End is up to snuff, as one might say. There are some people in the city who have been caught, to repeat your own word."

"Really? Have some of the stockbrokers been getting nipped? I always understood they were a very sharp body of men."

"They are generally supposed to be, my lord, but in the case we were just speaking of, some of them tell me they have oversold; that is to say, they have promised to deliver shares which are not at present in their possession, a rather reckless thing to do."

"Oh! then it was the stockbrokers who made that mistake, was it?"

"Yes, some of them exceeded their instructions. They knew that there were in existence some two hundred and fifty thousand shares, and when our shrewd friend here, Mr. Mackeller, approached them for five or ten thousand, some of them imagining they could get practically as many more as they desired—for the stock had been kicking about London for a week with no takers, and, being temporarily blinded by the commission they were to receive, and the fact that the purchase was a cash transaction, which I imagine they had some doubt of Mr. Mackeller's ability to make good—they pressed upon him more shares than had been given them to sell, and now they are in rather a panic. I think I am correct in saying, Mr. Mackeller, that in several instances you were offered more shares than you asked for?"

"I didn't ask for shares at all," gruffly responded Mackeller, "but I learn from my brokers that in all instances they were offered more shares than they required, but my instructions were definite enough, which were to accept and pay for all the shares they could get. In one or two cases, my brokers telephoned to me for instructions, and I suppose that's how the news got out that they were acting for me, and if these brokers of yours thought they were pushing farther into a corner a man already there, they can't expect much sympathy from me when they find themselves in the corner instead."

"Ah, no one would be optimistic enough to expect sympathy from you, Mr. Mackeller," pursued the lawyer.

"Then they won't be disappointed when they don't get it," curtly commented Mackeller.

"I beg your pardon, Mr. Hahn," interposed Stranleigh, "but am I to take it you have come to see me on behalf of these unfortunate stockbrokers?"

"No, my lord. I represent Mr. Conrad Schwartzbrod and his colleagues."

"Oh! and who is Mr. Schwartzbrod?"

Before the solicitor could reply, Mackeller said, with lowering brows:

"He is the head of the syndicate, the president of your company, and his colleagues are the board of directors."

"I see, I see. Then Mr. Schwartzbrod and his friends are not sufferers by this little deal of mine?"

"Oh! bless you, no, Lord Stranleigh, except in so far as they have parted with their property a little more cheaply than they had intended. I believe Mr. Schwartzbrod considers that a fair price for the shares would have been from three-and-six to four shillings."

"I'm not very good at figures," complained his lordship, with a slight wrinkle in his forehead, "but if three-and-six is a fair price, then the loss of the syndicate is merely a shilling a share, and as they sold me three hundred thousand shares, that comes to—" He looked helplessly at Mac-keller.

"Fifteen thousand pounds," said Mackeller sharply.

"Ah, thanks. Fifteen thousand pounds. Well, that divided between seven amounts to——"

Again he turned an appealing eye to the somber Mackeller, who replied promptly:

"Two thousand one hundred and forty-two pounds, six shillings each."

"I'm ever so much obliged, Mackeller. What a deuce of an advantage it is to possess brains! I am told that east of the Danube people cannot figure up simple little sums in their mind, and so this gives the Jews a great advantage over them in commercial dealings, which adds to the wealth of the Jew, but detracts from his popularity. I fear the inability to count often begins west of Regent Street, and afflicts many of us who are accustomed to paying the waiter at the club exactly what he demands. But to return to our muttons, Mr. Hahn, I must congratulate you on the fact that your clients, who I understand are rich and estimable men, lose merely a couple of thousand each on a deal involving some hundreds of thousands, although it occupied but a few minutes of the time of forty stockbrokers acting simultaneously. I suppose as the amount of their loss is so trifling, you have not come here to make any appeal for clemency on behalf of the respectable Mr. Schwartzbrod and his colleagues?"

"Oh, not at all, your lordship. No, Mr. Schwartzbrod is merely anxious that the transfer should be made in such a way as to give you as little trouble as possible."

"I'm delighted to hear you say that, Mr. Hahn, because the sole purpose of my life is to avoid trouble. I employ no less than twelve solicitors to intercept whatever trouble comes to hand so that it doesn't get past them to me. I should be glad to take on another solicitor, but that would make thirteen, which is a very unlucky number, Mr. Hahn. Mr. Schwartzbrod and his partners, then, will put no difficulties in my way?"

"Oh, none in the least, Lord Stranleigh. They have commissioned me to convey their compliments and congratulations to your lordship on the acquirement of what they consider a very valuable property."

"Oh, not so valuable, Mr. Hahn. Only a shilling a share, you know. Still, I believe that's considered a reasonably profitable margin. I don't know exactly what per cent it runs to, but——"

"Forty per cent," snapped Mackeller.

"Is it really? Well, I think I'm only getting four on a large portion of my money. I must speak to my investment solicitor about this. If a mere amateur like myself can make forty per cent in ten minutes, don't you think a solicitor should do better than content himself with four per cent in a whole year?"

"Your investment solicitor probably takes no risk, Lord Stranleigh."

"Ah, that will be it. I knew there was a flea on the wall somewhere, but, you see, I'm not well versed in these things. But I interrupted you, Mr. Hahn. You were going to say———"

"I was going to say, my lord, that there are two hundred and fifty thousand shares in the company, all of which are now vested in yourself, Mr. Mackeller, and probably one or two others. Of course the unfortunate stockbrokers cannot produce the fifty thousand shares or more that are not in existence, and I don't suppose your lordship has any thought of forcing these people into bankruptcy merely because of a little overzealousness on their part. Noblesse oblige, you know."

"Ah, quite so. Noblesse oblige. I thought the phrase hadn't penetrated yet into the city." Again the solicitor laughed heartily.

"A fair hit. A fair hit, my lord. Well, as I was about to add, Mr. Schwartzbrod and his friends are prepared to transfer to you instantly this property if you desire this to be done."

"Yes, I rather think that is my desire. You see, when a man buys a thing, and pays the money for it, he usually expects it to be turned over, don't you know?"

"Quite so, my lord. I have brought with me the documents pertaining to the transfer, all duly made out, signed and sealed, ready for delivery. But it occurred to my principals that perhaps you did not care yourself to develop the property, and perhaps your intention was to take what you considered a fair profit on the transaction, and relinquish whatever claim you possess on this land. You would thus make a clear gain, and run no further risk."

"Mining is a somewhat uncertain business, isn't it, Mr. Hahn?"

"Personally, I have had no experience with it, my lord, but they tell me that gold-mining is about the most hazardous occupation that a man can adopt. If he is not a practical miner, he is swindled on all hands by those to whom he intrusts the operations."

"I'm afraid I am not a practical man, Mr. Hahn, and know as little about gold-mining as you do."

"In that ease, Lord Stranleigh, I think we should have no difficulty in arriving at an understanding acceptable to both sides."

"I should be delighted. What do your principals consider a fair profit?"

"That is a matter for mutual discussion, my lord. They propose to pay you back the amount you have invested, and in addition to that hand over to you, say fifteen or twenty thousand pounds. Or they would be willing that you should retain a substantial holding in the venture if you wish to profit by their experience, and that there should be a pro rata deduction from the amount they are to hand over to you."

"I see. Well, that is very good of them, but as I told Mr. Maekeller to-day, I am by way of being a plunger. It is all or nothing with me, and so, having in a manner of speaking been drawn into the vortex, I think I'll stay in and see what happens. That being the case, I think it would be most unfair to make others share a risk over which they could exercise no control. I dare say I am very stupid. My friend, Jack Hazel, who knows city men and their ways, says that it is a practice there to minimize risk by spreading it over a number of persons, but I shouldn't be happy, if my plans went wrong, to think that others were suffering through my foolishness. I should feel toward them as Mr. Schwartzbrod feels toward those unfortunate stockbrokers who exceeded his instructions, a sentiment which does him great credit. So, if you don't mind, I think we will confine our attention to the simple transfer you propose."

"Very good, my lord. Whatever plan commends itself the more strongly to your lordship will be cheerfully acquiesced in by my principals. Here, then, are the papers which make over the gold fields to you, and if you will just sign this formal receipt we may regard the transaction as complete."

"My dear Mr. Hahn, it is a pleasure to deal with a man of your courtesy and comprehension."

His lordship, with a bow, took up the papers the other had laid down on the table, glanced at them, and passed them along to Angus Mackeller, who scrutinized them with the eye of a hawk. His lordship then read very slowly the document he had been asked to sign, and he took a long time in his examination, during which period the keen eyes of the solicitor could scarcely conceal their apprehension. At last his lordship laid it down.

"I am somewhat at a disadvantage," he said, "among legal instruments. As I informed you, I am fortunate in possessing the services of a dozen sharper men than myself who are good enough, for a consideration, to advise me on these topics. But, alas! not one of them is present at this moment."

"Why, my lord, I don't think you have any reason to complain. I'm here alone, without any corroborative witness on my behalf, while there are three of you sitting here."

"Ah, now you speak, Mr. Hahn, as if we were contestants—combatants, as one might say—instead of being a quartette of friends. There is no need of witnesses where everything has gone on as smoothly as has been the case since you entered this room. You represent men who are only too anxious to do the right thing, and you meet, I hope, a man who is desirous of effecting a compromise, and I think I may say the same for my friend Mackeller. I am sure nothing would give Mackeller greater pleasure than to treat Mr. Schwartzbrod in the same generous, equitable way in which Mr. Schwartzbrod would treat him." The solicitor leaned back in his chair, while his smile became a sort of fixed grin.

"Precisely, precisely," he murmured.

"Of course I don't pretend to penetrate into all the intricacies of this apparently simple little receipt, but it seems to me that in Mr. Schwartzbrod's generous desire to protect his stockbrokers, he is doing so, doubtless unconsciously, at my expense."

"At your expense, my lord?"

"Well, that's the way it looks to me. These stockbrokers, poor devils, must produce some sixty or seventy thousand shares on which they cannot lay their hands, and this, as my ancient friend Euclid used to remark, is impossible. Now, if I sign this receipt, it appears that I waive all claim against these unfortunate, but nevertheless careless stockbrokers."

"I thought it was understood, my lord, that, as you obtained quiet possession of the gold field, you were not inclined to push to the wall—I think that is your own phrase—a number of men who, as things are going in the city this year, have not been overburdened with business. Indeed, the stagnation in financial circles, the high bank rate, and all that, doubtless accounts for the eagerness with which these men, regarding the honest commission they were earning, ventured to overstep the bounds set for them, thus placing themselves, as one may say, at your mercy. I somehow took it for granted that you had no animus against this unlucky score."

"Animus? Oh, no, bless my soul, not the least. Animus is an emotion I confess I scarcely know the meaning of. I think all my friends will tell you I am a most good-natured chap, who would rather forgive an injury than remember it."

"I am delighted to hear you say so, my lord, and admit that, for the moment, I was slightly apprehensive."

"Your apprehensions were quite groundless, Mr. Hahn; quite groundless, I assure you. I shall not injure one of your stockbrokers, and when you report my words to the kindly Mr. Schwartzbrod and his colleagues, I can fancy with what relief they will hear your repetition of them."

"Thank you, my lord, I shall have great pleasure in telling them what you have said."

"On the other hand, Mr. Hahn, justice is justice, as you yourself would be the first to admit. I am entitled to what Mr. Schwartzbrod and his coadjutors would call fair profit on these sixty or seventy thousand shares they cannot produce. Now, although I am so ignorant of business methods, I nevertheless believe that a principal is responsible for the actions of his agents. My chauffeur was fined, down in Surrey the other day, for exceeding the speed limit. I was not in the car, but here in my club. Nevertheless, I was compelled to pay the fine and the costs, because the chauffeur was in my employ. The syndicate of seven, animated, as I believe, by a desire to crush Mr. Mackeller and possess themselves, not only of all his stock, but of the shares of his friends who paid a pound each for them, forgot during one critical ten minutes that a buyer might happen along who had some money in his pockets. It is due to the energy and the persuasive powers of this young engineer here, formerly in their employ, that a purchaser materialized at the crucial moment. I think it is a fact that if Mr. Schwartz-brod and his distinguished company of pirates had not jauntily run up the black flag with the skull and crossbones on it, they would not be today in the place of jeopardy in which they stand. To continue my nautical simile, they thought Mr. Mackeller here was an unprotected merchantman, and proceeded to board and scuttle him, when over the horizon there appeared the latest thing in turbine twenty-five-knot-an-hour cruisers, armed with 4.7 guns, or whatever bally pieces of artillery such a cruiser carries. Now, after presenting the good Mr. Schwartzbrod with my compliments, tell him not to lose any sleep because of the unfortunate stockbrokers, because I am going to attack him, not them. If, in the scrimmage, any of the stockbrokers go under, I will set them up in business again, but I shall not do so at my own expense. I shall simply raise my price to the immaculate syndicate of seven."

All geniality had departed from the solicitor's face, leaving it hard as granite.

"I think you are threatening us, Lord Stran-leigh," he said.

"Oh, dear me, no. How can you put such a construction on my words? I am merely making a suggestion. You will leave with me all those transfer papers. You will ask Schwartzbrod and the six directors to send me their resignations. You will warn them not to draw a penny from the bank account of the company."

"The bank account of the company is already overdrawn," said the solicitor; then apparently thinking he had spoken a little prematurely, added hastily: "at least, so I understand. They have gone in largely for materials necessary for the development of the property."

"Oh, that is very interesting, Mr. Hahn. You don't happen to know at what time to-day the money was taken out?"

"I didn't say it was taken out to-day. I don't know when it was withdrawn."

"Of course not. Still, that is a trifle that really doesn't matter, and doubtless your principals will ask of me to allow them quietly to replace it."

"I cannot leave these transfer papers with you unless you sign that receipt. You know enough of business to understand that, I suppose. A man like myself, acting merely as agent, must have documentary proof that he has fulfilled his duty. If I leave the papers with you, I must bear away the signed receipt in lieu of them."

"I'll willingly sign a receipt, Mr. Hahn, simply acknowledging your delivery of the papers."

"My instructions were quite definite, my lord, and I dare not vary from them."

"Oh, I thought that Mr. Schwartzbrod had placed negotiations entirely in your hands, and would do as you advised."

"I shall, of course, give him my best advice, but I honestly could not advise him to part with all his advantages in the situation, and receive nothing in return."

"His advantages? What are they?"

"Well, my lord, they are probably greater than you imagine. He and his colleagues have been elected president and board of directors of the Red Shallows company. They hold office for a year. You spoke just now of the withdrawal of the money. It is quite within their legal right to not only withdraw the money, but to issue debentures against the shares that you hold.

If you read the articles of association, you will see that this is so. Although you hold all the shares of the company, you cannot compel them to resign, and you cannot vote your stock until the next annual meeting, which is nearly twelve months distant. During that time the president and board of directors, who are clothed with large powers, for I myself drew up the articles of association, and I know their contents—these seven men may do practically what they please with your property, unless we come to an amicable settlement."

"Ah, who is threatening now, Mr. Hahn?"

"I am not, my lord. I am merely telling you, in the plainest possible words at my command, just how the situation stands."

"I thank you, Mr. Hahn, for the clarity of your explanation. I take it, then, that you cannot leave these documents with me?"

"Not unless you will sign that receipt, my lord."

"As I feel disinclined to do that, Mr. Hahn, and suffer no qualms of conscience whatever regarding the unlucky stockbrokers, I hereby return them to you, receipt and all. Now, you tell Mr. Schwartzbrod that the price of Red Shallows shares is one hundred pounds each, and if there are seventy thousand shares coming to me which your principles cannot produce, their check for seven million pounds will do me quite as well."

"My lord, you pretend ignorance in business affairs. I suppose you are now trying to prove it. You cannot make the shares a hundred pounds apiece, nor can you enforce such an exorbitant condition through any court in the land. My principals would receive relief from any court of equity."

"It is not my intention, Mr. Hahn, to trouble the courts with the matter at all. In fact, I refuse to accept cash from your principals. They have sold me the shares, and I insist on the delivery of those shares. I happen to be the only person in the world who owns the shares, and my price for each share is a hundred pounds. Your principals will be compelled to beg me to sell them the shares. As a matter of fact, I do not intend to place any such figure upon them. I merely used a hundred pounds as an illustration. Of course, if I put them at that price I would break your principals, and no court in the kingdom could save them. To be perfectly frank with you, for I do not possess the mental qualification necessary to cope with business men of genius such as I doubt not your principals are, I will now tell you what I intend to do. I shall put the price of shares at exactly what your people sold them to the public for, that is, one pound each. They cannot complain of my doing what they have done themselves, now can they? It is true that I bought these shares at two-and-six, but that also was not my fault. They, by throwing their shares on the market, knocked down the price to the figure I have named, and I bought the shares from the stockbrokers of your principals. If you say their action was not done to embarrass Mr. Mac-keller, then I at once accept your statement as true. For some other reason they battered down the price from one pound to half a crown. A few weeks ago they had sold fifty thousand of these shares for one pound each, and because of their unexplained smashing of the market, these good people lost a large portion of the money they had paid out. Now surely, surely, being a just and equitable man, your Mr. Schwartzbrod cannot refuse to drink the cup he has himself brewed. He could not show even the court of equity that I was doing a usurious thing in placing the stock back at the figure he himself originally settled, in following the illustrious example of Mr. Schwartzbrod himself. Now, I leave it to you, Mr. Hahn, as a fair and just man, whose indignant expostulation at my figure of a hundred pounds was most laudable, and entirely to your credit, are you not surprised at my moderation?"

"I should hardly go so far as to say that, my lord. This stock cost you thirty thousand pounds."

"Oh, don't underestimate, Mr. Hahn, it cost thirty-seven thousand five hundred pounds."

"Even in that case you are asking my principals to pay double. In other words, you will have deprived them of their property, getting it not only for nothing, but with a bonus of thirty odd thousand pounds in cash. If that is not an act of piracy, as you said, what in the name of Heaven is?"

His lordship shrugged his shoulders, and spread forth his hands. His expression showed that he was grieved and disappointed.

"Then instead of thanking me——"

He sighed deeply and did not continue the sentence.

"As I have informed you, Lord Stranleigh, my principals are not liable to you for those seventy thousand shares. You must seek your remedy against the stockbrokers."

"That is exactly what I shall not do."

"Then you will be non-suited in the courts."

"But, my dear sir, haven't I been telling you I'm not going to the courts? Like all respectable pirates, I abominate a court of law. It's such a waste of time, don't you know. Not only shall I take no action against the stockbrokers, but if your principals do not agree in writing also to take no action against them the price of shares shall rise suddenly. I am so much in sympathy with Mr. Schwartzbrod's tender feelings toward the stockbrokers that I intend to protect them, and I am sure you will forgive me if I say that I very much doubt if any of the stockbrokers exceeded their instructions, even though times are hard in the city."

"Then," said Mr. Hahn, rising, and replacing the documents he brought once more in his inside pocket, "that is your ultimatum, is it?"

"I beg you, Mr. Hahn, not to give to my poor and stammering remarks so harsh a term. Ultimatum? Bless us all, no. I'm no President Kruger, but merely a somewhat lackadaisical man who is innocent of many of the ways of this wicked world. I hope you won't represent me to the virtuous Mr. Schwartzbrod as a hard, contentious fellow. Tell him that I'm the most easy person in the world to deal with. Tell him the moment he sends me his check for seventy thousand pounds—I hope it will be a little less—Mr. Mac-keller here will figure out the exact amount, and run it into shillings and pence, and even farthings if necessary—the moment I get that check, the resignations, the guarantee that no harm will be done to the simple-minded stockbrokers, the balance in the bank, and some account of everything the company has done since it came into existence until the time it fell into my hands, why, tell him he has no greater admirer or well-wisher than myself."

"I shall give him your message, my lord."

"Do, but add to it that charming Biblical text, 'Agree with thine adversary quickly.' I think there's something about squaring up things before the sun goes down, but I shan't be so hasty as all that. Stock will remain at a pound during tomorrow. Next day it will rise a shilling, next day another shilling, the third day a third shilling. It's so very easy to keep count of; just make a red mark on your calendar to-day, and if he allows two weeks to go past, why, there's fourteen shillings added to the twenty he would have had to pay before."

The solicitor, who would have made an excellent actor, forced a laugh that did not sound half bad.

"Ah, you are joking now, my lord."

"I don't think so, Mr. Hahn, although I do sometimes joke unconsciously."

"You will, I am sure, give us a week to think this matter over."

"Oh, very well. Anything for the sake of peace and quietness, and an amicable settlement. I should hate Mr. Schwartzbrod to think me exacting. Now, don't go away thinking I'm reluctant to make concessions, and big ones. That's seven shillings a share I am giving you, and on seventy thousand shares—how much is that, Mr. Mackeller, you know I've no head for figures?"

"Twenty-four thousand five hundred pounds."

"Why, look at that, Mr. Hahn. Here are you, who refuse to leave me those documents you carry, who have been thinking hard of me—there, don't deny it; I saw it by the expression of your countenance—here am I giving to Mr. Schwartz-brod and the delectable six a present of—of—of——"

"Twenty-four thousand five hundred pounds," prompted Mackeller the elder.

"Yes, twenty-four thousand five hundred pounds in hard cash, bestowing it upon men I never saw, and up till to-day never even heard of. I don't want to boast of my virtues, Mr. Hahn, but I doubt if you could find any man in the city who would so jauntily fling away twenty-four thousand five hundred pounds. I got the amount correct that time, Mackeller. I'm improving, you see."

"Very good, my lord. Shall I communicate with you further at this club?"

"No. Hereafter our interviews must be on a hard business basis. The generous nature of our '78 wine makes me a little open-handed. The next interview will take place at Mr. Mackeller's office in the city any time that suits your convenience, and I should be glad to have twenty-four hours' notice, because I mustn't devote my whole life to finance, don't you know, for I am rather fond of automobiling, and may be out of town."

"Thank you. Good afternoon, my lord. Good afternoon, Mr. Mackeller."

The solicitor departed, and Lord Stranleigh smiled at his two companions, who had sat so long silent.

"Well, my young chap," said the frowning Mackeller, drawing a deep breath, "if you ever get to understand finance, God help the city!" His lordship indulged in a laugh, then turned to Peter and said:

"I think you should resume your place at Southampton. You were seeing to the loading of a ship—what did you call it?"

"The Rajah—the steamer Rajah."

"Well, even if I am not president or board of directors, I ask you to resume that occupation. You are still officially engineer for the company, I take it?"

"Yes."

"Very good. Say not a word to anybody, but go down to Southampton, and proceed with getting the machinery and provisions into the steamer, just as if nothing had happened. If you meet any opposition, telegraph me, and I think I can overcome the obstruction."

So Peter took himself off to Southampton, and met with no obstacle in resuming his duties.

The syndicate consumed the full week, and made an appointment with Mr. Mackeller and Lord Stranleigh on the last day before the shares would begin to go up. This time Mr. Hahn did not appear, but Conrad Schwartzbrod, unmistakably German and unmistakably Hebraic, came cringing in. He spent hours trying to get improved terms, and indeed Lord Stranleigh made him several important concessions. At last he delivered over everything that was demanded, and got from Lord Stranleigh a signed document giving Conrad Schwartzbrod full acquittance of everything he had done up to date. This document was witnessed by Mackeller, and, placing it safely in his pocketbook, the old financier cringed out of the office with an evil leer that would have done credit to the late Sir Henry Irving's Shy-lock.

"I wouldn't have conceded an inch to him," said the stern Mackeller.

"Ah, well, what does it matter. If he'd treated a little longer I'd have given him easier terms yet, so I'm glad he's gone."

A telegraph messenger entered the room with a dispatch for Mr. Mackeller, who tore it open, read it, and swore. It was from his son.

"Do not settle with those scoundrels," it ran. "Three days ago when I was seeing to the storing of cargo in the Rajah, I was battened down in the hold, and the steamer sailed. I was put ashore with the pilot, and have just been landed at Plymouth."

"By God!" cried Mackeller, bringing his fist down on the desk. "That document you have signed and I have witnessed, gives him quittance for this theft of the steamer. Now they are going to loot the surface gold and recoup themselves. They have three days' start of us, and it will take a week to get a steamer and fit her out."

His lordship's countenance was serene, and he blew slowly some rings of cigarette smoke up into the air.

"I can't help admiring the courage of old Schwartzbrod," he said. "Think how fine he cut it! And yet it might disturb him to know I'm a friend of the

Honorable Mr. Parsons."

"What has that to do with it?" growled Mackeller.

"Nothing, except that the speed of the Rajah is seven knots an hour, and my large yacht, The Woman in White, lying in Plymouth Harbor, is fitted with Parsons's latest turbines and can, at a pinch, steam twenty-five knots an hour. Poor old Schwartzbrod! We're going to have some fun with him after all."

CHAPTER III—THE MISSION OF "THE WOMAN IN WHITE"

THE breakfast room of Lord Stranleigh's town house was a most cheerful apartment, and the young man who entered sat down to a repast which was at once abundant and choice. The appointments could scarcely have been bettered; the spotless linen, the polished silver, the prismatic cut glass, and the dainty porcelain, formed a pleasant table picture, enhanced by the pile of luscious fruit, the little rolls of cool, golden butter, the crisp white crescents, the brown toast, while the aroma of celestial coffee from the silver urn over a small electric furnace was enough to spur the longing of a sybarite. It is perhaps to be regretted that truth compels record of the fact that the languid person who found himself confronted by delicacies in season and out was healthily hungry, for some of us grumble that to him that hath shall be given, which seems unfair, and there appears to be a human satisfaction in the fact that John D. Rockefeller, the richest man in the world, is compelled to breakfast on a diluted glass of milk. But regrettable or no, Lord Stranleigh of Wychwood was preparing to do full justice to the excellence of the meal when his man said to him, in a hushed, deferential whisper:

"Mr. Peter Mackeller has called, my lord, and insists on seeing you immediately. He says it is a matter of the utmost importance."

"Oh, dim!" ejaculated his lordship, "how these conscientious, earnest people tire me. As if anything could be a matter of importance at this hour except breakfast! Well, I suppose there is no escape: show him in."

He heaved a deep sigh, and murmured to himself:

"This is what comes of meddling with the city." The stalwart young Mackeller entered, and his very presence seemed to put the refined room to shame, his grim force causing his surroundings to appear dilettante and needlessly expensive. He was even more than usually unkempt, as if he had been sitting up all night in the hold of the tramp steamer which had kidnapped him. A deep frown marked his brow, and heightened the expression of rude strength that radiated from his determined face.

"Ah, Mackeller, good morning," drawled his lordship, looking at the young man over his shoulder. "I'm delighted to see you, and just in the nick of time, too. Won't you sit down and breakfast with me!"

"Thank you," said Mackeller, in tones as hard as the other's were affected. "I breakfasted two hours and a half ago."

"Did you really? Well, call it lunch, and draw up your chair."

"No, I've not come to a banquet, but to a business conference."

"I'm sorry for that. My head is not very clear on business matters at any hour of the day, but in the morning I am particularly stupid. Do try a peach; you'll find them exceedingly good."

"No, thanks."

"Then have a cigarette?"

His lordship raised the heavy lid of a richly chased box of silver, displaying a quantity of the paper tubes, and pushed this toward his visitor.

"They are a blend that is made for me in Cairo, but perhaps you prefer Virginians?"

"I have no choice in the matter," said Mackeller, selecting a cigarette.

The butler snapped aglow an electric lighter, and held it convenient for the young engineer's use, who drew in his breath, and exhaled a whiff of aromatic smoke.

"Do sit down, Mackeller!"

"Thanks, no; I'm in a hurry. Time is of great value just now."

"Although I am very stupid in the morning, as I told you, nevertheless the moment you came in I surmised you were in a hurry. For whom are you working, Mr. Mackeller?"

"Working? What do you mean?"

"Who is your employer, or are you on your own, as the vulgar say?"

"Why, my lord, I understood I was in your employ."

"In that case why don't you sit down when I tell you to?" asked his lordship with a slight laugh.

Peter Mackeller dropped into a chair with such suddenness that the laugh of his chief became more pronounced.

"You see, Peter, my boy, it is a rule of the world that the man who pays for the music calls the tune. You say it is to be a quick-step: I insist upon a minuet. How do you like those cigarettes?"

"They are excellent, my lord."

"Not half bad, I think. You don't mind my going on with breakfast, and I am sure you will excuse me if I fail to regard this table as a quick lunch counter. I think our sturdiness as a nation depends very largely on our slowness at meals."

"Perhaps. Still, that slowness should not extend to every function of life," replied Peter severely.

"You think not? Well, perhaps you are right, although I must confess that I do dislike to be hustled, as the saying is. My mind works slowly when it condescends to work at all, and my body rather accommodates itself to my mental condition. You appear to be under the impression that my affairs at the moment need the spur rather than the curb. Am I right in that conjecture?"

"Why, my lord, if ever there was a transaction where speed is the essence of the contract, as the lawyers say, it is the present condition of your gold property."

"Why, I fail to see that, Mackeller. I buy a property for, say, thirty-five thousand pounds. I receive a check for sixty-five thousand from the estimable Mr. Schwartzbrod and his colleagues. I have therefore acquired what you state is a valuable property for nothing, and there is bestowed upon me a bonus of thirty thousand pounds in addition for taking it over. Whether or not any gold exists on the west coast of Africa, there certainly reposes thirty thousand golden sovereigns at my disposal in the bank; sovereigns which yesterday I did not possess, so I think I have concluded the deal very creditably for a sluggish-brained person like myself, and after such a profitable bit of mental exertion it seems to me I am entitled to a rest, but here you come, bristling with energy, and say 'Let's hurry.' In Heaven's name, why? I've finished the transaction."

"Finished?" cried Mackeller. "Finished? Bless my soul, we've only just begun. Do you understand that the tramp steamer Rajah, with some hundred and fifty hired thieves aboard, is making as fast as steam can push her through the waters, for your property, with intent to loot the same? Do you comprehend that that steamer has been loaded by myself with the most modern surface-mining machinery, with dynamite, with provisions, with every facility for the speedy robbing of those gold fields, and that you have given that pirate Schwartzbrod a document acquitting him of all liability in the premises?"

"Yes, Peter, I suppose things are very much as you state them, but your tone implies that somehow I am to blame in the matter. I assure you that it is not my fault, but the fault of circumstances. Then why worry about a thing I am not in the least responsible for? You are not censuring me, I hope?"

"No, my lord, I have no right to censure you whatever happens."

"Oh, don't let any question of right suppress a just indignation, Mackeller. If you think I'm guilty of negligence, pray give expression to your feelings by the use of any combination of words that brings relief. Don't mind me. I really very much admire the use of terse language, although I have been denied the gift of emphatic denunciation myself."

"Don't you intend to do anything, my lord?"

"Yes, I intend to enjoy my breakfast, and really, if you knew how tasty this coffee is, you would yield to my pleadings and indulge in at least one cup."

"Don't you propose to prosecute that scoundrel Schwartzbrod?"

"Prosecute? Bless my soul, what for?"

"For the trick he played on you and my father. He got that exculpating document from you under false pretenses."

"Not at all, not at all. I made certain stipulations; he complied with them. I then gave him the exculpating document, as you call it, and there it ends. If I had been gifted with second sight, this vision would have revealed to me that the clever Schwartzbrod had caused the Rajah to sail with you a prisoner in her hold. But Schwartzbrod is not to blame because I possess no clairvoyant power, now is he?"

"You will do nothing, then?"

"My dear boy, there's nothing to do."

"Don't you intend to stop these pirates from mining your gold, and getting it aboard the Rajah?"

"Certainly not: why should I?"

"Nor give information to the authorities?"

"Of course not. The authorities have more information now than they can use."

"Then you will not even tell the police?"

"The police are a land force: they cannot take a rowboat and chase the Rajah, and if they could they wouldn't catch her, so what's the good of asking impossibilities from either Scotland Yard or the Foreign Office?"

"You have no intention, then, of interfering with this band of gold robbers?"

"Oh, no."

"You're going to take it lying down?"

"No, sitting up," and with that his lordship pushed back his chair, threw his right leg over his left, selected a cigarette, and lit it.

"I should be glad, my lord, to head an expedition, fit up another ship, follow the Rajah, and force those claim-jumpers to abandon their raid on another man's goods."

"I don't like force, Mackeller. I don't mind possessing a giant's strength, but we must remember we should not use it like a giant."

Lord Stranleigh, a picture of contentment, leaned back in his chair, and blew rings of filmy cigarette smoke toward the ceiling. Peter Mae-keller, the gloom on whose face had grown darker and darker, watched the nonchalant young man opposite him with a curl of contempt on his lip, yet he realized that if his lordship could not be forced to move, he himself was helpless. At last he rose slowly to his feet, the first tardy movement he had made since he entered the breakfast room.

"Very good, my lord. Then you have no further need of me, and I beg you to accept my resignation."

"I'm sorry," drawled his lordship, "but before you quit my service, I should like to receive one well thought-out opinion from you."

"What is your problem, my lord?"

"It is this, Mackeller. I consider the after-breakfast cigarette the most enticing smoke of the day. A man who has slept well, and breakfasted adequately seems just in tune to enjoy to the utmost these enchanting vaporous exhalations. I wish to know if you agree with me."

"Oh, damnation!" cried Mackeller, bringing his huge fist down on the table, and setting the breakfast things a-jingling, and with this regrettable word and action, he strode toward the door. The butler was there as if to open it for him, but his lordship made a slight turning motion of his wrist, whereupon Ponderby instantly locked the door and put the key in his pocket, standing there as silent and imperturbable as if he had not just imprisoned a free-born British subject, which he certainly had no legal right to do. The enraged captive fruitlessly shook the door, then turned round, his face ablaze with anger. Neither his lordship nor the butler moved a muscle.

"Mr. Mackeller," drawled his lordship, "you have been conversing most interestingly, I admit, on subjects that did not in the least concern you. Now, perhaps, you will resume your duty."

"My duty? What is my duty?" demanded the engineer.

"Why, I hoped it would not be necessary to remind you of it. I sent you down to Southampton to look after my property; the Rajah, which I had hired, and the machinery, provisions, etcetera, which I had bought. Through your negligence, carelessness, laches, default, supineness, inattention, or whatever other quality it pleases you to attribute the circumstance, you allowed yourself to be hoodwinked like a schoolboy, trapped like a rat, tied like a helpless sack on a pack horse for an unstated number of miles, flung like a bundle into a pilot boat, and landed like a haddock on the beach. A man to whom all this happened must be well endowed with cheek to enter my house and berate me for indolence. So cease standing there like a graven image with your back to the door, and do not perambulate the room as you did a minute ago, like a tiger in his cage at the Zoo, but sit down here once more, light another cigarette, fling one leg over the other, and give me, slowly, so that I can understand it, a formal report of your Southampton mission, and the disaster which attended it. I shall be glad to receive and consider any excuse you may offer for your own utter incompetence, and you may begin by apologizing for dealing a deadly blow at my table, which is quite innocent, and for offending my ears by the expletive that preceded such action."

Mackeller strode over to the chair again, and plumped down like the fall of a sledge-hammer.

"You're right. I apologize, and ask you to pardon my tongue-play and fist-play."

His lordship airily waved his hand.

"Granted," he said. "I sometimes say 'dim' myself, if I may quote Sir W. S. Gilbert. Go on."

"When I went aboard the Rajah, neither the captain nor any of the officers offered opposition to my resuming command of the loading. The stuff was on the wharf, and in less than three days it was all aboard, well stowed away. During this time I had seen nothing to rouse my suspicion that anything underhand was to be attempted. I had informed the captain that you were now the charterer of the steamer, and he received the intelligence with apparent indifference, saying something to the effect that it mattered nothing to him who his owners were so long as his money was safe. The last material taken aboard was a large quantity of canvas for making tents, and lucky for me it was that I placed this at the foot of the ladder up from the hold. The workers had all gone on deck, and I was taking a final look around, wondering whether anything had been forgotten. I then mounted the ladder, and was amazed to see old Schwartzbrod standing there, talking to a tall, dark man who was, I afterwards learned, the leader of the expedition. This man, without a word, planted his foot against my breast, and heaved me backward down into the hold. Immediately afterwards I was battened down, and in darkness. By the running about on the deck above me, I realized that the steamer was getting ready to cast off, and within an hour I heard the engines and screw at work.

"It was night, and we were thrashing seaward through the Channel when the covering of the hatchway was lifted, and the man who had imprisoned me came down the ladder alone, with a lantern in his hand, which struck me as rather brave in the circumstances, but then he was armed, and I was not, so after all I had little chance against him. He placed the lantern on the bales of canvas upon which I had fallen, and began, with seeming courtesy, by begging pardon for what he had done. Throughout he spoke very quietly, and impressed me as a determined and capable person. He said that if I gave him my word that I should speak to no one aboard, or attempt to hail any passing craft, should such come near us, he would allow me on deck, and would send me ashore when the pilot left the ship.

"'And if I refuse to give my word?' I asked. "'In that case,' he replied, 'I shall supply you with food and water, and will carry you to the end of our voyage.'

"'And where is that?' I asked.

"'I don't know,' he said. 'I have nothing to do with the navigation of the ship. I believe we are making for some port in South America, but I couldn't say for certain.'

"I realized that I could do nothing while in the hold, and although I knew perfectly well they were making for the West African coast, and not for South America, I would be equally helpless once I reached there. Besides, it was of vital importance that I should telegraph to you and my father. In fact, I was amazed that, having taken the risk of placing me in confinement as they had done, they should allow me to get on shore so soon, but I suppose the crafty old Schwartzbrod knew that if I remained missing long, there would be an outcry in the newspapers, so he reckoned it was safer to risk my being put ashore, as he estimated we could not possibly fit out another steamer and start in pursuit under a week at the very least, and with that start they could have the channel of the river blocked, a fort or two erected, and so bid us defiance when we did arrive."

"But if they blocked the river," interrupted his lordship, "they would shut themselves in, as well as shut us out."

"Not necessarily," continued the engineer. "I have reason to believe that before I reached Southampton, a number of floating mines were stowed away in the front part of the ship. These mines could be planted in the mouth of the river, and a chart kept, which, in the possession of the captain, would enable him to thread the channel in safety, while a navigator without this protection and guide would run a thousand chances of finding his ship blown up."

"Why," said his lordship with admiration, "our seven syndicaters are brave as the buccaneers of ancient times. They are certainly running considerable risk of penal servitude for life?"

"I am not sure that they are, my lord," replied Mackeller. "You see, this property is situated in a native state. The concession was granted by the chief of the ruling tribe in that district. British law does not run in that locality, and I very much doubt if the steamer Rajah will ever again put into a British port. My notion is that they will load her up with ore, and make for some point, probably in the Portuguese possessions, where they will smelt the ore, sell the ingots, and in the shape of hard cash which cannot be earmarked, the product of your mine will reach the syndicate in London. Now, my lord, you spoke of negligence, culpability, and all that. There is the story, and if you can show me where I was negligent of your interests, all I can say is that my error was not intentional."

"Well, you see, Mackeller, you were acquainted with old Schwartzbrod, and I wasn't. I had not met him up to that time, and I knew nothing personally of the syndicate, whereas you did. I think you should have put some shrewd man on to watch the trains, and learn if any of these men had come to Southampton, or perhaps you should have given us the tip in London, and we could have had the immaculate seven shadowed. I expected to meet legal chicanery, but not bold swashbuckling of this sort."

"Yes, it would have been better to set a watch, but although I knew the men, nothing in their conduct led me to suspect a trick like this. However, as I am no longer in your employ, you shall not suffer further from my incompetence."

"I think, Maekeller, you ought to give me a week's notice, you know."

"Very well. This day week I quit."

"I am not sure but I am entitled to a month. How much should I have to pay you if I dismissed you?"

"Six months' salary, I believe, is the legal amount."

"Well, then, why not give me half a year's notice?"

"I suppose you are entitled to it, my lord."

"Then that's all right. Half a year from now we shake hands and bid each other a tearful farewell. Much may happen in twenty-six weeks, you know."

"Not if you're going to do nothing, Lord Stranleigh."

"Maekeller, you may not be a thing of beauty, but you are a joy forever. Still, there is one characteristic which I do not like about you. Perhaps it is oversensitiveness on my part, but it sometimes seems to me that you think I am lacking in energy. I hope, however, I am mistaken." His lordship paused and gazed with quaint anxiety at his visitor, who, however, made no response, whereupon his lordship sighed ever so slightly, and put on the look of patient resignation which becomes a misunderstood man.

"Silence gives consent, I think, and I may find it difficult to put your mind right on this subject. Let me give you an illustration, chosen from your own interesting profession of mining engineering. I am credibly informed that if a hole is drilled in a piece of hard rock, and a portion of dynamite inserted therein, the explosion which follows generally rends the rock in twain." Again he paused, and again there was no reply. It was but too evident that the serious Mackeller considered himself being trifled with. Unabashed, his lordship proceeded:

"That is energy, if you like. Shall we name it Mackellerite—this form of energy? Now I shall tell you of a thing I have seen done on one of my own estates. A number of holes were bored in a large bowlder, and instead of dynamite, we drove in a number of wooden pins, and over those pins we placidly poured clear, cold water. After a time the rock gently parted. There was no dust, no smoke, no flame and fury and nerve-shattering detonation, yet the swelling pins had done exactly the same work that your stick of dynamite would have performed. Now, that also was energy, of the Stranleighite variety. I suppose it would be difficult to make the stick of dynamite understand the stick of wood, and vice versa. By the way, have you seen your father since you returned from Southampton!"

"Yes."

"Did he tell you I possess a trim little oceangoing steam yacht at present lying in a British harbor!"

"No, he did not."

"But I thought I made him aware of what I intended to do!"

"Apparently he understood you no better than I do; at least he told me he did not know what course you proposed to take."

"I informed him that my yacht was fitted out with turbine engines, and could reel off, at a pinch, twenty-five knots an hour. Now, how far away is this bally gold property of yours!"

"About three thousand five hundred miles."

"Very good. Toward this interesting spot the Rajah is plodding along at seven knots an hour, perhaps doing a little less, as her owners guarantee that speed. How long will it take her to reach the what-do-you-call-it river? There is no use of my attempting figures when I have an uncivil engineer in my employ."

"About twenty-one days," replied Mackeller.

"Very well. If my yacht goes only twice that speed, which she can accomplish in her sleep, we'd get there in half the time, wouldn't we? I think that mathematical calculation is correct?"

"Yes, it is."

"Then we'd be Johnnie-on-the-spot in about eleven days, wouldn't we?"

"Yes, my lord."

"The Rajah has now four days the start of us. Then don't you see we can spend six more days over our porridge in the morning, and still reach our river before she does? Now don't you begin to be ashamed of yourself, Mackeller? Why rush me over my frugal meal when we have such ample time to spare? I'd much rather spend the six days here in London than up some malarious alligator-filled river on the west coast of Africa." Mackeller's stern face brightened.

"Then you do intend to chase them, after all, my lord?"

"Chase them? Lord bless you, no. Why should I chase them? They are the good Schwartzbrod's hired men. He's paying their wages. Chase them? Of course not; but I'm going to pass them, and get up the river before they do."

Mackeller sprang to his feet, his face ablaze with enthusiasm, his right fist nervously clenching and unclenching.

"Now, do sit down, Peter," wailed his lordship. "Do not let us display unnecessary energy. I've told you two or three times I don't like it."

Peter sat down.

"What I was trying to do when you went off prematurely was to show you the folly of underestimating a fellow creature. You come storming in here, practically accusing me of doing nothing, whereas I am doing nothing because everything is done, and you, on the rampage, have arrived from a total and grotesque failure."

"I apologized for that already, my lord."

"So you did, Peter. I had forgotten. A man shouldn't be asked to pay twice for the same horse and cart, should he? Ponderby," he continued, turning to his impassive butler, "would you be so good as to go into my business office, and bring me my telegraph duplicate book."

Then, turning to his visitor, he added:

"I am so methodical that I keep a copy of every telegram I send. I shall ask you to look through this book with the critical eye of an engineer, and you will learn that while you were raging up from Plymouth I was ordering by telegraph to be sent to my yacht the more important materials for the contest in which we may be involved. A man must make some move to protect his own property, you know."

"Why, my lord, that's just what I've been saying all along, but you gave me to understand you were going to do nothing."

"I cannot account for such an idea arising in your mind. I think you must have jumped at conclusions, Mackeller. Still, as long as I can convince you that I am really a practical man, everything will be all right between us."

The butler placed before Lord Stranleigh the book containing copies of the telegrams sent the day before, and his lordship handed it gracefully to Mackeller.

"Nothing like documentary evidence," he said, "to convince a stubborn man. I think even you will admit that I have risen to the occasion." Mackeller turned the leaves of the book, reading as he went along. His eyebrows came lower and lower over his gloomy eyes, and a faint smile moved the lips of his lordship as he sat there watching him. Finally, he snapped the book shut, and put it down with a slap on the table.

"Twenty-four dozens of champagne; fifty dozens of claret, burgundy, bock, Scotch whisky——"

"Oh, and Irish whisky, too," interrupted his lordship eagerly. "I haven't forgotten anything, you know. You see, I have some Irish blood in my veins, and I occasionally touch it up with a little of the national brew."

"I don't think your blood needs any stimulation," said Mackeller dejectedly. "Here you have ordered tobacco by the hundredweight, pipes by the score, cigars and cigarettes by the thousand. I suppose you think there's something funny in handing me these messages. Are you never in earnest, my lord?"

"Never more so than at the present moment, Mackeller. I am disappointed that you failed to detect genius in the commissariat."

"Are you going to fight this band of ruffians, my lord, by popping champagne corks at them, or smothering them in tobacco smoke?"

"I have told you once or twice, Mackeller, that I don't intend fighting any one at all, but if the band of ruffians should come to dine with me aboard the yacht, I'd like the hospitality shown them to do me credit."

"Very well, your lordship," said Peter with resignation. "You have reminded me that my time is not my own, but yours, so if it gives you any pleasure to befool me, don't allow consideration for my feelings to retard you."

"Ah, you got in a good left-hander on me there, Peter. That's where you score. Now, the proper time having elapsed after a meal when a man should talk business, even if, like me, he does not understand it, he can at least pretend to be wise, no matter how foolish, he is in reality. What is the name of that river of yours again?"

"The Paramakaboo."

"Thanks. Well, as I understood you, it reaches the sea by several channels. Is our property on the main stream?"

"The streams are all about the same size, so far as I was able to learn."

"How far back from the coast are the mountains?"

"You can hardly call them mountains. They are reasonably high hills, and I estimate the distance to be from twenty-five to thirty miles. Our property is twelve miles up the river."

"A steamer drawing the depth of the Rajah could get up there you think?"

"Oh, yes, and could lay alongside the rocks in front of the gold field without needing a wharf of any sort."

"If I took the yacht up another channel, would she be out of sight of any one stationed on our property?"

"The delta is rather flat for a few miles back from the coast, but if you go upstream for fifteen miles or so, there are plenty of hills that would conceal even a line of battle-ship, but any one on your property could see her sailing up the stream while she was in low-lying country."

"That doesn't matter. I intend to get there before our friends do, so there will be no trouble on that score."

"Don't you intend to arm your yacht?"

"Oh, yes; I shall have on board a few sporting rifles, some shotguns, and plenty of ammunition. Is there any game back in the mountains?"

"I don't know. How many riflemen do you propose to take with you?"

"I was thinking of inviting some of my younger gamekeepers; perhaps half a dozen."

"But they can't hold out against a hundred and fifty well-armed men, not to mention the sailors belonging to the Rajah."

"My dear fellow, why is your mind always running on fighting? This is no Treasure Island cruise, with stockades, and one-legged John Silver, and that sort of thing. We are not qualifying for literary immortality, not being filibusters, but merely staid, respectable city persons going to look over a property we have purchased. If we are discovered and attacked, we will valorously fly, and as, at a pinch, I can get twenty-five knots an hour out of the boat, I think with the current of the stream in my favor we can reach the sea in case these misguided persons become obstreperous. You forget that as a city man I am an investor, not a speculator."

"I don't see how that course of action will save your gold from being stolen."

"Don't you? Well, you'll have an inkling by and by. Now, I wish you to go back to Southampton. You negotiated for the charter of the Rajah, I believe."

"Yes."

"Who are her owners?"

"Messrs. Sparling & Bilge."

"Very well. I'll give you a blank check and ask you to return to Southampton. Discover, if you can, what is the reasonable value of the Rajah, then go to Sparling & Bilge and purchase the steamer. See that everything is done legally, and arrange the transfer to me."

"Is there to be any limit in the price I am to pay, Lord Stranleigh?"

"Oh, yes, of course we must place a limit; say ten times the value of the ship. Make as good a bargain as you can. Part of the arrangement must be that Sparling & Bilge write a letter to the captain, telling him that they have sold the boat, that it belongs to me, and that they have transferred to me whatever contract they made with him, the officers and the crew; that I will be responsible hereafter for the pay of the same. Then find out what can be done toward changing the name of the steamer. I wish to paint out the word Rajah and substitute, out of compliment to you, the name Blue Peter. Blue Peter means the flag of that color with a white square which is run up to the masthead when the ship is about to sail, and I doubt not the Blue Peter was flying over Peter Mackeller as he lay in the hold. Please learn if we can change the name legally, and if we cannot, why, we'll see what can be done when the ship is in our possession. I am not going to indulge in any amateur piracy, so I expect you to look sharply after the legal points of the transfer. Get the assistance of the best marine lawyer there is in Southampton. Do you understand what I mean?"

"Yes, my lord, and I will carry out your instructions to the letter. I think I see what you intend to do."

"I am the most transparent of men, Mackeller. There's no subtlety about me, so you can gain little credit by fathoming my plans. We will suppose that two days are required to put me in possession of the Rajah. Return then to London, pack your trunk, bid good-by to all your friends, and say nothing to them of what you have done, or what you intend to do, what you guess, or what you know, not even to your father, whom I have made president of the company, because I dislike unnecessary publicity, and desire to keep my name in the shade of that modest obscurity which has always enveloped it. Buy anything you think you may require for the voyage, and ship your dunnage to Plymouth, addressed, care of the yacht, The Woman in White. Then engage a berth in the sleeping car on the 9.50 Penzance express, Great Western Railway, first-class fare, and five shillings extra for your stateroom, and don't forget to charge it to me. At the unholy hour of 6.49 in the morning, you will arrive at Redruth in Cornwall, where you can indulge in an early breakfast, which you seem to delight in. In the environs of that village you will find a little property which is owned by me, and on that bit of land is an abandoned copper mine with a smelting furnace. I think the smelting apparatus is in reasonably good order, but I doubt if any of the other appurtenances of the mine are of much value. Now, having gone into the mining business, I intend to work this property for all it's worth, and I propose that you spend a day or two getting a suitable manager, rigging up windlasses, and that sort of thing, so that we will see whether there is more money in copper to-day than was the case when the mine was abandoned, years and years ago. I suppose that modern processes may enable us to extract more copper out of the ore than our fathers found possible. Anyhow, my idea is to get the blast furnace in working order once more, and by the time we return to England, we shall probably know whether there is any brass, in another sense of the word, in the mine. Do you think you comprehend that task as well as the buying of the——

"But why trouble with copper, Lord Stranleigh, when you have on your hands the most prolific gold mine, as I believe it to be, in the world?"

"You said it was in the other fellow's hands, Mackeller."

"Don't you intend to stop that crew in some way from lifting the ore?"

"Oh, no, I shall not interfere with them in the least."

"Then what are you going to West Africa for?"

"For the voyage. For the scenery. For the chance of big game in the back country. To drink some of that champagne I have ordered, and to smoke a few of those cigarettes which I sent aboard. I shall read all the latest books that I haven't had time to peruse here in London. By the way, is the neighborhood of our mine a healthy locality?"

"I should say it was rather feverish along the coast, but up toward the hills I think it as healthy as Hampstead."

"I shall induce a doctor friend of mine to come with us. I'm glad I thought of that. If you indulge in your predilection for coercion, giving free rein to your passion for fighting, a surgeon will be necessary for amputations, the dressing of wounds, and generally useful in attending to those exciting incidents that follow in the train of a conqueror like yourself, who believes in brute force rather than in alert brains."

"Then I am to set this copper mine of yours in operation down in Cornwall?"

"Exactly. And leave a competent manager to engage the men, renew the machinery, and all that."

"Is there to be any limit in the expenditure?"

"Limit? Of course there is to be a limit. Aren't we always limiting expenditure? Isn't my life spent in putting a check on the outgoings? Yes, you will instruct the new manager that this is merely a tentative experiment of mine, and that he is not to purchase machinery wholesale, nor engage many miners, but merely to test the capabilities of the copper vein, and smelt as much of the ore as he can until you return."

"Of course it's no business of mine, my lord, but it strikes me that this is an unnecessary and losing venture. The copper industry of Cornwall has been steadily decreasing in value, and I doubt if there are half as many copper mines in operation as there were ten years ago."

"Oh, Peter, Peter, how little of the foresight of your saintly namesake do you possess! Does not your imagination see the little harbor of Portreath, which means the sandy cove? Of course it doesn't, for you are probably ignorant that such a port exists. Our smelter is situated near this marine haven of rest. Stir up your fancy, my boy, and see in your mind's eye the steamer Rajah, loaded with ore, but renamed the Blue Peter, floating majestically into Portreath. What more natural than that the grasping Stranleigh should own another copper mine where there is no smelter, and that this ship brings copper ore to our Cornwall furnace? The Blue Peter shall probably first put into Plymouth, where she is less likely to be recognized by seafaring folk than would be the case at Southampton. We will there discharge the crew, giving every man double pay. We will compensate the captain and his officers, sending everybody away happy. Then we will engage another captain and another crew, who know nothing of where the steamer has come from, and thus we sail round Land's End, and put in to little Portreath."

"You propose, then, to capture the Rajah on the high seas, following it with your much more speedy yacht?"

"Oh, no, not capture. I'm going to take possession, that's all. The Rajah is mine as incontestably as the yacht is. The ore with which she will be loaded is also mine. Everything shall be done as legally as if we were transacting our affairs in the Temple or Gray's Inn. Doesn't that put to shame your wild

Scottish Highland ideas of fighting and slaughter? You ought to wear kilts and a dirk, Mackeller, but my instrument is a quill pen and nice red stamps embossed at Somerset House."

"And who will pay the men who are blasting out the ore on the banks of the river Paramakaboo?"

"Why, really, Mackeller, that is no affair of mine. These industrious people are employed by the saintly Schwartzbrod. If that astute financier elects to engage a large body of labor to get out my ore for me, then I think you will admit, Mackeller, much as you are prejudiced against him, that he is really the philanthropic benefactor of his race I have always said he was."

"But—but—but," stammered Mackeller, "when they discover how they have been befooled, there will be a riot."

"I don't see that. When I discharge the captain and crew at Plymouth, I shall have cut the live wire, if I may use an expression from your absorbing profession. The connecting cable between those deluded miners in West Africa and the amiable syndicate in London, will be severed. The captain knows nothing, I take it, of Schwartzbrod. He was employed by Sparling & Bilge. Going ashore at Plymouth, out of a job, he would probably look for a ship in that port, and failing to find one, might journey to his old employers at Southampton. But, although I discharge the captain, I don't intend to turn him adrift. I have already set influences at work which will secure for him a better boat than the Rajah, and the contented man will sail away from Plymouth, from London, or from some northern port, as the case may be. It is not likely that captain, officers, or crew know the nature of the ore they will be carrying, but I don't intend to leave the wire partially cut. I shall provide places on various ships for officers and crew, and scatter them over the face of the earth, casting my breadwinners on the waters, as one may say, hoping they will not return for many days."

"But when Schwartzbrod hears nothing of the Rajah at whatever foreign port he ordered her to sail, he will make inquiries of Sparling & Bilge."

"I very much doubt that."

"Why?"

"Because he has chartered their ship, and must either produce the steamer or renew the charter. That reminds me, for how long a period was the Rajah engaged?"

"For three months with option of renewal."

"Good. Toward the end of that time old Schwartzbrod will write to Sparling & Bilge extending the charter for another three months. He dare not go to see these shipping men because he has mislaid their steamship, and does not wish to answer embarrassing questions regarding her whereabouts."

"Yes, but Sparling & Bilge will merely reply that they have sold the Rajah to Lord Stran-leigh, and beg to refer Schwartzbrod to the new owner."

"Bravo, Peter. You are actually beginning to get an inkling of Mr. Schwartzbrod's dilemma. I had almost despaired of making this clear to you."

"Still, I don't understand the object of cutting the live wire, as you call it, if you leave another communicating wire intact. You take great pains to prevent captain or any of the crew meeting Schwartzbrod, yet you make it inevitable that Schwartzbrod will learn you are the owner of the Rajah. Perhaps you wish me to pledge Sparling & Bilge to secrecy?"

"Oh, dear no. I anticipate great pleasure in meeting Mr. Schwartzbrod. I picture him cringing and bowing and rubbing one hand over the other as he pleads for a renewal of the charter, and crawls away from all my inquiries regarding the whereabouts of the steamer. I will be back in London by the time the syndicate begins to get uneasy about the Rajah, and I shall renew the charter with the utmost cheerfulness, without insisting on learning where the Rajah is. But imagine the somewhat delicate position of a man compelled to negotiate with me for the hire of a boat to steal my own gold. The venerable Schwartzbrod will need to keep a close guard on his tongue or he will give himself away. It is a delicious dilemma. I hope you comprehend all the possibilities of the situation, but be that as it may, get you off to Southampton, and when you are done with the copper mine, report on board my yacht at Plymouth, where you will find me waiting for you. Then for the blue sea and red carnage if it is so written. Sixteen men on a dead man's chest, yo, ho, ho, and a bottle of champagne, and all that sort of thing, Peter."

CHAPTER IV—THE MAGNET OF THE GOLD FIELD

THE young and energetic Mackeller completed his purchase of the steamer Rajah in something less than three hours, instead of taking the two days which Lord Stranleigh had allowed him. It is very easy to buy a ship in Southampton if you happen to have the money about you. An excellent express on the South Western line whisked him up to London again, and he spent the afternoon in securing what he needed for the long voyage that was ahead of him, dispatching his purchases, as his lordship had directed, to the care of the yacht at Plymouth. As his acquaintance with Lord Stranleigh progressed, his first impression of the lord of Wychwood became considerably modified. In spite of the young nobleman's airy, nonchalant manner in speaking of what the young engineer regarded as serious subjects, Mackeller began slowly to realize that there was thought and method behind all this persiflage which he so much disliked, and he began to doubt his theory that Stranleigh's successful encounter with the syndicate had been merely a fluke, as, at first, he had supposed. The plan his lordship so sketchily outlined, of regaining his own property on the high seas, struck the practical mind of Mackeller as probably feasible, but although all the legality would be on his lordship's side; although his opponents were engaged in a gigantic scheme of barefaced robbery, nevertheless, Mackeller had knocked about at the ends of the earth too much to be ignorant of the fact that in certain quarters of the globe lawfulness of action was but a minor point in the game. Indeed, the law-abiding citizen was at a distinct disadvantage unless he held superior force at his command to compel rather than to persuade. There is little use in arguing with a man who holds a loaded revolver, so on one point Lord Stranleigh failed to convince his subordinate. Mackeller thought it folly to proceed to West Africa with a small body of men, and no more persuasive ammunition than champagne and cigarettes. Therefore, in purchasing his own equipment Mackeller took the precaution of buying a dozen of the latest repeating rifles, with many thousand cartridges to fit the same, and this battery he ordered forwarded to the yacht to supplement whatever sporting guns Lord Stranleigh provided for the gamekeepers and foresters whom he took with him. Mackeller believed that these would be stanch, stubborn, capable young men, and although few in number, they might, if well armed, put the rabble of a hundred and fifty to flight, should a contest arise.

The dark man who kicked Mackeller downstairs into the hold, and who afterwards interviewed him alone by lantern light, had impressed Mackeller as being a capable leader of men, and he would probably drill his following into some sort of shape during the long voyage to the south. That the captain, officers, and crew, or any of the hundred and fifty knew the piratical nature of the expedition, Mackeller very strongly doubted, but the prompt manner in which the leader, with his energetic foot, broke the law, and very nearly broke Mackeller's neck, convinced the engineer that the dark man was well aware of the criminal nature of his proceeding, and undoubtedly, when once the force was landed, he would be very much on the alert, expecting that as soon as the flight of the steamer became known, instant arrangements would be made for pursuit. He would doubtless send out scouts, and endeavor roughly to understand the lay of the land on which he found himself. It was morally certain, thought Mackeller, that one or other of those scouts would ultimately come upon the yacht, no matter how securely they hid her, and so soon as her presence came to the knowledge of the strenuous leader of the filibusters, an attack on the yacht was certain, and her capture or destruction most probable, unless they could escape quickly to the open sea. So, as Mackeller knew there were no gun shops along the Paramakaboo River, he took precaution to make provision beforehand without saying anything to his peace-loving master. A man whose daily walk is Piccadilly is scarcely in a position to predict what may happen on the Paramakaboo.

At 9.50 that night Mackeller was in occupation of his most comfortable little room in the sleeping car of the Penzance express, and an excellent night's rest followed his busy day. Seven o'clock next morning found him at breakfast in Redruth, and so resolutely did he go about his business that in two days he formed complete the organization which was to operate the old copper mine. Then he took train for Plymouth, and was rowed out in the evening to the white yacht at anchor in the harbor, resting beautiful as a swan on the placid waters. Mackeller was astonished to find her so great a boat. She was almost as large as the Rajah, but of much more dainty shape, her fine lines giving promise of great speed. Thin cables, extending from slanting mast to slanting mast, he recognized as the outside paraphernalia for wireless telegraphy, and although he saw from this that Lord Stranleigh treated himself to the latest scientific inventions, he was quite unprepared for the quiet luxury that everywhere met his eye once he was aboard of the yacht.

He found Lord Stranleigh aft, seated in a cane chair, his feet resting on another. He had been reading the latest evening paper brought aboard, and he laid this on his knee as he looked lazily up at his mining engineer.

"Finished with copper, Mackeller?" he asked. "Yes, my lord."

"I did not expect you before to-morrow night. I imagine, you gave your disconcerting energy full play down in Cornwall."

"I have been reasonably busy, my lord."

"Would you mind pressing that electrical button? It is just out of my reach."

Mackeller did so, and a cabin boy immediately put in an appearance.

"Go forward, and ask Captain Wilkie if he will be good enough to allow me a word with him." Captain Wilkie proved to be a grizzled old sea-dog of unmistakably Scotch extraction. He rolled aft, and saluted his owner.

"Everything ready, captain?"

"Everything ready, sir."

"Very well; up anchor and away."

The captain went forward and mounted the bridge.

"Draw up your chair, Peter, and let me have your verbal report, and as you drop into the chair, drop also that appellation 'my lord.' If you want to be extra respectful at any time, say 'sir' as the captain does, and I'll do the same by you, if you require it."

Mackeller gave him a full account of his occupation during the last three days, but whether Stranleigh was asleep or not throughout the recital, he could not be sure. At any rate he did not interrupt, but lay back in his chair with closed eyes. Then, without opening them, he remarked:

"You have done very well, Mackeller, and as a reward I will give you the choice of a spot in the Bay of Biscay or the Atlantic Ocean where you may wish your case of rifles and ammunition heaved overboard."

"Oh, have you been examining my dunnage, sir?" asked Mackeller.

"Dear me, no," replied Stranleigh languidly. "Your fool of a gunsmith did not understand your instructions, and not knowing where to find you, and supposing you were acting for me, he telegraphed asking which of two rifles named should be sent. Learning that twelve had been ordered, I thought of telegraphing in the old phrase, 'Six of one and half a dozen of the other,' but I finally took on a score altogether, ten of each kind with ammunition to match."

"Why purchase more guns than I did, if you're going to drop them in the Bay of Biscay."

"Oh, they'll make the bigger plump when they go down."

"What harm will they do aboard, sir? If we don't need them, we won't use them. If we do need them, then you'll be sorry they're in the Bay of Biscay."

"So you're going to choose the Bay of Biscay, are you? I thought perhaps you might toss them over farther along than that. I hope you understand, Mackeller, I am on a mission of peace, and if, for any reason, the yacht should be searched, your rifles and ammunition would be rather a giveaway, wouldn't they?"

"I don't see that. You've got more than a score of men aboard here, and the repeaters can be used for sporting purposes."

"All right, Mackeller, don't be alarmed. The boxes are stowed safely away in the forrard hold, and we'll not drop them overboard anywhere. After all, you know the locality for which we are bound better than I do, and so your rifles and ammunition may prove friends in need. I see the boy hovering about in the offing, and I am sure he wishes to conduct you to your cabin. By the time you've washed the railway dust from your sylphlike form, the dinner gong will be filling the air with a welcome melody. I've got my own favorite chef with me, and I understand we shall not need to live on porridge and tinned milk. And, by the way, Mackeller, did you happen to pack such wearing apparel as dinner togs in your dunnage, as you call it?"

"Dinner togs?" echoed Mackeller, aghast. "Why, hang it all, I'm a mining engineer. I haven't even a starched shirt with me, let alone a dress suit. I didn't know I was coming to an evening party?"

"No, you paid attention to the trivialities of life, such as rifles and ammunition, and quite neglected the more important affair of costume."

"I'll eat forward with the men," said Mackeller gruffly.

"Oh, there's no need for that. As you tried to bolt through the door from my breakfast room the other day, when Ponderby was on guard, I saw him measure your proportions critically with his eye, in case it should be necessary for him to use that force which I deplore, so I told Ponderby to make a guess at what would fit you, and to go to the extent of three evening suits of varying sizes made to order. You will find them all laid out in your room, and the able Ponderby will give you critical advice regarding which fits you best."

"Well, sir, if you expect me to look pretty every night——"

"Oh, no," interrupted his lordship, "I never expect the impossible, but, you see, Captain Wilkie is rather a stickler on etiquette. He will occupy one end of the table, brave in a uniform of gold lace made by the premier naval tailor of London, so we must play up to him, my boy, and do the best we can. Then there will be our chief engineer, also in uniform, and the wireless telegraphy operator, who is rather a la-de-da young man, and lastly there's the doctor, an Oxford graduate, and so we must do honor to the university. You and I are in the minority, and we'll just need to make the best of it."

Mackeller departed dejectedly to his room, which he found so spacious and so luxuriously fitted up that he stood on its threshold for a few moments, dumfounded, regarding it with dismay. He emerged when the gong rang, and entered the long broad saloon which extended from side to side of the ship. Lord Stranleigh occupied the head of the table, and he introduced Mackeller to Dr. Holden, and to Mr. Spencer, electrician and telegrapher. Neither the captain nor the engineer put in an appearance during dinner, the one waiting to see his ship in more open waters, and the other standing by to watch the behavior of the machinery at the beginning of a long run.

"You have a fine boat here, Stranleigh," said the doctor.

"It isn't half bad," admitted his lordship. "Still, there's always a fly in the ointment. I call her The Woman in White, after the title of Wilkie Collins's famous novel. You know the book, Mac-keller, I suppose?"

"I never heard of it. I don't read novels."

"Oh, well, we must convert you before the voyage is ended. You'll find plenty of fiction on board this boat. There's a copy of "The Woman in White" in every room, large and small, each copy in a style of binding that suits the decoration of the room, so I beg of you, Mackeller, to begin reading the story in your own apartment, and if, getting interested in it, you wish to continue in the saloon, or on deck, I hope you will take the saloon or deck copy, so that the color of the binding will not clash with your surroundings. I ought really to have the copies chained in their places, as was the case with the ancient books in our churches, for it is a terribly distressing sight to see a man reading a mauve book in a white-and-gold saloon, or a scarlet copy up on deck."

"Yes, I should think that would be appalling," sneered Mackeller.

"Now, don't be sarcastic, Peter, and thus lacerate my tenderest artistic tastes. You may come to know, some day, when you are starving in a wilderness on the West Coast, that these are really the serious things of life."

"I dare say," replied Peter gruffly.

"Then the fly in the ointment," said the doctor, "is the fact that your passengers persist in taking away the volumes from the rooms where they belong?"

"Oh, no; a man who calls his yacht Woman in White, should have a captain named Wilkie Collins. I searched England and Scotland for one of that name, and couldn't find him, so I was compelled to compromise, a thing I always dislike doing. My captain's name is Wilkie, and my chief engineer's name is Collins, and thus I divide the burden of congruity upon the shoulders of two different men, whereas one would have sufficed if his parents had only exhibited some common sense at his christening. I'd pay any salary in reason for a captain named Wilkie Collins."

"I think I'll write a book myself, some day," said the doctor, "and call it 'The Grievous Worries of a Millionaire.' Would you object if I took you as my model for my Croesus?"

"On the contrary, I should be flattered, and as you progress with the work I may be able to supply you with incidents to weave into your narrative."

Mackeller sat silent while this frivolous conversation went on, and this silence he maintained during the greater part of the voyage. Mackeller's mind was troubled. He was a serious young man, whose opinions were strongly grounded on common sense, and there were many elements in the situation that gave him just cause for anxiety. When it came down to finalities, he possessed a strong belief in the efficiency of force. So far as his knowledge went, the Lord was always on the side of the biggest battalion. He represented the American confidence in the big stick, the British faith in keeping your powder dry, the German reliance on the mailed fist.

And now here he was treading the deck of a confection in naval construction; a dainty flower of marine architecture, which slipped through the water as gracefully as if she were a living white swan. Her well-molded, snowy sides were of the finest quality of pressed steel, almost paper thin, and he was convinced that even a single shot from a small cannon would send her shivering to the bottom, shattering her metal covering as a pane of glass is shattered by a well-thrown stone, and for this delusion he was scarcely to be blamed, because his education had been concentrated on mining engineering, and the mechanism of air-tight and water-tight compartments did not form part of his curriculum. He knew that on the open sea The Woman in White could not be overtaken by any craft afloat except one or other of the most recent torpedo-boat destroyers, which were not likely to be encountered along the west coast of Africa, but he knew the locality to which The Woman in White was bound, and he pictured her from twelve to twenty-four miles away from the coast, where, if discovered, she would need to make her way down a narrow river, flanked on each side, after she left the shelter of the hills, by a flat country. In this position it would be impossible, owing to windings of the stream, to take advantage of her full speed, and being under the misapprehension that a single well-aimed shot would disable, if not sink, her, he pictured the beautiful yacht and her crew helplessly trapped somewhere between the hills and the lagoon, at the mercy of well-armed, desperate men, in a region where no law, save that of might, ran: men who would not feel the slightest scruple in removing from the earth, all trace of the vessel and those aboard of her.

If Mackeller had been told that the little craft might have been riddled like a sieve, and still keep afloat, and that so long as a stray shot did not destroy her motive power, she could, within a few minutes, get out of range of any land force, so long as there was a sufficient depth of water in the river, he would not have believed it. He strongly suspected that the Rajah was well provided not only with cannon and ammunition, but also with floating mines to seal up the river, rendering exit impossible. Into this fatal impasse Lord Stranleigh, with a levity that saddened Mackeller, was running his unprotected cruiser, armed only with luxury. Officers and crew would be of little use in a fight, and the extra men, whatever might be the shooting qualities of the gamekeepers and foresters whom Stranleigh had requisitioned from his estates, were quite undisciplined, and although most of them were doubtless expert enough with a shotgun, their efficiency with magazined arms of precision such as he had sent on board, was more than doubtful.

Once or twice during the early portion of the voyage, Mackeller had endeavored to imbue Lord Stranleigh with some of his own apprehension, but the young nobleman was usually in company with the doctor, or with the telegrapher, or one or other of the officers, and he invariably turned aside

Mackeller's attempts with a joke, refusing to discuss anything seriously. By the time they had arrived at that portion of the waters where they should have passed the Rajah, according to Mackeller's calculation, they were sailing through an empty sea. Day after day Mackeller, from the front of the vessel, swept the bald horizon with the most powerful of binoculars, but he saw nothing of the tramp steamer. The voyage had been monotonous with its good weather. Nothing had happened, either in the way of a breakdown of machinery, or the encountering of even a moderate storm.

Lord Stranleigh recognized his anxious search with an amused smile, but said nothing. At last Mackeller gave up scrutiny of sea and sky. It was no longer possible that the Rajah could have covered the distance The Woman in White had already traversed. Still, his earnest meditations had at last evolved a plan, and the adoption of that plan he must now urge upon his chief, so seeing that Stranleigh, for once, was alone, he strode aft to the spot where the head of the expedition lolled in a reclining cane chair, with his slippered feet extended on the adjustable rest. Like the woman for whom his ship was named, he was clad entirely in white, for the weather was warm, although the yacht slipped so speedily through the oily water that a comforting breeze greeted every one on deck. The young man placed the book he had been reading face downward on the little table at his elbow, and looked up at the on-comer with an expression of amusement on his face.

"Well, Mackeller," he cried, "have you found her?"

"Found whom, sir?"

"Why, the Rajah, of course."

"How did you know I was looking for her?"

"You've been looking for something these few days past, so I took the liberty of surmising it was the Rajah."

"You are quite right.'"

"I always am, Mackeller. Haven't you discovered that yet? Always be right and then you'll be happy, although you'll also be extremely disliked by everybody else. Still, I never aimed at popularity, not wishing to write a book, or stand for Parliament, so a lack of popularity does not matter."

"I never pretend to be always right, sir."

"Well, that's a good thing. I dislike pretense myself; nevertheless, it is so easy to be right that I sometimes wonder you don't practice the art. All that is necessary is knowledge and brains."

"I do not lack knowledge in my own line of business, and no one ever hinted before that I was lacking in brain power."

"I do not hint that at all, Mackeller. I bear willing testimony to your brain power, but I sometimes think you don't exercise it enough. For instance, you think things out in somber silence, when sometimes a question might throw a good deal of light on your problem. Take my own actions, for instance. Do you suppose I wish the whereabouts of my yacht reported in the marine columns of the English newspapers day by day, thus running the risk that certain people will begin to wonder what I am doing so far south?"

"Of course not."

"Very well. Why have we met none of the South African liners, or overtaken any of the tramps threshing their way to Cape Town?"

"I'm sure I don't know."

"Oh, yes, you do, if you'll only think. The reason is this: that having ample time at my command, the course of my yacht was deflected from south to southwest when we reached north latitude 40. We spun along merrily in that direction till daylight did appear, and then resumed our progress south. We passed outside of the islands, and out of the track of any steamer that might report us. Now turn your brain power upon that amiable gentleman who kicked you downstairs. He must at least strongly suspect that he's engaged on an illegal expedition. Would he deflect, do you think, and waste valuable time on the face of the ocean?"

"No, I don't think so."

"Of course you don't. He'd make for your what-do-you-call-it river on a bee-line. The course we have taken puts us two hundred miles, more or less, from his path, and as they tell me you cannot see more than thirty miles on the water, you may now conjecture how fruitless has been your scanning of the ocean. I had no desire to see the Rajah, but in any case I did not wish the Rajah to see me. We will steam as we are going until we are directly opposite your gold mine; then round at right angles and straight eastward is our course. You should do as I do, Mackeller, and read that incomparable sea writer, W. Clark Russell, then you'd begin to understand what you are about. He'd put you up to all the tricks of the trade. It's one of his books I'm perusing now, which accounts for my trickiness at sea. Have you ever read any of his novels?"

"No, I haven't."

"Very well, then, begin with the 'Wreck of the Grosvenor.' We've got all his works on board, and pretty soon you'll know what to do with a mutiny, how to conduct yourself when marooned, the proper etiquette to adopt if tackled by a cyclone, what to say when you and a nice girl are left alone on a wreck. Of course I admit that W. W. Jacobs is excellent, and that he puts forth most admirable text-books on navigation, but he is only good below-bridge, as you might put it; for rivers and other inland waters, and perhaps a bit of the coast. When you take to deep-sea navigation you must study Clark Russell, my boy. Take the advice of a tarry old salt like myself, and study Clark Russell. Do not be deluded by my white apparel; I am tar to the finger ends, and full of salt junk, because I'm three quarter way through his latest book."

"I suppose it would be useless for me to say, sir, that I believe you are running into a trap?"

"Oh, quite. Sufficient to the day is the evil thereof. You refer, of course, to our being bottled up in that unpronounceable river, and ordinarily I should give some attention to the matter, but I cannot now, as I am in the middle of the most exciting chapter in this most exciting book. Once we are inside the trap, Mackeller, we'll study its construction, and find a way out. There seems to me little practical use in studying an imaginary trap which may not be there when we arrive. That leads to disappointment. Let us first get into the trap if we can; then if there's no way out, we will console ourselves by the knowledge that there are plenty of provisions and books to read on board. If the worst comes to the worst, we will get our wireless telegraphy at work until we pick up a liner similarly equipped, and thus get into communication with Clark Russell, relate our position, and ask him what to do. I'll bet you a fiver he'll send a solution of the problem."

Mackeller compressed his lips, and turned on his heel without a word.

"Oh, very well," laughed Stranleigh, "have it your own way. Try Jacobs if you like, but I bank on Russell," and with that parting remark his lordship resumed his reading.

Mackeller grimly resolved to make no further attempt to instill common sense into an empty head, neither did he take to the reading of freshwater or salt-water authors. He devoted what time remained to him in poring over certain scientific works he had discovered in the library.

One night he woke up suddenly. The boat was strangely still. Light as had been the unceasing purr of the turbines, its cessation had instantly aroused him. He made his way to the deck. The steamer swayed gently in the heave of the sea. From the east came the low murmur of breakers on the shore, sounding like a distant waterfall. The dim outline of dark hills against a less dark sky could be distinguished, and that was all. Mackeller paced the deck until daylight, when the steamer got under weigh again, and cautiously approached the shore. One of the ship's boats was swung into the water, and under Mackeller's guidance sounded with a lead the depths of the channel, the yacht crawling after them, until at last it entered the river. By nine o'clock it was moored alongside the gold fields. A few minutes later Lord Stranleigh appeared on deck, well-groomed, clear-eyed, and fresh as a youth whose night's rest has been undisturbed. He expressed no surprise on seeing the position of his steamer, but merely remarked to his captain:

"That was rather a good shot, old man, considering the size of the target and the distance. When did you sight the coast?"

"At four bells, sir."

"Did you need to cruise up and down to find the spot?"

"No, sir."

"Look at that, now, and yet Maekeller thinks we're going to be trapped."

After breakfast Lord Stranleigh gave orders that the steamer should proceed upstream to the head of navigation, wherever that was, so they cast off, and began to explore. They discovered that the stream they were navigating was merely a branch, and not the main river, as Mackeller had supposed. About a mile above the mines the land began to rise, and both banks were clothed with splendid forests. Arriving at the head of the delta they found that the river itself proceeded due north, while a branch similar to that which passed the gold fields struck off through the forest to the southwest. The southwest branch was the smallest of the three streams, so they did not trouble with it, but went down the main river until they reached a defile with hills to the west of them facing the continuous range to the east.

"This will be our camping spot, I imagine," said Stranleigh. "We will return to it, but first I wish to investigate the channel at the mouth of the river."

They discovered, to Mackeller's surprise, that the stream flowed so far to the north that when at last it turned west the steamer could reach the ocean without any possibility of being seen from the gold region. Stranleigh laughed when this fact was made plain, and smote Mackeller on the shoulders.

"Where's your trap now, my boy?" he cried. "You would have saved yourself some worry if you had known that the lay of the land was like this."

"Nevertheless," said Mackeller, "if they discover this channel, they may fill it with floating mines."

"So they may the mouth of the Thames, but they won't. An engineer should stick to probabilities, Peter. Now we will return, and seek our secluded glen, mooring against the eastern bank, so that if we are discovered by our opponents, as the song says, they will have one more river to cross."

They reached the ravine in the evening, and Lord Stranleigh complained of a hard day's work virtuously accomplished, with the prospective dinner well earned, although his exertions had consisted mainly of sitting in an armchair at the prow, with his feet on the rail.

Next morning he crossed the river with Mackeller and a party of foresters, some of whom carried axes, one a huge telescope with its stand, and another a small tent. At the top the foresters cleared away intervening underbrush so that a view might be had of the distant gold fields. The telescope stand was placed upon the rock, and the tent erected over it. Stranleigh, adjusting the focus, gazed at the gold fields, then rubbed his hands with satisfaction.

"Why," he said, "we can see their inmost thoughts with this."

When they descended, Stranleigh sent another party to the top, one laden with wireless telegraphy apparatus, which the operator was requested to get into working order.

"If successful it will save us a telephone wire," said his lordship.

The rest were laden with provisions.

"Mackeller," he said, "I appoint you to the outlook, and your companion will be our second telegraph operator. One never knows what may happen in this locality, so if our steamer is compelled to cut and run, you people up on top, with everything so well concealed, can lie low, yet keep in touch with us so long as we are within the four-mile radius, or whatever is the limit of the wireless. I noticed a little spring about halfway up in the forest, and that will supply you with drink nearer than the river, and I counsel you it is better for you than champagne, although I have sent up a case of that. And now, to show you how economical I am, and thus make an appeal to your Scottish heart, I am going to send my woodmen into the forest alongside, and while here we will burn nothing but hard wood, and save coal. Indeed, I have consulted with my chief engineer, and with his consent I am going to fill our bunkers with the most combustible timber I can find. I take no further interest in your mountain top until the Rajah is sighted, but while the woodmen, with their axes and saws, are filling the bunkers, I shall attend to the larder with fishing tackle and gun, and here's where my gamekeepers will earn their wages."

Game proved to be plentiful, and many wondrous fishes were captured.

"Oh!" cried Stranleigh, one night after an exceptionally good fish and game dinner. "Piccadilly is a fool of a place to this. If the postal arrangements were only a little better, we would be all right. I must send a letter to the Times about the negligence of our Government, and score the postmaster-general, as all right-minded correspondents do. I have almost forgotten what a postman looks like, but I expect when we get our wireless at work we'll be able to give Signor Marconi some hints when we return."

The Rajah was three days late, according to Mackeller's calculations, but one morning Mac-keller recognized her slowly stemming the current of the Paramakaboo River, and at once the information was telegraphed to Stranleigh, who did not receive the message, as he was out shooting. The young man had taken his lunch with him, so the operator on the steamer informed those up aloft, and no one knew when he would be back.

Mackeller, his eye glued to the telescope, watched the landing of the army that the Rajah carried, and saw the two steam cranes, one fore and one aft, begin at once to swing ashore the cargo from the hold. He momentarily expected the arrival of his chief, but the dinner hour came, bringing no visitor to the hilltop. Mackeller and the operator descended, and there, to his amazement, on the after-deck he saw Stranleigh seated, calmly reading a novel, and awaiting the sound of the gong.

"Didn't you get our message?" demanded Mackeller.

"Oh, yes, a couple of hours ago. The Rajah has come in, you say? That's very interesting. You'll be glad to know, Mackeller, that I have had a most successful day's shooting."

"Yes, that, as you remark, is very interesting," replied Mackeller dryly. "I thought, if you got my message in time, you would have come up to the outlook."

"I am sorry to have disappointed you, Peter, but when I place an excellent man on the spot I never interfere with him. I should be quite superfluous on the hilltop, and it's so much more comfortable down here."

"You might have been surprised to know how many men they landed from the Rajah. Enough, I estimate, to clean us up in short order if they find us."

"Well, let us hope they won't find us, Peter."

"They've got a number of tents erected already, and they began blasting operations at one o'clock."

"They are not losing any time, are they?"

"No, they are not. I see they have arranged electric searchlights on the two masts, apparently to cover the field of operations, so I suppose they will be working day and night shifts."

"I do love an energetic body of men," said his lordship with admiration. "If there was a funicular to the top of your hill, I'd take up an armchair merely for the pleasure of sitting and watching them. Ah, there's the dinner gong, thank goodness. Peter, I shot some birds to-day that I think you'll enjoy."

"Thank you, but all I wish is a sandwich. I'm going back to the outlook. We haven't broken into the boxes of provisions yet. I must learn if these people are actually going to work all night."

"Take my advice, Peter, and don't. Enjoy a good rest in your comfortable bed. Those who sleep well live long."

"I am going back," said Peter.

"Ah, I see what you're trying to do. You'll force me to give you both a day and a night salary, or perhaps you are yearning to imitate the energy of those johnnies on the gold rock. Now do be persuaded, for my sake, to consume a good dinner when it is all ready for you. Place the sandwiches in your pocket, if you like, to munch during the watches of the night, if you will persist in climbing that distressingly steep hill."

Mackeller shook his head.

"I implore you to be persuaded, Peter, because if you will not succumb to gentle measures, I shall command you, and then if you refuse, I'll put you in irons. I'm not going to tramp all day over Africa on your behalf, and then have my bag ignored when I return. One concession I will make: don't trouble to-night about your evening clothes. Be not abashed by the splendor of your table companions, but devote your attention to the dinner, which I hope you will pronounce good, and I will order the steward to make you up a parcel of delicious sandwiches."

So Mackeller, being a hired minion, was forced to comply. At the head of the table that evening, Lord Stranleigh held forth eloquently on the wickedness of work.

"I don't agree with my friend, President Roosevelt," he said, "regarding the strenuous life. The President quite overlooks the fact that work was placed upon this earth as a curse, and now many unthinking people pretend to look upon it as a blessing. Roosevelt reminds me something of Mackeller here, except that he is more genial, and possesses a greater sense of humor. Mackeller, actuated by the promptings of duty, and assisted by porridge-fed muscle, is actually going to climb that steeple of a hill tonight, while we will be playing bridge. This will give him a feeling of superiority over us which to-morrow he will be unable to conceal. I always sympathize with those people who eliminated Aristides called the Just."

Mackeller remained silent through all this badinage, but nevertheless enjoyed his dinner, although the moment coffee was served and the card table set out, he rowed himself across the river, tied up his boat securely, and ascended through the darkness of the forest to see the electric lights blazing over the gold mine when he reached the top.

In spite of his apparent indifference, Lord Stranleigh appeared on the summit shortly after breakfast. He found Mackeller stretched on the rock, sound asleep, and did not disturb him, but turned his attention instead to the telescope, through which he saw enough of industry going on to satisfy the most indolent. He turned the telescope this way and that, and at last fixed it at a point covering the river lower down than the mine. There he gazed quietly for a long time, until interrupted by Mackeller sitting up, and giving utterance to an exclamation when he saw his chief seated on the stump that did duty for a chair.

"Good morning, Peter. Watchman, what of the night?"

"They worked all night, sir, both at the blasting of the ore, and the unloading of the ship."

"Then that means we shall soon need to be getting under weigh again. If they load the Rajah as quickly as they have unloaded her, she will be out in the ocean before we know where we are."

"That's why I came up last night, sir. I thought you didn't quite appreciate how speedily our visit here is drawing to a close."

"And yet," drawled Stranleigh, "what they are doing now seems to point to a lengthened stay on the part of the Rajah."

"What are they doing now?" demanded Mackeller.

"About half a mile below the gold fields they are planting floating mines in the river. They have just finished one row that goes clear across the stream, and are engaged upon the second series a quarter of a mile, as I estimate the distance, nearer the ocean. They have two ordinary ship's boats at work, and one steam launch. The river is sealed up, and there is a practical declaration of war, my boy, with Mackeller sound asleep."

CHAPTER V—AN INVITATION TO LUNCH

MACKELLER, now wide awake, sprang to his feet and gazed through the telescope. "You see," he cried triumphantly, "I was right after all!"

"Yes, you were right on one point and wrong on another. I confess I did not believe in the floating mine, because it is not an article you can buy at every ironmonger's; but you were wrong in predicting they would leave a channel for the Rajah to get out: they have completely sealed the river. Of course that is an advantage. When it is time for the Rajah to leave, you will see those mines picked up and brought inshore; so, by watching the mine field on the river, we will receive notice of the Rajah's departure."

"And do you intend to follow her out when the mines are cleared away?"

"Bless you, no. We will depart by the main channel."

"Then you will do nothing about this nest of explosives?"

"What is there to do? If we were Japanese, and reckless of human life, we might steal down there and set the mines adrift; but that would be a dangerous business, and if one or more got out into the ocean we might find ourselves practically responsible for the destruction of a Cape liner. But after all," continued his lordship dreamily, sprawling at full length on the place that Mackeller had deserted, "after all, what is the use of this gold? You can't eat it or drink it, except in London or Paris, or some such center of so-called civilization. You have just seen what brutes it makes of men in quest of it, when they will in cold blood prepare for the annihilation of their fellow creatures."

"But you knew all that, sir, before you left England."

"True, true, so I did; but here the fact has made a greater impression on my mind. I have arrived at a theory. I believe this spot to be the Garden of Eden. The soil and climate will grow anything. You may enjoy whatever temperature you like by simply rising higher and higher in the hills; the higher you get the lower the temperature. There is ample timber of all kinds, and yesterday I discovered a lovely waterfall which would give us enough electricity to endow a city with power, so I intend to found a modern Utopia, and have selected a spot where this very day we will begin to clear away the forest and build log huts. The nucleus of our colony will be situated at the head of the delta alongside the stream that passes the gold field and flows direct to the ocean. I shall move the steamer over there, and thus, Peter, you will be deserted, for I insist that you shall watch our potential enemies from this spot, and report by wireless what they are doing."

"So you intend to give up this mining property without a struggle?"

"Oh, I hate struggling. The climate is too perfect to struggle. Let us be happy when there is a chance of happiness."

The young man reclined there with his hands clasped behind his head, looking up quizzically with half-closed eyes at the bewildered Mackeller.

"By the way, Mackeller, there is something afloat on the river near the yacht that would interest you. Did I tell you I had picked up a little gem of a motor boat at Thomycroft's, actually armored and bullet-proof? In it we could go down and visit the mine, and return, letting them pepper away at us, while we lay full length on deck protected by the armored bulwarks. No one could be hit, unless the shooter were on top of a church steeple. I think I'll visit the mining camp."

"I strongly advise you, sir, to do nothing of the kind."

"Oh, very well, I won't, then, but this little craft will come in handy for visiting you. It is a nimble little beast, and much more effective on these waters than the row boat."

"Are you in earnest about that Utopia, sir?"

"Certainly, which reminds me I must make a beginning."

He rose, lazily stretched himself, nodded good-by to Mackeller, and proceeded in leisurely fashion down the hill.

The woodmen on board The Woman in White received the announcement of the new Utopia in a spirit quite differing from that of Mackeller, but of course they knew nothing of the gold that had been the object of the cruise. The yacht proceeded to the side of the plateau that Stranleigh had selected as the site of his first village, and presently the air was filled with a crash of falling trees, with the ringing sound of the ax, and the snarl of the saw. Gamekeepers and crew were all set to work, those who could not chop being useful at the two-handed saw, or the rolling of logs to the river bank, where Stranleigh ordered them to be piled.

Mackeller and the telegrapher occupied their lonely perch night and day, and sent in reports of progress. At last Mackeller announced that the loading of ore had gone so far that the Plim-soll's mark on the Rajah's side was already submerged, which fact, added Mackeller, showed that the steamer did not intend sailing to England. Within half an hour of the receipt of this message the swift little motor boat brought Stran-leigh and the doctor to the foot of Outlook Hill, and presently the two arrived at the summit.

"Mackeller," said Stranleigh, "turn your telescope upstream to the first bit of clear water you see."

While Mackeller was doing this, the chief turned to the operator—and said:

"Send a message to your colleague: these words—'Let'em all come.' Ask him to repeat them to show that he has understood."

"Are you expecting an attack?" asked Mackeller, putting his own interpretation on the familiar defiant phrase.

"A sort of an attack," replied Stranleigh. "You watch the surface of that water, and tell me what you see."

"Oh!" cried Mackeller, "there seems to be a raft coming down."

"No, they are separate logs. They have understood our signal, doctor, and have acted promptly. Now, Mackeller, turn your glass on the floating mines, and give up your place to the doctor. I have promised him the first sight. How many mines did they lay down, Mackeller?"

"I don't know, sir."

"Ah, yes, I remember; you were asleep at your post. Well, I'm happy to inform you that the number I saw placed in the river was exactly twenty-seven. Now, Mr. Telegrapher, stand up here and make yourself useful. If explosions occur, no man is to speak, but each is to keep count of the number of spurts of water he sees, then we will compare notes at the end of the fusillade."

"By Jove!" exclaimed the doctor, his eyes glued to the telescope.

A tall pillar of water, white as snow, rose into the air, paused, broke like a sky-rocket, and subsided in a misty rain, which the wind caught and blew along the surface of the water. Then three more shot up into the air as if in competition. A sound like distant thunder came across the delta, and now it seemed that one mine had set off another, or else the logs were even thicker than might have been expected, for a wall of water rose from the surface of the river, extending, with breaks here and there, from shore to shore, and instead of a rumble, a sharp thunderclap was heard by the four men on the mountain. This made counting impossible. For a few moments nothing further happened, then a quarter of a mile down the river the line of mines went off practically simultaneously, forming for a brief instant a Niagara in the sky.

"I think we've got them," said Stranleigh quietly, as he slung over his shoulder again the binoculars he had been using. "Turn your telescope to the land again, doctor, and see those comical people tumbling over each other in their haste to find out what has happened. They look like a nest of disturbed ants."

"What have you done with the yacht?" asked Mackeller. "If any of those people have seen sawn logs float down the river there will be an investigation very speedily to discover who has done the sawing."

"That is true, Mackeller. I have therefore taken the yacht across the river out of gunshot, or the sight of our abandoned Utopia. If they come by land they can't reach her."

"They are not coming by land," said the doctor. "The steam launch is being got ready, and three men are standing on the rock ledge preparing to go aboard, I fancy. They are armed with rifles, too."

"Just glance through the telescope, Mackeller," said Stranleigh, "and tell me if you recognize the three men."

"Yes; there is the tall manager, with the captain of the Rajah on one side of him, and the first mate on the other."

"Don't say 'first mate,' Peter," corrected Stranleigh. "Clark Russell says there's no such thing as a first mate. He is merely the mate, and then you have second and third mate, and I don't know how many more. Well, doctor, let us get away, and meet them in the motor boat. We're innocent lumbermen, searching for timber that has tumbled off the bank, remember."

"You are surely not going down there," protested Mackeller.

"Why, of course. We'll fill them up with our story before they even begin to ask questions."

"But you are unarmed."

"Quite."

"And they possess rifles."

"So it seems."

"Then it is a foolhardy thing to meet them without being accompanied by an equal body of armed men to protect you, at least. I should take all that the motor boat will hold."

"I know you would, Peter, but then, as I have often said, you are a bloodthirsty person. We can drop behind the bulwarks flat on our faces, before any one of the three can shoot; then in that recumbent position I will explain to them as well as I can that the Thornycroft motor boat possesses a submarine prow as effective as that of a battle ship, and if they don't want their steam launch rammed and sunk, they'd better drop their rifles to the deck. I shall insist that whoever speaks to me shall talk as one gentleman to another. I'll tell them I'm a member of the Peace Conference at The Hague.

Come along, doctor. We'll invite those johnnies to lunch, and cheer them up with the best wine and cigars that's to be had in Africa," and with that Stranleigh and the doctor departed for the waiting motor boat.

The steersman of the little motor boat crouched over his wheel, which had some resemblance to that of an automobile, as the swift craft sped up the river until it came to the branch that led to the mine, then into this watery lane it turned at full speed. Stranleigh and the doctor were standing up, and on rounding a bend came in sight of the steam launch laboriously churning up toward them against the current.

"Stop the engine," said Stranleigh. "Swing round the stem of the launch, and come up alongside at a distance of about twenty feet, then regulate her speed to suit that of the launch."

The manager, captain, and mate, all standing up, seemed struck into immobility with astonishment at seeing such a cutter in such a region.

They made no motion to raise their guns, or even to salute the oncomer. The motor boat came past them like a wild duck, without sound of machinery or sight of vapor, swung gracefully round, and came up alongside with a light precision which should have aroused the admiration of an old salt like the captain of the Rajah.

But the three men were filled with consternation. The ruddy, weather-beaten face of the captain turned to a mottled purple; his jaw dropped, and he stood there gaping, with fear in his bulging eyes. The erect, easy grace of Lord Stran-leigh, clad in white, instantly suggested to his experienced eye the British naval officer. This error was heightened by the natty, gold-braided hat worn by the doctor; but the attitude of the two men in white was not so disquieting as the demeanor and appearance of the boat herself. She was most expertly handled, and came alongside with that impudent, saucy air characteristic of midshipmen and the smaller units of the British navy. There was a touch of arrogance in her rakish build, as if she knew the whole power of a maritime nation was typified in her. The significance of her armored sides was not lost on the two seafaring men, even though the manager of the mine did not become immediately conscious of it, but all three recognized the sinister significance of that projecting prow of steel, which was plainly, if waveringly seen, through the transparent green waters, dangerous as the nose of a maneating shark.

Lord Stranleigh smiled as he realized the panic his sudden appearance had caused.

"Good morning," he greeted them pleasantly. "Have you seen anything of timber floating down this river?"

"Timber?" gasped the manager of the mine. "Yes—yes—we have."

"Is it lost, do you think?"

"I—I suppose most of it is bobbing about in the surf of the Atlantic Ocean."

"Not lost, but gone before," murmured the doctor.

Stranleigh surmised that captain and mate knew more of the piratical, thieving nature of their expedition than he had supposed. They were both well aware that British cruisers were nosing about in all sorts of odd comers of the world, mostly where they were not wanted, but even so a worthy seaman, if engaged in his lawful occupation, had no reason to fall into a state of nervous collapse at the sight of a craft which looked like a baby torpedo boat. He had hitherto believed that captain, officers, and crew of the Rajah were innocent participators in a scheme of villainy and theft, but now he knew that the captain and mate were equally in the plot with the tall, dark-looking manager, and this information he placed at the back of his brain for future use when he should meet the captain on the open sea.

"Are you a naval officer, sir?" stammered the captain, speaking for the first time.

"Oh, dear, no," replied Stranleigh airily; "merely a private person."

All three heaved a simultaneous sigh of relief, and their statuesque posture lost something of its stiffness.

"I'm cruising about the coast in my yacht."

"That isn't your yacht, is it?" asked the mine manager.

"No, my yacht lies a few miles farther up the river, and is an ocean-going affair. It is built with an eye to comfort and to the housing of a good number of men."

"Ah, how many men do you carry?" demanded the manager, his courage visibly returning.

"Blessed if I know," replied his lordship. "How many men have we, doctor?"

"I never counted them, sir," replied the doctor with a noncommittal air of indifference.

"They are scattered over the face of the country," continued the chief. "Many of them are woodmen, and the rest are gamekeepers from my own estates in England. They can all shoot a bit—trust a gamekeeper for that."

"And is your yacht built on the model of this boat of yours?"

"No. As I told you, it is built for comfort. I'd like very much to show her to you if you will honor me with a visit. Indeed, it is getting near to midday, so I should be delighted if you three gentlemen would be good enough to lunch with me. I can promise you a passable meal, some excellent wine, and cigars that will call up recollections of Havana."

The manager whispered to the captain, who somewhat doubtfully nodded his head, as who would say: "Well, I suppose we'd better see what's in this, anyway."

The manager then spoke up:

"Thank you, sir," he said. "We'll be very glad of a bite and a drink and a smoke. My friend here is captain of the Rajah, and this is Mr. Thompson, the mate. I am Frowningshield, representing the owners of this district."

"Delighted to make your acquaintance, gentlemen. My name is Stranleigh."

"And a very well-known name in Africa, Mr. Stanley."

"S-t-r-a-n-l-e-i-g-h," spelled his lordship. "I cannot claim the distinction of being a namesake of the explorer."

"May I inquire the object of your visit in these regions?" asked the manager.

"In a small way I am looking after big game, and so carry some of my gamekeepers with me. Then again, as you are probably aware, I am interested in timber, hence my woodmen with their axes and saws. We have cut a considerable quantity of firewood, with which we hope to supplement our coal. My third object may strike you as largely impractical. I had some thoughts of founding a settlement here, or on any other healthy and suitable spot not too far from the coast. I am delighted with this section of the country. Back in the hills while shooting I have discovered several waterfalls which could supply cheap power. Some days ago I gave orders to my woodmen to prepare logs for the building of huts. I was away shooting at the time they began operations, and I fear rather neglecting my duties as a settlement founder. Be that as it may, they piled the logs too near the brink of the river, where the incline is steep. This morning, like the Gadarene swine, the logs seem to have tumbled one after another into the water. I suppose one heap set another going. As I tell you, I was absent, but when word was brought to me, I took this launch and followed down the river, thinking perhaps the sawn logs had lodged or jammed somewhere, and might be towed back; but if, as you say, they are already in the ocean, I fear they are lost to us, and we'll need to cut some more."

Frowningshield listened to this recital with wrinkled brow, and intense gaze upon the speaker, who talked in an easy, indolent manner which impressed the manager with the belief that he had encountered some rich fool with more money at his disposal than was good for him, and gradually the nerve of the man who had kicked Mackeller into the hold began to reassert itself. He felt ashamed of his failure in courage when he had supposed he was confronted by the power of Great Britain.

"Perhaps you are not aware, Mr. Stranleigh, that the timber you are cutting is situated on private property."

"You are surely mistaken," protested the young man. "All the maps I have seen—I'll show you them when we come aboard the yacht—depict this district as a sort of no-man's-land."

"Such is not the case, Mr. Stranleigh. More than a hundred square miles of this territory has been acquired by a European syndicate, of whom I am the representative."

"You amaze me. From what government did this syndicate buy the property?"

"They did not buy it from any government, they acquired the concession from native chiefs. No European government holds jurisdiction over this section of Africa."

"That's what I thought. Are you forming a settlement, then, farther down the river? Is that where you have come from?"

"Yes."

"You arrived in the steamer you spoke of—I forget the name?"

"The Rajah. Yes. I am a mining engineer, and we are experimenting with the mineral resources of this country."

"I see. Then you are probably loading the Rajah with such ore as you can find, and are taking it back to Europe to test it."

"Exactly."

"What you tell me is most interesting, but surely you were not here when I came up this river in my yacht less than a month ago?"

"No, we were not here then, but we prospected, and secured possession more than a year ago."

"Then you are clothed with authority to order me to move on?"

"I assure you, Mr. Stranleigh, that so far as I am personally concerned you might form your settlement, or stay here as long as you please, but I am not acting for myself. In the interest of my employers, and to prevent future complications, should we discover valuable minerals, I fear I must warn you off."

"Could you oblige me with the address of that European syndicate?"

"It would be useless, sir. I was instructed that they do not intend to grant any concessions or franchises to outsiders. Whether they gain or lose, they intend to exploit this region for their own sole benefit. If you dispute my authority, I shall be pleased to produce documentary evidence corroborating what I say."

"My dear Mr. Frowningshield," protested Stranleigh, "I should not dream of disputing your authority. I confess I was rather taken with this upper country, though I don't think much of the stretch of land along the coast. However, Africa is large, and I do not doubt I may find some spot equally favorable for the carrying out of my plans. What you say merely shows how small the world is getting to be. Who would have imagined that in this seemingly virgin territory, thousands of miles from what we call civilization, the land should be all taken up, just as if it were a newly plotted piece of acreage in the vicinity of New York or London, to be exploited and covered with jerry-built villas. Well, well, we live and learn. It's rather disappointing, but it can't be helped. I hope you won't send in an exorbitant bill for the trees I have illegally felled, especially when you remember that I have lost most of the timber."

"Oh, no," said Frowningshield, with a laugh. "That will be all right."

"It seems so strange that I, of all people, should be a trespasser and a poacher, for when at home I am a stern upholder of the rights of property. I own several estates in England, and am a very pig-headed Tory when any of my privileges are threatened; so I should be the last man to trespass on the rights of others, and I hope, Mr. Frowningshield, when you are communicating with the proprietors, you will convey to them my humble apologies, with the assurance that if ever again I fell a tree, I shall take pains to know it has grown on my own land."

"Oh, that will be all right," repeated Frowningshield reassuringly.

"There!" cried Stranleigh, as they approached the triple outflow, and waving his hand to the right, "you see the gash I have made in your forest. That is the spot I had chosen for the nucleus of my settlement. There are the remainder of the logs, and I present them freely to you with no charge for the cutting."

"They are piled rather close to the edge," commented Frowningshield.

"Yes, we all realize that now, when it is too late. Locking the door when the horse is stolen. I must inquire how it happened. I have not seen my men since I heard of the disaster. I suppose they will present plenty of plausible excuses, and will fasten the fault of the occurrence on anything but their own stupidity. Ah, captain, what do you think of my yacht?"

"Very fine lines, sir," replied the captain, as he and the mate gazed at the white steamer lying on the other bank of the main stream.

"If you will excuse me," said Stranleigh, "I will precede you on board, to inform cook and steward that three more plates are to be provided."

He and the doctor sprang up the steps; the motor boat gave itself a flick astern, and then the steam launch came to the floor of the gangway. Stranleigh welcomed his guests at the head of the stair, conducted captain and manager to easy-chairs aft, and ordered the deck steward to bring them sherry and bitters. He made a mental note of the fact that the mate had remained in the launch, and from this surmised that he had not succeeded in allaying the suspicions of captain and manager. He resolved to give them an opportunity of consulting alone together, wondering what their action would be when they had come to a decision regarding recent events.

"I must go below to see about the wine. Like a prudent owner I hold the keys of the wine bin myself. With a mixed crew you know the wisdom of such a course, captain."

"Yes, sir, I do," and with this the genial host went down the companion way with the doctor.

"What do you think of him?" muttered the captain, when they were thus left in solitude on the after deck.

"Oh, he's all right," said Frowningshield confidently. "I've met plenty of that kind before. A rich ass, good-natured, without too much brains, blowing in the money he has inherited."

"I'm not so sure of that," replied the captain.

"Oh, you're suspicious of everybody. He has blundered in here, and I dare say has amused himself as he said, shooting and chopping, and what not."

"Do you see," murmured the captain, "that this boat is fitted up for wireless telegraphy? That's the meaning of the line between the masts."

Frowningshield looked aloft.

"Oh, that's it, is it? Well, I don't see anything to worry about, even if it is so. I suppose plenty of yachts are fitted with Marconi apparatus nowadays. It certainly can't be much use to him here in West Africa."

"He might be in communication with some one outside."

"Out in the ocean, you mean? What would be the good of that?"

"I don't know," replied the captain. "This chap is too smooth-tongued to suit my book."

"What do you propose to do? Sink his craft and drown the lot of them?"

"No."

"What then?"

"Keep an eye on him, and not drink too much of his wine."

"You don't need to give that warning to me, captain. It would come more pat applied nearer home."

"You are right," admitted the captain. "If you notice me becoming talkative, just give me a nudge, will you? We must sit together at table."

"I think you are unduly suspicious, captain. This boat must have left

England before we did."

"I'm not so sure of that. Some of these oceangoing yachts are very fast. She may be turbine-engined."

"Can't a sea-wise man like you tell whether she is or not by the look of her?"

"No, not from the outside. A question to one of the men would settle it."

"Ah, here comes a waiter with the drinks. Well, my man, this is a very nice yacht you have here."

"Yes, sir."

"Turbine engines, I suppose?"

"I don't know, sir. The engineer would be able to tell you."

"Yes, I suppose he would. How long is it since you left England?"

"Very sorry, sir, but I don't remember the date. The captain or the owner would know."

"Why, of course. Have you been stopping at many places since you quit the old sod?"

"Running in here and there, sir."

"Lisbon, or Teneriffe, perhaps?"

"Well, sir, I never had no head for them foreign places. They all look alike to me, sir. Plymouth, or Southampton, or Liverpool, sir, there's some difference between them."

"So there is, so there is," murmured Frowningshield, as the man respectfully withdrew.

"You see," said the captain, "even the stewards are on their guard."

"Oh, that's the noncommittal nature of the English servant. I imagine

Stranleigh is by way of being a swell. There's something of that 'You-be-damned' air about him, in spite of his politeness, and the servants of such people know when they're in a good place, and keep their mouths shut. Still, I can't imagine a la-de-da chap like this, with a fashionable yacht, and a gang of gamekeepers, sent out to interfere with us. What can he do?"

"The steel prow of that motor boat didn't look fashionable," growled the captain. "She could sink the Rajah, loaded down as she is, in about ten seconds, although she'd crumple herself up if she tried it, and as to what he can do, look at what he has already done. The tumbling of all that timber in the river may have been an accident, as he says, but I don't believe it. It fitted the case of the mines too cursedly pat to suit me. He couldn't have hit it off better, and at less cost to himself, if he had studied for a year."

"Yes, it does take a bit of explaining, doesn't it? Still, there's nothing to be done with his crew of landlubbers. He daren't attack us; there are too many of us."

"I think you'll change your opinion before the week is out, Mr. Frowningshield. See what he's already done. He's cleared the river, and the waterway from the ocean to the mine is open. I tell you what it is, Mr. Frowningshield; there's been a miscalculation, and that man Schwartzbrod isn't as clever as you thought he was."

"Why do you say that?"

"Because, according to your story, it should have taken them a week or two to fit out another steamer, and by that time you expected to get the river protected, and erect a few forts. Now what has happened? Instead of that they have chartered the quickest yacht they could find in England, and they have cut in here ahead of us. This fellow's smooth talk about founding a colony is all balderdash. They've been spying upon us ever since we came here. The other fellows in England have taken their time in fitting up a steamer, or perhaps two steamers, or perhaps three. This chap has cleared the channel for them, and any fine morning you may see three or four ships in the offing, carrying perhaps three or four hundred men. Then what are you going to do?"

"There wouldn't be anything to do, of course, if all that happened.

Nevertheless, all you say is mere surmise, but if the worst came to the worst they couldn't touch us. We're doing nothing illegal. I tell you old Schwartzbrod assured me he would get from the new owners a legal document covering everything he ordered done."

"But suppose he didn't get that document?"

"'We're both blooming prisoners, that's what we are!'"

"Oh, trust him! Of course he's got it, but even if he hadn't, we are doing nothing illegal. Here you are with your fortune made if you run three trips to Lisbon and back. You are quite safe, whatever comes, for you are bound to obey the orders of those who chartered the vessel. But apart from all that, we are out of British jurisdiction here, and you will be out of British jurisdiction at Lisbon. You've done nothing, and can do nothing, so long as you obey orders, that will render you liable to British law."

"I don't like the job a bit, Mr. Frowningshield; I tell you that straight."

"Nonsense, man. If any one is in danger, it's me, and I'm not afraid. You're protected by your ship's papers. You are under orders, and you must obey them. If anything is wrong, it is other people who must stand the brunt. It isn't criminal to sail a ship from Southampton to the West African coast, and it isn't criminal to make voyages to Lisbon and back. You are all right, who-ever's hurt, so don't get into a panic, captain, merely because a rich fool and his yacht appears to have discovered the Paramakaboo River."

The captain, sorely troubled, but somewhat comforted by the confident tone of his comrade, was absentmindedly turning the picture pages of the Sphere, which he had taken from the wicker table at his elbow. Suddenly something caught his eye.

"By the Lord, Frowningshield, look at the date of the Sphere! 24th of May, it says, and we sailed on the 13th—a mighty unlucky day I call it. He bought this paper more than a week after we left! I tell you, Frowningshield, we're done for. We're blooming prisoners, that's what we are!"

CHAPTER VI—AN ATTACK ON THE HIGH SEAS

Mr. manager frowningshield took up the copy of the Sphere in his hand, and gazed with troubled brow at this conclusive evidence of the date.

"Yes," he said at last, "he was in England a week later than we were, and must have come direct to this spot, passing us somewhere on the way; during the night, probably."

The captain was now standing up, his fists clenched.

"What do you propose to do?" inquired the manager.

"I should like to know first whether we are here as his guests or his prisoners. We were fools to have accepted his invitation without giving ourselves time to think and consult."

"But, hang it all, captain, he came on us so unexpectedly that there was no time to plan, or even to suspect. He seemed to speak so honestly and straightforwardly, and was so ready with his explanation that even up to a moment ago I believed he was but a blameless tourist, with, eccentric tastes, and the money to indulge them; a craze for big game shooting, like so many of them toffs have, and, of course, that kind of a man is mouching all over the world. You meet them everywhere: South America, Africa, Asia. Of course he's got us aboard here, and could steam away past your ship, and my settlement, with us two flung down the hold, and helpless, just as I put away that Scotch engineer on the Rajah at Southampton. By Jove, I shouldn't wonder a bit but that's what's in his mind: taking a leaf out of my own book. We would have no chance of self-defense with so many men on board, and our steam launch could not keep within sight of him if this boat has turbine engines. The mines are exploded, and the way is clear."

"Don't you think your men would give her a shot as she went by?"

"Not unless I was there to command them. I've left nobody in authority. I wonder what he's doing so long down below? If we are his guests, he should be here to entertain us."

"He is probably giving his orders," said the captain gloomily. "We are trapped, my boy. He wouldn't leave us this long to consult together unless he was sure of us."

"Why hasn't your mate come up from the launch?"

"I told him to stay there until I called him. You see, I had my doubts of this man from the first. If he attempts to lay hands on us, I'll shout to the mate to cut for it."

"What good could that do?" protested the manager. "The motor boat can overtake our launch even if she were half way to camp."

"Ah, here he comes," said the captain, as Stran-leigh, debonair and smiling, appeared at the head of the companion way. "I'll settle the question whether we are prisoners or not within two seconds."

"I hope you'll excuse me," began Stranleigh, coming forward, "but you are the first guests I have had the pleasure of receiving aboard since I left England, and I wish my to do his best, so I took the liberty of giving special orders for our lunch, and the gong will ring, they tell me, in about a quarter of an hour."

"I am very sorry, Mr. Stranleigh," replied the captain, "but I am a little anxious about my ship, so I have told my mate to remain in our launch, and I must ask you to excuse me. I cannot remain to lunch."

"Dear me, I'm sorry," said Stranleigh. "Why is that? What harm can come to your steamer?"

"Well, I've seen those logs piled up still very close to the brink of the river, and I fear if they tumbled down also, coming end on upon us, they might do the Rajah some damage."

"My men tell me," Stranleigh reassured him, "that there's no further danger of more logs getting into the river. Still, they are such fools that they may possibly be mistaken, and I quite share and sympathize with your anxiety.

By the way, did any of the other logs damage your boat?"

"That I don't know yet. Some of them certainly struck her."

"Then, captain, you must let me pay for whatever damage has been done; yes, and overpay, because, after all, I am the man responsible. Of course, you see, when we came up the river, there was no ship there, and no sign of any settlement. Still, that does not excuse my not having kept a better outlook. If the timber struck the steamer, is it likely the damage will be serious?"

"That, of course, I cannot tell without examination," replied the master of the Rajah.

"Well, captain, we come of a sporting race. I'll give you a hundred pounds here in gold, win or lose. If the damage is a thousand pounds, then you've lost. If there's no damage at all, you've won a hundred pounds. Come, captain, what do you say?"

"If no damage has been done, Mr. Stranleigh, I don't want any money from you. Even if the steamer is hurt, I am not sure I should have a valid claim against you. After all, the affair was an accident."

"Are you satisfied to give me a quit claim for a hundred pounds, cash down?"

"I'll be quite satisfied if you excuse me from attending luncheon, and allow me to go back to my ship."

"Oh, certainly, but I'd like you to take the money. Can't you send the mate, and order him to come back and report to you? It's a pity to miss a meal, you know."

"I'd feel safer if I went myself."

"Yes, I know exactly how anxious you must feel, and in your place I should do the same. Very well, captain, the only point between us is the hundred pounds or not. To tell the truth, I shall not object to pay full compensation to your owners for what I have done. I imagine, however, so stanch a ship as yours has come to no harm. She lies bow upstream, and the current is not so strong down there as it is up here. The timber, I think, if it struck at all, would glance off, carrying away nothing but a bit of paint; but if you must go, I shall insist on your taking the hundred pounds."

"Take the money, captain," said the manager, looking up at him with a smile. It was evident that his fears had once more been overcome, but the captain was not so easily cajoled.

"Very well," he said, anxious to end the situation and learn whether he was to be let go or not.

"And now, Mr. Frowningshield," continued Stranleigh, turning to the manager, "let us settle all our financial affairs before lunch, so that we may enjoy our meal without the thought of commercialism at the hoard. You have seen the damage I have caused in your forest, thinking all the while it was my own property. Of course, if you were acting for yourself alone, I am certain I could drive a very easy bargain with you, but you are responsible for the care of these lands to the European syndicate you spoke of, and so, on its behalf, you must be just, rather than generous. At how much coin of the realm do you place my depredations? I know it would cost me a pretty penny if I committed so unforgivable a trespass in England."

"How many trees did you cut down, Mr. Stranleigh?"

"Oh, Lord knows! Twenty, thirty, forty, fifty, sixty, or a hundred perhaps. That can easily be discovered. We'll send a man across in the motor boat to count the stumps."

"Oh, it isn't worth while. Would you be content to part with another hundred pounds?"

"Done; and you've let me off cheaply, Mr. Frowningshield. Just pardon me a moment until I get the money," and once more he disappeared down below.

But all this had not changed in the least the captain's apprehension.

"He's gone to give the signal," he said.

"Well, you know, captain, I've a great regard for you, yet I cannot find it possible to distrust the faith of that young man. He may be a fool, but he's a gentleman. I don't believe he would invite three men to a feast, and then imprison them. Now, I'm no fool, but then I'm no gentleman, either, and I'd do it in a minute, if I had an enemy in my power, yet I'm sure he won't. You'll see him come up with the money, and you'll miss a mighty good feed by going off to the Rajah."

"I'm willing to miss the meal, if I once get aboard my ship. I'll turn her round, and make for the ocean within the hour. You stop here as long as you can; all afternoon, if possible, and give the Rajah a chance to get out of sight before this fellow follows."

"But he can easily overtake you. Still, what could he do if he did? You surely don't expect him to seize your vessel?"

"I don't know what I expect, but I am afraid of him. I think him quite capable of following me to sea, and capturing the Rajah."

"Nonsense, that would be rank piracy. That would be a hanging matter. It would do him no good to sink you, and what could he do with the Rajah once he had her? There are too many witnesses on board. He wouldn't dare to sail into any port in the world. But then there's not the slightest danger of that. He's no pirate. The days of piracy are past. He may be a fool, but he's not such a fool as to try a trick like that."

"Will you stop here and give me a chance to get away?"

"Willingly."

"Very well, if I once get out of sight there are ten chances to one he can't catch me before I'm in the Tagus."

Stranleigh reappeared with some rolls of gold done up in paper, and these he divided equally between the captain and Frowningshield. The latter could not resist the temptation of asking a question.

"I've been looking at this illustrated newspaper, and I notice its date is very recent. You must have made a quick voyage from England, Mr. Stranleigh."

For a moment they had the young man on the hip, but he did not allow the knowledge of this to change the expression of his placid face. He took the journal in his hand, and looked at the date.

"Yes, they do these things quickly nowadays, but perhaps not so quickly as one unaccustomed to journalism would imagine. I believe that the illustrated weeklies are dated some time ahead, and I have been told they send forth their foreign editions as far in advance as possible. This, now, could have come from London, through by way of Paris to Lisbon, and reach that city probably several days before the date mentioned on the cover. I must ask the doctor where he bought this copy, whether at Lisbon or Teneriffe."

He flung the Sphere carelessly down on the table as if the matter, after all, was of no moment, and even Frowningshield, who was watching him like a detective of fiction, could distinguish no note of hesitation in his voice, nor catch any glance of annoyance from his eyes.

"Well, Mr. Stranleigh," said the captain, who was not equally successful in keeping an inflection of anxiety from his words, "I am very much obliged to you for your invitation, even though I cannot take advantage of it, so I shall bid you good-by."

"Oh, you're not away yet, captain," said Stranleigh, with a slight laugh, and the captain drew himself up with a little start of surprise. Stran-leigh walked to the head of the companion way, and said:

"Will you be as quick as you can down there?"

As his back turned on them, the captain grasped Frowningshield's wrist.

"He's playing with me like a cat with a mouse," he whispered.

"Nonsense," replied the other. "Your nerves have gone wrong. He's as transparent as glass."

Stranleigh turned, followed this time by a steward carrying a hamper,

"I don't like to think of your losing your lunch, captain," he said, "so I've had them put up a basketful for you and the mate on your way to the

Rajah. There is in the hamper several bottles of champagne that I think will commend itself to you, or to any other judge of a good vintage, and there is also a box of cigars. If these weeds do not elicit the highest commendation I'll insist that you bestow on me a better box the next time we meet. So good-by, captain, and good luck to you. May you sail the high seas prosperously and safely. Here's hoping I shall meet you again when you are not in such a hurry."

Basket and hamper had been placed in the launch, and Stranleigh waved his hand at the captain and mate as their craft steamed out into the current and made for the mining camp.

The gong sounded out at last.

"Well, Mr. Frowningshield," said the young man, returning from the side, "if you're as hungry as I am, you'll enjoy this meal. Come along."

The manager did enjoy the meal, and they lingered long over the consuming of it, coming up on deck after it was over to indulge in coffee, liquors, and cigars. The manager fell under the charm of the young man's conversation, and began to revise his first estimate that his host was a fool. He had drunk but sparingly of the generous wine, yet in the glow of contentment which it produced he laughed quietly to himself now and then at the unfounded fears of the captain, which had cause him to run away from so excellent a repast.

"If this is a cigar from a similar box to the one you gave the captain, the old man is to be congratulated."

"Yes, it is. The captain, of course, will see civilization long before you do, and so can provide himself with any variety of the weed he fancies; but you, in this out-of-the-world place, are not so fortunate, therefore I must beg of you to accept six boxes in remembrance of the enjoyable time I have spent in your society."

"Why, Mr. Stranleigh, I'm awfully much obliged, and I may tell you at once I am not going to refuse. A man doesn't get a present like that every year of his life, worse luck."

"Then to make up the average, Mr. Frowning-shield, you must let me add a few cases of our champagne."

"Really, you are most kind. I don't know how to thank you."

"Don't attempt it, I beg of you."

A steward approached and presented Stranleigh with a sealed envelope, which, begging the pardon of his guest, he tore open, saying:

"I give all my orders in writing, so that there can be no mistake, and I rarely receive verbal reports from any one."

"A good idea," said Frowningshield.

"Yes, it prevents disputes afterwards."

He read to himself the penciled words of the telegrapher who had transcribed a wireless message from the hilltop.

"The Rajah is turning round, and is evidently about to depart."

Stranleigh, with a pencil, wrote on the back of the letter the following dispatch to Mackeller.

"Report once more if the Rajah actually sails; then take with you anything you don't want to leave, and come down to the water. The motor boat will be waiting for you. Come aboard at the prow, and get immediately out of sight in the forecastle, for sitting aft with me is the man who kicked you down into the hold, and I don't wish him to recognize you."

Giving this to the waiting steward, Stranleigh resumed conversation with his guest, who showed no desire to depart. Shortly after came the second message: "The Rajah has sailed. Send motor boat now."

Stranleigh folded up the sheet of paper, and handed it to the steward.

"Give that to the captain," he said, and a few minutes later the purr of the motor boat was heard leaving the ship. The sound aroused Frowningshield.

"Are you sending away the motor boat?" he asked. "As our steam launch has not returned, I fear I must depend on you for getting me down to the camp."

"Oh, that's all right," replied Stranleigh easily. "The boat isn't going far; just to pick up two of my men who've been prospecting in the hills. In fact, this is the end of my trespass, for there is little use in my gazing on a Promised Land that has been promised to somebody else. As for the motor boat, and getting to camp, I can take you there more comfortably than on that little craft. You see, there's nothing further to keep me here, as I have said, unless I can make terms with your syndicate, and that very likely would not suit my book, because cheapness of land was one of my objects in coming so far. If your syndicate expects to find valuable minerals on this property, they are not likely to sell any of their holdings to me at such a price as I should care to pay, so I think I shall cast off and away, but whether I shall go north or south will depend on circumstances when I get out to sea."

"What, you are not going to sail to-night, are you?" said Frowningshield, sitting up.

"Yes, there's no use in stopping here any longer. Do you happen to know any place along the coast which would be suitable as a colonizing place for Englishmen? I should like it to resemble this as much as possible: hills, a large flow of pure water, free from any fever swamps, and good soil."

"No, Mr. Stranleigh, this is the only portion of Africa I am acquainted with."

"It's very likely the captain of the Rajah may be able to give me some hints. He has probably knocked around the world a bit, and doubtless has kept his eyes open. I wish I had thought of asking him before he left whether or not he knows this coast. Besides, I would like to learn for certain if I have damaged his ship. It's a good thing she wasn't facing the other way, otherwise a log might have wrecked rudder or screw, or both."

"I am afraid," stammered Frowningshield, "that you won't see the captain again. He was very anxious to be off, and I rather fancy by this time he's well out at sea."

"Ah, in that case," remarked Stranleigh indifferently, "I shall be consoled by the assurance that his steamer is uninjured."

In due time the motor boat returned, and its occupants entered the yacht without being seen by their master's guest. The motor boat was hoisted on board, and the captain, coming aft, said:

"Any further orders, sir?"

"Yes. Plymouth, if you please. And, captain, just stop on your way at the camp, which I am informed is on the left-hand bank of the river. Draw up at the landing if there is one; if not, perhaps Mr. Frowningshield's launch will be waiting for him. There are some packages to go ashore."

The steamer proceeded down the river with just enough speed on to give her steering way. Frowningshield sat very silent, but his host made up with loquacity for the other's taciturnity. He told entertaining stories, and related odd experiences, and all with a delicate courtesy, as if his guest was the most honored of men, instead of being merely an adventurer and a marauder on a gold quest.

The captain drew up expertly at the landing. Nothing was to be seen of the Rajah that so lately had been berthed there. In spite of the fact that they saw their boss stepping ashore, large groups of men had ceased work, and were standing twenty or thirty yards back from the landing, viewing with eyes of wonderment the trim white steamer that had come out of the wilderness. Frowning-shield stepped ashore like a man in a dream, and a couple of stewards placed the cases of champagne and the boxes of cigars on the rock beside him. Lord Stranleigh leaned against the rail, and bade farewell to the manager.

"Wouldn't you like to come on to Plymouth with us?" he said. "Penny all the way. County Council express boat. No stop between Chelsea and London Bridge."

"God knows I wish I could," said Frowning-shield, with a deep sigh.

"Well, at least," cried Stranleigh cheerfully, "we've had one pleasant afternoon, and I'm more than grateful for your company. I hope that you will find valuable minerals on this spot; a second Klondike or Kimberley in either gold or diamonds. Somehow I think you'll be successful, and so I'll leave you my best wishes. Good-by, good-by."

The steamer was moving off down the river as Stranleigh waved his hand at the choice gang of ruffians that manned the highest outcrop of the reef.

"After all," he murmured to himself, "they're Englishmen, poor devils, and we're all a long way from home!"

The manager standing there on the rock suddenly bethought himself, and raised his hat. A cheer broke forth from the outlaws, and they waved aloft tattered caps.

"Pull the whistle, captain, with a hip-hip-hip-hurrah," and the siren sounded across the delta.

The manager stood for a long while watching the retreating boat, with his hands clasped behind him.

"By God," he said, "I don't know what to make of that man! I believe the captain's right, and that he'll capture the Rajah before nightfall, yet he'll have no shot from my cannon."

The Woman in White, as soon as she was out of sight of the camp, made record time to the coast, traversed the deep channel between the river and the sea with some caution, then struck straight out to the west. The sun was still about two hours above the western ocean. Far to the north the Rajah could be seen keeping closer inshore than seemed quite safe, the captain's idea being doubtless to get out of sight behind the first headland he might encounter. The heavily laden boat was burning up coal with reckless prodigality, the slight wind from the shore carrying out to sea a great black banner of smoke. Stranleigh walked forward to the captain.

"Can you overtake him before sunset?" he asked.

"I think so, sir."

"Well, I imagine our best plan is to convince him as speedily as possible that he can't run away from us. I don't like to see him wasting coal like that. Coal is more valuable than the ore he carries until we reach Teneriffe. Full speed ahead, captain."

The hum of the turbines rose and rose, and the trembling of the yacht perceptibly increased as the sharp prow clove through the waters with the speed of a torpedo-boat destroyer. The steward, setting out cups and saucers for tea, on a wicker table, found some difficulty in keeping the jingling dishes from catastrophe. The Rajah had about four hours the start, and had probably worried away thirty knots of the long route she was to travel. Higher and higher she seemed to rise in the water, and the sun was still a good quarter of an hour above the horizon when The Woman in White came tearing up alongside to landward of her, carried now by her own momentum, for the turbines had been stopped some distance away. Apparently everybody on board was leaning over the rail watching the amazing speed of the swanlike craft, white and graceful, as she gradually slowed down. Stranleigh recognized the anxious face of the captain, and shouted up at him:

"Tell your stokers to economize on that coal." The captain replied truculently:

"No one gives orders on this steamer but me."

"Quite right," replied Stranleigh, with less imperiousness than had barbed his first shout. "That's why I'm asking you to give the command."

The captain, after a moment's hesitation, sent the order below, then turned again to the white vessel, which was now keeping exact time with his own black one.

"Captain," said Stranleigh, in his ordinary tone of voice, "both Frowningshield and myself were very sorry you could not lunch with us, so perhaps you will be good enough to come aboard this yacht and dine with me."

"A captain cannot leave his ship," curtly replied the master of the Rajah.

"Ordinarily, no, but this is an exceptional case. I've got a letter for you, captain."

"Then why didn't you give it to me at noon?"

"Oh, come now, a man can't think of everything when he is overjoyed at receiving an expected and very welcome guest. You must admit, captain, that once I undertook the work of ocean postman, I lost no time in giving you the double knock. I don't think there's anything in these waters would have overhauled you so quickly as I have done. Won't you then make an exception, and honor us with your presence?"

"No, I will not. If, as you say, you've got a letter for me, I'll throw down a line for it."

"Well, on the face of it, that seems fair. A man in England drops you a line, and you drop a line for his line. Nevertheless, this letter, although addressed to you, I do not intend to part with. There are several documents in my pocket which I'd like to show you, and I wish to make some explanations that will interest you."

"Look here, Mr. Stranleigh, I'm captain aboard this steamer, and I'm on the high seas. I warn you, before witnesses here, that any interference on your part is piracy. I shall not come aboard your steamer, nor shall I allow any one from your steamer to come aboard of me. I take orders from none but my own masters, the owners of this ship. I am now under their orders, and acting upon them. I won't stand any interference."

"Again I say quite right, captain. Your sentiments are admirable, and your views of nautical duty are correct. Nevertheless, it is necessary that you and I should enjoy a quiet talk together, and I ask you to favor me by coming aboard."

"Well, I won't."

"Then, as the mountain wouldn't come to Mahomet, Mahomet went to the mountain. I ask your permission to go aboard your vessel."

"I shan't give it. I've told you that before. Now, sheer off, or I'll put a cannon ball into your engine room."

414

"Oh, have you got a cannon ball on board? How jolly! We are entirely unarmed so far as ordnance is concerned, but I'd like to say, captain, that the chances are ten to one your cannon ball wouldn't do much harm. You might even plant a floating mine in front of The Woman in White, and although it probably would blow her prow up, yet I think, crablike, I could crawl backward to the nearest port, as the White Star liner Suevic made her way from the Lizard to Southampton."

"Are you going to sheer off, sir."

"No, and you are not going to fire, either, captain. It isn't etiquette at sea to shoot cannon balls at a man until you have finished the cigars he has presented to you. I dislike very much to allude to my own gifts in this way, but still I wish you to understand that I am well versed in nautical law."

"I want to get along with my voyage, Mr. Stranleigh, unmolested."

"Why, bless your tarry heart, captain, get along with your voyage. If you can run away from us, don't let me put any obstacle in your path."

"Will you sheer off, sir."

"Certainly not. I'm quite within my rights. This part of the ocean belongs as much to me as to the Rajah. I'm not delaying you in the least, and all your talk of interference is mere humbug. If I ran my craft close enough to endanger yours, you might have a right to object; but I call your attention to the fact that we are under perfect control, and I can keep the distance between the ships to an inch. If I went farther away, I should be unable to converse with you without straining my throat, which I decline to do. Now, you will neither come aboard my vessel, nor allow me to go aboard yours."

"That's right."

"Well, I don't think it is. Nevertheless, you force me to do what I should much rather, for your sake, not do, and that is I am compelled to read your letter, and the documents I have referred to, in the hearing of your crew and my own."

"You may read what you like to the crew."

"Captain, I ask you to reconsider that dictum. I grant that you might honestly have made such a remark on any other voyage you have ever taken during your long seafaring life, except this one. Just think for a moment. Don't reply rashly, and be assured that I mean no harm to you, nor to anybody else aboard your ship. Quite the contrary. What I intend to do will be greatly to your advantage, and to that of every man who is with you."

When Lord Stranleigh made reference to his present voyage, the captain, who had been leaning against the rail, stood up suddenly. The men were whispering with one another. The captain saw that Stranleigh had taken from his pocket several envelopes, and stood there awaiting his reply. At last the captain said huskily:

"Will you come aboard alone, sir?"

"Oh, quite alone, of course, since it is your wish, or you can come aboard here with half a dozen or a dozen men as your bodyguard, if you like. Bring the cannon, too, if it makes you feel any safer."

"I'd rather you came aboard here, sir."

"Very good. Fling over a slightly stronger line than you'd have sent down for the letter, and I'll be with you in a jiffy."

"But how am I to know some others won't climb up?"

"Well, hang it, arm your men with handspikes, and knock 'em down again. Don't keep me waiting here all night. It will be dark very soon, and I shan't occupy more than ten minutes of your time. You seem spoiling for a fight, but I can't accommodate you. I'm a man of peace, and that's why I shudder when you speak to me of cannon. I swear I'll tell Sir Henry Campbell-Bannerman and President Roosevelt the way you're behaving. You're a positive danger on the high seas, with your ultimatums, and your shots through the engine room, and all that. Heave over a line, and get your men to watch that the yacht doesn't spring aboard of you. No wonder we English are disliked for our browbeating."

The captain seemed rather ashamed of his fears in face of this bantering, and besides, some of his crew had laughed, which still further disconcerted him. A rope fell coiling through the air, and came slap on deck.

"Hang tight aloft there," cried Stranleigh, as he jerked the rope taut, swung himself free of his own boat, and clambered up the black cliff of the Rajah hand over hand, feet against the side like a monkey.

CHAPTER VII—THE CAPTAIN OF THE "RAJAH" STRIKES OIL

THE captain strode gloomily to the evil-smelling den he called the cabin, and Stranleigh went down the steps with him, seating himself at the table.

"Now, captain," he began, "can we be overheard?"

"No, sir."

"Well, I come here as your friend. I want to save you, if possible."

"Save me?"

"Yes."

"I don't need any saving."

"Yes, you do, and a good deal of it. I thought at first that Frowningshield was the sole culprit, and that you were merely an innocent victim. I learned to-day that such was not the case; in fact, I surmised it before, because when you assisted in planting those mines across the Paramakaboo River you must have known you were committing a capital offense."

"Then it wasn't an accident; you did send down the logs?"

"Of course I did."

"You watched us ever since we arrived there?"

"Yes, I came from England for that purpose. I left a week after you did, and was there a week before you, more or less. My man, Mackeller, whom you kidnapped on board this steamer at Southampton——"

"I didn't kidnap him, sir. It was Frowning-shield."

"Oh, I know all about it. Mackeller is on my boat now, within three hundred yards of where you are sitting. He was up on the hilltop with a telescope, scrutinizing every action of yours since you landed."

"But I'm compelled to obey orders."

"Oh, no, you aren't. If you are ordered to do a criminal action, you must not only refuse, but you are in honor bound to give information to the authorities."

"I had nothing to do with putting Mackeller into the hold. Frowningshield put him in, and I didn't know he was there till we were more than a day out. It was me insisted he should be sent ashore with the pilot. Frowningshield wanted to take him with us."

"That's neither here nor there, captain. Of course, whenever you knew a man had been kidnapped in that way aboard your ship, you should have turned, made straight back to Southampton, giving information to the authorities. But even if such an unlawful action did not arouse your suspicions you must have known perfectly well when you planted those mines that it wasn't toy balloons you were putting in the water. It's too late to pretend innocence. You've been bribed to commit a crime."

"The floating mines weren't set in English waters."

"My dear sir, your offense is against international law. No man is allowed to place floating mines in a river up which a British steamer may ascend, and so far as that is concerned, you deliberately put them there to wreck a British steamer. You are at this moment commanding a pirate ship filled with stolen ore."

"I know nothing about that, sir. This ship was chartered, and I was told by my owners to obey the orders of them that chartered her, and that's old Schwartzbrod and his gang."

"We're merely losing time, captain. You talk about charters and owners. Well, I am the owner of the Rajah. I bought her from Sparling & Bilge."

"So you say. That's nothing to do with me. Even if you bought the ship, you are bound by law to carry out the charter. Till a charter runs out and isn't renewed, owners are helpless. I obey the charter while it holds, and as long as I do that I'm doing nothing wrong."

"You are perfectly well aware of what you are doing. I am convinced of that. You were not born yesterday. Now, you are not sailing toward Portugal, you are sailing toward a policeman, and it is from that policeman I wish to save you."

"Oh, yes, you'd like to get possession of the ship and cargo for yourself, wouldn't you?" sneered the captain.

"Yes, exactly."

"Well, you won't get it!" cried the master angrily, bringing his huge fist down on the table. "Talk to me of thieving! What are you? Why, you're a pirate, that's what you are. I said so to Frowningshield, and he wouldn't believe me. He thought you wouldn't dare come aboard of me on the high seas; that you knew better. You and your policeman! Why, damn it all, I'd be justified in hanging you from the yardarm!"

"You couldn't do that, captain," protested Stranleigh, with great mildness.

"Why couldn't I?"

"Because those two masts of yours are not provided with yardarms. You might possibly hang me from the funnel, or allow me to dangle in chains from one of the arms of your steam crane, but that's all."

"Why don't you and your gang of ruffians climb aboard here like real pirates, and make me walk the plank?"

"I have climbed aboard like a real pirate, and I am going to make you walk the plank."

"The devil you are!" cried the captain, rising, his two clenched hands resting on the table, his naturally florid face still further flushed with wrath. "I'll show you—I'll show you what we do to men of your kind that dare to come aboard a ship on the high seas."

"Sit down, my dear man, sit down," pleaded Stranleigh soothingly. "Don't bluster. What's the use of making a fuss? Let's discuss the thing amicably."

"Make me walk the plank, will you?" roared the captain, a-quiver with resentment.

"Oh, well, well, if you object, of course that puts a different complexion on the matter. I thought that walking the plank was a customary nautical amusement. I seem to have been misled by friend Clark Russell. If it isn't etiquette, let's say no more about it. Do sit down, captain."

But the captain wouldn't sit down. His eyes glared, his face grew redder, and his lips quivered with animosity.

"You come alongside with your toy yacht!"

"It's a toy, captain, that spins along a little faster than this old tub."

"You and your jackanapes dressed up like naval officers, dare to come aboard o' me."

"That's splendid, captain. I like that phrase, 'aboard o' me.' I'm delighted to have Clark Russell corroborated from your mouth. Yes, I come aboard o' you. What then?"

"What then? Why, then you try to browbeat me in my own cabin, on my own ship. Who the devil do you think you are, I'd like to know?"

"I am Earl Stranleigh of Wychwood."

The captain now, without being told, slowly relapsed into his chair, and gazed across the table at the young man. That latent respect for the aristocracy which permeates even the most democratic of his Britannic Majesty's subjects caused an instant collapse of the truculence which had threatened an abrupt conclusion to the conference. Curiously enough, the honest captain never thought of questioning the statement, which had been made in a quiet, but very convincing tone.

"Earl Stranleigh!" he gasped.

"Yes; of Wychwood. We always insist on the Wychwood, though I'm sure I don't know why, for there isn't another Lord Stranleigh, and Wychwood is far from being the most important of my estates. Still, there you have it, captain. English life is full of incongruities."

"The rich Lord Stranleigh?" questioned the captain, with an accent on the adjective.

"I've just told you there's only one."

"Then why in the name of Neptune are you pirating on the high seas? Is that the way you made your money?"

"No, my money was more or less honestly accumulated by my ancestors, but I think their method was highway robbery rather than piracy. The looting of land that didn't belong to them seemed to occupy their spare time, and so, what with the rise of manufacturing cities in the midlands, on portions of our property, the discovery of coal mines, and what not, my family prospered better than it deserved, and here am I the twentieth-century representative of it."

"If that is so, why the deuce are you meddling in this affair?"

"Because I like to see a man minding his own business. The ship which you so worthily sail is mine. I bought her a few days after you left Southampton. Here is the deed of transfer, and here is the letter I spoke of, written to you by Messrs. Sparling & Bilge, informing you that I am the new owner, that I shall be responsible for your pay hereafter, and as a consequence they will be much obliged, as, indeed, so shall I, if you do what I tell you."

The captain read the documents with slow care, then looked up.

"It's Sparling & Bilge's signature all right, and nobody knows it better than I do, but what about the cargo? Do you intend to unship at Lisbon?"

"No, I intend to run it to Plymouth."

"But even if the ship's yours, the cargo isn't."

"Surely you knew they were stealing the ore, captain?"

"They told me they had a right to it for three months. Mr. Schwartzbrod showed me papers to that effect. That's why they were in such a hurry. Wanted to get as much out in the time as they could, and offered me a bonus of five thousand pounds over and above my wages if I ran three voyages to Lisbon, and two thousand for each extra voyage within the time."

"Then, captain, why didn't they concentrate their energies on the mining of the ore, and not bother with the mining of the river?"

"Why, Frowningshield told me that they were on the lookout for some pirates that was going to interfere with them. We didn't intend to blow up any vessels unless they were determined to come up the river in spite of us. That's why we didn't put the mines at the mouth of the river. On the high ground west of the camp, Frowning-shield had two men on watch all the time. If they saw any ship approach, they were to go down the river in a boat that was kept below the mines, and order the steamer to go back. If the captain wouldn't go back, then he came on at his own risk."

"I see. And did Frowningshield tell his men to inform captain and crew that the river was mined?"

"I don't know."

"Now, captain, talking as one seafaring man to another, didn't all this, in conjunction with the large sums of money promised you, strike you as rather fishy? Did this appear to you an honest trading?"

"Well, earl, I've sailed to all parts of distant seas, and I've known things done that would have looked mighty queer in Southampton Harbor, and yet they were all right as far as ever I knew. Things happen in the South Seas that would seem rather odd in Bristol Channel, you know."

"You didn't think you were running any risk, then?"

"Oh, risk! A seafaring man runs risks every time lie leaves port. If this was a risk, there was good money at the end of it, and that isn't always the case when a man ships on a tramp steamer nowadays, what with everything cut to pieces by foreign competition. You see, earl, men born to money don't always appreciate what people will do who're trying to pile up a little cash against their old age. I've got a wife and family in a hired house in Southampton—three girls I've got at home, earl, and girls is helpless left poor—not to mention my old woman."

The captain's eyes took on a dreamy, far-away look that seemed to penetrate and question the future. He had, for the moment, forgotten the young man sitting opposite him, and went on as if talking to himself.

"There's a piece of land running down to Southampton water—five acres and a bit more. Somebody built a cottage there and put up a flagpole on the lawn in front. Then they got tired of it, and it's for sale. A thousand pounds they want for the place, everything included. There's a few trees, and there's outhouses; splendid spot to raise chickens. Then there's a veranda in front, and an oldish man might sit in an easy-chair smoking his pipe, and see the American liners come sailing past. And my family's living in a rented house on a back street. I've always wanted that bit of land, earl, but never had the money to spare, and when I come to settle down, like as not somebody else will own it, and we couldn't afford it, anyhow. Risks? Of course there's risks, but when I think of that little cottage—well, I took the risk, earl."

"My dear captain," said the earl softly, "your bit of land makes me ashamed of myself, and of my moral lectures. I have so much land, and others have so little. Here's a hard-working man like you, landless, and here's a loafer like me with thousands of acres! Hang me if I wouldn't turn Radical were it not for the awful example of William Thomas Stead. Well, captain, that plot of land is yours from this moment. If somebody else has bought it in your absence, we'll evict them. I'll go bail that old Schwartzbrod will pay you all he promised whether you make the voyages or not. Indeed, you are not going to make the voyages, as a matter of fact. I don't believe Schwartzbrod ever intended to keep his promise, and I very much doubt if you could collect. Now, I'm an excellent collector, and I think I can persuade Schwartzbrod to plead for the privilege of paying you. You see these city men are much too sharp for simple, honest chaps like you and me. After you had done their work, they would have left you in the lurch if you were caught, or cheated you out of your compensation if you escaped. You may depend upon it, Schwartzbrod and his crowd have done everything in the most legal manner.

Indeed, as a matter of fact, the last time I saw him he wheedled a document from me which I have reason to believe covers the villainy of this expedition. I do not in the least doubt that if I took the case into the law courts I'd get beaten. That's why I preferred to fight the case on the high seas, where an injunction can't be served till it's too late. You and I, captain, are not shrewd enough to be a match for these rascals."

There was almost a smirk of self-satisfaction on the captain's face as he found himself thus linked with a man of Lord Stranleigh's rank.

"Well, earl," he said, "what do you want me to do?"

They were interrupted by the heavy steps of the mate coming down the stairs.

"What do you want?" roared the captain. "Get out of here."

"Beg pardon, sir," explained the mate, "but they're getting uneasy on the yacht, and want to know what's become of the boss."

"Just excuse me for a moment, captain," said Stranleigh, "and I'll speak to them. You know you did rather tyrannize over us when we first hailed you, and they probably think you've Mac-kellered me. I rather flatter myself I've made a pun there, for 'keller' is the German for cellar." The young man sprang lightly up the steps, and went over to the bulwarks.

"Is it all right, sir?" shouted Mackeller.

"All right, thank you."

"It's getting dark, you know. Hadn't I better heave a revolver up to you, and if they try any tricks you can fire it off, and we'll be aboard before you can say 'Schwartzbrod.'"

"Ah, Mackeller, Mackeller, you're always thinking of deadly weapons and acts of piracy! No wonder I get a bad name in marine circles. Everything's going smoothly, and I expect to be with you within ten minutes."

Stranleigh returned to the cabin, where he found the captain sitting, staring into vacancy. Some one had lit an odorous oil lamp.

"Well, captain, before answering your question, I wish to say that I am interested in mercantile traffic aside from my ownership of the Rajah. Before I left England I reserved for you the berth of captain on a new steamer called the Wychwood, twice the size of this boat, that is intended for the South American trade. I think she will be ready for you by the time we reach Plymouth, and the moment we are in Plymouth I shall hand you a check for a thousand pounds to secure that bit of land by Southampton water. What sort of a crew have you aboard here? A mutinous lot, or easy going?"

"Oh, the crew's all right, earl. They're Devon men, most of them. It was a rough lot of passengers we took out under charge of Frowning-shield, but they herded most by themselves, and held no truck with the crew. The crew's all right, sir."

"Do you think any of the crew knew what was going on?"

"No, I don't suppose anybody knew what was going on but me and Frowningshield."

"Would you like to have your present crew with you on the new steamer?"

"Yes, sir, I would."

"Officers, too?"

"Yes, I would. Officers, too."

"Very well, I want you to come aboard my yacht, and be captain of her from here to Plymouth. Take the mate with you, if you like, or any of the other officers, and take such of the crew as are not Devon men. I'll put some of my own fellows aboard in their place."

"You mean me to leave the ship, my lord?"

"Yes. The yacht's captain and mate will take the place of you and your mate."

The captain's face was a study of indecision and doubt.

"It doesn't seem quite right, my lord."

"Your late owners have told you to obey me, and I am your new owner. It is quite right. I have merely transferred you to the yacht as if I were transferring you to a ferry boat, in order to take you the more quickly to your new command. We'll reach Plymouth in a fortnight, or three weeks before the Rajah does. I'd rather you didn't go to Southampton, but if you think you can keep out of sight, I don't mind your running across there, seeing your family, and securing that property. Indeed, if the property is still in the market, and the house empty, there's no reason why you shouldn't move your people into it. You'll have time enough, then you can return to Plymouth, see to your new ship, and engage what men you need to supplement the Rajah's crew when she arrives."

The captain made no reply: bowed head and wrinkled brow showed that a mental conflict was going on.

"I suppose you are very well known in Southampton?"

"No," he said; "not so well known as you might think. I'm there for a little while, then off on a long voyage. Not as well known as might be."

"You see, captain, I'm determined to get out of old Schwartzbrod the money wherewith to pay not only you, but Frowningshield and his men. I don't intend to leave them marooned there while Schwartzbrod sits safe in London, so I wish no rumor of what has taken place to reach the ears of Schwartzbrod and his syndicate, therefore I don't want you to be seen and recognized by anybody, if possible, and if you are recognized I am anxious that you should not talk about what has occurred."

"I see. You want to get all the witnesses shipped off to South America. Well, you know, my lord, meaning no disrespect, your way of doing things seems a little fishy, too, as you said a while ago."

"Of course it looks fishy, but you must fight a whale with a shark if you haven't got a harpoon. I must either go to law, which is the harpoon, with old Schwartzbrod, who is the whale, or else adopt his own methods, and play the shark. You've got to choose which course of fish you're going to take, and you've got to give your order to the waiter now."

"Suppose I refuse, what will you do? Attempt to capture us?"

"Bless you, no. I'll merely follow you, just as a shark follows a doomed vessel. The moment you approach a port that contains a British consul, I'll dash on ahead, show my papers, and set the law in motion, which, as I have informed you, I am reluctant to do. The moment that happens I can't save you, captain. I don't know what the penalty is, or whether there is a penalty. Perhaps your obedience to orders may allow you to slip through the meshes of the net, and then again perhaps it won't. If it doesn't, then that little cottage on Southampton water, which was yours a moment ago, will never be occupied by your family. Oh, hang it all, I'm either coercing or bribing you now, whichever it is. You must make a free choice. Whatever happens, I'll buy that piece of land, and present it to your wife, if you will tell me where it is, and give me her address. Now, captain, make your choice: the whale or the shark."

The captain heaved a deep, almost a heartrending sigh, that seemed to come from the very bottom of his hoots. He rose slowly and ponderously, and stretched forth his hand.

"Lord Stranleigh," he said solemnly, as one about to cross the Rubicon, "Lord Stranleigh, I am ready to walk the plank."

When Lord Stranleigh emerged from the captain's cabin of the Rajah, and drew a long, satisfying breath of the sweet evening air outside, he saw that the moon had risen, while the glow from the sunset still tinted the western sky. The slight breeze from Africa had completely died away, and the sea lay around the two ships smooth as a polished mirror. At a word from Stranleigh the captain of the yacht drew her alongside the Rajah, and the engines of both steamers stopped. Captain Wilkie, forewarned, had all his belongings packed, and they were speedily swung aboard the black steamer. The captain of the Rajah, and his mate, flung their possessions into boxes, and thus the transfer was made without loss of time.

"Mackeller," said Stranleigh, "I fear that luxury is thrown away on you, and besides, experience on the yacht has shown you that there is little chance of anything exciting happening. It must discourage you to remember that none of your repeating rifles have even been unpacked, so I will cause the cases to be swung aboard the Rajah, with sufficient ammunition to massacre our entire naval force, and I'll give you six of my gamekeepers. You can either use the gamekeepers to shoot the crew, or arm the crew and eliminate the gamekeepers. I had intended to take the crew of the Rajah upon the yacht, and put the crew of the yacht on the Rajah, but I am so selfish that I cannot bring myself to trust those clumsy seafarers from a tramp steamer with the somewhat delicate organization of my yacht. Will you accept the commission, and sail for home on the comfortless Rajah?"

"I shall be delighted, sir," said Mackeller. "You see, I feel just a little uncertain about the wisdom of leaving Captain Wilkie unprotected with what is, after all, a strange crew. Their captain gives them a good character, but Captain Wilkie, who is a martinet in his way, may get at loggerheads with them, so it is well that he should have a bloodthirsty commander and irresistible force at his beck and call. But remember, Peter, that for every sailor you shoot, one of your gamekeepers must take to the sailoring trade, which might turn out inconvenient in a storm, so repress your war spirit until the captain orders it to belch forth. I imagine your frowning appearance as, resembling the German Emperor, you walk the deck, will quell any incipient mutiny in the bud, if buds are quelled. Nevertheless, it is safer to hold the rifles in the background in case of an emergency. So call for six volunteers from among my men, and then fling your trunk aboard the lugger, after which it will be good-by till I meet you again at Plymouth." When the exchange was completed the white yacht drew away from the tramp and speedily disappeared to the north like a ghost. Captain Wilkie watched her departure with regret, and was unhappy at his promotion to the unkempt and dirty tramp steamer, with her slouching crew, dressed like scarecrows. The new commander of the yacht felt equally out of place in this trim, scrupulously clean, nickel-plated, bride's-cake of a ship, while the sailors, in their spick-and-span natty uniforms, gave him the impression of being in a nightmare where an uncouth private had been placed in charge of a company of officers. As he was about the same size as Wilkie, the useful Ponderby, at Stranleigh's orders, fitted him out next morning in a gorgeous uniform which added to the beauty of his outward appearance without materially augmenting his inward comfort. However, the bluff captain understood his business, no matter what costume he wore, and Stranleigh, studying him very unobtrusively as the voyage went on, came to place a great confidence in him, and felt rather ashamed of the distrust that had caused him to transfer the captain from the Rajah to the yacht. Before a week was past, he was certain that this gruff sea dog would have taken the Rajah direct to Plymouth once he had given his word, quite as faithfully as Captain Wilkie was doing. Although Stranleigh said nothing of this trust, and even doubted if the simple old man had seen the reason of the change, he nevertheless resolved to make amends, though not in words. The weather throughout had been almost obtrusively gentle, and Stranleigh complained that the voyage was falsifying all of Clark Russell's novels. He grumbled to the doctor that his faith in Clark Russell was undergoing a tremendous strain.

"When we reach a dead calm in one of Clark Russell's novels," he said to the doctor, "we always know what to expect. Suddenly out of the west comes a ripping cyclone which lays us over on our beam ends. Then wild, blinding rain and utter darkness, lit up only by vivid flashes of lightning. Every one has to cling to whatever is nearest him: overboard go the chicken coops, and there is such a general pandemonium that the voice of command cannot be heard. Crash go the masts, funnels, and what not: we right ourselves, staggering under the mountainous waves, and find ourselves a dismantled hulk next morning, with the cook missing, and no hot rolls for breakfast. Now, in reality we have had evenings without a zephyr afloat, then follows a peaceful night, and morning comes with a maidenly blush, like that on a new-born rose. I imagine the ocean has improved since Clark Russell's time, or perhaps the Government weather bureau has regulated tilings. We are a wonderful people, doctor, and at last Britannia really does rule the waves."

Fast as his yacht was, the young man had become tired of the voyage. He yearned for his morning paper and a stroll down Piccadilly. When well across the placid Bay of Biscay, he called up one of his wireless telegraphers, and said to him:

"I say, my son, cannot you tune up your heavenly harp, and pull us some news down out of the sky? Aren't we within the Marconi range of civilization yet?"

"Yes, sir. Several private messages have come through, and some scraps of news, but nothing important. The chancellor of the exchequer is speaking in the House of Commons on some bill, so far as I understand it, to regulate the Bank of England."

"I fear that wouldn't be very exciting reading, my boy, and besides, I don't understand finance, and never did. Still, I'd welcome even the words of a politician this evening, so if the chancellor is still talking, write out what he says. And, by the way, if you get a chance to talk back, you might ask the horizon what races were on to-day, and which horses won. After all, it is encouraging to know that the chancellor of the exchequer is on his feet. That shows that old England is still a going concern. It seems a year since I was there."

The operator departed for the telegraphic cabin, and Stranleigh went on with his cigar and after-dinner coffee. Presently the young man returned with a grin on his face.

"He's at it again, sir," he said, and handed Stranleigh a sheet of paper headed:

"CHANCELLOR EXCHEQUER.

"During the past decade our bank rate has been in a state of constant fluctuation, changing many times, and ranging from two-and-a-half to seven per cent., a variation which has exercised anything but a beneficial effect upon business. The gold in the issue department of the Bank of England usually amounts to about thirty millions of pounds, which are shown to be inadequate to the needs of our time. On the other hand, the Bank of France rarely allows its reserve to fall below a hundred millions of pounds, with a consequence that the French bank rate remains steady at from two-and-a-half to three per cent., and has not risen to four per cent for thirty years. In the twelve months preceding the report of 1904 the bank rate of France had not been changed once, while our own bank rate had jumped from——"

Here Stranleigh crumpled the paper into a ball in his hand, and flung it into the ocean.

"Great heavens!" he cried. "I wonder what kind of a brain revels in that sort of rot! And not a word about the races! What do these telegraphers imagine news is, anyhow?"

The ignorant young man little dreamed that the message he was reading would exercise an astounding influence on his own career on that day when the Bank of England was compelled by the new Act of Parliament to raise its reserve of gold from thirty millions of pounds to one hundred millions. A world-wide financial disturbance lay ahead which Stranleigh did not suspect any more than did the wise lawmakers who passed the bill by a large majority. Most of them, including his lordship, thought the races more important and interesting.

The captain strolled aft. More and more as the days went on the frivolous young man's liking for this veteran of the sea had increased, in spite of the fact that the captain had endeavored to carry away his gold mine.

"Sit down, captain," he cried. "What will you drink?"

"A cup of coffee, to keep me awake. I expect to be up all night, or at least till we pass the Ushant."

"Right you are, and coffee it is. Oh, by the way, I have changed my mind, and you must change your course. Instead of striking straight across from Ushant to Plymouth, steer your course up the Channel for Southampton."

"Very good, earl."

"And I've also changed my mind regarding that bit of land of yours."

"Oh, have you, earl?" said the captain, with a catch in his voice, and disappointment visible on his countenance.

"Yes, that's the reason we're going to Southampton. You will lay this yacht up—I think that is the nautical term—alongside your bit of land. As you know, I am anxious that you shouldn't be seen, and also that nobody aboard should have a chance to talk."

"I'll see to that, earl."

"My dear man, don't call me earl. I told you I was an earl in strict confidence. Haven't you noticed that everyone addresses me as 'sir,' and I don't even insist on that. We are all free and equal at sea, except the captain, who rules over us. When we reach Southampton water I'll go ashore in the motor boat, will call on the land agent, secure the estate of five acres, give the deeds to your wife, and invite her and the family to come up and view the cottage."

"She knows where it is, sir. We've often been there together."

"Then you'll grant no shore leave, not even to yourself. You'll keep the lads busy while I'm ashore. Take the yacht to the nearest coaling station, wherever it is, and fill her up with black diamonds. We may want to go to New York, for all I know. What time do you expect to pass Ushant?"

"About one bell, sir; half an hour after midnight."

"How long is the run from Ushant to Southampton?"

"We should do it easy in eleven hours."

"Then we'll reach there at noon to-morrow? Very good. You had better, perhaps, run me right up to Southampton, attend to the port formalities, see to the coaling, and be lying off your bit of property by six o'clock next evening. I'll stop the night at a hotel, so you needn't trouble about me. How large is your family, captain?"

"The three eldest are at sea, and the three girls at home with the missus."

"Three girls? Oh, that's jolly! Very well, I think we've everything arranged. You will see that the motor boat is ready for me at the landing both to-morrow afternoon and all next day. I shall probably want to run up the bay to the bit of land, or down, whichever it is. I suppose you can point it out to me as we pass?"

"Oh, yes, sir. I never enter or leave Southampton without looking at that bit of ground."

"Very well. At about five o'clock p.m. day after to-morrow I shall invite the missus and the three girls to take a trip with me in the motor boat. Arriving there I shall hand the keys and the deeds to the lady of the house, and if you come ashore I'll introduce you to the family. You may stop all night ashore. Next morning take the yacht, and navigate her slowly round to Plymouth. There you may give everybody shore leave, but don't overdo it. You understand what I want, which is that no man shall talk about the mine in West Africa or the transfer in midocean, so I expect you to keep your section of the crew in hand. I can answer for my fellows. Oh, yes, by the way, I'll take my woodmen off at noon to-morrow, together with all that are left of my gamekeepers, and send them home, including the excellent Ponderby, so you will have none to deal with except those belonging to the yacht."

The Woman in White did even better than the captain anticipated, and landed her owner in Southampton at ten minutes to eleven. He bade farewell to his men, and dispatched them to their homes, none the poorer for their long voyage. He visited the land agent's office, transacted his business within ten minutes, drew his check, and told the manager to have the papers ready by twelve o'clock next day. Then he went to the back street, and knocked at the number the captain had given him. The door was opened by a buxom young woman, in whose flashing eyes he recognized her father.

"Well, my dear," he said, chucking her under the chin, "are you the gallant captain's daughter, as we say in the revised version of 'Pinafore'?"

The girl drew back in righteous anger, and if a dagger glance of the eyes could have slain, he would have been in danger, but the callous young man merely laughed.

"Mother at home?" he asked.

"Who are you?" demanded the offended girl.

"That's the same question your father asked me. It's a secret, and I'll tell it only to your mother."

At this moment the mother, hearing the high tones of her daughter, and fancying something was wrong, appeared in the hall; a stout, elderly woman, who frowned at the tall, nattily dressed stranger.

"My name is Stranleigh, madam, and I am by way of being a shipowner. Your husband is one of my captains."

"He is nothing of the sort. He is captain of the Rajah.'"

"Quite right, and I am the owner of the Rajah. Your husband has just bought that little bit of property down the bay; the one with a cottage and a flag pole, you know."

"What are you talking about, sir? My husband is hundreds and hundreds of miles away at sea."

"Oh, no, madam, it's you who are at sea. Of course, he didn't buy the property personally. I have acted as his agent, and I come merely to tell you of the transaction. The deeds are promised by noon to-morrow, when I am promising myself the pleasure of handing them to you."

"Then his venture has turned out a success? I had my doubts of it."

"So had I, madam, but we who predict disaster are often confounded. Everything is all right, as you remark." Then, turning to the one who had let him in, he said reproachfully: "Please don't scowl at me like that, but close the door and invite me into the parlor. Don't you see I'm a visitor?"

The girl said nothing, but looked at her mother.

"Come this way, sir," said the woman, opening the door at the left, whereupon the girl, with visible reluctance, closed the front door.

"Where are the other two girls'?" demanded Stranleigh.

"They are in the kitchen, sir."

"Please send for them. I wish to see the whole family, being so well acquainted with the captain."

The still unmollified door opener, at a nod from her mother, disappeared, returning shortly with the two younger children shrinking bashfully behind their elder sister, who quite evidently ruled the household.

"Ah," said Stranleigh, "what a fine family! It is evident that these girls did not depend for their beauty solely on their father."

"I think," said the elder girl haughtily, "that my father is the finest looking man in the world."

"You'll change your mind some of these days, miss, or I'm greatly mistaken. I admit the worth of your father, but you'll never see his picture on a beauty post card. And now, if you're prepared for a bit of news, and if every one promises not to faint, I'll tell you what it is."

"Oh, he isn't arrested?" cried the wife in alarm.

"Arrested? Of course not. Why should he be? He is coaling my yacht at this moment somewhere in Southampton harbor, within half a mile of where you are sitting."

There were some shrieks of surprise at this intelligence, but Stranleigh went on unheeding.

"Now, as I have told you, the cottage is yours, and I wish you to do something very enterprising; to hustle, as they say in America. My motor boat is down at the landing, and can take you to and from the cottage as often as you like, and it will be speedier than tram or cab or railway carriage. Missus, you will be chief of the finest burst of shopping Southampton has ever seen. Your husband will land at the cottage at six o'clock tomorrow night. The chances are that the empty house will not be any the worse for a little cleaning, so your eldest daughter here should take with her a host of charwomen, and scrub the edifice from top room to basement. Then, madam, you are to go to whatever furniture shop you choose, ignore all that you now possess, and furnish every room in that house before four o'clock tomorrow."

"But, sir, that will cost a mint of money, and we——"

"Yes, I didn't expect it done for nothing, and I haven't the remotest idea what the total will be. But here are three hundred pounds to go on with. I got this purposely to-day in crisp Bank of England notes. Whatever more is needed I will pay you to-morrow."

"But how are we ever to pay you, sir?" asked the astonished woman.

"No need of that, madam. Your husband did me a very great service, and I am merely arranging this as a pleasant surprise for him, and also because of the intense admiration your eldest daughter exhibits for me."

The girl tossed her head.

"He's a humbug, mother; don't believe him. There's something bogus in all this. I'll warrant you those notes are counterfeit. He wants to get us out of the house, and then steal the furniture. I read about a person like him in the papers. He got seven years."

Lord Stranleigh laughed.

"Why, how sharp you are, unbelieving creature. You've guessed it the first time. Is the furniture in this villa worth three hundred pounds?"

"No, it isn't," said the girl promptly.

"Very well. Take those notes to the bank, and get golden sovereigns for them, leaving your mother on guard till you return. They'll probably ask you where you got them, and you will answer thus: 'They are the proceeds of a draft for three hundred pounds which Lord Stranleigh of Wychwood cashed at the London and County to-day, at half-past eleven.' If they still wish to know how you came by them, say that Lord Stranleigh is the owner of several steamships, and that your father is captain of the largest of them. Say nothing of the Rajah, because he is now chief of a steamer twice her size. I took notes because they were lighter to carry, but when you get the gold I hope you will do what I ask of you, and leave this house promptly, so that I can steal its furniture without molestation."

"Are you Lord Stranleigh?" gasped the mother.

"Yes, madam, and there's one other favor I beg of you, and of these three charming girls. Mention to nobody that your father has returned. Neither he nor I wish this known for a while yet, and I am quite sure four women can keep the secret, even if one man can't."

"There's nothing wrong, is there?" asked the anxious woman.

"Nothing wrong at all. It's merely a matter concerning his new ship, which lies at Plymouth, where he must go on the morning of day after tomorrow."

Energetic as the captain's family was, they never put in such a day and a half of nervous, capable speed in their lives before, and this included the intervening night, during which none of them slept.

By five o'clock in the afternoon everything was ship-shape, although not quite to the satisfaction of the eldest daughter, and at six Lord Stranleigh had the felicity of introducing the captain to his possessions, human and material, old and new. Then he rushed back in his motor boat, and took the train to London.

CHAPTER VIII—THE "RAJAH" GETS INTO LEGAL DIFFICULTIES

A CAB from the London terminus speedily deposited Lord Stranleigh at his favorite club in Pall Mall. Two acquaintances coming down the steps nodded to him casually, so casually that the salutation, taken in conjunction with the lack of all interest displayed in the smoking room when he entered, caused him to realize that he had never been missed, and this indifference keeps a man from becoming too conceited when he has victoriously pitted his intelligence against bears or brigands in far-away corners of the earth, and lives to tell the tale, or keep quiet about it, as the case may be. As he was attired in the ordinary business suit that had done two days' hard duty at Southampton, he could not commit the solecism of entering the dining room. Indeed, gleaming, snowy shirt fronts were so prevalent in the smoking room itself that he experienced the unaccustomed, but rather enjoyable feeling of being a wild and woolly pioneer, who had strayed by mistake into a stronghold of fashionable civilization. The dining room being forbidden ground, Stranleigh contented himself with a couple of sandwiches and a tankard of German beer. As he partook of this frugal fare, a broad shirt front bore down upon him that reminded him of the sail of a racing yacht.

"Hello, Stranleigh," said Sir William Grainger, the owner of the shirt front. "Remember me telling you last week that Flying Scud was sure of a place in the Maple-Durham stakes?"

"I don't remember having received that information from you," replied Stranleigh. "Did Flying Scud pull it off, then?"

"Pull it off? Why, the race isn't run till tomorrow."

"Oh, I beg pardon, I had forgotten the date."

"Well, Stranleigh, I've got it straight that Flying Scud will romp in a winner. It's a sure thing. Don't you give it away, but act on the hint, and you won't be sorry. Odds are twenty-five to one at the present moment, and for every blooming quid you put up, you'll get a pony."

"That's very attractive, Billy."

"Attractive? Why, it's simply found money."

"Ah, well, such chances are not for me, Billy. I've had to pawn my evening togs in order to get a sandwich and a glass of beer. I'm a hornyhanded son of toil trying to pick up an honest living. Why don't you follow my example, Billy, and do something useful? This deplorable habit of betting on the races will lead you into financial straits by and by, and what is worse, the gambling fever may become chronic if you don't check it in time."

Sir William Grainger laughed joyously at this. He was a young man who had already run through a large patrimony left him by his father, and since that time had developed a genius for borrowing which would have done credit to Harriman, the railway king.

"Come, Stranleigh, don't preach, or at least, if you do preach, don't hedge. You know what I want. Lend me a pony till next Monday, there's a good fellow. That sum will bring me in six hundred and twenty-five pounds before to-morrow night. I've figured it all out on a sheet of club paper, but I'm stony broke, so fork over the twenty-five, Stranleigh."

Lord Stranleigh, without demur, took from his pocketbook some Bank of England notes of ten pounds each, selected three of them, and passed them on to Sir William, who thus getting five pounds more than he had asked for, lovingly fingered the tenacious, crisp pieces of paper, then put forward a bluff of getting one of them changed, that he might return the extra money.

"Oh, don't trouble about that," said Stranleigh, somewhat wearily. He had had a tiring day at Southampton, and beer and sandwiches were not a very inspiring meal at the end of it. "Don't trouble about that. If you take another sheet of club paper, you may be able to calculate how much more the extra five pounds will bring you in to-morrow night."

"By Jove, that's true," said Sir William, much relieved, and then the ease with which he had made the haul seemed to stir up his covetousness and still further submerge all self-respect.

"Talking of the extra amount I will gain reminds me, Stranleigh, that if you will give me one more ten-pound note, the whole loot will be an even thousand at twenty-five to one, you know. I'll pay it all back on Monday, but it seems a pity to miss such a chance, doesn't it?"

"How wonderfully you can estimate the odds, Billy. If forty pounds will bring you a thousand, then, as you say, it would be a pity to miss such an opportunity. Well, here you are," and he passed the fourth ten-pound note into the other's custody.

Still Sir William lingered. Perhaps it would have been more merciful if his lordship had demurred rather strenuously against accommodating him with the so-called loan. The sight of the other's notes now returning to his pocket filled him with envy. He felt some remnant of reluctance in attempting to increase his acquisition, so he put it in another form:

"I say, Stranleigh, if you'd like me to lay a bit on for you, so far as Flying Scud is concerned, I'll do it with pleasure."

"Thanks, old man, but I shan't trouble you. I intend to put on some money, but it will be against Flying Scud."

"What! have you heard anything?" cried Sir William in alarm, but the other interrupted——

"I know nothing about the horse at all, but I know a good deal about your luck, and I'll have that forty pounds back on Monday, without troubling you, except by betting against you." Sir William laughed a little, shrugged his shoulders, and walked away with the loot.

"Yes," murmured Stranleigh to himself, "this is dear old London again, sure enough. The borrowing of money has begun."

In spite of being touched for varying amounts, Lord Stranleigh enjoyed to the full his return to the Metropolis, and for many days strolled down Piccadilly with the easy grace of a man about town, the envy of less fortunate people who knew him. This period of indolence was put an end to by the receipt of a telegram from Mackeller. That capable young man had sent his message from the northwest corner of Brittany, having ordered the Rajah to be run into the roadstead of Brest. The communication informed Stranleigh that Mackeller had hoisted up a portion of the cargo, and placed it aboard a lugger, which was to sail direct for Portreath. This transhipment of part of the cargo had brought Plimsoll's mark on the side of the Rajah into view once more, and the steamer might now enter the harbor of Plymouth without danger of being haled before the authorities, charged with overloading. He expected to reach Plymouth next day.

Stranleigh was lunching at home that day because in the morning he had been favored with a telephone call, and on putting the receiver to his ear, had distinguished the still, small voice of Conrad Schwartzbrod, who appeared to be trying to say something with reference to the Rajah. Stranleigh was afflicted with a certain dislike of the telephone, and often manifested an impatience with its working which he did not usually show when confronted with the greater evils of life, so after telling the good Mr. Schwartzbrod to stand farther away from the transmitter, to come closer, to speak louder, he at last admitted he could not understand what was being said, and invited the financier to call upon him at his house that afternoon at half past two, if what he had to say was important enough to justify a journey from the city to the West End.

At the luncheon table Mackeller's long telegram was handed to him, and, after he had read it, Stranleigh smiled as he thought how nearly its arrival had coincided with Schwartzbrod's visit, and he wondered how much the latter would give for its perusal if he knew of its existence. He surmised that the Stock Exchange magnate was becoming a little anxious because of the nonarrival of the Rajah at Lisbon, where, doubtless, his emissaries awaited her. In spite of his pretense of misapprehension, he had heard quite distinctly at the telephone receiver that Schwartz-brod had just learned he was the owner of the Rajah, and that he wished to renew his charter of that slow-going, deliberate steam vessel, but he could not deny himself the pleasure of crossquestioning so crafty an opponent face to face. He had been expecting an application from Conrad Schwartzbrod for some days, and now it had arrived almost too late, for he directed Ponderby to secure him a berth on the Plymouth express for that night.

The young nobleman did not receive the elderly capitalist in his business office downstairs, as perhaps would have been the more suitable, but greeted him instead in the ample and luxurious drawing-room on the first floor, where Stranleigh, enjoying the liberty of a bachelor, was smoking an after-luncheon cigar, and he began the interview by offering a similar one to his visitor, which was declined. Mr. Schwartzbrod, it seemed, never smoked.

The furtive old man was palpably nervous and ill at ease. He sat on the extreme edge of an elegant chair, and appeared not to know exactly what to do with his hands. The news which had reached him from Sparling & Bilge in Southampton, that Lord Stranleigh was the new owner of the Rajah, had disquieted Schwartzbrod, and his manner showed this to his indolent host, who lounged back in an easy-chair, calmly viewing the newcomer with an expression of countenance that was almost cherublike in its innocence.

"Sorry you don't smoke," drawled the younger man. "You miss a great deal of pleasure in life by your abstention."

"It is a habit I never acquired, my lord, and so perhaps I do not feel the lack of it so much as one accustomed to tobacco might suppose. I lead a very busy life, and, indeed, a somewhat anxious one, since times are so bad in the city, therefore I have little opportunity of cultivating what I might call—I hope with no offense—the smaller vices."

"Ah, there speaks a large trader. You go in for the big things in life, whether in finance or in vice."

"I hope I may say without vanity, my lord, that I have always avoided vice, large or small."

"Lucky man; I wish I could make the same confession. So times are bad in the city, are they?"

"Yes, they are."

"Then why don't you chuck the city, and come and live in the West End where life is easy?"

"A rich man may live where he pleases, my lord, but I have been a hard worker all my life."

"Poor, but honest, eh? Still, when all's said and done, Mr. Schwartzbrod, I really believe that you hard workers enjoy your money better when you get it than we leisurely people who have never known the lack of it. I believe in honesty myself, and if I were not of so indolent a nature, I think I might perhaps have become an honest man. But a busy laborer like yourself, Mr. Schwartzbrod, has not come to the West End to hear me talk platitudes about honesty. In America the man goes West who intends to work hard. In London a man comes west when he has made money.

"'You miss a great deal of pleasure in life.'"

"He has his pile in the city, and expects to cease work. You have come west temporarily to see me about some matter which the telephone delighted in mixing up with buzzings and rattlings and intermittent chattering that made your theme difficult to comprehend. Perhaps you will be good enough to let me know in what way I may serve you."

"At the time when I expected to operate the gold field, which you know of, my lord, I chartered a steamer, named the Rajah, at Southampton."

"Oh, the Rajah!" interrupted his lordship, sitting up, a gleam of intelligent comprehension animating his face. "The Rajah was what you were trying to say? I thought you were speaking of a Jolly Roger. Roger was the word that came over to me, and 'Jolly Roger' means the flag of a pirate ship, or something pertaining to piracy, so I, recognizing your voice, thinks to myself: 'What, in the name of Moses and the Prophets, can a respectable city personage mean by speaking of the Jolly Roger, as if he were a captain of buccaneers.' Oh, yes, the Rajah! Now I understand. Proceed, Mr. Schwartzbrod."

The personage seemed to turn a trifle more sallow than usual as the other went on enthusiastically talking of pirate ships and buccaneers, but he surmised that the young nobleman meant nothing in particular, as he sank back once more in his easy-chair, and again half closed his eyes, blowing the smoke of his cigar airily aloft. Presently, moistening his lips, Conrad Schwartzbrod found voice, convinced that the other's allusion to marine

444

pillage was a mere coincidence, and not a covert reference to Frowningshield and his merry men, or to the mission of the Rajah herself.

"I was about to say, my lord, that I had chartered the Rajah from a firm of shipping people in Southampton, intending to use her in the development of the mineral property in West Africa. That property having passed from the hands of myself and my associates into yours, my lord, I determined to employ the Rajah in the South American cattle trade, as we own an extensive tract of territory in the Argentine, the interests of which we are endeavoring to forward with the ultimate object of floating a company."

Again the prospective company promoter moistened his lips when they had safely delivered this interesting piece of fiction.

"So the Rajah has gone to the Argentine Republic, has she?" said Stranleigh.

"Yes, my lord."

"Filled with dynamite and mining machinery, eh? Surely a remarkable cargo for a herdsman to transport, Mr. Schwartzbrod?"

"Well, you see, my lord, the dynamite and machinery was on our hands, and as there are many mines in South America, we thought we could sell the cargo there to better advantage than in Southampton."

"Of course I don't in the least doubt, Mr. Schwartzbrod, that you own large ranches in South America, but I strongly suspect——"

He paused, and opened his eyes to half width, looking quizzically at his vis-à-vis.

"You strongly suspect what, my lord?" muttered Schwartzbrod.

"I suspect that you own a mine in South America that you are keeping very quiet about."

"Well, my lord," confessed Schwartzbrod, with apparent diffidence, "it is rarely wise to speak of these things prematurely."

"That is quite true, and I have really no wish to pry into your secrets, but

445

to tell the truth, I felt a little sore about your action with regard to the Rajah."

"My action? What action?"

"You must admit, Mr. Schwartzbrod, that when I acquired those so-called gold fields, I became possessor of everything the company owned, or at least I thought I did. Now, in the company was vested the charter of the Rajah, and it was the company's money which bought all the materials with which you have sailed away to South America. It therefore seemed to me—I don't wish to put it harshly—that you had, practically, made off with a portion of my property."

"You astonish me, my lord. It never occurred to me that such a view could be held by any one, especially one like yourself, so well acquainted with facts."

Stranleigh shrugged his shoulders.

"Acquainted with the facts? Oh, I don't know that I'm so very well versed in them. I'm not a business man, Mr. Schwartzbrod, and although I engage business men to look after my interests, it seems to me that sometimes they are not as sharp as they might be. I thought, after the acquisition of the company's property, that the charter of the Rajah and the contents of her hold belonged to me, just as much as the company's money in the bank did, or as its gold in West Africa."

"I assure you, my lord, you are mistaken. The Rajah and her charter were not mentioned in the documents of agreement between you and me, while the money in the bank was. But aside from all that, my lord, you gave me a document covering all that had been done previous to its signing, and the Rajah had sailed from South America several days before that instrument was completed. Everything was done legally, and under the advice of competent solicitors—yours and mine."

"Do not mistake me, Mr. Schwartzbrod; I am not complaining at all, nor even doubting the legality of the documents to which you refer. I am merely saying that I thought the Rajah and her cargo was to be turned over to me. There, doubtless, I was mistaken. It seems to me after all, Mr. Schwartzbrod,

446

that there is a higher criterion of action than mere legality. You, probably, would be the first to admit that there is such a thing as moral right which may not happen to coincide with legal right."

"Assuredly, assuredly, my lord. I should be very sorry indeed to infringe upon any moral law, but, unfortunately, in this defective world, my lord, experience has shown that it is always well to set down in plain black and white exactly what a man means when a transfer is made, otherwise your remembrance of what was intended may differ entirely from mine, and yet each of us may be scrupulously honest in our contention."

"Yes, you have me there, Mr. Schwartzbrod. I see the force of your reasoning, and a man has only himself to blame if he neglects those necessary precautions which you have mentioned, so we will say nothing more about that phase of the matter, but you will easily understand that having thought myself entitled to the use of the Rajah, I may not feel myself inclined to renew your charter now."

"Ah, there again, my lord, it is all set down in black and white. The charter distinctly states that I am to have the option of renewal for a further three months when the first three months has expired."

"You corner me at every point of the game, Mr. Schwartzbrod. I take it, then, that my purchase of the Rajah does not invalidate the arrangement made with you by her former owners?"

"Certainly not, my lord. If you buy a property, you take over all its liabilities."

"That seems just and reasonable. So your application for renewal is a mere formality, against which any objection of mine would be futile?"

"Did not Sparling & Bilge explain to you, my lord, that the steamer was under charter?"

"I never saw those estimable gentlemen, Mr. Schwartzbrod. The purchase was made by an agent of mine, and I have no doubt Sparling & Bilge made him acquainted with all the liabilities I was acquiring. If you insist on exercising your option, Mr. Schwartzbrod, I suppose I must either postpone the development of my gold-bearing property, or charter another steamer?"

"I should be sorry to put you to the trouble and expense of chartering another boat when the Rajah is so well suited to your purpose, my lord. It is possible that, even before the first charter is completed, the Rajah may have returned to Southampton, and our experiments in the cattle trade may end with the first voyage. In that case I shall be very pleased to relinquish my claim upon your steamer."

"That is very good of you, Mr. Schwartzbrod. By the way, where is the Rajah now?"

"She is probably in some port along the Argentine coast, south of Buenos Ayres."

"Really? Then perhaps you can tell me where Mackeller is?"

"Mackeller? You mean the mining engineer, son of the stockbroker?"

"Yes, I thought he was in my employment, and sent him down to attend the loading of the Rajah, but he has disappeared. Did you engage him?"

"No, I know nothing of him."

"I thought perhaps he had sailed with the Rajah."

"Not to my knowledge. Doesn't his father know where he is?"

"His father appears to know no more than I do. Just as much, or just as little, whichever way you like to put it."

"He's no employee of mine, my lord."

"I think he should have given me notice if he intended to quit my service. Probably he has gone hunting a gold mine for himself."

"I think there are many mining engineers more valuable than young Mackeller, my lord. He always seemed to me a stubborn, unmannerly person."

"Yes, he lacked the polish which the city gives to a man. I suppose his life in the various wildernesses he has visited has not been conducive to the acquirement of the art of politeness. Still, as you say, there is no lack of mining engineers in London, and doubtless, when the time comes that I need one, I shall find a suitable man for the vacancy."

"I shall be very glad to help you in the selection, my lord, if you care to consult me."

"Thanks, I'll remember that. I take it with regard to this charter that I have to sign something, haven't I, although I suppose I shouldn't sign until my solicitors are consulted; still, I feel quite safe in your hands, Mr. Schwartzbrod, and if you will send me the document, and mark with a lead pencil where my signature is to go, I shall attend to it."

"I have brought the papers with me, my lord," said the financier eagerly, extracting them from his pocket.

"Could you also oblige me with a fountain pen? Ah, thanks. You go about fully equipped for business, Mr. Schwartzbrod. That's what it is to be a methodical man."

His lordship cleared a little space on the table, and wrote his name at the bottom of two documents, which, however, he took the precaution to read with some care before attaching his autograph to them, in spite of his disclaimer that he understood nothing about these things. He complained languidly of the obscure nature of the papers, and said it was no wonder lawyers were so much needed to elucidate them. Schwartzbrod put the papers in his pocket with a satisfaction he could scarcely conceal, then, standing up, he buttoned his coat, ever so much more alert than the weary young man, half his age, who stood up from his writing as if the exertion had almost exhausted him. He, however, made a quiet, casual remark in parting that suddenly electrified the room and made his guest shiver and turn pale.

"When did you say you expected the Rajah from Lisbon, Mr. Schwartzbrod?"

For a few moments there was intense stillness. Stranleigh was lighting another cigar, and did not look up at the terror-stricken man, whose bulging eyes were filled with fear.

"Lisbon—Lisbon?" he gasped, trying to secure control of his features. "I—I never mentioned Lisbon."

"Oh, yes, you did. You said she was at some point south of Lisbon, didn't you?"

"I said Buenos Ayres."

Stranleigh made a gesture of impatience as if he were annoyed with himself.

"Why, of course you said Buenos Ayres. How stupid of me. I am always mixing these foreign places up. I suppose it is because the Argentine Republic is one of those former Spanish possessions, and Lisbon being in Spain, I confused the two."

"Lisbon is in Portugal, my lord; the capital of Portugal."

"You are right. It was Madrid I was thinking of Madrid is in Spain, isn't it?"

"Yes, my lord."

"And it isn't a port, either?"

"No, my lord."

"And is Lisbon on the sea?"

"On the river Tagus, my lord."

"I am an ignoramus, that's what I am. I ought really to go to school again. I have forgotten everything I learned there. Well, good afternoon, Mr. Schwartzbrod. Anything else I can do for you, you know, don't hesitate to call on me. We financiers must stand by one another, while times are so bad in the city."

The young man stood at the head of the stairs, a cigar between his lips, and his hands deep in his trousers pockets, seeing which Mr. Schwartzbrod, who had tentatively made a motion to shake hands in farewell, thought better of it, and went down the stairs, at the bottom of which the silent Ponderby waited to open the door for him. When he reached the floor below Schwartzbrod cast one look over his shoulder up the stairs. The young man still stood on the landing, gazing contemplatively down upon his parting guest. He nodded pleasantly, and "Ta-ta," he said, but the expression on Schwartzbrod's face could not have shown greater perturbation if Satan himself had occupied Stranleigh's place.

"A very uncomfortable companion is an uneasy conscience, even in the city," said Stran-leigh to himself, as he turned away.

Schwartzbrod hailed a cab, and drove to his office in the city; anxious about the Rajah; glad he had secured the renewal of the charter without protest or investigation; uneasy regarding Stranleigh's apparently purposeless remarks about pirates and Lisbon. Arriving at his office, he rang for his confidential clerk.

"Any word from Lisbon?" he demanded.

"Yes, sir. The same code word. No sign of the Rajah there, sir."

"How long is it since you sent warning to all our agents along the Atlantic coast and the Mediterranean to look out for her?"

"Just a week to-day, sir, and a wire came in shortly after you left, from our man at Brest. I'd have telephoned you, sir, if I had known where you had gone."

"Give it to me, give it to me, give it to me," repeated Schwartzbrod impatiently. He clutched it in his trembling hands, and read:

"Steamer flying English flag, named Rajah Wilkie captain, in roadstead to-day. Unloading ore into lugger."

The moral Mr. Schwartzbrod now gave way to a paroxysm of bitter language that was dreadful to hear, but his stolid clerk seemed used to it, and bent his head before the storm. During a lull for lack of breath he ventured one remark:

"It can't be our ship, sir. Our man is Captain Simmons."

"What has that to do with it, you fool?" roared Schwartzbrod. "That old scoundrel Simmons can easily change his name. He's sold me out, the sanctimonious hound. Very likely he and Frowningshield are both in the plot against me. Simmons is a thief, for all his canting objections when we were striking a bargain. I don't believe Frowningshield's any better, and he's got more brains. They'll smelt the ore in France, after carrying it to some suitable spot along the coast in sailing boats. But it'll take two or three days to unload, and I'll give old Simmons a fright before that is done. See if there's a steamer from Southampton to St. Malo to-night. If not I must go to Brest by way of Paris. I can't trust this job to any one else."

As it happened there was a boat that evening for St. Malo, and so the two persons who had indulged in a long conversation regarding the Rajah that afternoon were each in pursuit of her, moving westward; Schwartzbrod in his berth on board the St. Malo boat, Stranleigh in his berth on the Plymouth express, while between the two the stanch old Rajah was threshing her way across the Channel between Brest and Plymouth, heading for the latter seaport.

Next day Stranleigh greeted Mackeller with something almost approaching enthusiasm. Neither of them entertained the least suspicion that the stop at Brest might put Conrad on the trail; but even if they had, they must have known that the arrival of the Rajah at Plymouth would have entailed similar consequences if Schwartzbrod's minions were looking sharply after his interests.

The Rajah's stay at Plymouth was very short, merely giving time for the crew of the yacht to take its station aboard the Rajah, under command of Captain Wilkie, while the crew that had brought the Rajah into port was placed in the care of Captain Simmons, whose big steamer, the Wychwood, was not yet ready to sail. The Rajah then rounded the southwest corner of England, and found a berth in the little haven of Portreath, within easy distance of the smelting furnace. The Rajah was unloaded with the utmost speed, and the ore conveyed as quickly as possible to the inclosure which surrounded the smelting furnace. Stranleigh thought it just as well to get his raw material under cover with the least possible delay, for, although Portreath was not a tourist center, one could never be quite certain that some scientific chap might not happen along, who, picking up a specimen, would know that it contained gold and not copper. Besides this, the engineer of the Rajah reported certain defects in engines and boilers that needed to be seen to and amended before it was safe to face so long a voyage again; therefore, that no time should be lost, the Rajah was hurried back to Plymouth to undergo the necessary repairs.

When, after its long abandonment, Lord Stranleigh, with the aid of Mackeller, restarted his ancient copper mine in Cornwall, he, knowing nothing of figures, as he said, turned over the mathematical department of the business to an accountant, one of the twelve business men who kept his affairs in order. Just before leaving London for Plymouth, he requested this accountant to furnish him with a statement of profit and loss, so far as the mine was concerned. This statement he merely glanced at, saw with satisfaction that the working had resulted in a deficit, and put the document into his pocket. When the Rajah left Plymouth to worry her way round the toe of England to Portreath, Lord Stranleigh and Mackeller took train from Plymouth, and reached Redruth in two hours and fifteen minutes, from which station they drove together to the copper mine, Stranleigh having given Mackeller the statement of profit and loss, and instructing him what he should say when he met the manager of the mine, whom Peter himself had installed in that position.

Arriving at the office of the works, Mackeller consulted with the manager, while Lord Stranleigh, beautifully attired in fine garments quite unsuitable for such a locality, strolled round, taking such intelligent interest in his environment as a casual tourist displays in unaccustomed surroundings. The grimy, hard-working smelters gazed with undisguised contempt at this dandified specimen of humanity, who had so unexpectedly wandered in among them, and made remarks on his personal appearance more distinguished for force than courtesy. To these uncomplimentary allusions the young man paid not the slightest attention, but dawdled about, one of the men complained, as if he owned the place. At last the manager and Mackeller came out of the office together, and word was sent down the pit that all the miners were to come up. Ribald comment ceased, and an uneasy feeling spread among the employees that something unpleasant was about to happen. Their intuition was justified when all the men were gathered together, and the manager began to speak. He informed them that the reopening of the mine had been merely an experiment, and he regretted to add that this experiment had failed through the simple elementary fact that the amount of copper produced cost more than it would fetch in the metal market of the world. Operations had been conducted at a loss, and the proprietor was thus reluctantly compelled to disband his forces, all except four smelters, who would remain to assist in converting into ingots the remnant of the ore which had been mined. This intelligence was received in doleful silence by those whom it affected. Each of them before now had faced the tragedy caused by lack of work, but custom had made its recurrence none the more welcome for all that.

The manager, after a pause, continued. The proprietor, he said, was Lord Stranleigh, and he had given orders which, for generosity, the manager in all his experience thought was unexampled. Each man was to receive a year's pay. At this announcement the gloom suddenly lifted, and a resounding cheer went up from the men. The manager added that he himself had been given an important position in one of his lordship's coal mines in the north, whereupon the good-natured crowd cheered the manager, who appeared to be popular with them.

"And now," concluded the manager, "as Lord Stranleigh is himself present, he will perhaps choose from the six smelters the four whom he wishes to employ."

Stranleigh had been standing apart from the group, listening to the eloquence of the manager, and now every one turned and looked at him with more than ordinary interest. His hands, as usual, were in his pockets, a cigarette between his lips, which nevertheless did not conceal the humorous smile with which his lordship regarded the six smelters, who were quite evidently panic-stricken to learn that they had been exercising their robustious wit on the man with the money; the important boss who paid the wage. Lord Stranleigh slowly removed his left hand from his pocket, and took the cigarette from between his lips.

"I think, Mr. Manager," he said, "we will retain all six," and so the congregation was dismissed.

The hoisting gang was retained until all tools and movable ore were hoisted from the bottom of the mine to the surface of the earth. Stranleigh himself went down when the cage made its last trip, and there, by torchlight, examined the workings, listening to explanations by Mackeller. When he reached daylight again he ordered the dismantling of the hoisting apparatus, which work of destruction was taken to mean the final abandonment of the copper mine. Mackeller, thrifty person, protested against this demolition.

Stranleigh smiled, but did not countermand the order. He and Mackeller took up their quarters in the manager's house, its late occupant having taken his departure for the north. The six smelters were rude, unintelligent, uneducated men, who saw no difference between one yellow bar and another, so there was little risk of discovery through their detection.

"What are you going to do with the gold ingots?" asked Mackeller.

"I was thinking of placing them in a safe deposit vault."

"You will need to look well to its locks, bolts, and bars," said the cautious engineer.

"There will be no bolts and bars," said Stranleigh. "I shall leave the ingots open to the sky, without lock or latch. Nobody will interfere with them."

"Bless my soul, you'll never be so foolish as that?" cried Mackeller. "Why, even the copper was protected by the strongest and safest locks I could secure."

Lord Stranleigh merely shrugged his shoulders, and made no further explanation of his intentions.

At the first smelting the gold was run into ingots weighing about a hundred pounds each. When the smelters had departed for the day, and the gates were closed, Stranleigh said to Mackeller:

"Come along, and I'll show you my safe deposit vault."

With this he hoisted to his shoulder one of the ingots; still warm, walked to the mouth of the pit, and flung it into space.

"Not a bad idea," growled Mackeller, as he followed the example of his chief, until between them all the gold from the first smelting rested on the deep and dark floor of the mine.

One day, as the two were sitting together consuming the frugal lunch that Peter had prepared, a telegram was brought in to Lord Stranleigh. The young man laughed when he read it, and tossed it across the table to Mackeller, who read:

"Rajah ready to sail, but to-day was taken possession of by legal authorities under action of a man named Schwartzbrod. I am under arrest charged with stealing the Rajah. No objection going to prison, but await instructions. Wilkie, captain."

"By Jove, the enemy has tracked her," ejaculated Peter. "I wonder how they did it!"

"That isn't the point to wonder over, Peter, when you remember that the arrival and departure of shipping is announced in every morning paper. The wonder is that they didn't get hold of her some days ago. Oh, dear me, how I am pestered by obstreperous men! Here are you constantly trying to involve me in a fight, and now here is Schwartzbrod entangling me in the meshes of the law, while, peaceful man that I am, I detest equally battles or lawsuits, but the righteous have always been persecuted, and I suppose I must accept my share of trouble. Nevertheless, I anticipate some amusement with my friend Schwartzbrod. If you don't help me, Peter, don't help the bear, and you'll see the funniest legal fight that ever happened."

With this Stranleigh retired to dress for town.

"Peter," he said, on emerging from his bedroom, attired as if he intended a dawdle down Piccadilly rather than a scramble over Cornish hills, "Peter, I

456

am going to desert you. Continue the smelting as if we had not parted, and fling as many bars of gold down that pit as you can, thankful that for our purposes it is not bottomless, even though the possession of too much gold may lead to such. It is not that I like your cooking less, but that I love the cuisine of my club more."

"You are going to London, then?"

"Ultimately to London, my son, but first to Redruth station; then to Plymouth. I cannot allow my captain courageous to be flung into prison merely to please Conrad Schwartzbrod, who ought to be there himself. I must foregather at Plymouth with some one learned in the law, and so disconcert, delay, annoy, and at least partially beggar that old thief Schwartzbrod; therefore, ta-ta, my son, and be as good as you can during my absence, and when you feel proud because of your ever accumulating wealth, remember how difficult it is for a rich man to enter heaven, and thus resume your natural modesty. Good-by."

CHAPTER IX—THE FINAL FINANCIAL STRUGGLE WITH SCHWARTZBROD

ARRIVING at Redruth, Stranleigh sent off three telegrams, one instructing his chief solicitors in London to request the leading marine lawyer of Plymouth to call upon him at once at the Grand Hotel in that town. The second telegram bade Captain Wilkie cheer up, as ample bail was approaching him by the next train from the west, requesting him, if at liberty, to call at the Grand Hotel about six o'clock. The third telegram secured a suite of rooms at the Grand Hotel, and this task finished, Stranleigh had just time to catch the 2.49 train for Plymouth.

On driving up to the Grand Hotel shortly after six o'clock, he found both Captain Wilkie and Mr. Docketts, the marine lawyer, waiting for him, and the three went together up to the engaged apartments.

"So they haven't put you in quod, captain," said the young man, as he shook hands with him.

"No, sir; they thought better of that. In fact, there seems to be a good deal of hesitation about their procedure. They placed men in possession, and then have taken them out again. Just before I left the ship a fresh lot came aboard. At first they were going to put handcuffs on me, then they consulted about it, and asked if I could provide bail. Not knowing whether you wished me to go to prison or not, I refused to answer."

"Safest thing in the absence of instructions," put in Mr. Docketts. "What is it all about, my lord?"

"It's rather a complicated case, Mr. Docketts," said Stranleigh, throwing himself into the easiest chair he could find, "and it is not necessary to go into the whole story at the present time."

The lawyer shook his head doubtfully.

"If I am to be of any assistance, Lord Stranleigh, I think you should tell me everything. A point that may seem unimportant to the lay mind, often proves of the utmost significance to the legal student."

"You are wrong, Mr. Docketts. What you are thinking of is the detective story. It is the detective that the slightest incident furnishes with an important clew. You mustn't insult my intellect by calling it a lay mind, Mr. Docketts, because I take my marine law from that excellent practitioner, Clark Russell; therefore, when it comes to ships I know what I am talking about. The first point I wish to impress on you is that I am not to appear in this case. No one is to know who engages you. The second point is that no action will be fought in the courts. I could settle the case in ten minutes merely by going to the venerable Conrad Schwartzbrod, who has heedlessly set the law in action; but such a course on my part would be most unfair to an eminent limb of the law like yourself, who wishes to earn honest fees."

Mr. Docketts bowed rather gravely, an inclination of the head which contrived subtly to convey respect for his lordship's rank in life, and yet mild disapproval of his flippant utterances.

"I always advise my clients, my lord, to avoid litigation if they can."

"Quite right, Mr. Docketts. That is good legal etiquette, so long as the advice is conveyed in such a manner that it does not convince the client. Now this steamer, the Rajah, belongs to me, but it has been chartered for a number of months by the aforesaid Conrad Schwartzbrod—I trust I am using correct legal phraseology—and the aforesaid Conrad Schwartzbrod is one of the rankest, most unscrupulous scoundrels that the city of London has ever produced, which statement is regrettably libelous, but without prejudice, and uttered solely in the presence of friends. The law, of course, is designed to settle, briefly and inexpensively, such disputes as may be brought before it, nevertheless it is my wish that the law shall be twisted and turned from its proper purpose, so that this case may be dragged on as long as may be, with injunctions, and restraints, and cross pleas, and demurrers, and mandamuses, or any other damus things you can think of. Whenever you find you are cornered, Mr. Docketts, and must come into the light of day before a judge, you telegraph to me, and you will be astonished to know how speedily everything will be quashed."

Again the lawyer bowed very solemnly.

"I think I understand your lordship," he said impressively.

"I am sure of it, and I hope you will do me the pleasure of remembering your quickness of comprehension, so that you may charge extra for it when you send in the bill. I assure you, quite candidly, that nothing gives me such delight as the paying of an adequate fee to a competent man. If these people should attempt any further molestation of Captain Wilkie, you are to protect him, and I will furnish bail to any amount, reasonable or the reverse. And now, Mr. Docketts, if you will let me have your card, with your address on it, I shall leave the case in your hands."

Mr. Docketts complied with the request, and took his deferential departure. Captain Wilkie also rose, but Stranleigh waved him to his seat again.

"Sit you down, captain. Has the Wychwood sailed yet?"

"No, sir, she has not. I met Captain Simmons yesterday. He came across to the Rajah to take away some of his belongings that were still in his cabin. He said the Wychwood might be ready for sea to-morrow or next day."

"Well, I think I'll go over and call on him. I can do that before dinner. The estimable Mackeller has been my cook for some time past, and if this lucky action had not been begun by that public benefactor, Schwartzbrod, I do not know what would have become of me, for I did not wish to cast any reflection upon Mackeller's kitchen skill by desertion. But now that I have been compelled by law to desert him, I hope, captain, you will take pity on a lonesome man, and dine here with me at eight o'clock. I'll order such a dinner as will make this tavern sit up. You'll stand by, won't you, captain?"

"Thank you, sir, I'll be delighted."

"Well, that's settled. Now, if you will guide me to the Wychwood, I'll go aboard for a chat with Captain Simmons, and you will meet me in the dining room at eight o'clock."

The two parted alongside that huge steamer, the Wychwood, and

Stranleigh climbed aboard, greeting Captain Simmons on deck.

"Well, captain, you haven't got off yet?"

"No, sir—my lord, not yet," said the astonished captain. "If you'd sent word you was coming, earl, I'd have had dinner prepared for you. As it is, there's nothing fit to eat aboard."

"I am accustomed to that, captain. I was just complaining to Wilkie, who brought me here, that Mackeller was my cook, and he seemed to sympathize. No, it's the other way about. You're coming to dine with me. I've invited Captain Wilkie, and we will form a hungry trio about a round table at the Grand Hotel to-night at eight. Three Plymouth brethren, as you may call us: you two practical salts, and me an amateur. Have you been back to that little cottage on Southampton water?"

"No, my lord—sir, but I keep a-thinking of it all the time with great pleasure, and the wife or one of the girls writes to me every day. They are delighted, sir—my lord. I didn't know till after you left that 'twas you had bought all that furniture, but you must let me pay for that, earl, on the instalment plan."

"Oh, that's all right, captain. You wait till I send round a collector. Never worry about payment till it's asked for. That's been my rule in life. Now, captain, take me down to your cabin. I wish to have a quiet chat with you, and on deck, with men about, is a little too public."

The captain led the way, and Stranleigh, standing, gazed about him.

"Ah, this is something like. This beats the Rajah, doesn't it?"

"Yes, it does, my lord—I mean sir. I never expected to find myself in a cabin like this, sir, and a fine ship she is, too; well found and stanch. I'd like to sail her into Southampton water some day, just to let the missus and the kids see her."

"I'll tell you what you must do, captain. Send a telegram to Mrs. Simmons and the girls, asking them to lock up the shop, and come at once to Plymouth. I'll make arrangements for them at the Grand Hotel and they'll stay here until you sail, which can't be for some days yet. And now to business, captain. Old Schwartzbrod has discovered where the Rajah is, and has jumped aboard with a blooming injunction or some such lawyer's devilment as that: tried to habeas corpus innocent old Wilkie, or whatever they call it; anyhow, something that goes with handcuffs, but the old boy was game right through to the backbone, and was willing to go to the Bastile itself if his doing so would accommodate me, but I've invited him to dinner instead."

"Then Schwartzbrod will be trying to find me, very likely?" said Captain Simmons, in no way pleased with the prospect.

"I shouldn't wonder, so I'd keep my weather eye abeam, if I were you, for very likely Schwartzbrod is in Plymouth. Still, I've told an eminent lawyer to go full speed ahead, and I anticipate Schwartzbrod will have quite enough to occupy his mind in a few days. Now, Captain Simmons, although our acquaintance has been very short, I am going to trust you fully. Since this action was taken by Schwartzbrod, it has occurred to me that the proper person to go to the Paramakaboo River is the redoubtable captain who has already been there, and that person is yourself."

"Well; sir, Captain Wilkie has also been there, in your yacht, and perhaps he'd like this new ship. I'm sure he doesn't care about the Rajah."

"Oh, he doesn't need to care about the Rajah. He's off the Rajah for good, and will take command of my yacht again. No, you are the man for the Paramakaboo. You know Frowningshield, and you know his gang, and he knows you. Now, I leave everything to your own discretion. If you tell Frowningshield how everything stands, there is one chance in a thousand he may seize the Wychwood, and compel you to sail for Lisbon, or wherever he likes. It all depends how deeply he is in with that subtle rogue, Schwartzbrod."

"I'll tell him nothing about it, sir."

"That's my own advice. I should say nothing except that they have furnished you with a larger steamer, so that you can get away with double the quantity of ore, all of which is true enough. But if circumstances over which you have no control compel you to divulge the true state of affairs, get

Frowningshield alone here in the cabin, and talk to him as I talked to you on the high seas. He's engaged in a criminal business, whether he is under the jurisdiction of the British flag or not; but the main point I wish you to impress upon him is this: I shall stand in Schwartzbrod's place; that is to say, I shall make good to him, as I made good to you, every promise that rascal has given. I know that virtue is its own reward, yet I sometimes wish that virtue would oftener deal in the coin of the realm in addition. It doesn't seem fair that all the big compensations are usually on the devil's side. Anyhow, I trust this ship and this business entirely to you. You act as you think best, and if they compel you to sail to Lisbon or anywhere else, telegraph fully to me whenever you get into touch with a wire. I don't anticipate any trouble of that kind, however. Frowningshield will know on which side his bread is buttered, even if he is a villain, which I don't believe. Now, Schwartzbrod promised you five thousand pounds extra for three trips to Lisbon, and two thousand pounds for every additional voyage. How many additional voyages could you have made?"

"I couldn't have made one, sir, with the Rajah."

"Well, let us call it two. That amounts to nine thousand pounds. I'll give you a check for that amount to-morrow, and you can hand it to the missus to put in the bank when she returns to Southampton."

"I couldn't think of taking that from you, sir," said the captain, with an unfeigned look of distress.

"It's not from me at all, Captain Simmons. I am going to make Schwartzbrod hand over that amount to my bank. I am merely anticipating his payments; passing it on from him to you, as it were. In a similar way I shall recompense Frowningshield, and I shall give you a sufficient number of gold sovereigns with which to pay all his men, and this will create a certain satisfaction in the camp, even although there is no spot within a thousand miles where they can spend a penny. So, captain, you will load up your ship with an ample supply of provisions for those in camp, and take out to them anything that you think they may need, charging the same to me, which account I shall pass on to Schwartzbrod."

"But isn't there a chance, sir, that Schwartzbrod may charter another steamer, in which case we may have to fight?"

"No, I don't think so. I am having old Schwartzbrod watched, and from the latest report he has not even chartered a rowboat. No, I have extended his charter of the Rajah for an extra three months, and he will hope to get possession of her. It will take him a few days to realize the extent of the law's delay, and with such a start, together with the speed of the Wychwood you will find no difficulty about filling this ship, and getting away without encountering any opposition. No, I don't want any fight. You see, I can't spare Mackeller, and it would break his heart to think there was a ruction and he not in it.

"Here is a suggestion which has just occurred to me, and you may act on it or not as circumstances out there dictate. When the Wychwood is fully loaded with ore, and ready to sail, you might ask Frowningshield to come aboard with you for that twelve-mile run down the river. The steam launch could follow and take him back. Inform him that you have something important to say which cannot be told ashore, then get him down here into your cabin, and relate to him everything that has happened. He cannot stop the Wychwood then if he wanted to. Your crew will obey you, and no matter what commands he gave them to put about, they would pay no attention to him. Show him that he can make more money by being honest than by following the lead of old Schwartzbrod. Tell him you have received your nine thousand pounds—and, by the way, that reminds me I had better give you the check tonight before dinner, so that you can post it to your bank at Southampton, and receive the bank's receipt for it before you sail. The deposit receipt will be just as cheering to Mrs. Simmons as the check would be—and then you can tell Frowningshield, quite conscientiously, that the money is already in your hands. I always believe in telling the truth to a pirate like Frowningshield if it is at all possible. Don't imagine I'm preaching, captain. What I mean is that the truth is ever so much more convincing than even the cleverest of lies. We will suppose, then, that Frowningshield comes to the same decision that you did, and agrees to join me in preserving my own property from an unscrupulous thief. In that case tell him that Schwartzbrod will very likely send some other steamer to carry away the ore, as soon as he realizes he cannot again get hold of the Rajah, and that I shall expect Frowningshield and his merry men not to allow such a vessel to take away any of my ore."

"Shall I tell him to sink Schwartzbrod's steamer?"

"Sink her? No, bless my soul, no. What would you sink her for? Tell him to use gentle persuasion, and not give up the ore. An ordinary crew cannot fill the hold with ore which a hundred and fifty men refuse to allow them to touch. You don't need to fight. If Frowning-shield will just line up his hundred and fifty men along that reef, one glance at their interesting faces will convince any ship's captain that he'd be safer out at sea.

"I think the Wychwood will answer our purposes very well. She is large and fast. Try to find out, if you can, exactly what Schwartzbrod promised Frowningshield and his men, and let me know when you return. Now, captain, I think you understand pretty well what your new duties are, so get off for the south just as quickly as you can. Meanwhile we must be moving on toward the Grand Hotel. I'm rather anxious to meet that dinner, and on the way we will send a telegram to Mrs. Simmons and the family. After that we three roisterers will make a night of it, for I must go up to London to-morrow."

Mackeller worked industriously at his smelting, dumping the gold down into the abandoned mine after his assistants had left him for the night. He was anxious to hear what had become of the Rajah, and what had happened to Captain Wilkie threatened with imprisonment, but no letter came from Lord Stranleigh, which was not to be wondered at, for all Stranleigh's friends knew his dislike of writing.

The third morning after Stranleigh's departure Mackeller received a long telegram which had evidently been handed in at London the night before. At first Mackeller thought it was in cipher, but a close study of the message persuaded him that no code was necessary for its disentanglement. It ran as follows:

"Take half a pound of butter, one pound of flour, half a pound of moist sugar, two eggs, one teaspoonful of essence of lemon, one fourth glass of brandy or sherry. Rub the butter, flour, and sugar well together, mix in the eggs after beating them, add the essence of lemon and the brandy. Drop the cakes upon a frying pan, and bake for half an hour in a quick oven."

Mackeller muttered some strenuous remarks to himself as at last he gathered in the purport of this communication. He detained the telegraph boy long enough to write a line which he sent to Lord Stranleigh's residence at a cost of sixpence.

"What have you done about the Rajah—Mackeller."

Late in the afternoon the telegraph boy returned, and bestowed upon the impatient and now irascible Mackeller the following instructions:

"For two persons alone at the mouth of a pit take one plump fowl, add white pepper and salt to suit the taste, one half spoonful of grated nutmeg, one half spoonful of pounded mace, a few slices of ham, three hard-boiled eggs, sliced thin, half a pint of water, and some puff paste crust to cover. Stew for half an hour, and when done strain off the liquor for gravy. Put a layer of fowl at the bottom of a pie dish, then a layer of ham, then the slices of hard-boiled egg, with the mace, nutmeg, pepper and salt between the layers. Put in half a pint of water, cover with puff paste, and bake for an hour and a half."

"I suppose," growled Mackeller to himself, "he thinks that's funny, but it will cost him a pretty penny if he keeps it up every day."

"Any answer?" said the telegraph boy.

"Yes," answered Mackeller, and being made reckless by example, he wrote a more lengthy message than was customary with him:

"Everything going on well here. The cooking I am doing consists in the production of hardbake cake, and the receipt is as follows: Take ore from Africa, salt and pepper to suit the taste, mix it with hard coal from the north, quick fire and a hot oven. When completely baked run into molds of sand, and place in a deep cellar to cool. Save the money you are wasting on the postoffice department by sending me, through parcel post, the cook book from which you are stealing those items, and use a telegram to let me know what has happened to the Rajah and Captain Wilkie."

In the evening an answer came.

"That's not a bad receipt of yours, Mackeller. I didn't think so serious a man as you was capable of such frivolity. The Rajah is in Chancery, in litigation, in irons, in Plymouth harbor, in-junctioned. I expect it will be a long time before the Rajah gets out of court. Captain Wilkie is all right, and back on my yacht. The Wychwood, with Simmons in command, is off to Paramakaboo. I expect to be with you after you have had time to study the volume which at your suggestion I send to-day by parcel post; 'Mrs. Beeton's Book of Household Management'; bulky but useful."

Lord Stranleigh did not return, however, as promised, to the Cornish mine. Although apparently leading an aimless life at home, or in one or other of his clubs, or at an interesting race meeting, he was keeping his eye on Schwartzbrod by means of an efficient secret agent. He wondered how soon so shrewd a man as the financier would come to the knowledge that the Rajah was tied up with the red tape of the law, as immovable in her berth as if she had been chained to the breakwater by cables of steel. He was determined that Schwartzbrod should not further complicate the situation by sending out another steamer on an ore-stealing expedition to West Africa; and when at last he received a report from his agent that Schwartzbrod's men were in negotiation once more with Sparling & Bilge of Southampton, the indolent young man thought it time to strike, so he telephoned to Schwartz-brod, asking him to call at his town house next morning at half past ten, bringing his check book with him.

Schwartzbrod, spluttering at his end of the telephone, wished further explanation about the request for the check book. The charter money, he said, was not due. Nothing had been said in the document signed about payment in advance, but Stranleigh rang off, and left the financier guessing. When, some minutes later, Schwartzbrod got once more into communication with the house, the quiet-voiced Ponderby told him that his lordship had left for his club, but would expect to see him promptly at half past ten next day.

When Schwartzbrod arrived, he was shown this time into Lord Stranleigh's scantily furnished business office on the ground floor. He had been so anxious to know what the cause of the summons was that he found himself ten minutes before the half hour, and that ten minutes he spent alone in the little room. As the clock in the hall chimed the half hour, the door opened, and Lord Stranleigh entered.

"Good morning, Mr. Schwartzbrod. There are several little business matters which I wish to discuss with you and, as I expect to leave London shortly, I thought we might as well get it over." Stranleigh sat down in a chair on the opposite side of the table from the keen-eyed city man, who watched him with furtive sharpness.

"As I was telling you, my lord, there is nothing in the papers you signed saying that any payment was to be made in advance on account of the Rajah."

"You object, then, to paying in advance?"

"I don't object, my lord, if it's any accommodation to you. The first payment, you see, was made to Messrs. Sparling & Bilge."

"Of course, I've nothing to do with that."

"Well, the second amount I did not expect to be called on to pay until the steamer had earned some money."

"Ah, yes, I see. That seems quite just. The steamer, then, hasn't been earning money, I take it."

"It is too soon yet to say, my lord, whether she is earning money or not."

"Is she still at South America?"

"Yes, my lord."

"Has she not returned since I saw you last?"

"No, my lord."

"That's very strange," murmured Stranleigh, more to himself than to the other. "Shows how blooming inaccurate those newspapers are."

468

He took out from his inside pocket a thin memorandum book, searched slowly among some slips of loose paper, and at last took out a cutting from some daily journal.

"The paper from which I clipped this was issued a day or two after we last met. My attention was called to the item by the fact that so shortly before we had been in negotiation regarding the Rajah; successful and pleasant negotiation, if I remember rightly, and I signed the papers you presented to me without consulting a solicitor, and the impression left on my mind is that you went away satisfied."

"Oh, I was perfectly satisfied, my lord, perfectly satisfied. Yes, you very kindly signed the renewal of the charter."

"You said, if I remember rightly, that the trip of the Rajah was merely an experiment. It had something to do with the cattle business; a ranch, or several ranches, in the Argentine Republic."

"Quite right, my lord. I regret to say the business has not been as prosperous as I had hoped."

"I am sorry to hear that. I have always looked on ranching as a sure way to wealth, but it seems there are exceptions. Now, you said to me that if the experiment did not prove successful, which, regrettably, seems to be the case, you would turn the Rajah over to me when she returned."

"But she has not returned, my lord."

"Then what does this journal mean by stating that a few days after we foregathered in this house the Rajah arrived at Plymouth from Brest, in France?"

"That must be a mistake, my lord. Would you let me read the item?"

Schwartzbrod extended his hand, trembling slightly, and took the slip of paper, adjusting his glasses to see the better, visibly gaining time before committing himself further.

"The item is very brief," commented Stranleigh, "still, it is definite enough. 'Steamer Rajah, Captain Wilkie, arrived at Plymouth from Brest.'"

"That cannot have been our Rajah," said Schwartzbrod at last, having collected his wits. "The captain on your steamer, my lord, is named Simmons."

"Simmons? Oh, Captain Simmons of Southampton? Why, I know the man. A fine, bluff old honest tar, one of the bulwarks of Britain. So Simmons was the captain of the Rajah, was he? Still, he may have resigned."

"He couldn't resign in midocean, my lord."

"Oh, I've known the thing done. I've known captains transferred from one steamer to another on the high seas."

"I've never heard of such a thing, my lord, unless one vessel was disabled, and then abandoned when another came along."

"My dear Mr. Schwartzbrod, accept my assurance that these daring devils of sea captains do things once they are out of our sight which we honest men ashore would not think of countenancing."

"I thought you said just now they were the bulwarks of Britain?"

"So they are, so they are, but bulwarks, Mr. Schwartzbrod, need to be made of stouter and coarser timber than that which lines the cabin. You must not think I am attributing anything criminal to our captain, Mr. Schwartzbrod; not at all, but it has often seemed to me that they do not always pay that scrupulous attention to the law which animates our business men in the city of London, for instance. A captain out of the jurisdiction of England, much as it may shock you to hear it, will dare to do things that would make our hair stand on end, and send a lawyer or a judge into a dead faint. Now, there's the Captain Simmons, of whom you just spoke. He tells me that he has undertaken devilish deeds in out-of-the-way parts of the world which he would not think of doing under that arch in the main street of Southampton."

The company promoter moistened his lips, and stroked the lower part of his face gently with his open hand. Lord Stranleigh beamed across at him with kindly expectancy, as if wishing some sympathetic corroboration of the statements he had made. At last the city man spoke.

"You have perhaps had more experience with seafaring people than I, my lord. I had always supposed them to be a rough-and-ready sort of folk, as reasonably honest as the rest of us."

"It was to be expected, Mr. Schwartzbrod, that your kind heart would hesitate to credit anything condemnatory said about them. Because you would not do this or that, you think other people are equally blameless. Take Captain Simmons, for instance, and yet, when I think of him I remember, of course, there were mitigating circumstances in the case. Captain Simmons had set his eye on a little bit of property, something like five acres, stretching down to Southampton water. There was a cottage and a veranda, and the veranda seemed to lure Captain Simmons with its prospect of peace, as he passed up Southampton water in command of the disreputable old Rajah. But Simmons never could succeed in saving the money to buy this modest homestead, but at last far more than the money necessary was offered him if he did a certain thing. It was a bribe, Mr. Schwartzbrod, and perhaps at first he did not see where he was steering the blunt snout of the old Rajah. He did not completely comprehend into what miasmatic and turbid waters his course would lead him. But when at last he saw it was involving him in theft, in wholesale robbery, and in potential murder, in the sinking of ships, and the drowning of crews, Simmons drew back."

A gentle expression of concern came into Lord Stranleigh's face as he saw the man before him in visible distress, sinking lower and lower in his chair. His face was ghastly: only the eyes seemed alive, and they were fixed immovably on his opponent, striving to penetrate at the thought or the knowledge that might be behind the mask of carelessness he wore.

"Don't you feel well, Mr. Schwartzbrod? Would you like a little stimulant?"

Without waiting for an answer he rang the bell.

"Bring some whisky and soda," he said, "also a decanter of brandy."

Schwartzbrod took a cautious sip or two of the weaker beverage.

"Were any names mentioned?" he asked.

"Simmons told me the tempter was a city man; some rank scoundrel who wished to profit by another's loss, and did not hesitate at robbery so long as he was legally safe in London, and others were taking the risk. They were to take the risk, and he was to secure the property. I even doubt if he intended to give the recompense he had promised. It amounted in Simmons's case to nine thousand pounds, and only one thousand was needed for the purchase of the place on which he had set his heart."

"But Simmons must have known, if such a sum was offered him, that he was undertaking a shady transaction?"

"That's exactly what I told him, but, you see, he had committed himself before he realized what he was letting himself in for. 'Chuck the whole business,' I said to him. 'You've got friends enough who'll buy that little place and present it to you. I am willing myself to subscribe part of the money,' and so Simmons struck. He is off, I understand, on another steamer. He has influential friends who got him a better situation than the one he held. Now, as I have said, I am willing to put some money on the table to buy that little house near Southampton. How much will you give, Mr. Schwartzbrod?"

Schwartzbrod now took a gulp of the whisky and soda. His courage was returning.

"Do you mean to tell me, Lord Stranleigh, that you have called a busy man like me to the West End in order to ask him for a charity subscription?"

"But surely you subscribe to many charities, Mr. Schwartzbrod?"

"I do not. It's as much as I can do to keep my own head above water, without troubling with other people. I believe in being just before being generous. If I pay my debts, that's all any man can ask."

"Most true philosophy, Mr. Schwartzbrod, but a little hard, you know. Some poor fellows get under the harrow, and surely we may stop our cultivation for a moment, and lift the harrow long enough to allow him to crawl out."

472

Schwartzbrod finished the whisky and soda, but made no further comment.

"It was not altogether for charitable purposes that I requested the pleasure of your call. There is business mixed with it. But you, Schwartzbrod, try to place the worst side of yourself before the world. You are really a very generous man. At heart you are; now, you know it."

"I don't know anything about it, my lord, and I do not understand the trend of this conversation."

"Well, I have come to the conclusion that you are one of the most generous men in London. You have done things that I think no other business man in London would attempt. You do good by stealth, and blush to find it fame, as I think the poet said. You've been doing me a great benefit, and yet you've kept quiet about it."

"What do you mean?"

"Why, I mean Frowningshield and his hundred and fifty men on my gold reef."

"What!" roared Schwartzbrod, springing to his feet.

"The kidnapping of Mackeller I did not mind. That's all in the day's work, and a mining engineer must expect a little rough and tumble in this world."

"I had nothing to do with that, my lord."

"No, it was Frowningshield who did it. Am I not saying that you are perfectly blameless? When I learned about the Rajah's expedition, about the money offered to Captain Simmons, about the compensation that was to be given to Frowningshield, about the running of the ore to Lisbon; when I heard all this, so prejudiced was my brain that I said to myself: 'Here I've caught the biggest thief in the world.' But when I learned that you had done it, I saw at once what your object was. You were going to smelt that ore without expense to me, take it over in ingots to England, and say, 'Here, Lord Stranleigh, you're not half a bad sort of chap. You don't understand anything about mining or the harsh ways of this world. Here is your gold.'"

Schwartzbrod poured down his throat a liquor glass full of brandy, and collapsed in his chair.

"You see, Mr. Schwartzbrod, there were only two alternatives for a poor brain like mine to accept: first, that you are the most generous man in the world; second, that you are the most daring robber in the world. Do you think I hesitated? Not for a moment. I knew you were no thief. Thieves are in Whitechapel, and Soho, and the East End generally, but not in the City of London. They're all men of law there. You are not a thief, are you, Mr. Schwartzbrod? No. Then sit down, honest man, and write me a check for the nine thousand pounds I have already paid to Captain Simmons, and for the amount which you promised to Frowningshield. I accept the benefit of your generosity in the same spirit in which it is tendered. I do not ask you where the gold is, I'll look after that; but the new ship you are trying to charter must not sail for the Paramakaboo. I cannot accept further kind offices from you. All I ask of you is to write a check for such an amount that it will fulfill the promises you made to Simmons and Frowningshield. That's why I requested you to bring your check book."

Schwartzbrod, with a groan, sat down at the table and drew forth his check book.

CHAPTER X—THE MEETING WITH THE GOVERNOR OF THE BANK

THE mere accumulating of money does not call for a high, order of intelligence. A stealthy craft is more valuable in that business than the intellect of a Shakespeare. The low cunning of a fox is often successful where the brave strength of a lion fails. Of course there are estimable men who accumulate a fortune through manufactory, discovery, or invention: men who are benefactors to their fellow creatures, and to whom money comes through the fruition of their endeavors to enrich the world rather than themselves. But a Stock Exchange speculator like Schwartzbrod, equipped with the sneaking slyness of an avaricious but ignorant peasant, becomes a mere predatory beast, producing nothing; fattening on the woes and losses of others; stealthy and cruel as the man-eating tiger. It is probable that as civilization advances such a vampire will be secluded from his fellows as the leper is in Eastern lands.

Since his first disastrous encounter with Lord Stranleigh, Schwartzbrod had been animated by a vicious hatred of this seemingly happy-go-lucky young man, whose attention appeared to be concentrated mainly on dress, but as they met again and again, this rancor became tinctured with a slowly rising fear, not of the urbane nobleman's intellect, but of his amazing good luck, for nothing could have persuaded Schwartzbrod that Stranleigh possessed intellect of any kind. He regarded this junior financier merely as a polite but brainless fop. To one as rich as Schwartzbrod, the writing of a check to fulfill his promises to Captain Simmons and Frowningshield should have been scarcely more important than the tossing of a penny to a beggar by an ordinary man. But Schwartzbrod brooded over it, grit his teeth, and swore vengeance. Now, vindictiveness is a quality which does not pay. In our modern strenuous life the man who wastes thought on revenge runs a risk of falling behind in the procession, but in a time of crisis such deflection of thought upon trivialities, when all senses should be on the alert to prepare for the coming storm, may be fatal. Schwartzbrod was like a man in an open boat on the sea, with too much canvas spread, who, instead of casting his weather eye around the horizon, and shortening sail, was fuming because some one had spilled a cupful of water at the bottom of the boat, pondering over the method of mopping it up, and flinging the soaked rag in the face of him who had upset the cup. A financial typhoon was approaching which would unroof many a house in England and America before it had run its course. Shrewd navigators on the treacherous waters of finance were preparing to scud under bare poles until the clouds rolled by.

It may be admitted at once that Lord Stranleigh no more suspected what was coming than did Schwartzbrod himself, for, as his lordship frequently confessed, he did not understand these things. He had, without browbeating or recrimination, eliminated all chance of Schwartzbrod's further interference with his mine. Schwartzbrod knew that Lord Stranleigh was possessed of every fact in the case, and these facts, if brought forward in a court of law, might very well sequester the city financier in a prison for the rest of his life, and Stranleigh, quite correctly, counted on this fear restraining Schwartzbrod's hand.

The big steamer Wychwood passed unmolested from southern to northern seas and back again, and Mackeller's industrious smelters had tumbled down into the safe deposit some two thousand tons of solid gold.

It was when city men began to return from their summer holidays that a slight whisper floated round the halls of Mammon which sent a shiver up and down the backs of shrewd people here and there. The whisper was to the effect that the Bank of England was in trouble. On three separate occasions within as many weeks, the bank rate had been raised, and now stood at so high a figure that it threatened to check enterprise and speculation during the approaching autumn, when everyone had hoped business would mend in the city. Cautious bankers began calling in their loans, which is a bank's method of shortening sail. Ambitious projects were being abandoned here and there through fear of shortness of money. Companies whose promoters looked forward to a successful flotation before Christmas, were held over. Affairs in the city were stagnant, and weather-wise people feared worse was to come. About the beginning of October a sinister rumor went abroad, founded on a highly sensational article in a New York yellow journal. This rumor, on account of its origin, was discredited at first, but presently the world came to learn that there was too good a foundation for it. The New York paper said that as soon as the financial amateurs of the British Parliament had placed on the statute books an Act commanding the Bank of England by the first of January to maintain its gold reserve at a hundred million of pounds, a powerful syndicate of financial experts had been formed in Wall Street for the cornering of gold. Wheat had often been cornered, to the great benefit of some one individual either in New York or Chicago, and to the universal loss of a hungry world, but no one had hitherto attempted to corner gold. Wheat could not be produced at will. Once the sowing was done, the mathematicians could estimate very accurately, given a full crop, the maximum number of bushels of wheat likely to be placed on the market the coming autumn, and to this amount no man could add, because the production of wheat depended on the slow revolution of the seasons. With gold it was different: gold could be produced summer and winter, night and day, therefore no individual, be he as rich as Midas, and no syndicate, however powerful, had heretofore dared to attempt the cornering of gold. Wheat was consumed year by year, but gold was practically everlasting, preserved in the shape of ornaments, bullion, plate, and what not. Old coinage, minted centuries before the birth of Christ, was still in existence, and although a few grains of wheat grown in the time of the Pharaohs rested in the palms of certain mummies, the great bulk of year before last's wheat was already ground and baked and eaten. It would seem, then, that the boldest financial coup ever attempted had been successfully accomplished by the men of Wall Street. This, however, the New York paper pointed out, was not the case. Tremendous as might be the consequences of the corner, there was, after all, little risk to the operators. Gold, unlike wheat, was a staple commodity. Wheat rose and fell in price. Gold practically did not. These men had paid no exorbitant rates for gold, but merely kept silent, and through the help of their agents all over the world, they either secured actual possession of the available metal, or had obtained an option on it, which did not expire until June, while the Bank of England was compelled by the new law to acquire possession of at least a hundred million pounds sterling of gold on January the first. Even if the corner failed, this would entail no loss to the monopolists, because they possessed the actual metal for which everything is sold. No sensational fall in the price of gold could take place, as would have been inevitable in the case of wheat should the corner fail, while as a result of the hold-up, if the bank was forced to come to their terms, the profit to be divided would be enormous. It was also stated that the Wall Street men had secured bank notes and orders for gold upon the Bank of England which they would present at a critical moment, demanding the metal, thus facing this venerable institution with the drastic alternative of accepting their terms, or suspending payment. The Times in a leading article, intended to soothe the public mind, attempted to show that the proposed cornering of gold was impossible; that millions upon millions of hoarded gold would be brought out at the proper moment if enough were offered for it; that these millions were in the possession of people of whom Wall Street knew nothing and had no means of getting into touch with.

This article had some effect in staying the panic, or at least in postponing it. Those responsible for the management of the Bank of England kept silent, as is their usual course, and for a week it seemed, so great was the confidence of Englishmen in their most important financial institution, that nothing disastrous was about to happen. Then stocks of all kinds began to come down with a run. One important house failed, then another, and another, and another, and shrewd men realized that both England and America were face to face with the greatest financial disaster of modern times. It seemed that the punishment fitted the crime, because of the fact that in America, which originated the crisis, the panic was much more severe than in England, and throughout all the United States, especially in the West, there was a simultaneous denunciation of Wall Street, to which Wall Street, accustomed to popular ebullition, paid little attention.

In England meetings were held calling on the Government to rescind their bill, and give the bank more time, but, as was pointed out, the bank had not asked for time, and although the governor and directors were known to have been bitterly opposed to the bill, the Government could scarcely with dignity offer relief where relief had not been sought.

Lord Stranleigh sat at ease in one of the comfortable leather-covered armchairs which helped to mitigate the austerities of life in the smoking room of the Camperdown Club. His attitude was one of meditation. The right leg was thrown over the left; his finger tips met together, and those rather fine, honest eyes of his were staring through the thin film of smoke, and apparently seeing nothing. One of the men who had successfully borrowed money from him the day before, and whose salutation Lord Stranleigh ignored, not on account of the borrowed money, but simply because he had not seen the borrower, remarked to some friends that Stranleigh thought he was thinking, which caused a laugh, as these people did not know that the same remark had been made many years before, and were also under the delusion that Stranleigh was incapable of thought.

The Camperdown Club, as everyone knows, is more celebrated as a center of sport than as a resort of business men, yet it has two or three of the latter on its very select list of members. One of these entered, paused at the door, and looked about him for a moment as if wishing to find a chair alone, or searching for some friend whom he expected to meet. This was Alexander Corbitt, manager of Selwyn's Bank, a smooth-faced, harsh-featured man, under whose direction this bank, although a private institution, stood almost as high in public estimation as the Bank of England itself. As Corbitt stood there, the dreamy nature of Lord Stranleigh's gaze changed into something almost approaching alertness.

"Corbitt," he said, "here's a chair waiting for you."

The banker, without hesitation, strode forward, and sat down. There was a certain definite directness about each movement of his body which contrasted strikingly with the indifferent, indolent air assumed by most of the members; a decisive man of iron nerve, even one who knew little of him might have summed him up.

"What will you imbibe?" asked Stranleigh.

"Nothing, thank you. I just dropped in at the club for a bite of dinner, and having a few moments to spare, will now indulge in one cigar; then I must return to the bank."

"What, at this hour of the evening? I thought banks closed at four o'clock, or is it three?"

"I expect to be there all night," said Corbitt, shortly, as he held a match to his cigar.

"I wanted to ask you a few questions."

"Ask them."

"You know I am as ignorant as a child of all matters pertaining to finance, high and low?"

"Yes, I know that."

"What's all this fuss about, Corbitt?"

"What fuss?"

"Why, the accounts I read in the evening papers, and the morning papers, too, for that matter. They say there's a panic in the city. Is there?"

The banker laughed a little; a low, harsh, mirthless laugh.

"Yes, there's a panic," he said. "You are not nipped in it, I hope. I was told you were dabbling in the city a while ago. Is that true?"

"Oh, merely a small flutter, Corbitt, on behalf of some friends of mine."

"Have you been speculating lately?"

"Oh, no. I possess neither the brains nor knowledge requisite for success in the city."

"Brains and knowledge are at a discount just now. What is needed is cash. The biggest fool with ready cash can do more at this moment than the wisest man with a world of knowledge."

"Then I'd better jump into the turmoil," said Stranleigh, smiling.

"Take my advice, and keep out of it. There are rocks ahead. I see by to-night's papers that Conrad Schwartzbrod has gone under, and has carried down with him six or seven men who are considered the most acute financiers in the city. In ordinary times their standing might be supposed unimpeachable."

"Schwartzbrod bankrupt! Then it must be a fraudulent bankruptcy, surely?"

"No, it isn't. Everything has been swept away. He's had no time to hedge, or you may depend upon it he would have done so."

"Corbitt, what's the cause of the whole thing? Can't a man of your powerful intellect make it plain as A B C to an infant of my caliber?"

"The cause is simple enough. It is the attempt to do the right thing in the wrong way. The cause is the Bank of England's Gold Reserve Act, passed last May, and coming into force on the first of January next year. This Act makes it obligatory on the Bank of England to hold a reserve of a hundred millions in gold, where formerly it has only held, say, thirty millions. Do you understand so far?"

"Yes, Corbitt, I do. In fact, I remember last May picking up by wireless telegraphy part of the speech of the Chancellor of the Exchequer on this very bill, but I didn't understand it then, and don't now."

"Very well, the object which the Act sought to attain is one I have advocated for ten years past, but the way of accomplishing it is another instance of the conceited folly of a democracy meddling in a science that demands years of training and minds of a certain caliber. A democracy thinks that the right way to do a thing is the method adopted in bringing down the walls of Jericho. They beat drums and blow trumpets, and march round and round. Now, the exasperating feature of this case is that the Chancellor of the Exchequer knew at the time the folly of his own action, although, of course, he did not perceive the tremendous disaster it was going to bring upon not only his own country, but practically all the solvent nations of the world. He should have withstood the pressure of his unreasonable and ignorant followers. He should have arranged an interview with the managers of the Bank of England; should have told them that a bill of this kind was inevitable if they did not themselves put their house in order. He should have arranged with them quietly, without any beating of tom-toms, and blowing of horns, for the bank slowly to accumulate the needed reserve. Then he should have got up in his place in Parliament, and announced that the Bank of England already held the amount in gold which all thoughtful financiers believed to be necessary if we are to get rid of this eternally fluctuating bank rate.

"Of course, the Bank of England itself is also to blame; it being for all practical purposes a branch of the Government. It should have requested an interview, and come to some understanding before the bill passed into law. I expected that the lords would throw it out, and perhaps they thought the same. However, it passed both houses, received royal assent, and then the mischief was done. These very clever Wall Street men at once saw the possibilities of the situation, as they do with all amateur legislation. The bank remained silent and solemn; has given no word to this day, and then, at too late an hour, showed its distress by raising its bank rate again and again and again, hoping that would prove a magnet to attract gold, whereas it was merely hoisting a signal of distress, and acquainting the whole world with the fact it is drifting on a lee shore."

"Do you mean to say, Corbitt, that there's a chance of the Bank of England stopping payment?"

"No, I do not go so far as that. Here we come to the comic element of the tragedy, which shows the loose folly with which these Parliamentary bills are drawn. There is no penalty attached to the Act; it merely orders the bank to provide such a reserve by such a date. But if the bank doesn't do it, there can be neither a fine inflicted, nor can the governor be put into prison for contumely. If I were governor of the Bank of England, I would snap my fingers at Parliament, at the Act, and at the gold-cornering syndicate. I should say that as soon as was convenient to me I would accumulate this reserve of a hundred million, but that such action was impossible in the time given, therefore I should make no attempt to comply with the Act at the present moment."

"What would be the result of such a statement on the part of the governor?"

"I don't know. It would probably have a quieting result; or it might further accentuate the panic. Of course, when the governor began to perceive that it was going to be difficult to get the gold, he should have approached Parliament while it was in session, and got a relief bill, postponing the date, say for another year, but, as I have, said, he stood on his dignity; the Government stands on its dignity, and between the two of them they bring unnecessary ruin and disaster upon the country."

"Isn't it possible the bank will get the seventy extra millions by the first of January?"

"I see no possibility of it, unless they are prepared to pay two hundred millions for the accommodation to the Wall Street syndicate."

"Has the Wall Street syndicate got the gold? That is, the actual coin?"

"Yes, and showing its confidence, the money is actually in vaults here in London, so the syndicate seems to have no fear that our Government will commandeer the gold as Kruger did before the Transvaal War began. I understand that the syndicate has notified the Bank of England that the price of this metal will rise two hundred thousand pounds each day until the bank accepts their proposals."

"Corbitt, must the gold held in reserve by the Bank of England be in actual sovereigns, or raw metal?"

"Either one or the other."

"Suppose on the first of January the governor of the Bank of England were to announce that there are a hundred million pounds worth of gold in his vaults. What would be the effect on the country?"

"Stranleigh, there's more in that question than perhaps you think. I have never been just absolutely certain that you are as ignorant as you pretend. Most men in the city would tell you that such an announcement might instantly relieve the crisis, but if nothing were said until the first of January, and the announcement made then, I am not sure but it would be almost as disastrous as the former panic. It would be like the sudden releasing of a powerful and compressed spring, and anything sudden and powerful is apt to disarrange machinery. I think the inevitable result would be the instant soaring of stocks to much beyond their actual value. That, then, would bring ruin to many of those that had been spared by the fall of stocks. We should have a very disturbed market until things subsided to their proper level. And now you will have to excuse me, Stranleigh. I must be off."

The banker threw away the stub of his cigar, and marched out. Lord Stranleigh went over to one of the tables, and wrote several letters. Among them was a request for an interview at an early date sent to the governor of the Bank of England. Another was an order forwarded to Peter Mackeller in Cornwall. A third requested the honor of a meeting with Mr. Conrad Schwartzbrod. Then Stranleigh took the calendar of the dying year, and slowly counted the number of days remaining to its credit.

"I think there will be time enough," he said to himself, as he completed the count.

Four days after the lesson he had received on the crisis Lord Stranleigh kept the first appointment he had made by meeting Schwartzbrod in the little business office of the town house. The young man was shocked at the appearance of the aged financier, and, much as he disliked him, could not but feel sorry for him. He seemed almost ten years older than when last they met. His face was haggard, drawn, pinched; his shoulders stooping under the increased burden which misfortune had laid upon them. The only unchanged feature was his eyes, and from them gleamed the baleful light of unconquerable hate.

"I received your letter from the club," Schwartzbrod began. "I have come, you see, I have come. I am not afraid to meet you; you smooth, brainless sneak, you can do me no further harm. You have done your worst, and if you have called me here to triumph over me, I give you that pleasure, and freely acknowledge that you are the cause of all my misfortunes."

"I beg your pardon, Mr. Schwartzbrod, but you are quite mistaken in what you say. The cause of your misfortune goes farther back than any action of mine. The beginning was on the day when you resolved to crush the Mackellers. They had helped you, father and son. They were innocent men, and honest. Each in his own way had assisted you to the possibility of almost unlimited wealth. That did not satisfy you. You determined to take from them their just compensation, and to fling them, paupers, into the gutter. It happened through one of those freaks of fate which keeps alive our faith in eternal justice, that the day you came to this resolve you were a doomed man."

"That's what you called me here to tell me, is it, you human poodle dog, you contemptible puppy, rich through the thefts of your ancestors."

"Your language, Mr. Schwartzbrod, seems to have become tinged with the intemperance of the panic. I did not intend to refer to the past at all. You set the subject of our conversation the moment you entered the room, and I merely followed your lead, and strove to remove a misapprehension from your mind as to the original causes of things. No, my invitation to this house had quite another object. I shall not strain your credulity by asking you to believe that when I heard four days ago you were bankrupt, a feeling of slight regret was uppermost in my mind. I don't like to see people suffer."

The old man laughed, like the grating of a file on a saw.

"Of course I don't ask you to believe that, and should be sorry to put such a strain on whatever belief in human nature you may possess, so don't trouble any further about my statements, which you doubtless regard as absurd. Have you got any money left?"

"Not a stiver."

"How about your six colleagues; are they cleaned out?"

"Even if they had money, they would not intrust a penny of it to me. You talk about my belief in human nature. Well, the faith in human nature in me is gone. I have done my best for them, and lost every point in the game, together with their money and my own."

"Very well, Mr. Schwartzbrod, we must rehabilitate you. I possess what I think is the finest red automobile in London, and my chauffeur would add dignity to the equipage of an emperor. I will lend you chauffeur and car for the day, and if you drive through the streets round the bank for a few hours, those who turn up their noses at you will be lifting their hats instead."

"I suppose you think that's funny, Lord Stranleigh. You wish to exhibit me in your motor car after the fashion of the Romans parading their captives in their chariots when defeated. I don't know why I came here, but I warn you I did not come to be insulted."

"Of course not. It is incredible you should imagine it possible for me to insult a man in my own house. Now listen to me. My banker has asked as a favor that I should not draw any checks upon him until this flurry is over. Of course, if I did draw a check, he would honor it, but I have given him my promise. Under the back seat of this automobile I have hid away eight bars of gold, each weighing a hundred pounds or thereabout, and valued probably at five thousand pounds sterling. That means forty thousand pounds in exactly the commodity all London is howling for at the present moment. I don't know precisely what the position of a bankrupt is, and it may be possible that your creditors can take away those bars of gold if they knew you possessed them, therefore trade in my name if you like; act as my agent. Go in this automobile to your bank, and get the porters to carry the bullion inside. There they will weigh it, and estimate its value, giving you the credit for the amount. Now, pay strict attention to me. Buy the value of those bars in stocks which you know possess some intrinsic worth, but are now far beneath their proper level. Hold those stocks until the first of January, when you will see begin the greatest boom that London has ever known. I advise you to sell as soon after New Year's day as possible, because stocks are likely to shoot up to a higher point than they may be able later to maintain. This gold comes from a mine which was once in your possession, and my immature puppy mind is so absurdly constructed that I have felt uneasily in your debt for a long time, and now am glad of the opportunity to allow you a share in the prosperity of the mine, if you will be obliging enough to accept it."

The truculence of the ruined financier immediately fell from him at the mention of gold, and in its place came the old cringing manner, with a flattering endeavor to mitigate the harshness of his former remarks, a change of manner that made the young man shrink a little farther from him, and hurriedly end the interview.

"That's all right, Mr. Schwartzbrod. Words break no bones, unless they cause the recipient to fling the dealer in them down a steep stairway. The automobile is waiting for you at the door. The chauffeur thinks the metal under the seat is copper. Your banker will tell you it is gold, so keep an eye on it till it is safely in his possession. There, there, do not thank me, I beg of you. I assure you I am not seeking for gratitude, but I am a little short of time to-day. In half an hour I am to meet the governor of the Bank of England, so I must bid you farewell."

"Will you not come with me, then, in your own automobile, my lord?"

"Thank you, no. I think it best that you should be seen alone in the automobile if there have been rumors regarding your position down in the city. If anyone asks you what the machine cost, you can tell them its price is a net two thousand pounds. You will journey in that, and I shall take the twopenny tube, being a democratic sort of person. Good morning, Mr. Schwartz-brod, good morning."

So Lord Stranleigh went down the huge lift at the twopenny tube, and in due time emerged to daylight at the Bank of England. He arrived in the anteroom a few minutes before the time of his appointment, and exactly at the arranged moment was called for, and ushered into the presence, for punctuality is the politeness of kings, and—governors of the Bank of England.

The stern, almost commanding attitude of this monarch of finance abashed the young man, and made him feel the useless worm of the dust Schwartzbrod had indicated he was. Stranleigh, who was always more scrupulously polite to a beggar than was his custom with the king, resented the sensation of inferiority which came upon him when confronted with the forbidding ruler of the bank. He said to himself:

"Good Heavens, is it possible that if I meet a man who is big enough, I shall actually cringe in my soul as Schwartzbrod does with his body?"

Nevertheless, that slight hesitation in speech which was apt to incommode him at critical moments overpowered him now, and his dislike of any attempt to win the respect of the iron man before him sent him in the other direction, and he knew that for the next ten minutes he was going to be regarded as the most hopeless fool in London. Yet he did not consider himself a fool, and his latent sense of humor prevented him from making any attempt at endowing his conversation with that wisdom which seemed so suitable to this somber room.

When the governor's secretary had presented Lord Stranleigh's letter to him, the head of the bank had peremptorily refused to waste time with a member of the aristocracy of whom he knew nothing, but the secretary, whose business it was to know everything, dropped one word in a short phrase that arrested the governor's attention.

"It's the rich Lord Stranleigh, sir."

The word "rich" was the straw at which the drowning man clutched. So here was Stranleigh, the living contradiction of that phrase "The last of the Dandies." Here was the embodiment of the spirit of Piccadilly and Bond Street confronted with the rugged, carelessly dressed dictator of Threadneedle Street, a frown on the beetling brow of one man, an inane, silly smile on the lips of the other. At the sight of this smile the governor saw at once that his first thought had been right. He should not have wasted a moment on this nonentity, yet he had before him the herculean task of providing the institute over which he presided with seventy millions of pounds worth of gold within five days, or stand discredited before the world. Despair was strangling expiring hope as he realized that this simpering noodle could not be the god in the machine; godlike in stalwart form, perhaps, but that simpering smile would have discredited Jove himself.

"What can I do for you, my lord?" he bellowed forth, temper, patience, and time short.

"Well, sir," sniggered Stranleigh, "there's—there's several things you can do for me. In—in the first place you don't mind my sitting down, do you? It seems to me I can speak better sitting down. I've—I've really never been able to make a speech in my life, even after dinner, simply because a fellow has to stand up, don't you know."

"I hope, my lord, you won't think it necessary to make a speech here."

"No, no, I merely wished a quiet talk," said his lordship, drawing up a chair without invitation, and sitting down. "You see, I have no head for figures, and so little knowledge of business do I possess that I am compelled to engage twelve professional men to look after my affairs."

"Yes, yes, yes, yes," snapped the governor.

"Well, you see, governor, now and again I act without asking any advice from those men. Seems kind of a silly thing to do, don't you think? Keeping twelve dogs, and barking a fellow's bally self, don't you know."

"Yes. What has all that to do with the Bank of England?"

"I'm coming to that. You see, we are all imbued with the same respect for the bank that we feel for the church, and the navy, and the king, and sometimes for the Government, but not always, as, for instance, when they pass silly Acts about your gold reserve, instead of coming to you in a friendly manner, as I'm doing, and settling the thing quietly."

"I quite agree with you, my lord, but my time is very limited, and I should be obliged——"

"Quite so, sir, quite so. These ideas are not my own, at all. I didn't know much about the crisis until four or five days ago when Mr. Corbitt—Alexander Corbitt, you know, of Selwyn's Bank. You're acquainted with him, perhaps?"

"I know Mr. Corbitt—yes."

"Well, those are his opinions, and I agree with him, you know."

"Mr. Corbitt is an authority on finance," admitted the governor, as if, instead of praising the absent man, he was denouncing him.

"Now, what bothers me about gold is this. A sovereign weighs a hundred and twenty-three grains, decimal—well I forget the decimal figures, but perhaps you're up in them. I never could remember—to tell you the truth, the moment I get into decimals, I'm lost. I can figure out that two and two are four, but beyond that———"

"I assure you, my lord," interrupted the governor, "a great many people cannot go so far as that. If you will have the kindness, not to say the mercy, to tell me exactly what you want, I will guarantee that your answer will be brief and prompt."

"All right. To get directly at the nub of the business, then, do you have twelve ounces to the pound of gold, or sixteen?"

The governor's fingers were drumming on the hard surface of the table. He glared at his visitor, but said nothing.

"When I get entangled with decimals or vulgar fractions, it's bad enough, but when I don't know whether the pounds I am dealing with are twelve ounces or sixteen ounces, then the ease gets kind of hopeless—ah, I see you are in a hurry. Now tell me how much would be the value of a bar of gold weighing a hundred pounds, and we'll let troy or avoirdupois go. Just give me a rough estimate."

"My Lord Stranleigh," said the governor, with ominous calmness, "have you come here under the impression that the Bank of England is an infant school?"

Lord Stranleigh blushed a delicate pink, until his cheeks were as smooth and crimson as that of a girl receiving her first proposal. The contempt of the man before him was so unconcealed that poor Stranleigh thought, as he closed his open hand, he might feel it, so thick was it in the air. He plunged desperately into another tack.

"My dear governor," he stammered, trying to conciliate his opponent by cordial familiarity, "as I told you I have the utmost respect for the Bank of England. You see, I am rather well off, and within the last day or two I have plunged, and every available asset I possess except one I have put into stocks and shares. I've thought this thing out———"

"Oh, you've thought it out," said the governor.

"Yes, as well as I was able, and I believe that after the first of January

London is going to see the greatest boom in stocks and shares that has ever taken place in the history of finance."

"What are your grounds for such a belief, my lord?"

"The—the respect I hold for the Bank of England. We want to see the good old Bank of England buck up. It's humiliating to think that an upstart like Wall Street should be able to play Hey-diddle-diddle, the cat and the fiddle, with a venerable institution like this. Why, it's as if some one spoke disrespectfully of one's grandmother. I want to see the bank buck up, and that's why I'm here."

The governor bucked up. He rose like a statue of wrath.

"My lord, this interview must terminate. The Bank of England cannot assist you in your speculations. You should have consulted Alexander Corbitt if you wished further credit, should he happen to be your banker."

Stranleigh had risen when he saw the governor on his feet.

"I did."

"Then you had better go back to him. He surely never advised you to see me?"

"No, but what he told me of the situation filled me with a desire to meet you."

"I dare say. Well, Lord Stranleigh, you have met me. I bid you good morning, sir."

Stranleigh became a deeper crimson at what he considered this rude dismissal. He was not accustomed to being treated in such a way. His shoulders squared back, and the smile left his lips.

"Then you don't want the gold?" he said, almost as sternly as the other had spoken.

"What gold?"

"My gold."

"I thought you said that all your assets had been vested in the buying of stocks."

"I said, sir, all my assets except one. The one asset remaining is gold."

"Gold?"

"Yes."

"In what form?"

"In the form of ingots."

"How much gold have you got? What's its value?"

"Now, governor, I put it to you, as one man to another, you're a little unreasonable. Didn't I tell you that unless I can multiply a hundred and twenty-three decimal-whatever-it-happens-to-be, I can't even estimate it? I asked—I hope with courtesy—the favor of your assistance in calculating the value of my gold, but you began to talk about infant schools. You see, I have got a mine down in Cornwall that holds two thousand tons of gold."

"Nonsense," interrupted the governor, waxing impatient. "There are no gold mines in Cornwall."

"Sir, I did not say there were. The mine I speak of is a copper mine."

"I have had enough of this fooling, my lord, and I think I have already bade you farewell."

"Then you don't want my gold?"

"How many pounds of raw gold have you got?"

"Pounds? Oh, I don't estimate my gold in pounds. I hold at present upward of two thousand tons."

"Two thousand tons! In ore, do you mean?"

"Certainly not. If the Bank of England is not an infant school, I suppose it is not a smelting furnace, either. This gold, as I told you, has been smelted, and is in ingots. I came down by twopenny tube to keep my appointment because

I had lent my principal automobile to a man named Conrad Schwartzbrod. I see my automobile standing outside, and as I gave Schwartzbrod eight bars of this metal, telling him to take it to his bank, he seems to have taken it to this bank, so if this seminary for young ladies has purchased these eight bars, we may go at once and examine them. My two thousand tons is divided into ingots similar to those Schwartzbrod has sold you."

"Where is your gold?"

"A thousand tons of it is in Cornwall still, but can be delivered here within a day or two. The other thousand tons is on a special train of the Great Western Railway, which has already arrived in London, and its contents may be in your vaults this evening if your vans look sharp."

The governor sat down in his chair more hurriedly than he had anticipated, drew out a handkerchief and wiped his brow.

"Are you telling the truth, or is this—is this—What you say, my lord, is incredible."

"Very well, come up to the Great Western goods depot, and see for yourself. I have always avoided the city as a cynical place, but I had no idea that unbelief was so prevalent there as it seems."

"A thousand tons of gold! Worth a hundred and ten million pounds sterling!"

"There, you see how easy it is to calculate when a man who knows figures gets at it. Is that what my thousand tons is worth?"

"Where did this gold come from?"

"From the West African coast; a very valuable surface mine I own there. We've been working most of the year transporting the ore to Cornwall and smelting it, tossing the ingots down into an empty copper mine I own, which I call my safe deposit vault."

"How much do you demand for this gold?"

"Oh, I don't demand anything at all. I'm no business man, as I told you.

It struck me that the gold was quite as safe in your vaults as in my copper mine, therefore I engaged a special train to bring half of it up. You can have the other half if you wish."

"My lord, will you accompany me in my automobile to the Great Western goods depot, and show me that special train of yours?"

"Governor, I shall be delighted."

A few mornings later Lord Stranleigh sat at his appetizing breakfast, and smiled as he read the leading article in the Times:

"As our readers know, we did not join in the outcry of the sensational press which did so much to mislead public opinion both in England and America. Never for an instant, during all the tumult, did our faith in that greatest and most venerable of financial institutions, the Bank of England, waver. On October the fourteenth we pointed out the impossibility of cornering gold, no matter how powerful the financial syndicate might be which undertook his labor of Sisyphus. How long this treasure, whose very figures read like some romance of the 'Arabian Nights,' has lain in the vaults of the bank, no one but the governor, and those in his confidence, can tell. While the country was ringing with predictions of failure on the part of the bank to conform with a new and absurd law, those responsible for the direction of our leading financial institution quietly and in silence had gathered together the almost unimaginable amount of three hundred million pounds' worth sterling of virgin gold. Those journals which for the past four months have been foremost in deluding their readers, and bringing a crisis on the country, are now loud in their denunciation of the governor of the bank for not speaking sooner. But if the governor of the bank undertook to reply to statements, malicious or ignorant, concerning the institution over which he so worthily presides, there would be little time left for him to perform those functions that he has so ably accomplished. Those people who held faith in their country are rewarded. The almost unprecedented heights to which stocks and shares have risen means the enrichment of every investor who was not carried away by a senseless panic. As for ourselves, we have in season and out of season never swerved from———"

494

Lord Stranleigh laughed.

"Good old Times," he said, "how wise you are! A fitting companion grandmother to the Old Lady of Threadneedle Street!"

THE END

About Author

Robert Barr (16 September 1849 – 21 October 1912) was a Scottish-Canadian short story writer and novelist.

Early years in Canada

Robert Barr was born in Barony, Lanark, Scotland to Robert Barr and Jane Watson. In 1854, he emigrated with his parents to Upper Canada at the age of four years old. His family settled on a farm near the village of Muirkirk. Barr assisted his father with his job as a carpenter, and developed a sound work ethic. Robert Barr then worked as a steel smelter for a number of years before he was educated at Toronto Normal School in 1873 to train as a teacher.

After graduating Toronto Normal School, Barr became a teacher, and eventually headmaster/principal of the Central School of Windsor, Ontario in 1874. While Barr worked as head master of the Central School of Windsor, Ontario, he began to contribute short stories—often based on personal experiences, and recorded his work. On August 1876, when he was 27, Robert Barr married Ontario-born Eva Bennett, who was 21. According to the 1891 England Census, the couple appears to have had three children, Laura, William, and Andrew.

In 1876, Barr quit his teaching position to become a staff member of publication, and later on became the news editor for the Detroit Free Press. Barr wrote for this newspaper under the pseudonym, "Luke Sharp." The idea for this pseudonym was inspired during his morning commute to work when Barr saw a sign that read "Luke Sharp, Undertaker." In 1881, Barr left Canada to return to England in order to start a new weekly version of "The Detroit Free Press Magazine."

London years

In 1881 Barr decided to "vamoose the ranch", as he called the process of immigration in search of literary fame outside of Canada, and relocated to London to continue to write/establish the weekly English edition of the Detroit Free Press. During the 1890s, he broadened his literary works, and started writing novels from the popular crime genre. In 1892 he founded the magazine The Idler, choosing Jerome K. Jerome as his collaborator (wanting, as Jerome said, "a popular name"). He retired from its co-editorship in 1895.

In London of the 1890s Barr became a more prolific author—publishing a book a year—and was familiar with many of the best-selling authors of his day, including :Arnold Bennett, Horatio Gilbert Parker, Joseph Conrad, Bret Harte, Rudyard Kipling, H. Rider Haggard, H. G. Wells, and George Robert Gissing. Barr was well-spoken, well-cultured due to travel, and considered a "socializer."

Because most of Barr's literary output was of the crime genre, his works were highly in vogue. As Sherlock Holmes stories were becoming well-known, Barr wrote and published in the Idler the first Holmes parody, "The Adventures of "Sherlaw Kombs" (1892), a spoof that was continued a decade later in another Barr story, "The Adventure of the Second Swag" (1904). Despite those jibes at the growing Holmes phenomenon, Barr remained on very good terms with its creator Arthur Conan Doyle. In Memories and Adventures, a serial memoir published 1923–24, Doyle described him as "a volcanic Anglo—or rather Scot-American, with a violent manner, a wealth of strong adjectives, and one of the kindest natures underneath it all".

In 1904, Robert Barr completed an unfinished novel for Methuen & Co. by the recently deceased American author Stephen Crane entitled The O'Ruddy, a romance.Despite his reservations at taking on the project, Barr reluctantly finished the last eight chapters due to his longstanding friendship with Crane and his common-law wife, Cora, the war correspondent and bordello owner.

Death

The 1911 census places Robert Barr, "a writer of fiction," at Hillhead, Woldingham, Surrey, a small village southeast of London, living with his wife, Eva, their son William, and two female servants. At this home, the author died from heart disease on 21 October 1912.

Writing Style

Barr's volumes of short stories were often written with an ironic twist in the story with a witty, appealing narrator telling the story. Barr's other works also include numerous fiction and non-fiction contributions to periodicals. A few of his mystery stories and stories of the supernatural were put in anthologies, and a few novels have been republished. His writings have also attracted scholarly attention. His narrative personae also featured moral and editorial interpolations within their tales. Barr's achievements were recognized by an honorary degree from the University of Michigan in 1900.

His protagonists were journalists, princes, detectives, deserving commercial and social climbers, financiers, the new woman of bright wit and aggressive accomplishment, and lords. Often, his characters were stereotypical and romanticized.

Barr wrote fiction in an episode-like format. He developed this style when working as an editor for the newspaper Detroit Press. Barr developed his skill with the anecdote and vignette; often only the central character serves to link the nearly self-contained chapters of the novels. (Source: Wikipedia)

NOTABLE WORKS

In a Steamer Chair and Other Stories (Thirteen short stories by one of the most famous writers in his day -1892)

"The Face And The Mask" (1894) consists of twenty-four delightful short stories.

In the Midst of Alarms (1894, 1900, 1912), a story of the attempted Fenian invasion of Canada in 1866.

From Whose Bourne (1896) Novel in which the main character, William Brenton, searches for truth to set his wife free.

One Day's Courtship (1896)

Revenge! (Collection of 20 short stories, Alfred Hitchcock-like style, thriller with a surprise ending)

The Strong Arm

A Woman Intervenes (1896), a story of love, finance, and American journalism.

Tekla: A Romance of Love and War (1898)

Jennie Baxter, Journalist (1899)

The Unchanging East (1900)

The Victors (1901)

A Prince of Good Fellows (1902)

Over The Border: A Romance (1903)

The O'Ruddy, A Romance, with Stephen Crane (1903)

A Chicago Princess (1904)

The Speculations of John Steele (1905)

The Tempestuous Petticoat (1905–12)

A Rock in the Baltic (1906)

The Triumphs of Eugène Valmont (1906)

The Measure of the Rule (1907)

Stranleigh's Millions (1909)

The Sword Maker (Medieval action/adventure novel, genre: Historical Fiction-1910)

The Palace of Logs (1912)

"The Ambassadors Pigeons" (1899)

"And the Rigor of the Game" (1892)

"Converted" (1896)

"Count Conrad's Courtship" (1896)

"The Count's Apology" (1896)

"A Deal on Change " (1896)

"The Exposure of Lord Stanford" (1896)

"Gentlemen: The King!"

"The Hour-Glass" (1899)

"An invitation" (1892)

" A Ladies Man"

"The Long Ladder" (1899)

"Mrs. Tremain" (1892)

" Transformation" (1896)

"The Understudy" (1896)

" The Vengeance of the Dead" (1896)

"The Bromley Gibbert's Story" (1896)

" Out of Thun" (1896)

"The Shadow of Greenback" (1896)

"Flight of the Red Dog" (fiction)

"Lord Stranleigh Abroad" (1913)

"One Day's Courtship and the Herald's of Fame" (1896)

"Cardillac"

"Dr. Barr's Tales"

"The Triumphs of Eugene Valmont"

CPSIA information can be obtained
at www.ICGtesting.com
Printed in the USA
BVHW030922300720
585023BV00006B/49

9 789390 209293